THE PURSUIT

A MAX AUSTIN THRILLER – BOOK TWO

JACK ARBOR

HIGH CALIBER BOOKS

THE PURSUIT
(A MAX AUSTIN THRILLER - BOOK TWO)

ISBN-13: 978-1-947696-01-3
ISBN-10: 1-947696-01-7

Requests to publish work from this book should be sent to:
jack@jackarbor.com

Edition 1.0

Published by High Caliber Books

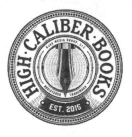

Cover art by: www.damonza.com
Bio photo credit: John Lilley Photography

For my mother, without whom none of this would be possible

"The enemy of my enemy is my friend"
-Proverb

ONE

Dubrovnik, Croatia

The Russian colonel's head wavered in the rifle scope as Max adjusted his sitting position. He switched from the scope to a wider-angle view through a Bushnell spotting lens. The target was sitting in a frothing hot tub, a melon-chested girl on each arm, sipping from a champagne flute. His mostly bald pate glistened with sweat, and reflections of multi-colored lights from the yacht's disco ball glinted from his head. Two bodyguards stood at attention several paces behind, their eyes roving restlessly over the undulating party.

Hoots and shouts and clips of music from the boat came through the open window. Three hot tubs were full of obese old men surrounded by hired girls. Partygoers carried bottles of Cristal in their fists. It was approaching midnight, and the festivities were in full swing.

Despite the cool breeze coming through the window, a bead of sweat dripped down Max's forehead. While he waited, he absently fingered the rabbit's foot he kept in his pocket, a token of safety given to him by his ten-year-old nephew.

Using a sniper rifle required that the assassin know exactly where the target would be ahead of time. That knowledge was usually hard to come by. Today, though, he knew. Max's handler at the CIA had a source in the colonel's organization – a Ukrainian sympathizer who had supplied minute details about the target's schedule. Despite the intel, this was a rush job, and Max hated rush jobs. He prided himself on a spotless record and preferred to spend months researching a target's habits. Killing a man was an intimate act, one not to be hurried. Still, Max's new boss at the CIA wanted to take advantage of the opportunity, so here he was, perched in a decaying tenement, about to end the life of a man whose sin was profiting from supplying weapons to the pro-Russian rebels in Eastern Ukraine.

His target was about the length of two football pitches away. At this distance, using the Leupold scope and a M2010 ESR rifle, Max's assignment was relatively easy, even with the long silencer attached to the barrel. The rifle was chambered for a .300 Winchester Magnum, a bullet proven to produce more long-range effectiveness with less weight than other .30 cartridges. It was probably overkill for this job, but that was how Max operated – he always stacked the deck in his favor. As he waited, he admired the workmanship of the matte-black, American-made rifle. Most of the gear he'd used in the KGB had been decades old and poorly maintained. Restlessly, his hand checked the SIG P226 at his side and the fighting knife strapped to his leg.

Max felt no remorse or conflict about killing a former colleague. He knew the FSB had played a role in his parents' death and he'd recently sold his soul to the CIA in exchange for the protection of his family. He owed the FSB nothing.

He moved his eye back to the spotting lens and watched the colonel tip his head back to laugh at something one of the girls had said. An oversized gold diver's watch glittered on the man's wrist. In contrast to the colonel's obese underlings, Konstantin Koskov was built like a rugby player – short and stocky, chest and arms rippling with muscle. He spent as much time working out as he did chasing girls and counting his money.

Max checked his own watch. Two minutes. He moved into firing position. The rifle's bipod legs rested on a wooden kitchen table pushed up to the window. Next to the rifle, a Nikon digital camera fitted with a long-range lens sat on a pocket-sized tripod. A cord ran from the camera's shutter to a foot pedal on the floor. A wireless data card in the camera would automatically transfer the photos to his smartphone. In his pocket was the remote control to a small block of C-4 he'd attached to the underside of the kitchen table. When the job was done, he'd activate the bomb and destroy the evidence. He reacquired the target in the scope. The man's head came through the view finder in magnified clarity.

Max reached into his pocket and fingered the lucky rabbit's foot again. He believed in making his own luck, but the little token reminded him why he was doing this job. He checked his watch again. One minute. He moved the chair back from the table, taking care not to make any noise, and took a wide stance. The flag on the pole visible through the window lay limp, but the spring air held significant moisture. Max went over his firing solution one last time, made a tiny adjustment, then re-acquired the target. The colonel was pawing at the girl next to him, who was trying to wiggle away.

As the second hand on Max's watch jolted to the 12 mark, a loud explosion sounded a block away. The table rattled slightly. Glass bottles chattered above the stove. Max watched through the scope as Koskov looked up, startled by the diversion Max had planted hours before.

Max ensured the scope's crosshairs were a shade above the colonel's temple, breathed out, and let his heartbeat slow. Using the pad of his index finger, he pulled straight back on the trigger, simultaneously pressing down on the camera pedal with his foot. The muted *thump* from the bullet passing through the silencer and the whir of the camera's servo motor were drowned out by the pounding music on the yacht. The target's head disappeared from the view through the scope.

Max switched to the spotting lens and watched Koskov's body slip into the roiling hot tub, the top portion of his head ragged and bloody. The two girls appeared frozen, their minds not yet registering what their eyes had just seen. The chest and neck of one of the girls was covered in a dark, silky liquid. Then, in unison, the girls started screaming. The bodyguards reacted more quickly, drawing weapons as they scanned the area. Their training made them act, but Max could see the incredulity in their eyes even from this distance. Max pulled the rifle back from the window and left it on the table.

Suddenly, he heard a creak in the floorboards behind him. To most, the sound would be imperceptible. To Max's tightly honed senses, it was like a rifle shot in a still forest. Instinct took over and he ducked and rolled away from the table, coming up on both feet, the SIG in his hand.

TWO

Dubrovnik, Croatia

An arm wielding a knife thrust through the air where Max had just been standing. He parried the arm with a swift slash of his left hand and tried to bring the gun around, but felt a stinging blow to his right wrist as the intruder punched downward with his free arm. His gun came loose and clattered to the wooden floor, out of reach. The attacker pounced, faster than Max thought possible, and slashed again with the knife. Max defended with a downward cut of his forearm, but not before the blade caught and sliced through his T-shirt, drawing a deep cut in his torso. Max felt the sticky sensation of blood on his skin.

Again, the attacker slashed toward Max's torso, sensing easy victory against a weaponless opponent. Max, however, had trained for this, spending countless hours on the mat, unarmed against a knife-wielding opponent. He shifted his weight and parried again, forcing the attacker's arm to his left. He caught the intruder's knife arm in his armpit and wrenched hard, trying to break a bone or dislodge the knife. Max sensed the man was too strong, too supple. His opponent's body felt like a steel pole grounded in cement. Max twisted his body under the man, flipping his opponent over his shoulder. The intruder fell hard to the ground on his back, landing with a soft grunt.

Max was on him in a second, happy to see the fight move to the ground. He'd excelled as a grappler at the KGB's Red Banner Institute, and had kept up the practice. Max regained his hold of the attacker's knife arm and twisted so he was on his back, then extended his legs across the man's torso. He torqued his hip on the man's elbow, attempting to break the joint, using a move called an armbar. Grunting in pain, the attacker dropped his knife. Max continued to apply pressure, waiting to hear the elbow snap.

His opponent shifted slightly and linked his hands together, and Max felt pressure on his knee. The attacker pushed up violently into a bridge, then twisted and pulled out of the armbar. The wiry man immediately leapt to his feet with the agility of a dancer and snatched his knife off the ground.

Max took the opportunity to jump back and draw his own blade. Blood dripped from his forearm as he held the blade in a fisted grip. He assumed the classic knife-fighting pose with both arms tight in front of his face, the free arm slightly in front, knife hand slightly cocked back. For the first time, he could study his opponent.

The attacker was Caucasian, tall, wiry, and of imperceptible nationality. His face was lined and weathered, but Max placed him in his early thirties. The man seemed vaguely familiar, but Max only had a moment to think before the attacker came after Max with a series of vicious swipes. Max circled away and retreated from each slash of the knife.

The assailant paused, as if to recalibrate his attack. Seeing an opening, Max pivoted on a planted foot and lashed out with his other leg using a rear side kick that had all his weight behind it. He caught the intruder in the hip, and the man tumbled backward. The table, rifle, and camera went crashing to the ground along with him.

The attacker rolled with the fall and leapt to his feet, coming at Max again. He was at least a decade younger than Max, and moved with the efficiency and grace of a highly trained fighter. His face was passive and devoid of emotion. This man was a professional.

The way the killer moved reminded Max of his own training. The attacker used very little of his own strength, relying instead on his body weight, points of support, rotation, and leverage. The way the man shrugged off the pain of Max's attacks was also familiar, and suddenly Max realized he was fighting a fellow member of the Spetsnaz, the blanket name for Russia's various special forces units. The Spetsnaz were famous for training under brutal conditions, like being forced to swim in a pool crisscrossed with barbed wire, being tied and dragged behind vehicles, and being hit in the bare skin by molten-hot metal poles. A Spetsnaz fighter could withstand pain like no other warrior.

A swing of the knife caught Max in the forearm, cutting through muscle and sinew and drawing more blood. As the attacker closed into Max's body, Max brought his forehead down onto the bridge of the attacker's nose. Because of the close range, Max had to shorten the arc of his movement, reducing the power of the strike. Still, he connected with a crunch, and the attacker staggered back. Max knew the killer was momentarily blinded by the shock. Blood covered the man's mouth and dripped onto his chest.

For the first time, Max saw emotion. Anger crept across the intruder's face, and he came at Max again, closing from a distance. Max planted his left foot and lashed out with his right, but his opponent anticipated the kick, shifted his weight, and parried. Then he came at Max with a blinding flurry of jabs and swipes, catching Max in the side with a long cut. Max parried the arm with his knife hand, then landed a glancing blow with a left jab that sent the attacker backward again. Max felt more wetness under his shirt, but steeled himself. He had no intention of dying in this dingy tenement in Croatia. Not with his nephew and sister waiting for him at the safe house back in the States.

The man's mouth curled up in a smirk as he saw Max's blood-soaked T-shirt. He came at Max again in a blur of speed. The knife sliced the front of Max's shirt, drawing a cut across his chest, then an elbow caught him in the side of the head, sending stars shooting through his vision. Another flurry of attacks came, and Max tried to deflect and spin away, but felt another sharp pain, then more wetness. His legs suddenly felt weak and a wave of dizziness came over him. He managed to deflect a blow to his side that might have finished him, landed a punch, and staggered back a few paces.

His attacker stood in the middle of the kitchen. Max's back was to the doorway. Around them were the broken pieces of the camera and the overturned kitchen table. Glass crunched under their feet. The rifle lay on the ground next to the wall. A quick glance failed to reveal where the SIG had landed. Max saw the small package of C-4 he'd attached to the underside of the kitchen table to use as a diversionary tactic upon his departure. The remote was in his pocket.

The attacker, relentless, came at him again. Steeling himself, Max parried a knife swipe with his left arm and thrust his own knife, catching the intruder in the thigh. It was a glancing blow, drawing little blood, but the attacker hesitated. Max lashed out with a fast left jab that caught the attacker directly on his already-broken nose. The attacker fell back. Max kicked out and caught the intruder in the gut, sending him tumbling. The man landed directly on the overturned kitchen table, his face next to the package of explosives.

Max saw recognition in the attacker's eyes. Shifting the knife to his left hand, Max brought the bomb's remote detonator from his pocket. His thumb pressed down on the detonator button, but froze with it half depressed. Max took a couple steps back toward the kitchen doorway, adrenaline surging through his veins.

As Max paused, he suddenly placed the man. Years ago, when Max had been a guest instructor at the FSB's training facility, he'd been introduced to the organization's rising star. Plucked from the Red Army's general population due to his viciousness, the young man had been trained as a special forces soldier by the Spetznaz, then trained to be a killer by the FSB. He'd been branded the FSB's newest killing tool; a ruthless assassin who pursued his target at all cost. A psychopathic killing machine. That man was now sprawled on the ground in front of him.

As the assassin started to get up, Max showed him the transceiver. The killer wavered. Max's mind was spinning. Why was the FSB's most ruthless killer targeting him? Was this part of the larger plot to kill Max's family? Or was this a coincidence, a second assassin sent to kill Koskov? His father's voice rang out in his mind, like an echo from the abyss.

Son, behind every coincidence is a cold and calculating mind.

"Don't move," Max said in Russian. "Or I'll push the button and turn you into a red mist."

THREE

Dubrovnik, Croatia

The attacker froze. He was on his side sprawled partially on the overturned table, legs splayed in the broken glass. Behind him lay the rifle. The man's eyes darted around, then lingered for a split second on a spot near the kitchen's broken-down cabinetry. Max followed his gaze and saw a dull glint of metal. Max's SIG. It was a only a couple of meters from the attacker.

"Go for it," Max said, holding up the radio-controlled detonator. He took another step backward, toward the kitchen door. Max had fashioned the explosive to be large enough to destroy the kitchen, but not level the building. His goal had been to create a small diversion and erase any lingering forensics evidence, not kill a neighbor.

The assassin remained silent, eyes still roving, looking for a way out.

"Who sent you?" Max asked.

The killer said nothing. He slowly pushed himself into a sitting position.

"Stop moving," Max ordered. "If I push this button, I'll make it into the hallway, but you'll be blown to bits." The assassin froze, holding himself up by one arm.

"How did you know where I'd be?" Max asked, more forcefully.

The assassin remained silent.

Max studied the man's face. He had a narrow face and sharp nose, like a bird. His black hair was cropped close, bangs cut straight across the front in a Caesar cut.

"I know who you are," Max said.

In response, the would-be killer directed a curse in Russian at Max, then sat up and brushed broken glass from his hands.

Max took another step backward, toward the kitchen door. The bomb was a small package of C-4. The radio-controlled blasting cap was attached to the plastic explosive with duct tape, and the entire package was attached to the underside of the table using another piece of the adhesive. He knew if he timed his jump into the hallway, pressing the detonator button as he went, he'd be shielded from the brunt of the blast.

The assassin glanced at the explosive. Max knew he was performing calculations in his mind. The distance between himself and the bomb. The size of the charge. The distance between Max and the bomb. The distance between him and the SIG. That's exactly what Max would be thinking were he in the man's position.

"KGB, right?" Max asked. "We met at the Institute. Who sent you? Were you after me, or Koskov?"

The assassin remained silent. They were in a hopeless standoff. This was only going to end one way.

Perhaps the assassin realized the same thing. He did the one thing Max would have done in his situation – he stalled. "Former," he said, sneering. "The KGB don't pay."

The Russian KGB had been officially disbanded in 2001 during the fall of the Soviet Union, replaced by an organization called the FSB. They were just two names for the same organization. Both perpetrated heinous repression and brainwashing against their own people. Russia was known to be the fifth most dangerous country in which to be a journalist, behind countries like Iraq and Syria.

"Contract pays better," the attacker said, leaning forward on an arm and shifting a leg. "Your father used to be our idol. Until you defected." He spat the last word out like it was poison.

"So the FSB hired you to kill me?" Max asked, ignoring the man's comment.

The assassin smiled an evil grin, thin bloodless lips curling up at the corners. His eyes, however, remained dead.

"No."

Again, the killer shifted his weight so now he was sitting on his haunches. Max noted that he'd shifted from the awkward position he'd landed in, and now was poised to spring. Max took another step backward and now stood next in front of the open door.

"Then who?" Max said, hoping to keep the man talking.

Instead of answering, the man nodded toward the window. "Are you sure you hit the right target?"

Caught off-guard, Max glanced away. In that split second, the intruder sprang.

Max caught the movement out of the corner of his eye and dove through the kitchen's doorway, pushing the transceiver's button as he launched himself into the air.

A loud *boom* sounded as he landed on his stomach in the hallway. Shards of wood and glass rained down on his back. Momentarily stunned, he willed himself to his knees and scrambled down the hallway. Adrenaline masked the pain from the deep wounds he'd received in the knife fight, and he left a trail of blood along the hallway's wooden floor. Max ignored the cloud of soot that enveloped him, forced himself to his feet, and stumbled forward. He needed to get out of the building before any first responders appeared.

He staggered down the length of the hallway and took the stairs down two at a time, holding on to the hand railings. He exited the building through the back door and jumped astride a small motorbike. He grabbed the helmet he'd left on the bike's handlebar and shoved it on his head. A turn of the key fired the engine, and he twisted the throttle and shot through a narrow alleyway and out into traffic.

Max's head was ringing, and he could hear muted sirens. He chanced a glance back at the building. Smoke billowed through the window and flames licked at the wooden frame. Max slowed the bike and blended into traffic. The motorcycle was a Honda Hero with a 97 cc engine, one of the most common motorbikes in Croatia. This one had a dented tank and rusted exhaust. He became just another Croatian on an errand.

As he threaded through traffic and pedestrians in the small resort town, he was alarmed by the significance of the killer showing up at his job site. Only three people knew where he was: his CIA handler – Kate – and two of her staff. The implication was staggering. His enemies must have deep resources, even within the CIA. He knew the Agency had a leak; that much had been evident when two of Kate's men tried to kill him in the facility outside Minsk.

Kate's internal investigation had been thorough, and had yielded nothing. Now he had evidence the leak was still very much in place.

Max gunned the throttle, putting distance between himself and the site of the attack. A wave of dizziness overcame him, and he fought to control the bike. His jeans were soaked with blood, and the pain from his wounds started to cut through the fading adrenaline. Max pushed the questions and the pain from his mind and focused on his escape. He dodged an oncoming lorry and made a sharp left turn onto northbound Route 8, heading for the bridge and the waiting fishing trawler that would take him to Italy.

FOUR

Undisclosed location outside Budapest

Wing Octavia's heels clicked on the slick cobblestone, sending an echo through the subterranean chamber. In the distance, she heard water dripping, a steady *plink, plink, plink* from somewhere in the darkness. The stone walkway was uneven, but her team had rigged up a string of dim lights to illuminate the passage. Behind her was the old freight elevator that had brought her down from her offices above.

Finding this place had been a boon for her team, one of the few things that had gone well since Nathan's death. The building had been a satellite office for the Hungarian secret police in the late forties and early fifties. Before the 1956 Hungarian uprising effectively shut the group down, the Secret Police operated as a brutal offshoot of the Soviet Union's own covert police force, conducting violent purges of anyone thought to be against Moscow's rule over Hungary. The facility, long abandoned, still had its torture chambers and prison cells intact. It was one of these rooms that Wing was walking to now.

She walked confidently, her outward appearance belying the turmoil she felt inside. Things weren't going well with her business, and the stress was starting to take its toll. She wasn't sleeping, and her diet consisted of soup and red wine – when she even took the time eat. She knew she was in a downward spiral that she needed to pull out of. Wing touched the pistol at the small of her back, taking a small measure of comfort from the hard steel.

Wing entered a small, square room. The ceiling was low and the same wet cobblestone floor was underfoot. A single bare bulb lit the room, and the air was dank with moisture and the scent of fear. In the center of the room, an obese, pale-skinned man was strapped naked to a board. The board was held in an upright position, and the straps strained to hold the heavy man secure. One of her staff, a thick-chested man named Walter, stood leaning against a side wall.

"Good morning, Henry," Wing said to the man strapped to the board. "Thank you for joining us. I know the abduction was unpleasant, but it's the only way I could ensure our privacy for our little talk."

Walter chuckled, and Wing shot him a glance. Walter was new to her team, and Wing wasn't sure she liked him. Henry didn't speak. His face was red from anger and shame, his eyes narrow slits. He glared at Wing with hatred.

She addressed her captive again. "Do you know why you're here?" Thus far, they had not harmed him, other than the chafe he was experiencing from the webbed straps holding him to the board and the blow to the head he'd received during the abduction. Wing had mixed feelings about using pain to extract information. To gain the upper hand during an interrogation, she preferred psychological punishment over force. Once the pain began, most people would make up any story just to end the suffering. She suspected she'd get more information out of Henry by toying with his mind rather than inflicting physical torture.

Once again, Henry didn't respond. Walter pushed away from the wall and slapped the prisoner. "Speak when the lady speaks to you," Walter said. Wing frowned at Walter, but remained silent.

The prisoner sputtered. "Do you know who you're dealing with? You can't just kidnap a baron and expect to get away with it. MI6 will be all over your ass so fast your—"

Wing nodded at Walter, who in turn slapped Henry again, cutting him off mid-sentence.

"I'll repeat," Wing said. "Do you know why you're here?"

She moved a step forward and looked into Henry's eyes. They were bloodshot, but flashed with anger. Normally, Wing would have her men break the subject down by using sleep deprivation, forcing him to stand for hours on end, and blasting heavy metal music. This would have spared her from dealing with the prisoner's anger, and allowed her to get right down to business. Unfortunately, she didn't have the luxury of time.

Henry's eyes flashed again. "Do you do this to all your clients? This kind of thing won't be very good for your reputation."

"Only former clients," Wing stated. "Dead men tell no tales."

Henry's face lost a shade of color, but he remained belligerent. "Fuck you. You wouldn't dare kill a member of the aristocracy."

Wing ignored him and crossed her arms over her chest. "You lied to me, Henry."

"Fuck you," Henry said again.

Without waiting for a nod from his boss, Walter launched a right-handed cross at Henry's head, connecting with a crunch. A cut opened on the prisoner's cheek and blood flowed freely. "Watch your language around her," Walter growled.

"I know why you lied," Wing said. "You're broke. You're an aristocrat by title only. Your bank accounts are empty and you owe more money than a small third-world nation. You don't even have enough to pay my bill."

Henry glared at Wing, but kept his mouth shut.

"Your ruse to pretend to have your wife kidnapped and killed so you could collect the insurance money was probably the worst-planned crime in the history of insurance fraud. And you hired us to take the fall, didn't you? What do you take me for, Henry? A complete idiot?"

Henry stayed silent, avoiding Wing's eyes.

"Answer the lady," Walter said, taking a step forward.

Henry said nothing, but his face had softened. He clearly hadn't thought Wing's team could uncover the truth about the job he'd hired her for.

Walter hit him again, this time with his entire weight behind it. His fist crashed into Henry's nose, causing blood to spatter on the front of Walter's tactical shirt. Henry cried out in pain.

"You understand why I can't simply allow you to get away with it," Wing said. "My business is built on my reputation. If I don't maintain that reputation, my business will suffer. If I allow you to walk all over me, then others may think they can do the same."

"How about I cut you in on half?" Henry said. His eyes registered hope.

Wing pulled the pistol from the small of her back and removed a black metal suppressor from her pocket. She made an elaborate show of screwing the silencer into the gun's barrel. Henry's eyes went wide.

Wing knew she was on thin ice. Lord Henry Bradley was indeed a powerful man in the United Kingdom. A former member of the British Parliament and a member of nobility with the title of baron, he had stature in Britain. Wing also knew he was all form and no substance, a land owner with no viable income.

"You can't do that," Henry blustered. "If I'm killed, they'll come after you. Scotland Yard, MI6. You can't kill a baron and get away with it—"

Wing placed the barrel of the gun up to Henry's temple. "We have ways of disposing of bodies so they're never found."

Any remaining blood that had been in Henry's face now drained out. Wing's finger tightened on the trigger. The pistol was a Glock 19 9mm, with a handle custom made for her small hand. She knew exactly the amount of pressure that would release the trigger. She was burning to get this over with, to move on, to kill the man and put this ugly situation behind her. She knew she was doing just as Nathan would do. He would have killed anyone who crossed him as a message to the world that you didn't mess with Nathan Abrams. She applied more pressure to the trigger.

"Wait!" Henry screamed. Reflexively, Wing let the pressure off the trigger. "I have insurance," he blurted.

Wing paused, confused.

"I mean, I've got materials in a safe deposit box. If I'm

killed or I disappear, I've instructed my attorney to release the materials to the police."

Wing cursed to herself. She was looking into Henry's eyes, but couldn't tell if he was lying. He was obviously a man in a desperate situation, and desperate men would say anything.

"What materials?" Wing asked.

"Your identity, your picture, the bank account information I used to wire you the money. It's not much, but I'm sure Scotland Yard will take it very seriously."

Wing still had the gun to his temple, her frustration mounting. On top of this mess with Henry and her struggling business, her other job wasn't going well, either. She hadn't heard from the assassin she'd sent to Croatia two days prior. She lost her cool and smashed the butt of the pistol against Henry's head. A cut opened on his temple and he looked momentarily dazed. Wing stood back and steadied herself, forcing herself to calm.

"How do I know you're not lying?" she asked.

Henry's eyes cleared and he looked smug. "I guess you don't."

"You're just coming forward with this now?"

"I didn't think you'd be dumb enough to kill a member of British aristocracy."

"It doesn't mean anything anymore," Wing muttered under her breath. Louder, she said, "How much time before the provision kicks in?"

Henry didn't answer right away, and seemed to be calculating. Wing folded her arms.

"Wouldn't you like to know," he said finally, a smile appearing on his face.

Wing's mind was spinning. Either he was bluffing, or he actually had materials stashed somewhere. If he had materials stashed somewhere, there would need to be some kind of trigger for their release. She looked at her watch.

As if reading her mind, Henry said, "It won't do you any good to break into my lawyer's office. Access to the safe deposit box requires either his thumb print or mine."

Wing smiled. "That won't be a problem. Walter, bring me Henry's thumb print, then get me the lawyer's name. Do whatever you have to."

Henry's face went white again, and Wing turned on a heel and strode from the room.

FIVE

Undisclosed location outside Budapest

As Wing banged open the metal door to the freight elevator, she heard a long howl of pain from behind her. She didn't know if Henry was lying, but she hoped Walter bound up the wound so he didn't bleed out. She knew she was taking a big risk, but she didn't see any other choice. She couldn't release Henry or she'd be forever under his thumb. Her only choice was to get that information before it got out.

The freight elevator was one of those old-fashioned models; a metal cage hanging by a wire-and-pulley system. She yanked the rusty lever that set the elevator in motion and watched as the wet stone and clay walls slid by. A few moments later, she emerged into the basement of her building. She walked on cracked yellow linoleum past rows of empty holding cells and storage rooms. Four flights of stairs brought her to her office, a large room with high ceilings rimmed with ornate crown molding. Several blood red oriental rugs from Pakistan were on the floor and she'd had an extra-large cherry wood desk brought in. A small cot sat in one corner along with a few personal effects. She maintained a flat in Budapest, but it was full of unopened boxes. She spent all her nights in this room, working late, rising before dawn, eating little and consuming vast amounts of coffee, in an attempt to keep the firm started by her late mentor, Nathan Abrams, afloat.

Wing was no stranger to adversity. Growing up an orphan in the slums of Malaysia, she'd outworked everyone and had earned a full-ride scholarship to Oxford. That's where Nathan had found her, adopting her as his own daughter and slowly moving her up the ranks at his company. Displaying the same work ethic that got her into college, she quickly proved herself and became Nathan's right-hand woman. Upon his death, it was natural she'd taken over the firm. The transition, however, hadn't been easy.

One wall of her office had been removed and replaced with a row of floor-to-ceiling glass windows. She strode over and looked down on her operations center. It pained her to see only two people typing furiously and talking rapidly into headsets. In Nathan's time, the operations room would have been a seething pot of activity, much like a trading floor just after the opening bell, with dozens of operations going on around the world simultaneously. Now, Wing only had two teams working: the group dealing with the Henry mess and the team pursuing Mikhail Asimov, AKA Max Austin. She yanked open the glass door and walked down the steps to where Marisa sat, her most loyal and effective comm specialist.

"We need someone in London," Wing said, perching herself on the edge of Marisa's desk. She filled Marisa in on Henry's revelations.

"He's lying," Marisa said as she started typing rapidly on her keyboard.

"Probably, but I can't take that chance," Wing said.

"Fulton is out of commission," Marisa said, referring to a contractor in their database known to operate in London. "In the hospital with pneumonia."

"What about Gema?" Wing asked. Nathan had built a database of external contractors who lived around the globe, people he could trust with any number of highly sensitive jobs. Jobs like breaking into a law office and raiding a safe deposit box.

Marisa looked up from her monitor. "She hasn't responded once since Nathan's death."

"Crap," Wing said. "Don't these people want to earn money?"

One by one, Marisa went down a list of names, and each one was dismissed as either out of commission or unresponsive. Wing realized she had some work ahead of her to build up her list of resources. "I'm going to have to go myself," Wing said, standing. "Can you get me on the first flight to Heathrow?"

Marisa turned and started typing, then looked at her watch. "A KLM flight leaves in two hours."

"Book it," Wing said, turning to go.

"All they have is coach," Marisa said.

"Fine. That's all we can afford anyway."

———

Her next stop was the desk of Enzo, a lanky, dark-haired, olive-skinned Italian with elaborate sleeves of tattoos up and down both arms. He was a twenty-five-year-old Nathan had made into a passion project. Enzo had Nathan to thank for saving him from a life of drugs and lengthy prison sentences, and had been crushed when Nathan had died. Now he'd pledged his services to Wing, telling her he was dedicating his life to finding Nathan's killer. Wing had put him in charge of hunting down and killing Max Austin, Max's sister Arina, and her son Alex.

"Any word from Bokun?" she said, planting her feet and crossing her arms in front of Enzo's workstation. Aleksander Bokun was the name of the assassin she'd sent to Croatia to find and kill Max Austin. Bokun was their most effective weapon, and had come at a steep price. Wing had personally met with him to plead for his assistance, ultimately telling Bokun that Asimov had been responsible for Nathan's death. Wing knew Bokun and Nathan had been close.

"None," Enzo said, looking up from a thick computer book. Wing knew he was teaching himself to be a computer hacker. Enzo banged on his keyboard for a few seconds, then shook his head. "He hasn't checked in."

"Crap," Wing said. "How long's it been?" The Asimov contract was her one paying gig. She needed the money, and she needed her demanding client off her back.

"Several hours," Enzo said. "A few headlines coming in now about Koskov's death. No mention of Bokun or Asimov." Enzo shifted in his chair, and she caught him looking at her with wide brown eyes. She looked away. It wasn't the first time Enzo had looked at her that way, and each time it touched a nerve deep inside she'd forgotten existed. Still, she didn't have the mental energy for such games.

"Asimov changed his last name to Austin," Wing said. "Part of his deal with the CIA. I'm sure he's got a completely new identity and everything. Maybe even plastic surgery."

Enzo leaned back in his chair and stretched his lanky frame, toying with the ends of his dreadlocks. "Where do you get all your information?" he asked. "You knew exactly where he'd be for the hit on Koskov, too."

Wing just looked at him.

"Oh, right," Enzo said, smiling, a trace of mock-scorn in his voice. "You can't reveal your source."

Wing wasn't about to be goaded into a response. "Any reaction from Moscow on the news of Koskov's death?"

"No, and I'd be surprised if there is one. I doubt the Russian government would pander to the Western media by legitimizing Koskov. Even if that country is run by the FSB and the mafia."

"All right. Keep after Bokun. I know he's eccentric and a loner. But if he wants to get paid, he's going to have to report in at some point. Meanwhile, start looking for another resource in case Asimov, I mean Austin, somehow got the better of Bokun."

"What? You think that's possible? Bokun's the best there ever was. I mean, he's a killing machine, right?" Enzo's brown eyes twinkled as he looked at her.

"Anything's possible in this business," Wing said, trying to ignore the flirting. "Remember that as your lesson for the day."

———

Wing bounded up the stairs to her office two at a time. She went to her computer and activated a secure email program using a randomly generated security token from an app on her phone. She had many such email accounts, but this one was used for one purpose only. She clicked a couple of times and the inbox came up in a secure browser. Each email was encrypted using a 128-bit AES cipher. Only one person had the email address. As the inbox appeared, she saw she had one new message. She clicked to open it.

Update? Koskov confirmed dead. What of Max Austin?

She looked at the time stamp. It had been sent only fifteen minutes ago. That meant her source also didn't have an update on either Austin or Bokun's status. That was definitely concerning. What could have happened to the two men?

She closed down the secure email program without responding. Let her source stew a little longer. In time, something would come to light. She undocked her laptop, shoved it into a small bag along with some personal effects, then carried the bag downstairs.

Walter was standing by Marisa's desk. When Wing walked up to them, he handed her a small, oblong object wrapped in gauze and packed in a small plastic bag.

"This what I think it is?" Wing asked.

"Yes, but how will you get it through airport security?" Walter asked.

"I have a fake diplomatic passport that allows me to bypass security," Wing replied.

"Handy," Walter said.

"He's still alive, right?"

Walter frowned. "Of course. Not a very happy camper, but he's still alive."

"Excellent," Wing said. Turning to Marisa, she said, "When I land, I need the location and security information for that lawyer's office."

Marisa bent over her workstation. "On it, boss."

SIX

By the time Wing landed at Heathrow, her concern about the health of her assassin was rising. There was still no word from Bokun, and according to her source, Max Austin still hadn't checked in with the CIA. She tried to stay focused on the task at hand. There was nothing she could do until one of them re-emerged.

Her heels clicked on the hard floors of Heathrow terminal as she hastened through the surging crowds. Someone had told her once that Heathrow was the third busiest airport in the world. As a small woman, she was used to fighting to succeed, and the trip through chaotic Heathrow was a metaphor for her life. The passport she'd used belonged to a fake, mid-ranking diplomat from Malaysia. She knew it wouldn't raise any flags. British customs was a breeze and, clear of the crowds, she marched out toward ground transportation.

Marisa had arranged for a driver from the list of contractors still willing to work for them, so Wing wouldn't have to wait in the notoriously long Heathrow cab lines. She walked up to a man wearing a turban and holding a sign with her assumed name and said softly, "I'm told Grey Lady is the pick in the third at Romford."

The man shook his head and said, "I like Sassy Prince in the third."

The code phrase was correct, and Wing followed the man out to a long black Audi.

"Soho Hotel, Richmond Mews," Wing said to the driver as she slid onto the dark leather seat. The sedan lurched away from the curb and merged into the heavy morning traffic. Wing thumbed the lever to raise the window between her and the driver, then removed her phone and resumed her secure chat session with Marisa.

Wing looked up from her phone twenty minutes later and noticed the car was exiting the M4 in Kensington, about five kilometers before reaching downtown London. Alarmed, she lowered the window so she could talk to the driver. "Why are we exiting?"

"Road construction and congestion on the M4, ma'am," the driver said, pointing at a smartphone attached to the dash. "We'll take Bayswater instead."

Wing grunted in reply, then closed the window.

The next time she looked up from her phone, the sunlight had faded and the bars of connectivity on her phone had disappeared. Startled, she glanced out the window and saw that they'd entered a parking garage.

"What the—?" She knew the Soho didn't have a parking garage. Annoyed, she thumbed the button to lower the window to the driver's compartment. The window didn't move. Alarm rose in her throat. She fumbled, pulling at the door latch. It moved in her hand, but the door didn't open. She jammed a finger on the door lock mechanism. Nothing. She banged her head on the head rest in frustration.

The car wound its way down several levels, and arrived at a cement wall where the parking level ended. They made a three-point turn and came to a stop facing the direction they'd come. Through the tinted glass, she saw no other cars. She glanced at her phone; still no connectivity. She tossed it into her bag. This was a sophisticated move, made by a sophisticated adversary. All she could do was wait.

Eventually, she saw a black Mercedes sprinter van roll toward them. It came to a stop directly in front of them and doused its lights. Through the front window, Wing watched as four large men in suits exited the van and took up positions around the perimeter. Almost in unison, each removed a machine pistol from under his suit jacket and stood at attention.

The passenger side door opened, and any remaining mystery of the day's events were erased. A tall, Germanic-looking man stepped from the van. He wore a light grey suit and blue tie. The man's features were stony and his eyes were dull, unfeeling. His skin was the color of limestone. Wing knew the man only as Mueller, personal assistant to the man Wing called the Wheelchair Man, for she did not know his true identity. Mueller gave a signal in the direction of Wing's car, and she heard the door locks release. The driver exited the car and opened her door. With no other options, Wing got out.

She was roughly frisked by the driver and the bag was taken off her shoulder.

Mueller approached. "Come," he said, taking her arm. His baritone voice was dry, deep, as if it had come from the bowels of the earth. He propelled her along the concrete to the open side door of the van. In the dimly lit interior, Wing could see an empty captain's chair facing the rear. Aided by Mueller, she stepped into the darkness of the van and sat down in the chair.

"Ms. Octavia," came a scratchy voice from the rear of the van. As her eyes grew accustomed to the darkness, she made out the scrawny figure of her client, clothed in a black suit three times too large for him. His skeletal body was perched in an oversized motorized wheelchair secured to the floor of the van. He looked older and more withered than when she'd last seen him, only four weeks ago. "Pardon me saying so," he continued in his high-pitched voice, "but you look tired."

"Yeah, well you look like death warmed over," Wing said.

A tense moment passed where she thought she'd over-stepped. Then he let out a squeal of laughter, and Wing saw his red, wet lips glinting in the dim light, curling around a large set of bright white dentures. A clawed hand reached up and tried to tame the wisps of white hair floating around his head, behaving as if there were extra static in the air.

"You may long for my untimely demise," he said. "But be careful what you wish for. The next man may not be as forgiving. Right now, my fondness for you is all that is between you and your own tragic departure from this earth."

"How did I become so lucky," Wing said, folding her arms over her chest. "What do you want? I'm on a schedule."

Another peal of laughter. Spittle flew from the old man's mouth as his body shook with mirth. "I know you are. Such a troublesome business with Lord Bradley. He's an old fool, a man who will not be missed."

Wing blanched. "How did you know—?"

"My dear, there is very little that I don't know. You would do well to remember that."

"And despite that power, you still have not managed to kill Max Austin."

The old man's look darkened and his smile disappeared. "Is that the name he's going by now? Now that he's disappeared into the safe confines of the CIA and their witness protection program?"

Wing's mouth dropped open for a brief moment.

"You are not the only one with sources, my dear. A man does not get to my level of power without cultivating a robust network of information. Most men—" he paused and nodded at Wing "—and women, have their price. So is he dead?"

"If you have so much information, why don't you tell me? You seem—"

"Do not toy with me," the old man growled, more spittle flying. "My patience only extends so far. I know you sent the KGB assassin. A wise choice. A move I would have made myself." His expression softened.

"I haven't heard anything," Wing said. "Both men seem to have disappeared."

"Do I need to remind you the price of failure?" the old man said. Without waiting for an answer he yelled, "Mueller!"

The tall assistant had remained standing next to the open door during the conversation. Now Mueller produced a small tablet and handed it to Wing. On the bright screen were two icons.

"Tap the first one," the old man said. "Technology is a wondrous thing, is it not?"

She tapped the top icon and a video sprang to life,

taking up the full screen of the tablet. The first image took her breath away as she watched the movie unfold. It was only a few seconds long. Even though she hadn't seen him in over twenty years, she recognized her father. He was sitting in a wooden chair holding up a newspaper. His long, flowing beard was all white. Deep lines creased his weathered face. Her heart skipped a beat. Wing's biological parents had been killed not long after her birth. This man had taken her in and raised her as his own, working several back-breaking jobs around the slum where she'd been born just to feed her and her adopted brothers and sisters. Now her client was holding him hostage. She peered at the newspaper. It was today's morning edition of the *Financial Times*.

"Is he ok?" Wing asked, blinking back tears.

"For now," the old man said. "Tap the second video."

She felt momentarily relieved. Wing minimized the video of her father and tapped on the second icon. Once again a video filled the entire screen, and Wing held her breath, steeling herself for anything. This time, a younger man sat in a metal chair, holding a newspaper. The background was different. Wing didn't recognize the man, but noted his Slavic, Eastern European features. He wore a dirty white oxford shirt, untucked, and black trousers. A pair of rimless spectacles were perched on his nose. Wing watched as a hand holding a pistol entered the video frame. She caught her breath as the man's head rocked sideways and blood and brain matter blew out the side of his skull. The man fell from the chair and the video ended.

"What the—?" Wing exclaimed.

The old man's face was frozen in a grotesque smile. "Three days ago you contacted an independent computer hacker code named GreyRabbit—"

Wing's face screwed up in horrified surprise.

"I warned you, my dear," he continued. "Do not hire computer hackers to try to dredge up information about me. Not only will you fail, but you will sign the death warrant of each person you hire. If you can live with that, then keep at it. You will not win. My resources are vast. My connections are beyond what you can even fathom."

Wing suddenly felt dull, like her brain wouldn't function. She'd hired the GreyRabbit without knowing his identity using a series of blind, secure email accounts and a wire transfer to an anonymous bank account in Samoa. How on earth had the hacker been discovered?

"Now go, Ms. Octavia. Go kill Mr. Asimov. Or Austin. Or whatever the fuck he is calling himself these days. I want him dead!"

Wing felt herself being escorted from the van and guided into the back seat of the Audi. She barely noticed the car ride into the city. When she was dropped off at the hotel, she checked in, locked the door behind her, poured herself a glass of wine, and walked to the balcony that overlooked Soho Square Gardens.

She watched lovers strolling hand in hand through the square, past the Bavarian-styled gardener's hut. A gentle breeze ruffled the lush trees and flowering plants that filled the square's gardens. She downed the wine, then poured a second. By the time she'd finished the third glass, her nerves had steadied, and the fear was replaced with anger and frustration.

Turning, she threw the empty glass through the open sliding door, and watched it burst against the wall next to the bed. She would be damned if she was going to let either the baron or her client defeat her. She was better than that, and knew if she focused on one thing at a time, she would prevail. First, get the information out of the safe deposit box. Next, kill and dispose of the baron. Then, kill the Asimov family. Lastly, she'd track down the old man in the wheelchair and kill him, too. One step at a time, she reminded herself. One step at a time.

SEVEN

Paris, France

Max opened his eyes and saw nothing but blackness. Beneath him, the sheets were damp, but luxurious. He put his wrist close to his face and noticed his watch was missing. It hurt just to move his arm. He propped himself on his elbows and waited for his eyes to adjust. His mouth felt like it was stuffed with cotton, and his body ached like he'd been in a car wreck.

Gradually, his eyes acclimated to the darkness and the room came into view. He was lying in an oversized bed. The satin sheets were black. There were no windows, and the door directly across from him was closed. On the wall next to the bed was a gigantic portrait of a nude, brightly tattooed woman. The picture was of the home's owner, and it jogged his memory. He was at Goshawk's, his former lover and current computer expert.

Max turned his head. On the nightstand was a small dish containing a handful of pills. Next to the dish was a bottle of water and a washcloth. He grabbed the bottle and drank half. Then he swung his legs off the bed, pushed open a set of double doors, and entered the bathroom, wincing as he flicked on the light. He relieved himself, then stood naked in front of a full-length mirror, fighting off a wave of dizziness and nausea. His body looked like he'd been attacked by a mountain lion. Three deep cuts had been stitched shut. The rest of his wounds looked like they'd been washed and treated with antibiotic cream. He noticed several days' growth on his normally shaved head.

He returned to the bed and lay back down. He looked at one of the pills from the dish. On one side was written the word *Vicodin*. He sighed with relief. With Goshawk, you never knew.

Just as he was about to doze off, the bedroom door opened and a tall, lithe form glided in, seeming to glow in the darkness. She wore a white silk robe and her long flowing hair had been dyed a bright pink. She came over to the side of the bed.

"Max, darling, you're awake," she said. She put a hand on his forehead, caressing his skin with long fingers tipped with pointed nails. "And the fever seems to have broken. Thank goodness. I was starting to get worried about the infection."

She undid the front of her robe and let it slip to the floor. Even though he'd seen her naked hundreds of times, he still marveled at the beauty and intricacy of her tattoos. She pulled the sheet down and with the grace of a ballerina, threw a leg over his body and straddled him. Letting her hair brush across his face and chest, she took two pills from the dish and held them up.

"You need to sleep, darling," she said. "These will help."

Max allowed her to put them into his mouth, and

accepted a slosh of water from the bottle. "How long have I been here?" he asked.

Goshawk trailed a sharp nail down his chest, avoiding the cuts and scrapes. "Three days, honey. You were in bad shape when you got here."

"Did I talk about what happened?"

"You were delirious when you arrived. I could barely get you into the house and up into the bed."

"Do you have my stuff? My phone and my watch?"

"Yes, dear."

Max breathed a sigh of relief.

"Now don't talk," she said. "You need to rest. After, of course. I've been waiting for this for three days. Somehow fucking you while you were out seemed, well, a little weird, even for me." With that, she gently guided him into her, and Max drifted off into a haze of pleasure.

———

When he woke again, Goshawk was gone. His head still felt woozy and heavy, but he experienced no dizziness when he used the bathroom. Looking around the bedroom, he found his jeans and yanked them on. They were bloodstained and cut in two places, but they were the only clothes he could find. He opened the door and padded down the stairs, shirtless and barefoot.

Goshawk's home was one of the more unique buildings Max had ever been in. As a hyper-paranoid computer expert, Goshawk had taken her own privacy to an extreme level. Her house was a two-story building, custom built inside a warehouse in one of Paris's commercial districts. The outer shell of the warehouse had been reinforced with a lead lining that blocked all radio waves from entering or leaving the structure. Max's mobile phone was useless in her house. Goshawk also had a rule that no foreign electronics were allowed in the building. She maintained a small storage locker on the outside of the interior building where her guests were required to leave their electronics.

He entered the kitchen and found Goshawk in jeans and a thin, sleeveless T-shirt in front of the stove. The black granite counter top was covered with baking supplies, and Max saw a red box of brownie mix. He sat on a stool at the kitchen's center island.

"Thanks for nursing me back to health," Max said.

"My pleasure, darling. We'll just add it to the tab." She smirked and gave the concoction on the stove another stir.

"I need something else," Max said. "Your computer expertise."

"Of course you do. What is it this time, sugar?" She moved away from the stove and poured a cup of steaming black coffee into a white mug and handed it to Max. He took it gratefully, then winced as the scalding liquid scorched his tongue. She poured herself a cup and perched on a bar stool.

"I can't remember how much I've told you about the people trying to kill my family," Max started.

"Not much, lover. Just that you're not sure who they are, but that you suspect the Russian FSB."

"Correct," Max said. "Abrams, the guy you helped me track down a few weeks ago, was just the hired gun, and he never revealed who hired him. I suspect it's connected somehow to my father's position with the KGB—"

"Your father was the Assistant Director of the Belarusian KGB, right? Are they still connected to Moscow?"

"Right. And yes, they are still very tight. Belarus is one of the last of the former Soviet territories to sever ties with

Moscow. My guess is my father must have done something to make enemies of the Russian FSB."

"The Russian FSB. Different name, same goals."

"Exactly." Max paused to take a sip of his coffee.

"So that's why you cut a deal with the CIA? You never did explain that to me."

"They offered to keep Arina and Alex safe in exchange for my services."

"Christ, Max."

"I know. My father is probably rolling over in his grave. I just didn't have any other alternatives."

"Fucking CIA," Goshawk said. "Not sure I can work for you anymore."

"I'm not sure I can fuck you anymore."

"Touché," she said. "So what do you need?"

"I found something the last time I visited my parents' house. It was hidden in a framed picture—"

"Wait, wasn't your parents' house completely destroyed by the bomb that killed them?"

"Yes. I found it back in the barn. Anyway, when I dropped it, a small memory card fell out."

"What's on it?" she asked.

"I don't know. When I put the card into a card reader, all I saw was gibberish. But whatever it is, I'm guessing it might be the reason why our family is being targeted. Whoever is after us probably wants whatever is on that memory card."

"Where is the card?"

"Hidden back at the safe house with Arina and Alex. But I put a copy on the hard drive of my phone."

"Well don't just sit there, sugar. Go get it."

Max left the table, exited Goshawk's building, and retrieved his smartphone. Called a Blackphone, his smartphone was an ultra-secure device that prevented cellular companies from infiltrating it using back-door hooks, utilized encrypted transmissions, and employed its own fire-wall to prevent external intrusions. He stepped outside into the bright sunlight, and used an encrypted email application to send Goshawk the contents of the memory card.

When he returned, he found her in her office. Large television monitors were fixed to the walls around the perimeter of the small room; some showed the health of various servers, while others were tuned into news and stock market channels. To her left was an electronic piano and bench. In front of her were arranged six large computer screens. She was sitting on a shearling covered desk chair, her long legs folded under her, pink hair pulled back into a ponytail. As soon as Max walked in, she hit a key and all the monitors went dark save for the one directly in front of her.

"Where's your tinfoil hat?" Max asked.

"Very funny, fuck toy. Take a seat."

Max sat on the piano bench.

She hit a key and a document flashed onto the screen showing a long string of nonsensical numbers and characters. "You're right about one thing," she said. "The document is encrypted."

Max said. "Can you break the code?"

She laughed. "Obviously you know little about encryption."

"Explain," he said, ignoring her comment.

"Encryption is actually a very simple concept," Goshawk started. "Rudimentary forms of it have been around in analog form for thousands of years. The first known use of cryptography was in Egypt back around 1900 BC—"

"Spare me the history lesson," Max said.

"Fine. Public key encryption is pretty basic. Someone uses a computer to encrypt a message using the public key, which turns the message into gibberish – a long string of alpha-numeric characters like you see here. The recipient of the message needs a private key to decrypt the message. The private key is mathematically related to the public key, but you can't derive the private key from the public key. With me so far?"

"The public key must be generated using the private key," Max said.

"Whoa, look at the smarty pants," Goshawk said. "You are correct. Also, keys are categorized by bit length. The more bits used to perform the encryption, the harder the code is to break. Nowadays, anything under 128 bit is deemed un-secure, given how much computing power is available."

She flashed another document on the screen, this one also filled with gibberish. "The second document you sent me was the public key," she said. "If you count the characters in the public key, you'll see there are 256. Each character is a bit. This is encrypted with 256-bit encryption."

"Got it," said Max. "Can't you throw tons of computing power at it and break the encryption?"

"I'm not the NSA, Max. Where am I going to get that kind of iron?"

Max looked at her. "So we need to find the private key."

"Bingo."

EIGHT

Safe house in upstate New York, USA

Max was barely out of the SUV before he was assaulted by a whirling dervish in the form of a towheaded ten-year-old boy. Alex launched himself at Max and clutched at his chest in a tight bear hug. Max had to stifle a yelp from the pain in his side as Alex gripped him. After four days of healing, the deepest knife cut was still causing him pain. Goshawk had given him a baggie of the Vicodin and he found himself popping one every now and then.

"Uncle Max, come see what Aunt Kate got for me! Come see, come see." He let go from his hug and tugged on Max's hand. Max let himself be pulled across the gravel drive. The safe house was located on a large tract of forested land. The house itself was situated off a long driveway that curved through a wooded patch hiding it from the main road. Situated between the trees and the house was a medium-sized horse paddock rimmed by a white fence. To the left of the house was a large red barn. Alex had been getting riding lessons from one of the compound's staffers charged with care of the animals. In addition to the caretaker and a live-in housekeeper, Max knew the compound was surrounded by a troop of unseen paramilitary security personnel. Kate had said the security was at a level just short of what the President of the United States got when he stayed at the property. Max saw Kate's helicopter off to the side of the barn.

Max wasn't sure he was going to like what 'Aunt Kate' had given his nephew. Aunt Kate was what Alex had taken to calling Kate Shaw, Max's CIA handler. Max followed the boy over to the paddock, and watched as Alex bent down and held up a squirming, golden-haired puppy. Max groaned and looked around. He saw the tall, athletic figure of his sister standing on the long front porch, her arms crossed. Next to her stood Kate, equally tall, impeccably dressed in a banker's pantsuit, her curly hair tamed with a barrette. She wore her usual tortoise-rimmed glasses. Kate also had her arms crossed.

"Do you think that was such a good idea?" he called out to the pair. Neither one answered him.

Max walked over to the house and hugged his sister, ignoring Kate as he walked through the front door. After he'd taken a shower, redressed his wounds, eaten a sandwich, drunk a gallon of water and poured himself a glass of bourbon, he led Kate out to the front porch. They sat in white Adirondack chairs and watched Alex play with the puppy. Max sipped his bourbon and lit a cigarette.

"Where the fuck have you been?" Kate said finally.

"Recovering," Max said. He took a drag on the smoke. "Do you think giving Alex a puppy is a good idea?"

"Did you lose your phone or something?" Kate asked, ignoring his question. "You're going to have to realize that you're no longer working alone. You're part of a team now. You have to communicate. You can't just go off the grid any time you want."

Max took a sip of his bourbon, then stood and lifted his T-shirt. He peeled back the large bandage and showed her one of his wounds. The rough stitches, applied by Goshawk, were still in. It would leave an ugly scar.

"Max, what the fuck?" Kate said, her hand going to her mouth. "How did that happen?"

Her surprised reaction seemed genuine. Max said nothing.

"Did you get caught by Croatian authorities?" Kate asked.

Max sat back down and took another sip. "I was attacked at the job site."

"Attacked? How?" Kate exclaimed. "Who knew—?" Her voice trailed off as she put it together.

"Exactly," Max said. "Only your team and I knew exactly where I'd be and when. The mole is the only explanation." Several weeks ago, the location where Kate had been hiding Arina and Alex on the outskirts of Minsk was leaked to Max's enemies, causing all four of them to be almost killed. Because of the mole, their current location was known only by one CIA employee: Kate. The farm was a Secret Service safe house. Kate had gone outside the Agency to try to ensure their safety.

"Fuck," Kate said. "This is worse than I thought."

"So I'm sorry if I wasn't in a hurry to alert you to my location."

"Understood," Kate said. She looked lost in thought. "What happened with the attacker? No other bodies were reported."

Max looked at her. He'd been so preoccupied with his

recovery and the mystery of the encrypted memory card that it hadn't occurred to him to check the news reports coming out of Croatia. "Someone must have buried the news story, or maybe someone got rid of the body at the scene," he said. He briefed her on the rest of the operation, leaving his physical condition vague. "Doubtful he survived the C-4 explosion," he finished.

Arina walked out onto the porch and leaned against the railing.

Kate stood and said, "I have to go. I'm working on your next job, so make sure you get rested and get that cut healed up." With that, she took the steps down from the porch. A second later, the blades started turning. Max and Arina watched as the helicopter took off, banked ninety degrees to the east, and disappeared from view.

"What cut?" Arina asked, sitting down in Kate's vacated chair.

"Nothing to worry about," Max said.

"What cut, Max?" Arina pressed.

Max stood again and lifted his shirt.

Arina sucked in her breath. "Oh my God, Max. That looks deep. Did you get that treated by a doctor?"

"In a manner of speaking," Max said. He'd run out of bourbon and used that as an excuse to walk into the house. Once he'd returned with a fresh glass, Arina took up where they'd left off.

"Max, Alex is starting to ask a lot of questions about what you do."

Max watched Alex chase the puppy around the paddock. "Did you talk with him about how he's going to have to take care of the dog? Walk it, feed it, pick up its poop?"

"Did you hear what I said?" Arina said, her voice a little louder.

They were entering well-worn territory. Arina was dead set on preventing Alex from growing up like Max had, under the direct influence of their famous spy father. Max had learned everything he knew about being an agent and an assassin from their legendary father. Each weekend while growing up, they'd visited a defunct KGB compound on the outskirts of Minsk and Max had practiced everything from shooting to counter-surveillance techniques. Arina wanted Alex to grow up as a normal boy. Max didn't see how that would be possible. Normal boys didn't have assassins for uncles and famous spies for grandfathers. Normal boys didn't live in the CIA's witness protection program. "What are you telling him?"

"I told him you're kind of like a policeman. That you hunt down and apprehend international criminals."

"Not far from the truth," Max said. "Don't you think, given our present circumstances, that we should teach him how to shoot a gun? At least give him some experience with a small pistol, and maybe a shotgun?"

"Absolutely not!" Arina exclaimed.

"This is America, sis. Guns are everywhere here. Don't you think we should teach him how to handle them safely?"

"I strictly forbid it! I'm serious, Max. If I catch you even talking with him about guns, we're moving out."

Max laughed. "You can't move out, Arina. We're stuck with each other for a while."

"Watch me," Arina said, and stood up. "I'm not kidding, Max. The kid deserves a chance at a normal life. Don't fuck that up for him." She stepped off the porch and walked out to where Alex was playing with the puppy.

Max's newfound love for Alex had taken him by

surprise. Arina's husband had been killed in the same bomb attack that had killed their parents, leaving Alex fatherless. Over the past several weeks, Max had developed a strong attachment to the boy. Before Max left for Croatia, they'd gone fishing together in the pond behind the house and Max had shown him how to drive the four-wheeled quads stored in the barn.

Max pushed himself up and walked into the house. Despite the two bourbons, the wound in his side throbbed, and he went in search of the Vicodin. In his bedroom, he glanced at the photo on his bedside table. The picture was of him, his sister, and his parents when Max had been about twelve. He'd found the picture in the barn on his father's work table. It was the one keepsake that had survived the explosion. He picked it up and stared at the photo, thinking momentarily of his father.

A few weeks ago when Max had first arrived at the safe house, he'd dropped the photo, breaking the glass. When he had reassembled the frame, he'd found the memory card, hidden between the photo and the frame's backing. Now he noticed someone had replaced the glass while he'd been away.

Maybe it was intuition. Maybe it was the knowledge that someone had been in the room. He stepped over to the closet and opened the door. He removed the two boxes containing his meager possessions, then used his knife to pull up the carpet in the left corner. Under the padding, he dug the knife's tip into a crack in the flooring and pried up one of the boards. He shone the light from his smartphone into the small cavity and his heart skipped a beat.

The box he'd stored the memory card in was gone.

NINE

Safe house in upstate New York, USA

"Arina!" Max yelled. Carrying the photo, he walked out of the bedroom and shouted for his sister again. The bedrooms were situated around an atrium that contained the living room and large, two-story plate-glass windows overlooking the pond in the back of the house. "Arina!" he yelled into the atrium.

His sister came running from the direction of the kitchen, an anxious look on her face. She held a dish towel in her hands. "What? What is it?"

Max held up the photo. "Did you replace the glass in this picture frame?"

Arina's face relaxed. "Max, you scared me. I thought something was wrong. Jesus." She recomposed herself. "Yes. Kate brought it with her a couple days ago. Same day she brought up the puppy. Said you'd asked for it. I thought I'd put it in the picture frame for you so it was there when you got home. Why are you asking?"

"Were you the only one who was in that room while I was gone?

"Yes, I think so. Except for maybe the house cleaner. They were here last week. Why?"

Max forced himself to calm. How could his sister have known about the card, or the hiding place? He hadn't mentioned it to anyone. Telling her about it now might put her life at risk.

"Never mind," he said. "No big deal." He walked down the wide, sweeping staircase to where she stood. "I thought I'd left something in a certain place. When I got home, it was in a different spot. Must have been the maid." He gave Arina a hug. "It's nice to be here," he said.

"Alex missed you," she said.

"And I missed him." Max pulled the rabbit's foot from his pocket. "Reminds me why I'm doing this."

Arina looked away. "What exactly are we doing, Max?"

"Trying to stay among the living," he said. "It's not my fault we're in this spot, but I'm going to fix it."

Arina turned and walked back into the kitchen. "This isn't living," he heard her say as she walked away.

———

Max set the picture on the credenza by the front door and walked outside. Alex, who was still in the front yard playing with the puppy, gave him a wave. Max smiled and waved back, then turned toward the barn.

The red barn was half allocated to three horses and the mowers, tractors, and other machinery necessary to make the estate run. The other half of the barn was devoted to the security team that kept the compound safe. Max turned left, away from the equipment, and found the large sliding door that separated the security offices from the rest of the barn. Above his head was a walled-off, second-floor loft where the security team bunked when off duty. He rapped hard on the metal door with his fist and waited. He knew the team could see him on the security camera mounted directly above the door.

He heard the sound of a latch being released, then the big door slid open on oiled runners. This was Max's first visit to the security office, and he was impressed at the gear. The Secret Service had spared no expense. The interior of the room was lined with displays, work stations, and racks of computer equipment. Blinking red and green lights were everywhere. A serious-looking soldier wearing a paramilitary uniform with no insignia sat at one workstation, his blond hair cropped in a crew cut. In front of Max stood a stout man, his face lined and weathered. Instead of the paramilitary uniform, he wore suit pants and an oxford-cloth shirt with the sleeves rolled up. His eyes were hard and cold as he looked at Max.

"Mr. Austin," the man greeted Max. "Can I help you with something?"

Max had been introduced to Ed Willson, the compound's head of security, when he'd first arrived. Kate had told him the man was a veteran agent of the secret service, and had earned this post as a semi-retirement position. Willson had given Max a brief overview of the security arrangements, clearly not happy revealing any of his strategies to a recent member of the KGB.

"Ed," Max said, being as polite as he could. "I'm afraid we might have had a breach while I was away."

Willson's eyes narrowed to thin slits. "Impossible. We didn't pick anything up." He took Max's arm and maneuvered them both out into the barn's main room, sliding the big security door closed behind him. "What makes you think—?"

"Something was stolen out of my bedroom," Max interrupted. "I know you have security cameras—"

"What was stolen?" Willson interrupted.

"The item stolen is a private matter. It was well hidden in my room. Someone would have had to know it was there, and spent time looking until they found it."

Willson's eyebrows raised, then lowered, resuming the scowl. "What was the item?"

"I'd rather not say. I know you have security cameras in every room. If we can look at your footage between last Monday and Thursday morning, I think we'll have a—"

"Not going to happen."

Max was incredulous.

"My guess is that it was one of your family," Willson said. "Maybe your son? I have a fifteen-year-old myself. Boys just like to get into everything. He probably found it and took it."

"Look," Max said, his own brow narrowing. "I'm happy to do the work with the security footage if you just point me—"

"I'm sorry, Mr. Austin. I'm sure you can understand that it would be against protocol for me to allow you to use our systems. Not only could I get fired, but it also violates my own principles."

"You mean to give a former KGB agent access," Max stated. He realized the security man was probably old enough to have served during the Cold War.

Willson just looked at him.

Max nodded. He knew pushing Willson any harder at this point would be counterproductive. Besides, he had another idea. Max turned and exited the barn, and joined

Alex in the paddock. By now, Alex had tired of the puppy and was tossing a tennis ball high into the air and trying to catch it. The puppy waited expectantly for the ball to fall to the ground.

"Have you named the puppy yet, Alex?" Max asked.

"Yes," Alex exclaimed as he flung the ball as high into the air as he could. "His name is Spike!"

Max laughed. "That's a great name."

"I can't get him to chase after the ball, though," Alex complained. "He's not much of a retriever."

"Give him time, Alex. He's still too small to fit the ball into his mouth." Max watched as Alex deftly caught the ball, then turned and winged it back up into the air.

"Say, Alex, you didn't go into my bedroom while I was away, did you?"

Alex turned, the smile vanishing from his face in an instant. The ball fell to the ground, and the puppy dashed over and tried to bite down on it. "Gosh no, Uncle Max. I would never. Mom gave me very strict instructions to never enter your room, unless you invite me."

Max gave his hair a tussle and picked up the tennis ball. "Ok, that's what I thought. Nothing to worry about."

"Ok, Uncle Max. Want to play catch?"

"Sure. Let me make a quick phone call, then we can play." He turned his back on the barn and removed the Blackphone from his pocket. The smartphone was the same size and shape as an iPhone, but had software on it that would scramble all of his voice and electronic transmissions, as well as his geo-location. Max had no doubt that Willson and his team would listen in on all cellular traffic originating from the compound. The encryption on his Blackphone would scramble the transmission, making it undecipherable to Willson's team.

Max tapped a speed-dial button and listened. Goshawk's voicemail came up. Max said, "Text me when you're free. I have a job for you that I think you'll find intriguing."

He hung up, placed the phone in his pocket, then tossed the ball to Alex.

TEN

Undisclosed location in upstate New York, USA

Max's phone buzzed with a text message. He removed it from his pocket with one hand, while tossing the tennis ball back to his nephew with his other. *Call me.* It was Goshawk.

He and Alex had been throwing the ball for an hour, and the sun was starting to set over the back of the house. The puppy darted between them, hoping for a chance at the ball.

"Gotta make a call, buddy," Max said.

Alex looked crestfallen.

"It's almost time for dinner anyway. Go see if your mother needs any help in the kitchen. And don't forget to feed little Spike."

"Ok, Uncle Max," Alex said as he ran off toward the house. The puppy looked on for a moment, then followed more slowly. Alex seemed to remember the puppy, and turned to scoop up the wriggling furball.

Max tapped a speed-dial button on his phone, then waited. He knew the network was routing the voice over IP call through an encryption device and several anonymous proxy servers. A few seconds later, Goshawk's voice came on the line, slightly garbled with distortion from the security.

"Where are you?" she asked.

"Trust me, you don't want to know."

"Well, wherever it is, these people you're dealing with have some serious state of the art firewalls. Impressive shit, actually."

"I guess that makes me feel a little better," Max said. "Able to get through?"

"I have to say, sugar, that hacking into the US government is pretty thrilling. Scary and dangerous and exciting at the same time."

"And we all know how much you like that kind of thing," Max said. "Get on with it."

"I got through and found their security camera footage. Even their camera tech is impressive. I went back a week, to just after you left for Croatia. I'm downloading a copy now. They'll never know I was there."

"Excellent," Max said.

"I'll put it out on one of my servers. Do you remember the IP address for Hemingway?" Goshawk named all her servers after dead writers.

Max read off the number from memory for confirmation, promised to wire Goshawk payment, and hung up the phone. Walking into the house, Max knew getting the footage to his laptop for his review would be tricky and time consuming. Ed's team would be monitoring all the internet traffic in and out of the house. Even if he encrypted the transmission, Max figured Ed's team would sniff the string of internet gibberish and shut it down just to be safe.

He went up to his bedroom and rummaged around in a box in the closet. During Max's rapid departure from Paris to their current hideout, Kate's team had put most of his belongings into secure storage. This box, however, he'd asked to be delivered to the safe house. He yanked out a boxy satellite phone, then rummaged some more and found the charger. He wrapped the two items in a towel, then put his laptop under his arm and left the bedroom.

The safe house was a rambling two-story, modern home built partly from logs and partly from stone. It had exposed beams and a cathedral ceiling in the main living area, a stone fireplace that dominated one corner of the living room, and large windows facing over a duck pond. Two wings stuck out from either side of the house. One contained a large kitchen, pantry, and staff quarters. The other housed additional bedrooms, a library, a large television room, a game room, and a mud room. When Max had first arrived, he'd toured the house, paying particular attention to the location of the surveillance cameras. To the security team's credit, the home was very well covered by an array of small, inconspicuous cameras. Max had made note of each of the blind spots — areas in the house where the cameras couldn't see.

Carrying his equipment with the satellite phone hidden by the towel, he made his way into the library. The walls were covered with shelves of books from floor to ceiling. Four large leather wing chairs were arrayed in the middle of the room. A cart was positioned next to them with crystal bottles of bourbon and brandy. The room smelled vaguely like cigar smoke, and contained a small alcove also lined with shelves. A leather chaise was against one wall of the alcove. The configuration of the security cameras prevented the surveillance team from seeing into the nook. Max sat down on the chaise.

He plugged the unit into the wall outlet and waited while electricity revived the battery. Leaving the satellite phone plugged in, he connected it to his laptop via a USB cord. Then he used his computer to activate the internet network on the satellite phone, waiting patiently for the tiny green light to come on indicating a successful connection.

Max knew he'd get a slow connection using the satellite, and speed would be even slower when he encrypted the transmission. If he was lucky, the files would download overnight.

When the green light appeared, he used a secure file transfer protocol application to locate Goshawk's server. When the window refreshed, he saw a *read me* file and a list of .mp4 files. The browser window indicated there were sixty-eight files. He clicked on the *read me* file.

Your friends have surveillance technology that only turns on the camera when the camera senses activity. It uses motion detection to achieve this, which then also saves them from storing too much video files. I sorted through all their archives for the cameras located in your bedroom and the hallway outside your bedroom. There were only these files from the time you were gone. Enjoy. xxoo

Max closed the text file and dragged the .mp4 files to his hard drive. A status bar appeared and indicated two hours of download time. Max left the laptop and satellite phone on the chaise, selected a book from the shelves called *Annals of the Former World* by someone named McPhee, poured himself a bourbon, and sat down to read. Forty-five minutes later, he was called to dinner, and left the laptop on the chaise.

———

When he returned from dinner, the file downloads had completed. Max poured himself a second bourbon, and sat down to browse through the video footage. He used fast-forward to move through the files. He sipped his bourbon and watched.

The first several were uneventful. They showed either Alex or Arina walking down the hallway, obviously on the way to their own bedrooms or the bathroom. He poured himself another bourbon, and this time left the crystal decanter balanced on the chaise next to him. He was developing a taste for the American spirit.

After the fortieth file, he was starting to think maybe he wasn't going to find anything. Then he reminded himself that the memory card couldn't just walk out of his bedroom on its own. Someone had to have walked in and searched the room, disassembled the frame, found the card, then reassembled the frame and left it exactly where it had been. Max sipped and clicked and watched.

By the sixtieth file, he was preparing himself for disappointment, and letting his mind wander to his next move. He clicked on the sixty-first file and sipped the bourbon. Five minutes into the movie, he sat up and tapped on the 1x icon to slow the film back down to normal speed. A man had entered the frame. Max noted the time stamp: it was 3:12 a.m., four days after Max had left for Croatia. The picture was dim, but Max could see the shadowy shape moving down the hallway from the direction of the staircase toward the camera. The man looked average in height, and wore a jacket and a ball cap pulled down tight, hiding his face from the camera. He looked trim and fit and moved confidently down the hallway. Max watched as the man walked under the camera and disappeared from view. The file ended, the camera having ceased recording with no more motion in its field of view.

Max clicked on file number 62 and saw the hallway facing in the opposite direction. He fast forwarded the footage until he saw the man's back appear. A second later, the man turned and opened the door to Max's bedroom. The video file ended.

Max clicked on file number 63. The interior of his room came into view, from the perspective of the camera mounted over the bedroom door. Max saw the man enter and, moving with the speed of a pro, begin a systematic search of the room. When the man finally disassembled the picture frame, Max saw him grab something, glance at it, then put it in his pocket. After reassembling the frame, the man exited the room. The next few files showed the intruder walking down the hallway until he finally exited from view.

Max shut the laptop and wrapped up the satellite phone in the towel. The implications to this were staggering, Max knew. The presence of the video footage meant only one thing. Whoever had taken the card from Max's room had entered the property with the full knowledge of Ed Willson and his staff. Max replaced the nearly empty decanter of bourbon on the beverage cart and left the library. It was time he and Ed Willson had another chat.

ELEVEN

Langley, Virginia

Kate Shaw tossed a pen against the beige grey wall in frustration. She'd been in the tiny observation room going on eight hours, with barely a break to pee. One side of the room was taken up by a large plate-glass window with light tint. A small table sat in front of her covered by coffee cups, food containers, and empty water bottles. The room had the perpetual stink of body odor and moldy cheese.

Through the window, she could see a large man with a flattop and a smaller man with skin the color of lightly roasted coffee. The larger man wore a blue suit, which did a terrible job of disguising his military bearing. He was packing machinery into a large case on a trolley. The smaller man wore a white oxford-cloth shirt and a blue silk tie with a large knot like some football players liked to wear. His name was Kaamil; he held the title of Special Operations Officer and worked on Kate's team. Kaamil was in the process of rolling his sleeves down. When he was done, he looked over at the window and rolled his eyes.

Kate smiled to herself. She was happy to see that her favorite officer was taking the polygraph in stride. She'd passed the lie-detection exercise off as routine, making reference to the CIA employee handbook which indicated that all members of the CIA from the Director down to the mailroom clerk could be expected to take a polygraph once every three years on average. She didn't have the official results, but she knew her staff had all passed with flying colors. She thought it highly unlikely that one of them could be the mole.

Kaamil was the last one of the day and Kate was looking forward to a glass of white wine and a long hot shower. Her mobile phone buzzed on the table, and she smiled when she saw the name on the screen.

"Yes, sir?" she answered.

Bill's gruff voice came over the earpiece. "Need you up here right away."

Kate frowned. It wasn't like Bill to get right to business. William Blackwood was her immediate superior, and held the official title of Director, Special Operations. They'd worked together for almost a decade. "Ok, where?"

"Director's office," Bill said.

"On my way," Kate said into the phone, but Bill had already hung up.

———

When Kate arrived in the ante-chamber to the Director of the CIA's office, the capable-looking assistant immediately ushered her in to the Director's inner office. Not many CIA staffers got to see this office, and it was Kate's first visit since the new Director had taken over. The previous tenant, a CIA lifer, had been forced to retire when the investigation into the bombing of the American embassy in Tunisia revealed gross incompetence and serious intelligence missteps.

She entered and was amazed to see the room's transformation. Gone were the large portraits of former Directors, all white males in either military garb or severe suits. Gone was the sterile grey cloth furniture. Instead, large, colorful modernist paintings hung on the walls and white leather furniture was tastefully arranged in the large room. A flower rested in a crystal vase. A teak conference table had been positioned by the window surrounded by black leather chairs. It seemed the new Director was already putting her mark on the staid institution of the Central Intelligence Agency.

As Kate entered, a tall woman with short blond hair rose from the conference table and came forward. Two men in dark suits, one of them Bill, remained seated.

"Piper Montgomery," the woman said, offering her hand. "I've heard great things and am delighted to finally meet you."

Kate's hand was nearly crushed by the Director's grip. She found herself speechless, a rare occurrence. She'd heard rumors about the new Director, but in her presence, was awed by the charisma and force of her personality. Kate was still fumbling for words by the time the Director had sat back down.

"Please, Kate," the Director said. "Have a seat."

Kate sat in one of the conference table chairs, crossing one leg over the other. Each of the other three had coffee. None was offered to her.

"Congratulations on the Croatian operation," the

Director said. "I read the report this morning. It was well executed."

"Thank you," Kate said, unsure what else to say. The Director was leaning forward with her elbows on the table.

"I was also just briefed on the situation with your asset, Max Austin."

Now Kate was worried. Only she and Bill knew the details of Max's arrangement. She glanced at Bill, who avoided her gaze.

"Kate, I'm intimately familiar with the concepts of compartmentalization, need-to-know, and plausible deniability. They are the pillars of how this organization has subsisted for generations. I realize those processes are in place to reduce the risk of information leakage and also to obfuscate the details of actions to protect senior leaders of the organization. If I don't know we sent an assassin to kill a Russian colonel, then I can't very well provide details in a senate hearing, can I?"

Kate stayed quiet. She wasn't sure where this was going, but didn't like the direction of the conversation.

"My mandate, as communicated to me by the President, is to open this organization up and bring it into the twenty-first century. The reason my predecessor failed can be directly linked to the little islands of information that are created and hoarded by this organization's staff."

Kate glanced at Bill again, who seemed to have found something interesting in his coffee. Then Kate looked at the man sitting across from Bill. Charles Tedford III was the Director of Clandestine Operations, Bill's direct superior. Charles was one of the Director's immediate reports, and along with the Directors of Intelligence, Science & Technology, and Support, sat on the Director's leadership team. Charles was old-guard CIA, a lifer who'd been passed over by Senator Montgomery's appointment. Charles was a deft political animal who would do anything to survive. He was looking right at the Director, nodding his head to everything she said.

"So now we find ourselves in somewhat of an awkward position," the Director said. "Are you familiar with Executive Order 12333?" Without waiting for an answer, the Director went on. "It prohibits assassination by any person employed by or acting on behalf of the United States. You can thank Reagan for that little gem." The Director paused, looking hard at Kate.

"I am not a naive woman, Kate. The world is a crazy place. Between radical Islamists devising their own oil supply chains to the massive rape of our country's intellectual property by the Chinese through computational invasion, things are only going to get crazier. We need every weapon at our disposal, and if killing some Russian colonel who was smuggling weapons to Ukrainian rebels gives us some strategic advantage, then I'm all for it."

Kate silently breathed a sigh of relief.

"So therein lies the challenge. How do we utilize all the weapons at our disposal without getting locked up in jail? How do we share information among ourselves, and with our colleagues in other departments like the NSA and FBI, without increasing the risk of leaks?" She paused again. "Any ideas?"

"None come to mind immediately, ma'am, but I'll put some thought into it."

"You do that. Until such time as we can figure it out, your man there makes me extremely uncomfortable. A former KGB agent who was not only conducting assassinations on behalf of private clients for years, but who will do anything to protect his family – including defecting to his sworn enemy? What part of this did you think was a good idea?"

Kate figured she had about ten seconds to defend her hard-fought prize. "I've weighed all the risks and I believe he's a tremendous asset to our fight. In our business, we have to take risks. Sometimes—"

"Don't lecture me on risk, young lady," the Director said.

"No, ma'am, I'm sorry," Kate said. She steeled herself and continued. "I believe this asset will pay off for us for years to come. He is a legend, a machine. I've been in the field with him. I've seen him in action. He is the real deal. Trained agents that operate at his level are very difficult to find, much less harness into effective tools. Not only did we steal him right out from under the Russians' noses, but we also put him right into play. He took Koskov out with a perfectly executed operation—"

"He's a dangerous loose cannon who can't be trusted," the Director broke in. "Can you actually say you know for sure where his loyalties lie?"

"His loyalties are with his family," Kate said quietly, feeling herself falling into the Director's trap. "As long as we are perceived to be helping to keep his family safe, he'll do whatever we want."

"And can you keep his family safe?" the Director asked. "Can you keep the charade up long enough to get value out of this man?"

Kate finally capitulated, and said nothing.

"Exactly," the Director said. She sat back in her chair and crossed her arms. "How many men did we lose bringing him in?"

"Four, ma'am," Kate said quietly.

The Director sat back in her chair, crossed her arms,

and sat for a moment, as if she were about to render a judgment.

"At this point, I'm not telling you to shut him down," the Director said. "But he's a dangerous loose end to have running around and it makes me nervous. If I see anything I don't like, I'm going to end it and ship him back to Moscow in a spy trade. Do I make myself clear?"

"Yes, ma'am," Kate said. "You won't be disappointed."

"That'll be all."

Kate tried to catch Bill's eye on the way out of the office, but he studiously avoided her. Perhaps he was no longer her ally after all. She was going to need something stronger to drink tonight than wine.

TWELVE

London, UK

Wing stood in the large antechamber of the office of the branch manager of C.H. Lore & Sons, an exclusive private bank in London's Soho district. The floor was marble, and covered with ornate Persian rugs. The walls were hung with art by the renaissance masters. Frescos covered the ceiling that towered above her head. Behind her, the main lobby of the bank was silent. She could have heard a pin drop. There were no administrative assistants clattering on keyboards, no customers milled about, no light music sounded in the vast lobby. Wing wondered if anyone ever came here to do business, or if this institution was destined for extinction now that most banking had gone electronic.

A somber man appeared in front of her wearing a black suit and a silver tag above the left breast with the name *Paine*. His face was impassive, and he stared at her through thick rimless spectacles perched on a long, curved nose. "May I help you?" His voice was slow and nasal.

She produced a brass-colored key from her left suit pocket, roughly two inches long. "I need access to my safe deposit box."

He glanced down briefly, taking in both her left hand with the key and her right hand encased in a thick ace bandage.

"Judo accident," Wing explained.

The man's eyebrows went up. "Indeed. Box number?"

"Forty-six," Wing said.

Mr. Paine stared at her for a moment, then turned and walked back into his office. A moment later, he reappeared and said, "Follow me."

Obtaining the key from the law offices of Cadd, Otley & Sandell, Esquires, had been relatively easy. The security officer in the lobby had disappeared as planned and a key had been left in the front door to the interior office. Dressed in black with a balaclava around her face and hair, looking like a modern ninja, Wing had easily slipped into the offices. A ten-minute search of Sandell's office had yielded a folder with a key taped to a piece of paper. A further search offered no additional information, such as the number to the box. After a call to Walter, Henry had revealed the box's number.

Wing followed Mr. Paine down a long, brightly lit hallway filled with more Renaissance art, her heels clicking on the marble flooring. After they passed several doors, the banker turned and entered a large vault. The thick metal door was open and a red carpet led through the portal into the inner vault. Mr. Paine paused at a raised dais in the center of the front room. The dais had a place for two keys and a small, oval indentation the size of a thumbprint. A keyboard and small LCD screen were on the backside. Mr. Paine inserted a key into one of the key holes, then took a position behind the keyboard.

Wing inserted her own key, then paused, looking at him. He looked back disdainfully and said, "You'll need to supply your thumbprint, madam."

"Does it matter which thumb?" she asked, holding up her bandaged hand.

Mr. Paine's brow furrowed. "Did we not fully explain the procedure when you opened the box, Mrs.—?"

She flashed a smile at him, ignored his implied question, and said, "Yes, but it was so long ago and I'm just so busy these days. One forgets easily."

"Right," Mr. Paine said, offering her a sour smile. "We require the right thumbprint, as each print on each finger is unique."

"Of course they are," Wing said, smiling brightly. "What do you do in cases where someone's thumb might be maimed or damaged?"

"We have procedures," Mr. Paine said, not moving.

With a sigh of resignation, Wing made a show of fiddling with her bandage. In a single move, she pulled back a flap with her left hand and placed her thumb in the indentation, flashing the bank manager an irritated look. She hid her right hand from view by holding the ace bandage flap open with her left hand. Mr. Paine raised his eyebrows and tapped a few keystrokes. Wing held her breath.

The bank manager frowned, and tapped a few more keys. Wing's stomach tightened. She was tense, ready to yank the pistol from her purse if needed.

"Please, remove your thumb and try again," he said. "You may need to try a slightly different position."

Wing lifted her thumb, paused, then placed it back in the indentation, in a slightly different position.

Mr. Paine smiled and said under his breath, "Yes, there you are, you little devil. Damn technology. Only works half the time."

Wing relaxed and withdrew her thumb, hiding the severed finger of Lord Bradley with the bandage.

"Follow me," Mr. Paine said, smiling at her as if they were new friends.

She smiled back and followed the bank manager through the second door into the inner vault. Several small alcoves were off to her left, each covered by a heavy black velvet curtain. "Wait here," the bank manager said, and disappeared through another vault door. A few minutes later, he reappeared with a long, flat, grey metal box. "You may use an alcove if you like."

Her heart in her stomach, Wing took the box and went behind one of the curtains. She lifted the hinged top and peered inside. She saw two manila envelopes, both the size of a sheet of paper. In the back of the box were a few packets of pounds sterling. Otherwise, the box was empty. She took the cash and stuffed it in her purse. Then she grabbed the envelopes and stuffed those into her purse. She left the curtained alcove and handed the empty box back to Mr. Paine. Her legs shaky, she bid Mr. Paine good day and exited the bank into the morning sunshine.

————

Wing squinted at the line of taxis waiting at the hotel next to the bank. She jumped into the back of one of the distinct black vehicles and said, "Heathrow."

The driver pulled out of line and shot into traffic.

She yanked the two envelopes from her bag. One was thinner and felt like it might contain photographs. The second was thicker, and was lumpy on the bottom, like it held a sheaf of papers and something else. She opened the second one and dumped the contents into her lap. A file folder fell out, along with a USB thumb drive. The thumb drive had the logo of Cadd, Otley & Sandell, Esquires. She set it aside and opened up the file folder. She was staring at a picture of herself, and her heart began racing. The picture had been taken from a distance, using a telephoto lens. She was walking down a street she didn't immediately recognize. She flipped the picture over and found a stack of about ten more photographs, all of them surveillance-style pictures of her on the street. Underneath the photos, she found a dossier, and her eyes went wide in shock.

To be successful in her business, Wing needed to remain a ghost; she needed to be anonymous. Her identity had to be hidden from her clients and she needed to remain off-the-grid with regard to various government entities and other institutions. All her personal financial transactions were done under an assumed identity. She even paid taxes as that assumed identity. Her business operated almost entirely in the black market; no official record of it, its owner, or its employees existed. The business itself was organized under a string of impenetrable shell companies at offshore locations. The building she bought had actually been purchased by one of these shell companies. Her anonymity was crucial to her survival. Now she was looking at a dossier that contained her entire life story. How many copies of this were in existence?

The file started with records of her childhood adoption, then moved to her high school and college transcripts. Thankfully, the period just before she was hired by Nathan was a gap, but the file picked up recently with details of several of her most recent operations. There was also a ledger showing financial records of her firm, its location just outside Budapest, and details of her staff. Wing swallowed, her dry throat clicking. There was only one way Lord Bradley would have this kind of information. It had to come from someone inside her organization.

Thumbing on her smartphone, she dialed Marisa. "I'm on the way in. I'll be there in a few hours."

"Were you able to—?"

Wing cut her off by hanging up her phone. It pained her to do so, but her mind was reeling. She didn't know who she could trust.

THIRTEEN

Undisclosed location in upstate New York, USA

It took Max and Goshawk only a few minutes to work out a plan. It was sketchy, but it was the best they could do considering the circumstances. Max was hyper-aware of the risk he was taking going after the very security staff that was protecting his family. Between the attack in Croatia and the man entering their so-called safe house unimpeded, however, Max knew their safety was at risk anyway. The plan called for alerting Kate at the onset of the operation. Afterward, he'd have to work out a new place for them to stay, away from Kate's staff. It was 9:00 p.m. He had four hours until they got started.

After watching the rest of the video footage, Max had helped Arina and their housekeeper clean up the kitchen, then had played video games with Alex until Arina had shooed the boy to bed. They put the puppy in its crate in Alex's room, where it promptly fell asleep. Now, Max sat on the side of Alex's bed.

"Are we going to live here forever, Uncle Max?" Alex said. He was wearing a set of pajamas with the Avengers characters stenciled in bright colors.

Max tussled his hair. "Do you like it here?" he asked.

"I like it when you're here," Alex said. "But when you're gone, it's boring. There are no other kids around, and Mom won't take me anywhere."

"I can see what you mean," Max said. Alex needed kids around him. "Do you like the horses and the paddock and the barn?"

Alex nodded his head. "Can we take the quads out for a ride tomorrow?"

"Maybe, sport," Max said, tussling his hair again. "Let's see how things go." He said goodnight and closed the door behind him. Max knew there would be no quad riding tomorrow.

———

Max sat on the chaise lounge in the library, reading the McPhee book and sipping water. At 12:45 a.m., he washed back a Vicodin, shut the book, and took it with him to his room, where he stretched out on the bed and started reading, taking care to stay as still as possible. If everything was going according to plan, Goshawk would be hacked into the compound's camera system and recording a video file of Max lying on his bed, reading. A few minutes later, his smartphone buzzed and he saw a text message that showed a single word. *Go.*

He swung his legs off the bed, reached under the mattress, and retrieved a pistol, which he shoved into his waistband. He darted out the door, down the hall, descended the sweeping stairs, and strode out the front door. If Goshawk was doing her job, each video camera in Max's path would show an image with no movement. This was for the benefit of the security team, who would be monitoring the cameras as part of their surveillance protocol.

Max stole along the side of the house, making his way toward the barn. He darted across the open ground, then hugged the side of the barn and made his way around to the back. A half moon shown silver light on his path. He saw no movement. At the back door to the barn, he bent down, removed a sliver of metal from his pocket, and picked the door's lock. He slid into the barn's darkened interior.

As his eyes adjusted to the darkness, he saw farm implements, several quads, and stacks of hay bales. He moved around the equipment and found the sliding door to Ed Willson's operations room. About five feet from the door was a rusted 1963 Ford Fairlane sitting on flat tires. He hunkered down behind the old car, hidden from the door to the operations room, then slid an earbud, its wire attached to his smartphone, into his ear. Max checked his watch: three minutes until all hell broke loose. He watched the second hand move, steeling himself. He only hoped Kate would forgive him once she was presented with evidence of Willson's illicit activities.

As the second hand on his Rolex chunked into the twelve mark, Max looked up to watch the door of the security men's bunkhouse. At that moment, he knew Goshawk was cutting off the electricity to the entire compound, which would force their backup generator to kick in. Goshawk would then launch a massive denial-of-service attack on Willson's computers and phone systems. Max knew Willson would recognize it as an attack and mobilize his team.

As he predicted, the upstairs door to the bunkhouse banged open and two men trooped down the stairs and entered the operations room. Max's intel, provided by Goshawk, indicated there were four security men on duty in the operations room at all times, including Ed Willson. Max also knew there were four men on rotation on the compound's perimeter. His plan was risky, but he'd weighed the alternatives. By containing the four operations personnel, he'd control their movements and prohibit them from alerting the men on the perimeter.

Max removed the pistol from his waistband, slid out from behind the Fairlane, and approached the operations room door from the side, his back against the wall, keeping away from the video camera. When he reached the door, he used the butt of the pistol to bang on the aluminum portal, imagining the chaos going on inside. There was no response.

He banged again, harder and longer. Finally, the door slid open and Ed Willson appeared, an irritated look on his face. Max pointed his gun at him and pushed him back into the room. "Everyone on the floor or I will blow his head off," Max shouted. "Do it. Now!"

Willson's face became a mask of anger and hate. Max saw movement out of the corner of his eye. One of the security men went for his sidearm. Max shifted the gun and pulled the trigger, firing once just above the guard's shoulder. The pop of the gun was deafening in the small room. The bullet burst into a computer monitor, showering the guard with sparks and glass shards and making him pause.

Willson took advantage of the distraction to make his move. With his left hand, he struck at Max's gun arm, attempting to push the gun down and away. With his right fist, he jabbed at Max's kidney.

Max had been ready for the move, knowing Willson wouldn't go down without a fight. He let him connect with the left and felt a stabbing pain in his wrist. Instead of fighting the force of the blow to maintain his position, Max let his weight follow the momentum of the strike and twisted away from the right-handed jab. Willson lost his balance, and tried to recover. Instead, Willson found Max behind him, left arm curled around his windpipe and the gun barrel pointed at his head.

"Everyone on the floor," Max roared. "Or Willson is going down. I'm a desperate man right now, and you don't want to test me."

The guards all froze.

"Tell them to get down," Max said.

A few seconds ticked by in which no one moved. Max removed the gun from Willson's head and pointed it at the man's right quad muscle. His finger flexed on the trigger, adding just enough tension to keep the gun from firing.

"He's a fraction of a second away from taking a bullet in his thigh," Max said.

Another second ticked off the clock.

"Do what he says," Willson growled through clenched teeth.

The three guards lowered to the ground, glaring at Max until they were prone.

"You too," Max said to Willson. He reached down and took the man's pistol, shoving it in his waistband. Willson sank to the floor, his hands interlaced on his head.

Max moved from guard to guard, removing their weapons. He grabbed four plastic riot cuffs from a peg on the wall and tossed them at the nearest man. Holding his pistol to the guard's head, he instructed him to bind the wrists of the others. When he was done, Max shoved him down and bound his wrists.

"Big mistake," Willson growled from his position on the floor.

Max ignored him, grabbed a roll of duct tape from the pegboard, and wrapped tape around each man's face, covering their mouth and eyes. He didn't want the security men seeing what he was going to show Willson, and he wanted them disoriented. Max wrapped the tape around each man's ankles, then stood and pulled the sliding door closed. He pressed the speed dial to Goshawk's phone and said, "Room secure." A second later, he heard a *chunk* as Goshawk remotely activated the sliding door's electric lock. He was sealed in with the four bound prisoners. Max yanked the tape from Ed's face.

"Time for you and me to have a little talk," Max said, squatting down next to the prisoner.

Hatred blazed in Willson's eyes. "My external teams will be here any second."

"Bullshit. Right now, they're receiving electronic messages from my colleague to remain on the perimeter."

"Kate isn't going to like this. You can't just take down the security team without repercussions—"

"Kate's on her way up here right now," Max said. "I've already talked to her. I think she'll be more interested in what's in your video surveillance files."

"What are you taking about?"

"Either you let the man on to the property, or one of your men did," Max said. "At 3:10 a.m. four mornings ago, a man entered the property, searched my room, and stole something that belonged to me."

"You're delusional."

Max hauled Willson up by his shirtfront and helped

him sit in a chair, facing a computer. Max read a number from a label on the monitor into the phone's microphone. "Workstation four." He could hear Goshawk on the other end, typing furiously.

A few seconds later, a large, grainy image appeared on workstation four's monitor. The image began to move and Max watched as the tall man in the ball cap walked down the hallway. Then the image was replaced with the video of the man searching Max's room.

"First time you've seen this?" Max asked.

Ed's face was blank.

"Either you're complicit, or you're grossly incompetent. I've seen enough of this operation to know you're not incompetent."

"Fuck you," Willson said.

"All I want to know is who hired you. I know you didn't think this up yourself. Someone reached out to you and paid you some money to allow this to happen. Just give me his name."

"I want a lawyer," Willson said.

Max laughed. "We may be in America, but we're playing by my rules now. There are no lawyers when it comes to the protection of my family. Last chance—"

Willson's eyes narrowed to slits and he remained silent. Max shoved the pistol into his waistband. Back when Max had been a young agent in the KGB, he'd been trained to inflict pain slowly. He also knew that pain wasn't always the best motivator, as the victim may say anything just to get it to stop. He was desperate, though, and didn't have much choice.

Max had been prepared to use his fists, but he saw a collapsible police baton hanging on the wall among a jumble of other gear. He grabbed it and flicked his wrist to extend the series of steel tubes. Willson's eyes narrowed as Max approached.

"I'm going to try not to kill you," Max said. "See, I'm trying to rehabilitate myself. My sister doesn't think killing provides a very good role model for my nephew." Max swung the baton at Willson's chest, connecting with a *thunk*. Willson yelled out in pain.

"But it's hard to stop killing when your family has a price on its head," Max said. He swung the baton again, hitting Willson in the same spot. Willson cried out, his face going white.

"Is it better to kill to save a life, or not kill and not save a life?" Max put his weight behind the next swing, connecting at the same location as the first two strikes. Willson screamed.

"How many ribs will I have to break before you decide you've had enough?" Max wound up for another swing.

FOURTEEN

Undisclosed location in upstate New York, USA

"Ok, ok," Willson held up his hands, panting from the pain. "No more."

Max kept his arm cocked, but didn't swing the baton. "Talk."

The security man looked away, then glanced at his trussed-up men. Max read shame on his face.

"Spill it," Max demanded. "They're going to find out eventually."

Finally, the story came out. "It was an anonymous email," Willson said. "It offered me money for helping with a task."

"What was the task?" Max asked.

"The first email didn't say," Willson said. "I tried to determine the sender, but it had been routed through too many blind proxy servers."

"Why didn't you report it?" Max asked, although he knew the answer.

The senior security officer glanced back at his men.

"You needed the money," Max said, his voice soft.

Willson nodded his head, and looked at the ground.

"How much?" Max asked.

"A hundred grand," Willson said, his voice barely audible. "When I didn't answer right away, a second email came doubling the amount."

Max whistled. "What was the task?"

"Simple, really," Willson said. "I just had to let a man onto the property for a few minutes and look the other way. The emailer promised there would be no violence. I figured they were looking for something."

"So you accepted the task," Max said.

Willson hung his head. "I needed the money. I'm getting old, I want my son to be able to go to college. All I have is my pension—"

"Tell me about the night of," Max said.

Willson paused again, then spoke. "It was simple. I gave the emailer the details of our security rotation and the locations of our motion sensors. Then I programmed a simple video loop of empty hallways for an hour during the operation so my men here in the operations center wouldn't see the intruder."

"Why didn't you erase the footage?" Max asked.

"I was getting around to it," Willson admitted. "I just didn't think anyone would be able to penetrate our firewall."

"My person is an expert in penetration," Max said.

Through the barn walls, Max heard the distant sound of an approaching helicopter. A few minutes later, someone was pounding on the door to the security room. Max glanced at the monitor above the door and saw the tall form of Kate surrounded by four armed paramilitary types and a tall man wearing a tweed jacket and a turtle-neck. He hit the button that unlocked the door and yanked it open.

"Max, what the fuck?" Kate exclaimed when she saw the inside of the room. Max had propped each of the captives against a wall and removed the tape from their heads. Willson sat in a chair facing the door.

Max smiled at the man in the turtleneck and shook his hand warmly. "Good to see you, Spencer."

"Likewise, Max. Wish it were under better circum-stances," Spencer said. Spencer White, one of Kate's black ops officers, had played an instrumental role in bringing Max and his family over to the CIA. Max and Spencer had gone through several ordeals together, and the two men had forged a strong bond. Max was glad to see Kate had brought the senior field man with her.

"I assume you watched the surveillance video we sent you?" Max asked.

"Yes, but what the fuck?" she repeated, shock evident on her face.

Max wondered if the shock was because of Ed Willson's betrayal or the seeming ease with which Max had disman-tled her security team. Leaving her soldiers to secure the room, Max steered Kate out into the barn with Spencer following. He explained everything to both of them. When he was done, he said, "I can get you Ed's bank records and more copies of the footage."

"Max, you should have just called me instead of taking things into your own hands," Kate said, clearly exasperated.

"Stuff with you isn't exactly secure these days, Kate. I didn't know what I was dealing with."

"Goddamn it, Max. We could have done it together. You shouldn't have hidden this from me."

"Somehow I don't think you would have let me do what I needed to do to get him to talk," Max replied.

Kate's stared at Max. "What did you do?"

"Nothing that won't heal after some time," Max said.

"MAX!"

"At least I didn't shoot him in the leg," Max said. "I thought about it."

"Jesus," Kate said. "Did you at least find out who the intruder was?"

Max looked at her. "No. Everything was done via secure, anonymous email."

"Fuck," Kate said, echoing both of their sentiments. She looked thoughtful, having recovered from the initial shock of the scene. "I wonder why the intruder didn't kill Arina and Alex? Have you considered that?"

Max had, and the mystery perplexed him. "The only explanation I can think of is that the people stealing the memory card are different than the people who want us killed," Max said.

They stared at each other. The mystery had just deepened.

———

Max's smartphone buzzed with a text message. *Call me now*. It was Goshawk. He peeled off from the group and exited the barn. The cool air felt good on his skin and he looked up. Above his head was a canopy filled with millions of pinpricks of light. Off to his left, he could see the haze of the Milky Way. He walked over to the paddock and stepped awkwardly on an object in the grass. He bent down and picked up a tennis ball. He dialed Goshawk's line and held the phone to his ear while tossing the ball in the air.

Her voice came on a minute later. "I've been poking around Willson's servers," she started.

"Ok," Max said.

"You're really going to owe me for this one."

"Stop playing games and just tell me, for fuck sake," Max said.

"Is that any way to talk to your favorite person right now?" she said, her voice sounding hurt.

He breathed in. "Ok, my dear. You are right. I owe you big time. Now what did you find?"

She laughed. "That's better, sugar. So I was looking through his servers—"

"Yes. You've said," Max said.

"—and I found a pretty clear image of the intruder's face from the security footage of him entering the property."

Max's heart rate quickened.

Goshawk continued. "I've started a facial recognition search using the FBI's database, but this might take a while, if I even get anything back."

"Ok, you're right," Max admitted.

"Right about what, darling?"

"You are my favorite person right now."

Gales of laughter came over the earpiece. Then she severed the connection and Max was left in silence, standing under a million stars.

FIFTEEN

Undisclosed location in upstate New York, USA, Undisclosed location outside Budapest

Max, Kate, and Spencer adjourned to the library to figure out their next move. After the chain of command and security teams had been reestablished, the surveillance of the library had been disabled, allowing the three of them to talk in private. The breach of security at the compound left them with few alternatives for the protection of Alex and Arina. Max no longer felt safe at the compound, and Kate couldn't argue with him. Spencer had come forward with an idea that met with Kate's strenuous objections. After an hour of hashing things out, Kate had capitulated, and the final plans were laid.

Max departed the library in search of his sister, leaving Kate and Spencer behind to make the final arrangements. One of Kate's soldiers had taken over temporary control of the compound's security and was making preparations to transport Ed Willson and his staff to a CIA black site located in New Jersey, just outside of Manhattan. Ed was steadfast in his assertion that he and he alone had orchestrated the plan to allow the intruder access to the house, but Kate wasn't taking any chances. Each man would be interrogated until the truth was known.

He found Arina in her bedroom, packing her things as he'd instructed her to do. Clothing was strewn all over the bed and a single large duffle bag was open on the floor. She looked up, tears in her eyes.

"How much longer are we going to have to do this?" she said. "I'm getting tired of running, Max. I want our life back."

Max came forward, and for the first time in a long time, took his sister in his arms. At first she resisted, then she hugged him back. The tears came harder, and she sobbed into his shoulder until she was cried out. Finally, she pulled back and turned away, using the blouse she was holding to dab at her eyes.

"I just want Alex to have a normal life," she said. "School, friends, sports. Just like other kids."

"I know," Max said. "I want that, too."

She found a tissue box on the side table and blew her nose. "Where will we go?" she asked.

Max held his finger to his lips, then pointed to the surveillance camera. "I can't tell you right now, but you and Alex will be safe."

She looked disappointed for a moment, then her face returned to neutral. "You're not coming with us?"

Max shook his head.

Arina looked at the floor. "Alex is going to take that hard," she said. "He's really grown to like you."

"And I like him too, Arina. I want to be there for him.

But I also need to go fix this situation. It's not going to go away on its own, and I can't count on Kate and the CIA."

"How are you going to fix it?" Arina asked, her eyes narrowing.

"The best way I know how, Arina. I know you don't want to hear it, but these people will stop at nothing until we are dead. There is only one way I know of to stop them. The CIA can't help. The FSB is corrupt and probably involved. We're on our own now."

A tear came to her eye. "Why, Max? Why do they want us dead? I don't even know what we did to deserve this—"

He hugged her again. "I don't either. But I'm going to fix it."

She hugged him back, but didn't say anything.

"How about we give you a gun to carry?"

She gave Max an angry glance. Since their parents' death, this had been a constant source of conflict between the two siblings. Despite having been trained to shoot by their father, she'd steadfastly refused to have guns anywhere near Alex.

"What if you're the only one standing between the bad guys and Alex?" Max asked. "Wouldn't you rather have a weapon to try and save your son's life?"

Arina shifted her weight and looked at the floor.

"We can find a pistol that fits in your hand, something compact and powerful like one of those Springfield .45s. I'm sure Kate will have some good ideas."

Arina looked up at the sky for a moment, and Max heard her sniffle.

"Do it for Alex," Max said gently.

She wiped her eyes with the back of a hand, then turned back to him, resolution in her eyes. "Fine, I'll do it. But only for Alex."

Max smiled at her and helped her with the bags. They roused a sleepy Alex, who gave Max a long hug. Then Max helped them into the black suburban idling in the driveway, and handed Alex a squirming Spike to hold. Spencer was in the driver's seat, a silenced pistol next to his leg. He gave a curt wave as they drove off. As the suburban rolled away, Alex's face was plastered to the side window, tears in his eyes.

Max held up the purple lucky rabbit foot and waved. Alex instantly brightened and waved back. Max stood in the drive watching the back of the suburban recede into the darkness, wondering if he'd ever see them again.

———

Wing stood outside the tiny holding cell where Lord Henry Bradley reclined on the threadbare mattress. The five other cells lining the stone wall were empty. Behind her, the door was closed and locked. Wing had ordered the security cameras in the dungeon where she stood turned off. Six bare bulbs, one for each cell, lit the chamber, and the yellow light cast long shadows that flickered on the wall. She pulled a scratched wooden chair over and sat down facing her captive. She removed a Glock 30S .45 ACP pistol from a leather shoulder holster. The gun was compact enough to fit into her hand, but its double-stacked magazine held ten rounds. She made a show of screwing in a silencer.

Henry did not look well. He lay on the cot, naked and shivering. His face was bruised and dried blood was caked on his chin and chest, and his hand was wrapped in a bloody bandage. His skin had a slight green tinge to it, and he periodically burst out in coughing spasms. When she'd first arrived, he'd tried to spit phlegm at her, so she was keeping her distance. He didn't seem to have enough energy to spit very far.

"Sounds like you've come down with something," Wing said. "Sleep deprivation and the damp air can take its toll."

The baron peered at her from behind swollen and bloodshot eyes. "I'd imagine the authorities will be showing any minute," he managed. Then he was overtaken with a wet and phlegmy coughing fit.

When he'd recovered, she said, "No one's coming, Henry. I found your little dossier on me. Quite a file."

Henry's head seemed to sag, then he looked up. "Prove it," he said.

Wing looked at him, and wondered why she felt no pity for the man. Maybe it was because he had tried to fuck her over. "There were two files in the box."

As soon as she said that, the man's head sagged forward again and he groaned.

"I have to give it to you," Wing said. "I'm impressed at your resourcefulness. You proved to be a better adversary than I gave you credit for. You managed to put together quite a file on me. But it was the other file that really impressed me. How did you get photographs of the Prime Minister in such a compromising position? I mean, who knew he was into that kind of thing?"

Henry remained looking at the floor, silent.

"You do have one card left to play, Henry."

That made him look up. Using his good hand, he tried to tame the tangle of hair on his head. After a moment, he gave up. "What's that?"

"The information you had on me could only have come from one place. Tell me where you got it and I'll spare your life."

Henry laughed, which turned into a spasming cough.

"Bullshit," he managed. "I don't see any scenario where you'd let me live. Not with what I know about you and this place."

Wing aimed the pistol at his right leg.

"Do you know what a .45 hollow point can do to a man's knee?" Wing asked.

Any remaining blood in Henry's face drained, but he remained quiet. "You wouldn't—"

Wing pulled the trigger and the Glock rocked in her hand.

Henry cried out and tried to grab his knee, but found it a shredded mess. He fell back on the cot, howling in pain.

Wing stood and walked closer to the bars. Large drops of blood had spattered on the floor and Henry's knee was covered in the crimson liquid. "I'm out of patience. I'm going to keep shooting you in the knee until you tell me. Then I'm going to get Walter down here to bind it up so you don't bleed out. Then I'm going to shoot you in the other knee." She pointed the gun at his left knee.

Henry held up a hand. "Wait, wait," he managed. "Don't shoot. I'll tell you. Fuck. I'll tell you."

Wing waited, her finger tensed on the trigger.

"I don't actually know—"

Wing adjusted the gun down slightly, and pulled the trigger. The front of Henry's calf burst open and blood spattered on the stone floor in front of Wing's shoe. He cried out, his voice turning into a long wail of pain.

"Fuck, fuck!" Henry yelled. "I was just telling you I don't know the man's name, but I can give you a description."

"I'm listening," Wing said.

"Tall, white, male. Salt-and-pepper hair, cut short. Light grey suit. Deep voice, spoke with a German accent—"

Wing cursed under her breath. Unbelievable. The man Henry was describing could be only one person – Mueller, her client's assistant. She aimed the gun at the baron's head and pulled the trigger. A dark hole appeared in the middle of his forehead and Henry fell over dead.

SIXTEEN

Newark, New Jersey

"I have another gig for you," Kate said. She and Max were sitting in a dingy office with a broken window overlooking a mostly empty warehouse floor. Four monitors in front of them showed close-up shots of each of the captives. The captives had been segregated into individual holding cells, served food and coffee, and permitted to smoke. Ed Willson sat with his shirt off, being examined by a doctor.

Max was surprised. Given everything that had just occurred, he figured Kate would want him to lay low for a while. "You're forgiving me for beating the crap out of Willson?"

"No, I'm not. You were way out of line. But I don't have a choice," Kate said. She blew on the coffee in a Styrofoam cup to cool it.

Max found a crumpled pack of Camels in the pocket of his leather jacket. The filterless smokes were the closest thing he could find in the States to his beloved Russian

Belomorkanals. He shook one out and cast about for a light. With an audible sigh, Kate got up, rummaged in a desk drawer, and threw Max a pack of matches. He lit the smoke and blew a cloud at the ceiling, then looked at the logo on the matches. "What's the Stone Pony?"

"Bar down in Asbury Park. In New Jersey." Kate said. "Where Bruce Springsteen made his start."

"Born to run, huh?" Max said absently, looking at the end of his cigarette. When she didn't answer, he looked around the tiny room and asked, "What is this place?"

"Black ops site. Belongs to my group. We have several on the East Coast. This one is a staging area for New York City."

"Like a safe house kind of thing?"

"Sort of. But we also keep supplies here like ammunition and assault gear, and in forty-eight hours can have it fully stocked to support special ops teams. Five semi-trucks can unload at once at the loading docks. It also backs up to the Hudson and can be supplied by ship. We built the facility after 9-11, but we haven't used it much."

"And it can serve as an off-the-books brig to hold prisoners you don't want in the system."

"Correct. Guys at Ed's level never end up in the system. We have a private tribunal for these sorts of things. My guess is Ed will be court-martialed in a sealed proceeding and the other guys will be busted down a few grades."

"In light of the mess at Guantanamo Bay, you guys still mess around with off-the-books prisoners?"

"Guantanamo was a fiasco," Kate agreed. "It got too public, in my opinion. I do believe that the US government needs to be able to treat terrorism prisoners as prisoners of war, and leave them outside the US prison system. We're living in a new day and age where the old rules of war don't apply, and we need all the weapons at our disposal. Plus, every government, like it or not, has a system for dealing with off-the-books prisoners. We just fucked up by letting it become public."

"But you guys did some crazy shit in there," Max said. "You made prisoners bark like dogs and wear bras and smeared them with menstrual blood."

"First, that wasn't us. The US Military runs that prison. The KGB doesn't exactly have a perfect track record in human rights violations."

"Fair enough," Max said. "But still—"

"Listen, I'm not condoning all the shit that happened down there," Kate said. "God knows there was some stuff that went too far. But I do contend that in a world where ISIS, or ISIL, or daesh, or whatever the fuck they are called, is going around raping and killing innocent women and children, destroying national treasures, and selling women as sex slaves, we need aggressive weapons at our disposal. 9-11 will happen again, on our soil, and then the same people who are judging our treatment of detainees will judge us for not doing enough to stop terrorism in our own country."

"I'm not arguing," Max said. "You know me. I'm in favor of doing whatever needs to be done to get the job done. I just don't see how making a prisoner bark like a dog achieves anything."

"Agreed," Kate said. "That went too far. Plus, I'm well aware that the abuses that went on in that prison are not helping US-Arab relations."

"That's putting it mildly," Max said. "You can bet that any so-called detainee that is released has effectively been turned into either a terrorist, or at the minimum, a supporter."

"Regardless," Kate said. "What I'm doing with these

guys is perfectly legal within the US government's system. The law works differently when national security is involved. These men will be treated humanely, and at the appropriate time, given access to US government lawyers."

"What will happen to Willson?"

"He'll probably be sent to Leavenworth under the oversight of the Midwest Joint Regional Correctional Facility operated by the US Army. He'll be an old man by the time he gets out."

Max pondered that for a while. It was a stiff price to pay for the opportunity to earn a couple hundred grand. Max did not, however, feel sorry for him. Willson had put Max's family's life in danger. As far as Max was concerned, the man was lucky to be alive.

"So before we talk about the new gig, we should talk about the elephant in the room," Max said. He was referring to the mole in the CIA that had dogged them from the beginning of their working relationship. Someone in the CIA wanted Max dead, and seemed to be supplying Max's enemies with critical information.

Kate looked thoughtful. "I'm working on it." She got up and walked over to the coffee maker. On the screens, Max could see one of the detainees being interrogated. It looked stressful, but the subject was not being mistreated.

"What does that mean?" Max asked. "So far, two of your staff flipped and tried to kill me back in Minsk, which also resulted in four of your men being slaughtered. Someone leaked my location in Croatia to an assassin. Now Ed here," Max pointed at the screen with his cigarette, "let someone waltz into my supposedly protected house. You'll forgive me if I'm not excited to go on another assignment for you."

"Max, you don't have any choice. I get that there seems to be a mole somewhere—"

"Seems to be?" Max said, letting the front two legs of his chair hit the ground. "It's pretty clear to me, Kate."

"Ok. But we can't bring the entire operation to a screaming halt. Besides, I spent a ton of political capital bringing you over, and let's just say not everyone above me is supportive. The more targets we can pick off, the more justification we have."

Max leaned back in his chair and let that sink in. The fact that the higher ups in the CIA might not approve of their deal wasn't a surprise. He was familiar with office politics from his days in the KGB. Still, he found it unsettling.

"Who is the target?"

"Russian mafia boss who is funneling weapons into Eastern Ukraine to support the pro-Russian rebels."

"Name?"

"Victor Volkov," Kate said.

Max raised his eyebrows and whistled. Volkov was one of Russia's most powerful crime bosses. He didn't relish going after such a high-profile target while vulnerable to the mole in Kate's organization. He leaned back with his arms crossed and thought for a moment, his gaze fixed on Kate's face. Then he got an idea. He stayed silent while he mulled it over. The only question was whether Kate would go for it.

"There is only one way I can do this mission—" he started.

Just then, Max's phone buzzed in his pocket. He retrieved it and saw a text message from Goshawk. *Call me.*

"Excuse me," he said and stood, tossing his cigarette butt into an empty Styrofoam cup. He tapped Goshawk's speed-dial button as he walked out of the little room.

"I got a hit on the facial recognition of the intruder," she said by way of an answer.

"Good girl," Max said. "Tell me."

"According to the FBI's database, there is an eighty-nine percent likelihood his name is Peter Orlov, a KGB—"

"I know exactly who he is," Max said, cutting her off. "I'm surprised I didn't recognize his face. Fuck me—"

"If you say so," drawled Goshawk on the other end of the phone.

"Very funny. Thanks, darling. I gotta go." He hung up and returned to the tiny office. Kate's feet were up on a table and she was sipping coffee, watching the monitors. She had the volume up as she listened to one of the interrogations. Max stood in front of her, his arms crossed.

"You were saying?" she asked. She turned the sound down on the monitor.

Max smiled at her, liking his plan more now that he had an actual lead. "There is only one way I can do that gig," Max said.

"How?"

"Solo," Max said. "Like I used to operate. My people, my plan. No support from the CIA. I go in dark and I come out dark."

Kate was shaking her head before he finished speaking. "No fucking way," she said. "No way I can sanction that."

"It's the only way, Kate. If your team runs this operation, I'm a dead man."

"Max, it'll never fly. I can't get approval for that."

"You're right, you can't get approval for it – I'm not asking you to."

Kate was shaking her head. "No fucking way—"

"It's the only way, Kate, and you know it. Take it or leave it."

She was silent for a long time. Max turned toward the door. He knew she would go for it. They both knew it was the only way. The only thing he wasn't telling her was that he had no intention of carrying out the assignment. At least not right away. It was a simple ruse to buy himself some time to chase after the thumb drive.

When his hand was on the knob, she sighed. "Fine. What do you need?"

He turned back and smiled at her. "Only a couple things."

SEVENTEEN

Istanbul, Turkey

Max was the first one off United flight 6904. He walked up the jet bridge and into Istanbul's Ataturk airport carrying only a small backpack. He'd slept soundly in the horizontal recline chairs in the first-class section, eaten two nutritious meals served by a smiling United crew, and managed to skip the alcohol. Despite the sleep, his side still ached and his forearm burned from the cuts sustained in the fight with the assassin. He'd used a Vicodin to help him sleep, and had a packet of the little white pills in his pocket.

At customs, he presented a US passport along with an entry visa application indicating he was a technology consultant arriving for two days of meetings. Max had only asked Kate for one thing – a numbered bank account with 500,000 in US dollars. She'd initially balked, until Max explained that he was going to have to replicate her staff and support network, and that was going to take some cash. He had immediately wired $50,000 to Goshawk to settle his tab and pre-pay for future services. He breezed through customs and stepped out into the haze of Istanbul.

Max ignored the hoard of taxi hawkers, found the limousine stand, and paid cash for the twenty-minute ride to the Four Seasons Hotel, located in the heart of historic Istanbul. He was thankful for the air conditioning in the silver Mercedes. Outside, the summer heat made the pavement shimmer and drove even the heartiest of locals inside, where the marble floors offered some respite from the heat. His T-shirt was already soaked through, and he reminded himself to pick up a couple tropical shirts before his meeting that evening.

He tipped the driver and entered the hotel's lobby through the broad marble-facade entryway. Inside, the cool air gushed at him as he strode through the marbled lobby. The interior of the hotel was busy with well-heeled Caucasians wearing linen and talking in hushed voices. Max paid cash in advance for three nights and was ushered to his room, a sprawling suite with floor-to-ceiling windows trimmed with dark woods and a gently curved ceiling that towered overhead. The floor was a rich, brown hardwood and the trimmings were Persian. Max locked the door, yanked the shades closed, and lay down for a nap.

When he awoke and opened the curtains, it was late afternoon and the shadows had started to lengthen. His stomach growled, and he grabbed his backpack and found the hotel's cafe, an open-air restaurant on a veranda with a stunning view of the Blue Mosque. Max stuck with water, but downed a small-plate appetizer of beans and salad called meze, a small Turkish pizza called pide, and an order of kofte – a stew of ground beef and lamb balls for which the region was famous.

He tried not to worry about his nephew and sister. He

trusted Spencer implicitly and knew the venerable security agent would take good care of them. Instead, he focused his thoughts on his current mission. Max knew Peter Orlov. Orlov was a mid-level Belarusian KGB agent who worked for Victor Dedov. Dedov was the Director of the Belarus KGB, and also had been Max's father's boss. Although Max had never worked directly for Dedov, he knew of the man. He was called 'The General' behind his back, in reference to his little-big-man attitude. Dedov had led the official investigation into Max's parents' death, and had determined the bomb was placed by Chechen terrorists. Max knew the official conclusion was a sham, and had ultimately killed the bomb maker who had placed the device. Max still didn't know why Dedov had declared the killing a terrorist act, and as yet had no evidence of Dedov's direct involvement in his parents' death. The only way Orlov could have found his way into Max's bedroom was if Dedov was behind it. Now, Max was in Istanbul to find Dedov. And to find Dedov, he needed the help of a local.

He paid the tab in cash, grabbed his bag, and went out into the street. The Four Seasons was located in Istanbul's Old City, a district teeming with open-air cafes, narrow alleys, thriving markets, and a robust tourist scene. The skyline was dominated by the Blue Mosque and the red roofs of buildings leading up the hillside away from the water. Colorful ferry boats bobbed against their moorings, waiting to haul tourists across the Golden Horn River to Istanbul's new city. Istanbul was one of Max's favorite cities, and he wished he had more time to poke through the markets and sample the delicacies. Instead, he turned right, away from the hotel, and disappeared into the crowd.

He had two hours until his meeting, and he decided to

run a surveillance detection route, also known as an SDR. The concept was simple: perform a series of maneuvers designed to flush out any surveillance he might have picked up since arriving in Istanbul. It was unlikely he had a tail, but you could never be sure in this line of work. A crowded evening among bustling tourists was the perfect environment in which to run an SDR. He turned right and walked up Kabasakal Street next to the Blue Mosque, which took its name from the cool hue the building gave off in the evening light and for the blue tiles in its interior. He followed a group of Americans toting cameras and bags overflowing with purchases.

In the surveillance game, anyone could be disguised as a pursuer – from the stooped old lady pushing the cart of groceries to the ten-year-old boy kicking the ball down the street. The KGB was famous for training young, beautiful women to follow Western spies, and Max had worked with more than a few old men who were professionals at blending into the surroundings. Max turned left and strode up a street named Divan Yolu and walked past a small open market full of mosaic tile and other gifts. Ahead of him towered the famous Roman Column of Constantine.

Max began to dip into the various stalls, pretending to look at merchandise. More than once, he doubled back to another stall, as if to compare prices. Thus, the game began. Any experienced operator on Max's tail would immediately know Max had started an SDR. After browsing the stalls for ten minutes, Max turned up the street behind the Blue Mosque, then doubled back and cut through Mahmet Park. On the far side of the park, he jumped into one of Istanbul's bright purple CNG busses. The bus was standing room only, and Max hung onto a hand strap as the vehicle jolted away from the curb. Through the window, he thought he saw the furtive glance of a tall, bearded man. The man had olive or sun-tanned skin and a blue taqiyah on his head, the traditional Muslim skullcap. Max stored an image of the man's face in his memory.

Three blocks later, Max jumped off the bus and hiked north up a narrow street toward the Grand Bazaar, one of the world's largest and oldest covered markets. The market spanned sixty-one covered streets and contained over three thousand shops. Someone had once told him it was among the world's most-visited tourist attractions, and the teeming masses moving through the crowded streets in front of him seemed to prove that. Above his head was a curved, stone ceiling that ran the length of the corridor. On both sides were endless stalls selling brightly colored textiles, handbags, gold jewelry, carved wooden chess sets and silly-looking shoes with pointed toes. Both locals and tourists jostled for position in the narrow corridor. A group of giggling high school students passed next to him, and in front of him, what looked like a Turkish family of children, parents, brothers, sisters, and elders slowly picked their way through the offerings.

Max turned a corner and stole a glance behind him. He thought he could see the same man he'd seen from the bus – the same beard, but this time without the skullcap. The man's shaved head glistened from the overhead lights. It was the stranger's eyes that gave him away, though. Rather than being captivated by the market's offerings, this man's eyes were alert, roving.

Max's mind raced through the last twenty-four hours. He'd used cash everywhere. He'd used his own credentials to pass through immigration into Turkey. Had his ID somehow triggered an alarm at the border? The only person who knew he was heading to Turkey was Goshawk, whom he trusted completely. Was it possible she'd been compromised? Anything was possible, he reasoned. No matter now. His first order of business was to get clear of the tail before his meeting.

EIGHTEEN

Istanbul, Turkey

Aleksander Bokun guessed he'd been made the instant he locked eyes with the man calling himself Max Austin. He cursed under his breath, but held his ground. If he turned away too quickly, he could be assured of giving himself away. Instead, he let his eyes glaze over so he wasn't locked with his target, then casually returned his gaze to the afghan he was pretending to admire. It was a subtle gesture, but one of strength.

Out of the corner of his eye, he saw Austin duck down a corridor and decided to let him go for now. Bokun darted to another stall and paid cash for a black and white linen scarf called a shemagh. Bokun pulled the scarf over his head and up around his mouth and nose. It was hot in the market, and he didn't see many men wearing the traditional Muslim garb, but there were a few. It might confuse Austin enough to make him doubt what he'd thought he'd seen.

Attempting surveillance on a well-trained operative was very difficult alone. Usually, this kind of thing would be performed by teams of four to six men and women, each picking up the subject for a few minutes before handing them off to the next person on the team. However, Bokun didn't have a team. He never worked with a team. He slid through the crowd without making a ripple and went up the same corridor where Austin had disappeared.

He was the cat, and Austin was his mouse. Sometimes the cat liked to toy with the mouse, and Bokun relished the game. He let his hate for his quarry surface, but then funneled the hate into a heightened sense of motivation rather than letting the emotion consume him. Bokun subconsciously touched his face and felt the beard, something he wasn't quite used to yet. He'd grown it to hide the disfigurement. The scabs and wounds still itched, and he cursed Austin for detonating the bomb that had marred his beautiful face. A face that could instantly disarm, and then disrobe, a woman. As he shouldered his way through the crowd, he shrugged it off. A part of him knew he was lucky to be alive. And if he was alive, he could still sample the delicacies offered by beautiful women. Now he'd just have to take them by force instead of guile. He could feel the itch, the burn in his groin, at the thought. He forced it away. Later there would be enough time. Perhaps a reward for a successful day's work. Now, he focused his hatred on the man who had bested him. It was time to even the score.

He picked Austin up again a few minutes later. Bokun saw him standing in front of a stall of brightly colored spices, head bent, sniffing a yellow powder. Bokun paused, pretending to admire a table made from a mosaic of tile. When he looked up, Austin was gone. He looked around, not seeing the tall man. A moment later, he felt a jab in his kidney and the words in Russian, "That's a silenced pistol in your back. Now move."

Bokun paused, anger rising like a volcano. This was a bold move made in a public place. Would Austin really shoot him dead in the middle of a busy, crowded market? Bokun thought that if the roles were reversed, he himself wouldn't hesitate to shoot, especially if the pistol was silenced and muffled by the clothing. The victim would go down and Bokun would easily be able to disappear into the crowd, just as Austin would. The two men were cut from the same cloth, products of the same system. He decided his best course of action for now was to cooperate, and see what games Austin had in mind.

To irritate his abductor, Bokun moved slowly. He stepped out into the aisle and shuffled his feet. He felt a sharp jab in his back and heard the words, "Walk at a normal pace, toward the exit."

Bokun smiled. Austin had just committed his first error. Now Bokun knew where they were going. It was a little thing, but every advantage stacked up. He moved his arms slightly and felt another jab in his back. "Don't move your arms, or I'll shoot you dead right here."

Bokun frowned. He had a tactical knife in his waistband within easy reach. Point to Austin.

As they wove their way through the market's crowded aisles, he kept his head forward, but scanned the crowd with his eyes. He was looking for any backup that Austin might have. He was also looking for a child or a group of children. The detailed file Bokun had on Austin mentioned one thing that he interpreted as a weakness. Austin seemed to have an affinity for his ten-year-old nephew. Bokun interpreted this to mean Austin had a weakness for children. Bokun's gaze took in everything. There. A group of Turkish teenagers was coming toward them, each one wearing a school uniform and a backpack. They were jostling and yelling, getting in the way of shoppers and knocking over produce displays.

Bokun kept looking straight ahead as he and Austin came abreast of the school children, waiting for just the right moment. He was patient, like a big cat hunting her prey. He knew restraint meant survival. He watched for his opening.

His patience paid off when a dark-haired boy in a navy-blue school uniform pushed a smaller boy, laughing. "Get out of here, Ali."

The smaller boy was sent reeling toward Bokun, who simultaneously grabbed the child and twisted so the gun was no longer jabbing him in the back. In one instant, Austin was holding the gun to him, and in another, Austin was pointing the gun directly at the child. Bokun had taken advantage of the split second of hesitation he knew Austin would have when he saw the child. The assassin danced away into the crowd. After rounding a corner, he turned to look behind him. The school kids were still jostling around Austin. Then Bokun saw something that made him flush with shame. Austin caught his eye for a moment and held up a yellow banana, then mock-fired it at Bokun through the crowd.

Bokun turned away, his embarrassment turning to anger, and slid through the throng of people. Austin would not best him again.

———

Max extricated himself from the schoolboy and hastened

after his assailant. Despite his casual mockery, Max was roiling inside. He had easily seen through the new beard and the Turkish garb and recognized the assassin. Max wouldn't forget those eyes for a very long time. He took little satisfaction from the fact the man's face had been marred by the bomb. How had Bokun survived the explosion? And more importantly, how had he found Max here in Istanbul?

Max turned the corner where Bokun had disappeared and scanned over the heads of the crowd. He saw plenty of bearded, dark-skinned men, and he saw a few wearing the traditional head scarf called the keffiyeh. But none matched the exact description of his pursuer. Max pushed forward down the corridor, looking left and right, trying to see if the man had disappeared into a stall, but he was nowhere in sight. Max darted through a narrow access path between two stalls and found himself in a cramped service alley. Here, the floor was slick with mud and vegetable matter and Max had to work to keep his footing. He scoured the back alley for a few minutes, then went back out into the main market area. The man had disappeared.

In the past week since Max's first encounter with the assassin, he'd racked his brain to remember everything he could about the man. During his encounter with Bokun at the FSB training facility, he'd witnessed the assassin destroy opponent after opponent in the sparring ring, using a combination of grappling, close-body moves borrowed from Krav Maga, and vicious kicks and punches from Muay-Thai. The man had been a machine, and Max remembered thinking he was glad they were on the same team. Now that had changed, and Max realized he'd better watch his back.

Cursing, Max exited the market. Even in the late evening, the air was stifling hot with humidity. For the next hour, Max performed an elaborate SDR using busses, a rented bicycle, a rickshaw, and his own two feet. He noticed no additional surveillance. Satisfied that his encounter had been with a lone pursuer and confident that he was not being watched, Max set off for his meeting.

NINETEEN

Undisclosed location outside Budapest

Wing felt small and alone in her oversized office. Everything about the room was grandiose, including the massive desk, the huge Persian rugs, and the high ceilings. Even the crown molding seemed larger than it needed to be. In the center of the room hung a lavish crystal chandelier that dominated the space and drew the attention of every visitor. She was beginning to hate the room and everything it stood for; it was a grim reminder of the men who'd terrorized the Hungarian population into submission. She was considering moving downstairs to a workstation closer to her team. It would mean giving up some privacy, which was the only reason she hesitated, particularly now that she didn't know who to trust. So she sat in her office, feeling very alone.

She consulted the oversized digital clock on her desk and watched the seconds tick down. At the appointed time, her desk phone rang. She scooped up the headset and put it on. She waited a few moments, listening to a series of hums and clicks, then the light on the console flashed green, indicating the line was now secure. "Report," she stated.

"Picked him up at Ataturk. No luggage. He hired a car, which dropped him off at the Four Seasons. He's in room 523, a suite. He napped, ate, then ran a very long surveillance detection route."

Wing had known Aleksander Bokun for many years. He had been one of Nathan Abrams' most ruthless and effective weapons. The man was a true psychopath, but he always got the job done. Now, however, Wing heard something different in his voice. Always an unimpassioned, robotic killer, now she thought she heard emotion in his voice. Maybe it was anger. "And?"

There was a short pause on the line. "I lost him."

"Damn it," she said, before she could catch herself.

"Actually, I didn't lose him. He made me."

Even worse, she thought. "Fuck. Stop toying with him and just kill him," she said. "I don't have time to wait for you to play your little games."

The line went silent, then the call ended. She slammed her headset onto the phone and walked over to the broad window overlooking her operations room. She was fuming, and she found herself thinking about Nathan. He'd built this company up using raw willpower, intellect, and hard work. She missed him, and the empty space was painful to bear. As she watched Marisa talking into her phone, she somehow dug up new resolve. The thought of Nathan's legendary resilience combined with the knowledge of what she'd overcome to get this far in life steeled her will. She wasn't going to let a few setbacks get her down. She'd taken care of the Lord Bradley, and she would take care of Max Austin. She'd root out her mole and make an example of them, then she'd set about rebuilding this business from the ground up.

The buzz from an alert on her mobile phone startled her out of her thoughts and she walked back to the desk to retrieve it. It was an email notification from her source in the CIA. She opened up the secure email application and accessed the note.

Austin has disappeared. Off the grid and out of the sanctioned operational team. The sister and nephew have also disappeared from Secret Service protection. Will keep digging and apprise when I know more.

For the first time that day, Wing smiled. For once, she knew more than her mole in the CIA. She returned to the window. Marisa was still talking animatedly into her headset. Walter was nowhere in sight. Enzo walked back to his workstation from the coffeemaker, balancing a mug and a plate of food. Her long-time friend and confidante, her new hire, and her rising star. One of them was betraying her. She would have to vet them one at a time. She watched Enzo sit down and work a mouse with one hand while he sipped coffee with the other. Suddenly, she had an idea of where to start. The idea galled her, but she knew she needed to use every weapon at her disposal. That's what Nathan would do.

TWENTY

Budapest, Hungary

Wing rolled off Enzo's tattooed body, swinging her legs to the floor, and walked naked into his cramped kitchen. The air in the apartment was stifling so she forced up a window, letting in a hot breeze and the din from the street below. She rummaged around and found two fairly clean juice glasses and a half bottle of red wine. Returning to the bedroom, she handed him a glass of the ruby liquid and sat cross-legged on the bed in front of him.

"Fenékig," she said, raising her glass.

"Fenékig," he said clinking his glass with hers. Enzo was reclined on one elbow, naked against the dingy sheets. His dreadlocks were a rat's nest and a silver ring hung from one nipple. He looked like the cat who caught the canary. Wing supposed that's exactly what he was.

She reminded herself to proceed with caution. The first time she'd seduced him, she made quick work of him on the desk in her office before sending him on his way with a

confused look on his face. The second time, she invited
herself over to his rundown apartment and took it slow
while forcing herself to listen as he rambled on about his
parents. That night, she slipped out after he fell asleep. The
next night she stayed over, made love to him in the morning,
and then dutifully ate a plate of runny eggs before
departing for the office. That morning, it was she who felt
confused.

"There's a band at A38 tomorrow night," Enzo said,
after he had drained half his glass of wine.

Wing inwardly groaned. The last thing she wanted to
do was listen to bad music with a bunch of twenty-some-
things. She needed Enzo wrapped around her finger, but
without herself getting too involved.

"Enzo—" she started.

He held up his hand. "I know. I'm sorry. Too fast—"

"I'm just not the kind of woman who has time for social
activities."

"I get it."

Wing saw disappointment in his face. "It's not the life
we lead. And my business is struggling, in case you haven't
noticed."

Enzo's face softened, and he put his hand on her knee.

"This business ruined Nathan's marriage and ultimately got him killed because he took his eye off the ball,"
Wing said. "Social activities are for normal people. We've
chosen this life, or it chose us, and the reality is we can't live
ordinary lives."

"Can't, or won't?" Enzo asked.

Wing looked away for a moment, steeling herself, then
turned back and said, "If I'm going to pull this thing out of a
nose dive, it's going to require all my attention. Or I'll end
up dead."

"So why —" Enzo started to ask.

"Some things I can't explain," she replied. "Emotions get the better of us, and our bodies do things our minds try to resist." She touched his hand. "I can't explain it, but even a little physical intimacy helps me."

He chewed on that while she refilled their wine glasses. Wing had had several lovers in her life, but all of them were designed merely to address physical needs. Each had ended badly, usually with both walking away with hurt feelings. She had since vowed never to get involved in a relationship again.

"Anything else I can do to help?" Enzo asked. The hurt look on his face was replaced by his usual earnest gaze.

Finally, the hook was set. She looked away and sipped her wine, as if thinking, before she looked up and found herself caught in the warm pull of his brown eyes. A breath of air from the open window ruffled the drapes, cooling the sweat on her skin. She shivered and smiled to herself, excited by the razor edge where she was perched.

Wing held his gaze for a moment, her face a mask hiding her compassion for the young man. "Someone on my team is fucking me over," she said. "Someone is providing information about me, about us, to our client." She watched his reaction as his eyebrows went up and surprise covered his face.

"Seriously?"

"Someone gave our client a complete dossier on me, which ended up in the baron's safe deposit box. Before I killed him, Bradley admitted he'd gotten the information from our client."

Enzo sat up, concern etched on his face. "What can I do to help?"

"Walter is the newest member of the team. He's the

only one I've hired since Nathan's death. I think he's a plant. I think he's here undercover, working for our client."

Enzo nodded his head. "Ok. So what do we do?"

"Dig into Walter's life, and see what you can uncover. You need to go deeper than our normal background check. I want to know every financial transaction he's ever done. I want to know every woman he's slept with, and who his high school sweetheart was. I think the background we found on him was fake. And, of course, do it without anyone else knowing."

"I'm on it," Enzo said, an eager look on his face. He took the wine glass from her hand and set it on the floor along with his before gently pulling on her arm. She tried to resist, her mind on her problems, but once she felt the warmth of his body against hers, she let him guide her into the sheets.

TWENTY-ONE

Istanbul, Turkey

As the evening progressed, the streets of the Old City turned from a tourist Mecca to a party in full swing. Many of the outdoor cafes converted into late-night drinking establishments filled with locals and foreigners alike, smoking and drinking a local beer called Efes Pilsen from squat bottles with blue labels. Turks liked their cigarettes, and the air in many restaurants and cafes was thick with smoke.

Having just completed a successful SDR, Max was confident he was alone. He ducked into a small cafe named Lucca and wormed his way through the crowded bar area. The patrons were mostly young, dark-haired locals – women and men moving in packs, flirting, talking, laughing. Max caught the eye of the bartender, a heavyset man with no neck and a scruffy beard that touched his chest. The man, who was slowly polishing glasses, nodded at Max, then looked away. The signal was imperceptible to anyone else watching, but Max knew it meant the meeting was to go forward as scheduled. Max pushed through the crowd toward the back and shoved aside the strands of beads covering a doorway and ducked into a back hallway. He was about to rap his knuckles on the door opposite him when it swung inward. A man who looked identical to the bartender stepped out and embraced Max with a massive bear hug. Tabor and Tadeo were Turkish twins who owned the cafe. Max could never tell which man was Tabor and which was Tadeo, but he knew the pair from his years in the KGB and knew he could trust their discretion. Max clapped him on the back, and the big man stepped aside so Max could enter the room. Max knew the twin would stand guard at the closed door and prevent anyone from bothering them.

"Well, this is a first," a quiet voice said from across the room. The room was hazy, as if the previous occupants had left a cigarette burning in an ashtray. Max saw an old rickety desk along one wall, piled high with papers. A low, leather couch rested against another wall and a chair sat at an angle to the couch. Standing at the far end of the couch was a tall woman wearing a cream-colored linen pantsuit. Her arms were crossed, but she wore a bemused smile on her face. Despite her seventy-plus years, Julia had the face of a woman twenty years younger. Max gave her a hug, and after a moment's hesitation, she hugged him back.

"Hello, Julia," Max said. Despite having known her for a few weeks, Max still didn't feel comfortable calling her *mother*. Theirs was a relationship still in development. Julia, his father's former mistress, had revealed herself to be Max's true mother just a short time before. United by his father's death, it was a situation they were both still feeling their way through. "What's a first?"

"You arranging to meet without trying to shadow me first."

"I think I've learned that you're better at picking up a tail than I am at tailing someone," Max said, laughing. He had picked up on the fact that his mother either had been, or still was, some kind of intelligence agent. But thus far, Julia hadn't revealed any details about her background, nor how she'd come to be involved with Max's father.

"It's a nice surprise to see you," Julia said. "And this time you called ahead of time."

"Sorry I didn't give you more than twenty-four hours' notice," Max said. "Preservation tactics."

"I get it," Julia said. "More than you know."

Max pointed to the seats. Julia sat on the edge of the couch. Max sat back in the chair, produced a cigarette, and pulled out the matchbook from the Stone Pony. Julia signaled with her fingers. Max leaned forward and shook one out of the crumpled pack, then held a match to the end as she inhaled. Soon, the tiny room was filled with the sticky scent of the Camels.

"American cigarettes, I see," Julia said, waving the smoke in the air.

"When in Rome," Max said.

"And how's little Alex?"

"As good as can be expected." Max filled her in on the latest developments, then finished with why he'd come. "I need your help finding Dedov. He's somewhere here in the city, and I need to know where."

"What makes you think I'm in a position to help?"

"Hope, I guess," he said. "I know that you moved here after the mess in Prague. I assume you're plugged into the intelligence scene here—" He left his statement open, hoping she'd take the bait.

Julia looked away and took a drag on her cigarette. It

looked like she was trying to determine how much to tell him. He waited patiently.

"I don't want to keep running, Max," she said finally. "I'm an old woman. I've been chased out of Zurich and Prague. I like it here. I'd like to stay for a while. Put down some roots. Life is different now."

"I understand," Max said. He left the cryptic statement alone, figuring if she wanted him to know more, she'd tell him.

"Yes, I suppose you do," she said. She got a faraway look in her eyes, and Max wondered where she'd gone.

Max waited. She didn't say anything for a long time. Finally, he changed the subject. "Did my father ever tell you about a memory card he had hidden?"

At this, Julia turned her head and looked at him. Did he see a flicker of recognition in her eyes?

"I think it was why he was killed," Max went on. "Sometime before the bombing of our house, my father's study – a room out in our barn – was ransacked. I think they were looking for a memory card. I found it hidden in the back of a photograph."

Julia's eyes narrowed. "Do you still have it? The memory card, that is?"

"No," Max said. "It was stolen from our safe house. I think one of Dedov's men was the operator who stole it."

Julia nodded. "Yes. I know of the memory card," she said.

"Did he tell you anything about it?"

Again, Julia got that faraway look in her eyes, making Max feel like he was intruding on an inside joke, or maybe the secrets of two lovers. "He said it was the future of the Russian state," Julia said. "And your father was not given to making rash, sweeping statements like that. He told me that he couldn't tell me what was on it, for my own safety."

"The future of the Russian state?" Max asked. The statement didn't make much sense, and Julia had avoided his eyes as she'd said it, making Max wonder if she was lying, or perhaps covering up the truth. He guessed she knew exactly what was on that thumb drive.

"Yes. Those were his exact words. I remember because, as I said, he didn't often make those kinds of statements. Have you been able to determine what kind of information is on it? Did you look at it?"

"It's encrypted," Max said.

At that, Julia got a peculiar look on her face, which disappeared almost as soon as it appeared. Max read it as recognition, or perhaps she'd put something together that had previously perplexed her.

"What is it?" he asked.

She shook her head. "No, nothing. So you said you think Dedov took the memory card?"

"Correct." Max explained the connection between Peter Orlov and Dedov.

She nodded her head. "What will you do with Dedov?"

"That depends," Max said. "Can you arrange a meeting?"

She looked at him for a long moment, and Max got the impression she was playing out a chess match in her head. Finally, she said, "Call me in an hour."

Max thanked her profusely. They talked long enough to smoke another cigarette, then Max hugged her and said goodbye.

As he turned to go, Julia said, "Something else, Max." Max stopped and turned back.

"You know who might have information about your father's death?"

Max just looked at her.

"Do you remember Dmitry Utkin?"

The name didn't immediately ring a bell. Max had to search his memory. Then an image of his father flashed in his mind. His old man was standing in the rain next to a door, wearing a massive wool overcoat. Max, as a young boy, was standing next to him. *Do not speak unless spoken to, my boy,* his father had said, before opening the door and leading Max inside. Dmitry Utkin was among the most powerful men in Russia, and the door had led to his inner sanctum, a place only a few privileged men came to witness.

Max nodded at Julia. "I do. He's still alive?"

Julia nodded. "I believe Utkin would honor your father's memory by agreeing to take a meeting with you. Whatever you do, do not tell him I mentioned his name."

Max held her eye for a moment and realized she would offer no further information. He nodded, then turned and left the room. He exited the cafe by threading through the cramped kitchen and out the back door. As he walked down the alleyway, he wondered for the hundredth time what was really going on in Julia's head, and when she might confide in him.

———

The boy scampered from the rear kitchen door of Cafe Lucca and dashed through the crowded streets, his ragged sandals slapping on the cobblestone and splashing in puddles. He knew he would lose his job at the popular cafe for abandoning his post, but the potential reward was worth it. Two blocks up and one block over, he dashed into a narrow alleyway, ran through a narrow door, and took a set of rickety stairs two at a time. He'd left the tourist part of the Old City and had entered the narrow and grimy residential area where many of the city's service workers, students, and poor families resided. It wasn't quite the gecekondular, the Turkish slums, but it was a poor neighborhood. The boy's family would profit from what he'd just seen, as long as he could report the information in time.

The boy raced down a corridor and burst into the cramped two-room apartment he shared with his extended family. His father and grandfather were reclining on cushions, smoking the hookah and sipping raki, the anise-flavored alcohol favored in Turkey. They looked up, startled, when the boy burst in.

"Father, father. I've seen him. The man." Stumbling over his words, the story spilled out of him. While refilling water pitchers in the kitchen, he'd seen the tall Caucasian man with the shaved head walk through the kitchen. At first he hadn't been sure, but then he saw the bandage on the man's forearm, just as it had been described, and he'd known.

His father, better able to hide his excitement, reached into his robes and removed an ancient flip phone along with a ragged slip of paper. The phone was missing a few buttons and a green cord stuck out of the hinge where the two pieces met. The boy held his breath while his father fumbled with the phone, attempting to dial with his calloused and misshapen fingers. Finally, the man held the phone to his ear. A minute later he spoke a few words in Turkish into the handset, then hung up. Smiling, he hugged his boy. The money they'd just earned would feed the entire family for a month.

TWENTY-TWO

Istanbul, Turkey

His meeting with Dedov was to take place in a restaurant called Venezia, located in a quiet neighborhood on the edge of Old Town Istanbul. The entry to the cafe was in a tight alleyway, and according to intelligence provided by Julia, the restaurant only had four tables in the main room. Venezia was off the beaten tourist path, but Julia had assured him the one-man operation served the best Italian cuisine outside of Italy.

Because of the tight confines around the restaurant's entrance, Max had a tough time finding a covert location from which to perform surveillance. Finally, he broke into an abandoned third-floor flat that afforded him a partial view of the restaurant's front door. He dragged a battered wooden chair with burn marks on the seat over to the window and sat down to wait.

The meeting was scheduled for 10:00 p.m. that night, and Julia had indicated that the proprietor, a long-time

Dedov confidant, would close his doors early to allow the private conversation to take place. Dedov had stipulated that Max come alone, un-armed and un-wired. He – Dedov – would have one bodyguard in place to ensure Max's compliance with the rules. Max didn't trust Dedov any further than he could throw the man, so he had arrived five hours early to watch.

As he waited, Max removed a soft pack of Turkish cigarettes from his pocket and lit one using a match. After his meeting with Julia, he'd tossed the caustic American smokes and purchased something more local. The pack had the name Murad on the front and showed a colorful image of a beautiful woman reclining on a chaise. Max admired the artwork while he enjoyed the aromatic smoke, and his thoughts turned to his father. The former KGB master spy was known for his fondness of the pungent yet mild tobacco, and had seldom been seen without one between his fingers. As Max watched couples entering and exiting the restaurant, he recalled one of the many teachings his father had bestowed upon him while growing up.

"Stand against the side wall with your arms crossed and stare at the prisoner," his father said, "But don't say a fucking word."

Two months shy of his eighteenth birthday, Max was already looking forward to shipping off to basic training with the Red Army. In the past two years, the intensity and urgency of his father's training had increased. By that time, Max was an expert marksman, could use a set of picks to open a lock in under five seconds, knew how to escape from a set of plastic cuffs using his shoe laces, and could perform a surveillance detection run like an expert. His father had promised only a year in the general population of the Red Army before Max would be singled out for special forces training.

With his mind on the future, Max followed his father's bear-like form into the holding cell. Two of his father's agents followed and took up positions on either side of the room's sole occupant.

The first thing Max noticed was the stench. The over-powering odor was a combination of urine, feces, rotting flesh, and something else. Something intangible. It wasn't the first time he'd sensed it, but he couldn't get used to it. It was the smell of fear.

The room was formed out of cinderblock and had several openings to the outdoors. Overhead, the metal roof radiated heat, turning the structure into a sauna. The dirt floor had turned into a sea of mud, and Max's boots sucked into it as he walked.

In the center of the room, the naked prisoner was hunched down on his knees, bent at the waist, forehead to the muddy ground. His arms were secured behind him, and his body was filthy and marked with red welts along his back and arms. Max walked to the side wall, shifted his sidearm on his belt, lit a cigarette, put a foot up on the wall, and glared at the prisoner.

His father stood in front of the captive. "Untie him," his father demanded. The man remained hunched over as one of his father's men complied.

"Get him some water," his father commanded. "And bring two chairs." His father squatted down and asked the man if he wanted a cigarette.

Max watched over the course of two hours as his father coaxed information from the man, using a mixture of gentle threats, promises, and rewards like cigarettes and food.

Finally, his father rose and patted the prisoner on the shoulder, then indicated for Max to follow him outside. They sat in folding chairs, and Max breathed deep, thankful to be out of the stench.

"Why didn't you simply torture him?" Max asked, shielding his eyes from the hot sun. "Wouldn't that have been quicker?"

"That's why I brought you," his father said, leaning back in his chair and lighting a cigarette. "Pain has its place in interrogation, but I'd caution you to use it sparingly. A man in physical pain will tell you anything just to make the pain stop. Instead, you want to get into his mind. We use a series of techniques to break down a man's will. We strip him, we force him to stand for days on end, deprive him of sleep. Force him to listen to terrible music. The pain is mostly psychological. Then we build him back up again. Give him hot food, a place to sit comfortably, cigarettes. At that point, he'll usually tell you what you want to know in order to prevent repeating the same experience."

"Isn't that the same?" Max asked. "A man will tell you anything in order to prevent the psychological pain?"

"The two kinds of pain work differently on the mind," his father replied. "Physical pain will make a prisoner suddenly reply with anything, just to get the pain to stop. Emotional pain builds up over time. We break down his fortitude slowly. When we build him back up, he has hope. Hope that he'll still get out of the mess alive. It's that hope for escape, combined with the need to avoid the pain, that will make them open up."

"What happens to him now?" Max asked.

As if in answer, the crack of a pistol shot reverberated through the compound, and Max looked at his father, alarmed.

"We got what we needed from him," his father said, looking intently at his cigarette.

A black sprinter van pulled up to the front door of the restaurant, pulling Max back to the present. His watch read eight p.m., two hours before the scheduled meeting time. Four men emerged from the van, none of whom were Dedov. They all wore suits, had cords running to their ears, and Max saw a shoulder holster flash under one man's jacket. The first man to step out of the van was big as a bear, at least six feet, ten inches tall. The last man out carried a long flat case, like it might contain an electric guitar. Or a sniper rifle.

Two of the men disappeared into the restaurant. A third stayed with the van. The man with the case walked down the alley and disappeared through a door. Max noted he entered the tallest building on the block. Nothing happened for ten minutes. Then the man who had stayed with the van jumped into the driver's seat, started the vehicle, and pulled away from the curb.

Max let the front legs of his chair hit the ground, pocketed his cigarette butts, and exited the building through a narrow alley. Dedov obviously wasn't sticking to his own rules for the meeting. Max didn't intend to, either.

———

The big man's name was Leonid, but everyone called him Leo, and he took pride in the nickname. At six-foot-ten, with broad shoulders and no body fat, he cut an imposing figure. Leo walked in what he imagined was a prowl – slow, taking it all in, a beast that demanded respect. After eight years in the elite Russian special forces, he'd been recruited by Victor Dedov to lead the Belarusian KGB Director's personal bodyguard unit. For the past several years, Leo had performed that role with distinction, and he prided himself on his unit's performance, dedication, loyalty, and effectiveness.

Leo's earpiece chirped. "Unit four in position. I have clear line-of-sight to the restaurant's door."

A second chirp came a few seconds later. "Unit three. In position. I also have clear line-of-sight."

Leo toggled his mic. "Excellent." Unit three was unit four's spotter. "Remember the drill. Nothing happens until after the meeting. If you hear me say *drook*, stand down and let the target pass. If you hear *vrag*, take him out the moment he steps out the restaurant's door."

"Roger that," he heard both men report.

Leo prowled the small room and ensured the interior was set up correctly. All the tables save one had been pushed back to the wall. The lone table in the center of the room had a linen cloth set with two place settings and two chairs set up opposite each other. He ran his hand along the table's underside to ensure the .38 pistol was in place.

Next, he walked into the kitchen and watched Yakov, one of his men, drill a small hole in the wall separating the dining room from the kitchen, up near the ceiling. The man placed a tiny surveillance camera in the hole and ran the closed-circuit wire up through another hole in the ceiling. The cord ran to a TV monitor located in the room directly upstairs from the kitchen. Yakov would be in that position, heavily armed, in case of a problem.

Lastly, Leo found the proprietor and quizzed him one last time about the restaurant's layout. "You're sure there is only one way in, and one way out of this restaurant?"

"Of course," the old man said. "I've owned this building for thirty years. If there was another way in, I'd know about it."

Leo placed a thick envelop in the man's hand and shooed him into the kitchen to start meal preparations.

At precisely 9:45 p.m., a long black Mercedes appeared at the front door of the restaurant. Two guards got out and surveyed the streets. Seeing no sign of a threat, one pulled open the Mercedes' rear door and the small form of Victor Dedov stepped out and entered the restaurant. Per the plan, both guards accompanying Dedov remained outside, flanking the front door.

Leo stood, his eyes cast downward so he didn't look the great man directly in the eyes, and reported, "All units are in place, sir. The entire facility has been swept. We're clean."

"Excellent," Dedov said, then strolled into the kitchen and took the chef by the shoulders and kissed the man's cheeks. Dedov accepted a glass of red wine and listened as the chef went on about his wife's gout and his daughter's ne'er-do-well boyfriend.

At ten o'clock p.m., Dedov took his seat facing the door and accepted another glass of wine. Leo stood behind him and to the left, eager to catch sight of Mikhail Asimov, the famous assassin.

TWENTY-THREE

Istanbul, Turkey

By 10:15 p.m., Dedov was growing impatient. If he wasn't so eager to hear what Asimov had to say, he might have left. He suspected the operative had somehow figured out that he, Dedov, had been behind the theft of the memory card. Dedov was interested to know what Asimov would pay, or barter, to get the memory card back. He'd already lined up a buyer who had agreed to pay Dedov's stiff price, but it didn't hurt to test the market. He accepted another pour of the silky Sangiovese from the chef, and tried to calm his growing irritation.

If his plans to sell the memory chip worked out, Dedov would take an early retirement from the KGB and disappear to his country estate in the South of France. He would live out his days as a semi-wealthy man. Asimov, however, had a fairly substantial price on his head. If Dedov could combine a bounty for Asimov with the sale of the memory card, he could retire as a very wealthy man, and perhaps buy that yacht he'd always dreamed of.

He figured it was a long shot, but if Asimov agreed to Dedov's price, Asimov could walk free. If not, Asimov would step out of the restaurant directly into a 54mm $7N14$ round loaded with a 9.8g projectile containing a sharp hardened steel penetrator fired at a muzzle velocity of 830 meters per second. Dedov had reminded his men not to stand directly behind Asimov when he left the restaurant, as the slug would penetrate clean through his chest. Dedov sipped his wine, and asked the proprietor to bring a plate of bruschetta and some olive oil.

———

Max pointed a pistol at the chef's head and put his finger to his lips. Blood drained from the man's face and he almost dropped a plate of toasted bread covered with fresh tomatoes and mozzarella. Max gestured for the chef to turn and prodded him with the barrel of the gun through the swinging doors and into the dining room.

In front of him, Dedov sat at a table, his back to Max. To Max's right, he saw the enormous guard who had emerged from the van several hours ago. When the guard saw Max, he made a quick move toward the pistol in his holster.

"Don't," Max said. The big man froze, his hand hovering above the butt of his pistol. From the corner of his eye, he saw Dedov's right hand disappear under the table, signaling the man had a weapon available to him. "Freeze, Dedov, or the chef bites it."

Dedov froze.

"I come in peace," Max said.

Dedov rose from the table and turned, then spread his

arms out wide, his hands empty. "Mikhail, it's so good to see you. Why all the theatrics? Put the gun away and let's share a meal."

"I'm just evening out the playing field a little, Victor," Max said, still holding the gun steady on the chef. "Why don't you tell Dolph Lundgren there to toss his weapon. Also, why don't you get rid of that gun you have hidden under the table." Max saw Dedov glance toward the back wall. "Oh, and your man upstairs might have a bit of a headache when he wakes up. At least we'll be able to talk in relative privacy, and not worry about being recorded."

Max saw Dedov's face flush, but he regained his composure quickly and retrieved a .38 from under the table, handing it to Max butt first. Max collected the Makarov supplied by the big guard, then came around the table and sat down. He placed his pistol, barrel facing Dedov, on the corner of the table within easy reach.

"Now, let's talk," Max said, as the chef poured him a glass of wine with a shaking hand.

Dedov straightened his tie and took his seat at the table. Max noticed the experienced KGB man's hand was steady when he took a sip of his wine. Dedov had always been a cool customer under pressure.

"You can't blame me, Mikhail," Dedov said. "Men such as ourselves must take precautions, no?" Then Dedov raised his wine glass and said, "To your father, may he rest in peace."

Max paused, surprised, then raised his glass. "To my father."

They sipped and watched the chef lay out a spread of antipasti, bruschetta, and a plate of fresh mozzarella and tomatoes covered in balsamic.

Dedov said, "How's your sister? I was always fond of her. Must be difficult to raise a son without a father."

Max tensed at the mention of his sister and nephew. "She's a warrior," Max said.

"That she is," Dedov said. "I remember when she was a teenager and your mother had gotten her a puppy. One of the neighbor's dogs, a vicious Doberman, if I recall, attacked your sister's puppy, almost killing the poor thing. Arina beat that Doberman within an inch of its life with a cricket bat. I still remember the pride on your father's face when he told me."

Max had heard that story too, and wondered briefly why Dedov was mentioning it.

"Go on and eat, Mikhail. Before it all gets cold."

"I'm not eating, and I can't stay long," Max said.

Dedov's smile froze on his face. "Mikhail, my friend. You must eat. Salvadore here makes some of the best food in all of Turkey."

Max crossed his arms.

"Believe me, it's not poisoned. If you'd like, I can have Leonid taste each dish prior to you eating."

"Of course it's not poisoned. You'll just blow my head off when I step through that door instead," Max said, his arms still crossed.

Dedov looked aghast, and Max realized the man was a great actor. "Are you kidding?" Dedov asked. "We go way back, Mikhail. I would never do that. As you can probably understand, I can't be too careful when traveling. We both have many enemies."

"So you're not tempted by the large bounty on my head?"

Dedov spread his arms. "I'm a humble public servant. I have no use for such riches."

Max laughed. "So why did you go to all the trouble and expense of bribing Ed Willson to help you steal the memory card?"

Dedov's face grew somber. "Sometimes, in the course of an investigation, one must, how do you say, make sacrifices."

"So you admit to having it?"

"I admit nothing, Mikhail," Dedov said. His eyes said he was not a man to be bullied.

"What investigation are you referring to?" Max asked.

"The death of your father and mother, of course," Dedov replied. Max watched as Dedov ate some antipasti. He ate with the grace of a man used to formal settings. "It's still an ongoing investigation."

"I thought you said it was Chechen terrorists," Max said. "Isn't that what you said right after the explosion?"

Dedov shrugged his shoulders. "As you said, there is little proof of that. The case is still open as far as the KGB goes. What is on the memory chip, anyway?" Dedov asked.

"I thought you could tell me," Max said. "Since you went to so much trouble to get it, I assumed you knew."

The two men watched as the chef brought plates of fresh seafood farfalle and mozzarella stuffed with ham and vegetables. When the chef departed, Dedov said, "You must try this. It's simply amazing."

Max watched him dig in with a fork and spoon. "Quit stalling, Victor. You have something I want. The only reason you'd agree to meet with me is to see how much I'm willing to pay for its return. Or to try to kill me and turn me over to my enemy."

Dedov chewed, then swallowed. "Just like your old man. Direct and to the point. All business. Very well. Have it your way." Dedov folded his napkin and put it on the table, then pushed his chair out. "I have one buyer for the memory card. I'm here to see if you'll counter the offer."

Finally, they were getting somewhere. Max thought for a moment, then replied. "If I do, you'll let me walk out that door so you can collect. If I don't, you'll shoot me the moment I walk out so you can collect the bounty. Early retirement, Dedov?"

Dedov's face remained passive. "Do you want to bid, or not?" he asked. "Besides, seems like there is another way in and out of this restaurant."

"What's the current bid?" Max asked.

"You'd have to start at five million US if you want to be taken seriously," Dedov said.

Max whistled. "That card must contain some valuable information."

Dedov shrugged. "It's encrypted, as you no doubt discovered. All I can go on is what the market is willing to pay."

Max leaned forward. "I'll give you ten million US, but I need something else in return for the extra five."

Dedov's eyebrow's raised. "You can get that kind of money?"

"Don't worry about that," Max said. "I'll need forty-eight hours, but it can be done. Do we have an agreement?"

"What is this additional condition to the deal?" Dedov asked.

"I want you to set up the sale to your first buyer, then disappear and let me deliver the merchandise," Max said.

Dedov's eyebrow's narrowed. "You want me to set up my buyer so you can take them out. Not sure how healthy—"

Dedov was cut off by the sound of semi-automatic gunfire and the tinkle of broken glass. Slugs started pouring through the windows and the tiny room plummeted into chaos.

Instinctively, Max grabbed his pistol and rolled to the ground. He saw Dedov react with similar speed and flip up the table as a blockade to the gunfire. As Max rolled, he saw the bodyguard take several bullets to the chest, a blossom of red appearing on his white oxford shirt. The big guard grunted, jerked from the impact of the bullets, then fell to his knees. He finally fell to the ground like an ancient redwood felled by a chainsaw.

Max tipped over a thick table and took cover. Bullets continued to chew up the inside of the restaurant. Glass from the windows and shards of wood from the walls and tables flew through the air. Based on the amount of carnage, Max figured there had to be at least two, maybe three shooters. Max glanced at Dedov. The man had a pistol in his hand, but was holding his fire. He looked calm.

"Friends of yours?" Max called out. He knew firing blindly toward the front would be a waste of ammunition. His only hope was to exit the way he'd come in – through the skylight in the third-floor bedroom.

"Maybe friends of yours," Dedov called. "You're the one with the price on his head."

The barrage of bullets ceased. Max knew their time in the tiny dining room was limited. Any moment, a group of men might storm the room, perhaps preceded by a few grenades.

"Follow me," Max yelled. He started firing through the broken windowpanes on the front door. As he fired, he backed up toward the kitchen, almost stumbling on the chef's dead body. The man's torso was riddled with bullets and his kitchen whites had turned dark red. Dedov followed suit, firing as he backed up, finally joining Max in the kitchen.

"The world just lost a great chef," Dedov said, his face dark with anger.

"Up those stairs," Max said. "You first."

Dedov hesitated. Then an explosion was heard from the direction of the dining room, followed quickly by a second explosion. Dedov moved, scampering up the stairs. Max followed and they emerged into a small living area. Max pointed to a second set of stairs and they found themselves in a bedroom, its dusty skylight propped open. With no other choice, Max shoved his gun in his belt, hoping the prospect of a large payday might keep Dedov from killing him. Max boosted Dedov up, then stood on a dresser and pulled himself through the hole, emerging onto a roof covered in black tar paper.

"Thanks for not shooting me," Max said as he and Dedov scampered over buttresses on a beeline for the end of the row houses.

"I try to never kill my investments before they pay off," Dedov said, breathing hard from the run.

TWENTY-FOUR

Unknown Location

Darkness enveloped her. From somewhere in the distance, Wing could hear the sound of classical music. She instantly recognized the iconic notes of Beethoven's Fifth Symphony. A variety of smells assaulted her through the velvet hood. Moist, damp odors she associated with nursing homes and cellars. Through the must, she caught the wavering fragrance of a male – leather or sandalwood – then it was gone. She shivered against a draft and wished she'd grabbed a jacket.

She worked to control her fear. To get to her current destination, a helicopter had arrived at her office unannounced, containing Mueller and two heavily armed men. The chopper had whisked her to a regional airport, where she'd boarded a small Lear jet and been hooded. After a short flight and a long car ride, she'd been paraded up and down stairs and along various corridors to the spot where she now stood. Her leg muscles felt weak and she fought the urge to just collapse, willing herself to be strong.

The black velvet hood was yanked from her head and she blinked to clear her eyes. In the dim light, she saw her client directly in front of her, a bemused look on his withered face. Then she looked around, catching her breath.

"Ah yes, my dear," her client said. "Take it all in. You are privileged to see something few people in the world get to."

She was standing in a long hall that resembled the nave of a huge, medieval cathedral. The main source of illumination came from beams of sunlight streaming through long, thin, stained glass windows evenly spaced along two sides of the hall, high overhead. Underneath the stained glass windows were dozens and dozens of paintings. The only other source of light came from tiny lamps above each picture. Wing saw the distinctive brush strokes of several Van Goghs and the muted spring colors of more than a few Monets before the old man's voice cut through her thoughts.

"You are standing before what is undoubtedly the world's largest collection of Renaissance, impressionist, and expressionist art. Over the years, I've carefully curated this collection, liberating many of these from museums and . other collectors."

"These are all stolen?" Wing asked.

"It depends on how you look at it," the old man said. Once again, he was smiling as if he knew a joke unknown to the rest of the world. "In many cases, I've simply re-taken what others had stolen, and left exact replicas in their place. Many private collectors couldn't tell a fake from the real thing if it bit them on the nose." A peal of laughter reverberated around the room as the old man laughed at his own joke.

Wing said nothing, and gazed around. Then she gasped, catching sight of a painting of a small ship on stormy seas. "Is that—?"

"'The Storm on the Sea of Galilee'?" The old man interrupted. "Yes, that's the original. Come."

He piloted his chair closer to the painting in question and Wing followed, sensing someone behind her. Turning, she saw the ever-present form of Mueller towering over her. Turning back, she said, "That's from the Gardner Museum heist. How did you—?"

"My dear, money is power. Power to get anything you want."

She gazed in wonder at the lost masterpiece by Rembrandt. The painting showed an image of Christ attempting to calm stormy seas. The work was regarded as the most priceless work of art ever stolen.

"I come here when I need to be cheered up," the old man said, maneuvering his chair so he was facing Wing. "You know why we're here now?"

Wing remained silent.

From somewhere in the folds of the black suit draped over his withered body, her client produced a handgun and pointed it at her. Wing noticed his hand was steady.

"When I was a younger man, I did most of my killing myself. It helps garner respect, you see. Now, I have others to carry out my wishes." He waved the gun, and Wing noticed it was an old revolver. A six-shooter, like American cowboys used to carry.

The old man kept talking. "I see you're admiring my weapon." He held it up so she could see it better. The handle looked to be made from white bone. "It's a .45 Smith & Wesson," he said. "Used to belong to Jesse James, before I had it lifted out of the NRA's museum over in the States. Its handle is mother of pearl."

"You sure it'll fire, and won't blow up in your face?" Wing asked.

That made the old man laugh, and he set the gun down on his lap. "Doesn't matter. I'm not going to kill you today."

Silently, Wing breathed a sigh of relief.

"But we are going to change our little arrangement. It's clear you're not equal to Nathan in skills or capabilities. Your organization is falling apart, your staff is turning against you, and you're spending your valuable time trying to figure out who I am instead of completing your assignment. You're out of money and no one will work for you. You're self-destructing. Even if you were to catch Max Austin, he'd probably tear you limb from limb."

Wing felt herself deflating with every word.

"Even the threat of your father's imminent death has done little to motivate you to success," the old man continued. "Maybe you don't belong in this game, eh? Most businesses fail, Ms. Octavia. Maybe yours is destined to be one of those many failures. Maybe you just need a job."

At the mention of her father's name, Wing lost the will to stand and looked around wildly for a place to sit. She hobbled over to a nearby bench and plopped down on the cold leather surface. The old man motored closer.

"Come work for me, Ms. Octavia. I can use someone of your logistical talents. You and Mueller here would make a wonderful team. Let me do all the thinking, and you can simply carry out my strategies. You can forget all of your responsibilities. You would be handsomely compensated and your father could retire in comfort."

Wing buried her face in her hands. She couldn't believe it had come to this.

"Take some time, my dear. I know this is sudden. Mueller will return you to your offices and provide you with a special mobile phone you can use to contact me. I'll give you a day or two to make up your mind. But don't dally. I suspect our mutual acquaintance, Mr. Bokun, will enjoy having a new quarry to pursue. Stay as long as you'd like. This room can be soothing, something you may benefit from."

Wing listened as the whir of the wheelchair's motor disappeared into the distance. Finally, she was left in silence. Looking up, she saw Mueller standing in the distance by the door. She gazed around at some of the world's most exquisite works of art, and wondered if she could sink any lower.

TWENTY-FIVE

Istanbul, Turkey

The bullets started flying faster than Max had anticipated. He leaped over a brick buttress dividing one roof from another and started to weave, his shoes grinding on the gritty surface of the roof. A bullet sang by his head and another punched a hole in an aluminum vent right next to him. To his right, he could see Dedov pick up his pace as more bullets ricocheted off the balustrade lining the front of the roof.

"You sure someone didn't get wind of your retirement plan," Max yelled.

"More than likely, you led someone to our meeting spot," Dedov yelled back.

They reached the end of the row of houses, where a black nylon rope had been fixed to a drain pipe. Max stowed his gun, grabbed the rope, and stepped off the side of the building, using the rope to spin himself so his feet slapped against the brick wall. Favoring speed over safety, he let go of the rope and let himself fall, periodically grabbing hold to control his speed. The nylon burned into his palms, but it was only a matter of seconds before his feet hit the ground. He rolled and came up with his pistol in his hand. A second later, Dedov dropped to the ground, crying out as his ankle twisted under him.

Max grabbed his arm and tried to pull the KGB boss along. "We need to move," Max urged.

Dedov stood and took a step, but his leg buckled under him and he fell against Max. Keeping his pistol in his right hand, Max reached around and grasped the man around his back, locking his hand under the man's armpit. He practically picked up the smaller man and carried him forward. As he did so, his hand felt a wetness on Dedov's suit jacket.

"Are you hit?" Max yelled. They were moving more slowly now, staggering down an alleyway, Max's shoes splashing through puddles. He knew any minute the hail of bullets would resume as the pursuers reached the end of the row houses. They needed to put as much distance between them and the building as possible.

"No. Don't think so," Dedov said through clenched teeth.

Max didn't believe him. His hand felt slimy, a feeling he knew all too well. He needed to prevent Dedov from dying – the man was his one connection to the memory chip, and his pursuers. All Max needed to do was come up with ten million dollars, and he knew Dedov would help him identify his enemies. But Dedov couldn't do that if he was dead.

The gunfire started again and Max instinctively picked up his pace, urging Dedov forward. He could see a corner a few paces away. If he could get Dedov around the corner, they might at least be sheltered from the gunfire. If the attackers had left any men outside during their raid – which is what Max would have done – they'd be in touch via radio, and would already be in pursuit. *One step at a time*, Max reminded himself. A bullet ricocheted off the cobblestone in front of him. He pushed himself harder, the corner almost within reach.

A bullet pinged off the wall next to his face, the chips of concrete stinging his neck. He pumped his legs and heaved both Dedov and himself around the corner, the combined weight of both men almost sending them pitching headlong onto the ground. Max fought to steady himself, but his grip slipped from Dedov's shoulder, and the smaller man fell face first onto the cobblestone.

Relieved to be out of the line of fire, at least for the moment, he grasped Dedov under each armpit and heaved. "Come on, Victor," Max grunted. "Help me. We need to keep moving."

Dedov struggled and managed to push himself up with Max's assistance. A moment later they stood, panting, with Max still supporting the smaller man. Dedov felt in his jacket and came out with a mobile phone. He flipped it open and held it to his ear. A moment later, he barked a few commands in Russian, then stowed the phone.

"We need to go," Max said. "They'll be mounting a search."

"We should split up," Dedov said. He was still breathing hard. "My team, what's left of them, will be here any minute. You shouldn't be here when they arrive."

"Why not?"

"I won't be able to explain why we're still together. The team on its way are not my most trusted men. We should split up and meet back up in forty-eight hours. You bring the money. I'll arrange the setup." The man's breathing had evened slightly, and he looked around, taking in their surroundings.

What Dedov said had merit, but Max didn't like the idea of splitting up. Still, he knew he stood a better chance of escaping if he was on his own. "How do I contact you?"

Dedov reeled off a string of numbers, which Max instantly memorized. "Call me at that number," Dedov said. With that, he started hobbling away, moving fast for someone with an injured ankle. A minute later, he disappeared down an alleyway.

Max briefly considered turning back to see if he could take out any of their pursuers. Then he reconsidered and took off down the alley. He had no idea how many men were back there, and he was vastly out-gunned. Keeping the pistol by his leg, he made a left, then another right, and found himself on the sidewalk of a major roadway. He put the gun in his waistband and let his jacket hide the handle. Then he flagged down a cab, thrust a wad of lira in the driver's hand, and said, "Drive fast."

TWENTY-SIX

Moscow, Russia

Max kept his pace brisk, like he was a businessman late to a meeting. Wind swirled trash around his feet, and overhead the sky threatened rain. Not violent rain like a thunderstorm, but a steady cold rain that could chill even the heartiest Russian to the bone. Around him, smartly dressed men and women with Gucci bags or leather briefcases moved with urgency. It had been several years since Max had visited Moscow, and he marveled at the changes, like the sidewalks made narrower to accommodate new bike lanes and the food carts on every block.

Coming to Moscow was unbelievably risky. Officially, Max was a traitor. Despite having been mostly forgotten by the FSB in recent years, he'd given himself over to the organization's arch enemy, the CIA. Russians hated traitors more than anything. If Max was caught, he could look forward to a long stay in the worst gulag Russia had to offer, if he wasn't outright killed.

He hoped the trip was worth the risk. He'd come to meet a man – someone who had forgotten more about the KGB than Max would ever know. He was a recluse, a member of the old guard, and a long-time acquaintance of Max's father. Max's mission was to arrange a meeting and escape the country before the FSB was alerted to his presence.

Something caught his eye and Max stopped short. He backtracked two steps. He'd just walked past a corner kiosk that sold newspapers, coffee, and other sundries. The news-stands were another relatively new addition to the streets of Moscow. This one had a rack of newspapers facing out, and he'd recognized an image on the front of one of them. Something that made his blood go cold.

Max grabbed the *Izvestia* from the front rack and tossed a few rubles at the proprietor. The *Izvestia* was a long-running national newspaper with close ties to the government. Glancing around to see if he was being watched, Max folded the paper and slipped it under his arm. He saw no one watching, but that meant nothing in Moscow.

The picture on the front page was alarming, but he didn't want to call attention to himself by standing in the crowd of pedestrians gawking. His nerves were already on edge just being in the Russian capital.

Moscow, and much of Russia for that matter, was famous for having the eyes and ears of the FSB every-where. Foreign spies attempting to work in Moscow during the Cold War had coined the term *The Moscow Rules*. These were rules adhered to, as a matter of survival, by anyone attempting clandestine activities in Russia. They included such missives as *assume nothing*; *everyone is potentially under opposition control*; *don't look back – you are never completely alone*, among others. Max had always chuckled about the reputation of the rules. He wasn't laughing now.

Max kept a steady pace through the cold spring evening, and angled for the tenement where he'd arranged to stay. He was itching to look at the cover story of the newspaper, but forced himself to keep walking. As he turned into a narrow street, a light rain began to fall, and he turned up the collar of his coat. He wore a short-brimmed fedora, a bushy fake mustache, and large, thick glasses that made him look like a university professor.

Glancing back to ensure he was alone, he used a key to enter through the side gate of a small house. The residence contained three small flats plus the owner's rooms on the first floor. He ignored the old babushka in the common room and trudged up three flights, then used another key to enter his room. He tossed the paper on the tiny table and hung up his overcoat on a nail by the door.

Finally, he sat down and flipped open the paper. On the cover was a portrait of Victor Dedov, resplendent in his Belarusian KGB dress uniform. "KGB Chief Victor Dedov Found Dead," the headline screamed.

Max read the article, his heart sinking with every word. Afterward, he got up and made some strong Russian black tea, then read the article again. Something about the story seemed off to Max, even though he knew he couldn't believe everything he read in Russian newspapers.

Details were sketchy, but the article described how Victor Dedov had been on holiday in Istanbul with his family. His wife and children had returned from shopping to find Dedov dead in his study from an apparent gunshot wound to the side of his head. A Makarov pistol was found on the floor next to his chair. No note was in evidence. The paper further went on to speculate that Dedov may have suffered a nervous breakdown from the investigation of his number two, who had recently been killed by a bomb. Max winced when he realized the statement referred to his own family.

Max knew the media in Russia served only one purpose: to further the interests of the Russian government and maintain the high approval ratings of its president. Max had no doubt Dedov was dead. But he didn't believe for a second the man had killed himself. Max guessed Dedov had been captured by the men who had attacked them the previous night. The nature of the story made Max think the Russian FSB had been onto Dedov's plans to sell the memory chip and enter an early retirement. Did that mean the FSB was now in possession of the memory card? Max had to assume so. Suddenly, Max's mission in Moscow had become that much more critical.

He folded up the paper and took his tea to the window. Standing hidden behind the curtain, he peeked out. The rain was coming down heavier now. The occasional car that passed down the narrow side street next to his room cast off sprays of water. Max watched for a long time while he sipped his tea. He saw no indication he was being watched. There were no suspicious sedans driving slowly by, no people loitering in doorways. He might be clean now, but he knew that would not last long.

Max checked his watch, then finished his tea. The rain was keeping most people off the streets, and that suited him just fine. The low grey clouds meant the rain was here to stay and it was perfect operational weather. One more long look through the glass suggested he was clean. The Moscow Rules told him that his sense of security was false.

He put his hat back on, checked his mustache and glasses in the mirror, then donned a long grey trench coat.

In the right pocket of the jacket, he slipped a Russian-made Makarov pistol. The gun was an older model, holding only eight rounds in the magazine, but was the perfect size to keep in a coat pocket.

Max looked around the tiny room to ensure he'd left nothing behind, then gave it a brisk wipe-down. He wouldn't be back. He'd brought little with him and would need little where he was going. With any luck, he'd be leaving Moscow within a few hours.

TWENTY-SEVEN

Moscow, Russia

Max exited the flat using the back staircase. He stepped through the back door and into the rain, the drops making a *pat, pat, pat* sound on the brim of his hat. He glanced around and saw no one. In the distance, he heard the sound of a car approaching, its wheels splashing through puddles. He paused a moment, half hidden behind a tree, and watched as the car passed.

One of Max's favorite Moscow rules was *Don't attract attention, even by being too careful.* The phrase caught the paradoxical essence of the Moscow Rules – that no matter what you did, you were fucked. He reminded himself of that maxim and exited the yard through the back gate. He raised a black umbrella and started down the street at a pace that would be expected of any man walking in the rain.

His journey would not be far, and Max elected to refrain from performing an SDR. He thought it likely a low-ranking FSB foot soldier was keeping tabs on him much as they might any foreign business man, without realizing Max's true identity. Max's fake passport had been French, and he'd stated his business was with a small gas pipeline company. His passport had many Russian visas stamped on its pages, showing Max was no stranger to Moscow. Max didn't need an SDR tipping them off to the fact that he might be some kind of agent. Still, he glanced back several times, not once seeing anyone suspicious. Still, he knew they were there.

From memory, Max made a left turn down an alley. He'd only been here once with his father, but he remembered it like it was yesterday. He splashed through a few puddles and emerged in an industrial neighborhood filled with small factories and distribution warehouses. The area was more rundown than he remembered. Faded graffiti marked the sides of buildings and parked delivery vehicles. It was a Sunday, and the streets were silent.

He turned down another alley between two squat brick buildings, stopped, and leaned against the wall. He removed a pack of Belomorkanols and used a match to light one, putting a foot up on the wall while he smoked. He saw no one.

About twenty meters down the alleyway, Max could see a double metal doorway with an unobtrusive fisheye security camera above it. The door had no markings of any kind. As he smoked, the rain grew stronger, reminding Max of the last time he'd visited Dmitry.

"What is this place?" Max asked, slowing his pace. The low clouds had threatened all day, and Max could feel the cold moisture seep through his great coat. Up ahead, his father had stopped in front of an unmarked metal door.

"You'll see. Hurry now. This isn't the type of man you want to keep waiting," his father said.

"Is this place safe?" Max asked, catching up with his father. He noted they hadn't performed their standard surveillance detection route.

Andrei Asimov snorted. "Dmitry controls this entire neighborhood and owns most of the buildings in it. Nothing moves here without him knowing. He's a friend, as much as anyone in this godforsaken city can be a friend," his father said, pausing with his hand about to knock. "I need you to remember a few things."

"Anything," Max replied, his curiosity piqued.

"Do not speak unless spoken to," his father said in a hushed voice. "Avoid eye contact with anyone. And most of all, offer no opinion on anything that could be construed as a State matter. Make no sudden movements. Register no surprise if you recognize anyone famous. Got it?"

Max nodded, his throat suddenly too constricted to speak.

With a last stern glance at him, his father knocked on the door.

Trusting Julia's word that Max could visit Dmitry without fear of being turned over to the FSB, Max strode down the alley and knocked on the door. The rain came down harder, splashing on his leather shoes. Finally, the door opened and Max was ushered inside a small antechamber. Immediately, he felt the air go from damp and cold to a hot, sticky steam that made his clothes cling to his skin. A rotund man stood in front of Max with his arms crossed over his chest. The other man shut the door and moved to stand next to his partner. They each had square faces with flat noses and buzz cuts.

Max spoke a word in Russian, a password, dredged up from a twenty-year-old memory, which caused the two men to look at each other. Then Max removed his coat, took off his mustache and glasses, shoved them in the coat's pocket, and put the coat on a hanger. One of the two men searched him thoroughly.

"That's a very old password, my friend," the other man said in Russian, his arms still crossed. He wore a red shirt one size too small and the buttons strained to cover his immense belly, showing flashes of white flesh. The one who had frisked him moved back and re-crossed his arms.

"Tell him Mikhail Asimov is here to see him," Max said, using his given name.

"Who the fuck is Mikhail Asimov?" the man in the red shirt asked. He seemed to be in charge.

"You can go tell him," Max said, "or I'll go tell him myself while you're on the way to the hospital. Either way, he's going to want to see me."

Red Shirt's eyes narrowed at the threat. He was a foot shorter than Max, but he was built like a bull and his nose looked like it had been broken a few times. He stared at Max for a few beats, then used his head to indicate something to the other man. The other man turned and disappeared through a door.

They waited in silence in the stifling humidity. When the other man returned, he whispered something into Red Shirt's ear.

Red Shirt's brow wrinkled and he turned to Max. "Follow me."

They walked down a gently sloped hallway covered in pale yellow and light green tiles. The walls were slick with moisture and Max could smell a faint musty odor masked by the overpowering scent of eucalyptus and menthol. Red Shirt ushered him into a room with worn wooden benches and a few bent and rusted lockers. A cracked mirror hung over a stained sink. Red Shirt stood and crossed his arms.

"I can find my way from here," Max said.

Red Shirt didn't move.

Max sighed. He took off his clothing and stowed them in a locker. He removed a dingy terrycloth robe from the locker and put it on. Then he followed Red Shirt out of the locker room and through another tunnel.

Bathhouses were a favorite pastime among Russian men, the most obvious reason being the long, cold winters. Another equally important reason, though, was that it was difficult to hide a recording device or a weapon when everyone was naked. For this reason, Russian men liked to conduct their business in the damp confines of a bathhouse.

The hallway finally gave way to a large cavernous room with an arched ceiling covered in a patchwork of chipped frescos. Massive pillars, discolored from years of exposure to moisture, held up the ceiling and disappeared into the murky pool. A set of wide, tiled stairs led from the front of the room into the water. The pool itself spanned the entire room, and Max could see the heads of several men bobbing in the dark water. The rear of the large room was obscured by dim light and billowing steam.

"He's in the back," Red Shirt said, and used his head to indicate Max should walk down the side pathway. Max complied, and the guard followed. The path led to a smaller room and Max noticed the temperature rising a few degrees. Here, the steam rose off the water and filled the room, making it hard to see. Gradually, Max could make out a small head covered in white hair bobbing in the water. This room was where Dmitry Utkin did all his business, and it hadn't changed in the twenty years since Max had been here with his father.

Dmitry Utkin emerged from the haze, taking each step out of the pool slowly. He'd been old when Max had first met him, and now Max guessed he was easily in his nineties. Despite his age, Dmitry looked spry and as fit as a man thirty years his junior. He gathered up his long white hair and tied it into a knot behind his head. The man's darkly tanned skin completed the impression of an ancient swami.

"Well, I'll be damned," Dmitry said, speaking in a slow, measured cadence. He peered at Max as if the younger man were his long lost son. Dmitry's voice was soft and melodic. "That'll be all, Roman." To Max, Dmitry gestured at the pool and said, "Please. Join me." With that, the old man slid back into the water.

Max tossed his robe onto a small table and slipped into the pool. The hot water stung his wounds, but the heat crept into his bones, and complete relaxation overtook him. He floated toward the back of the pool where he found Dmitry sitting on a submerged stone bench. Max sat next to him. From his vantage point, the steam hid the other side of the pool. Max looked around, unsure whether they were safe.

"We are alone," Dmitry assured him. "Those look like some wicked wounds. They look relatively fresh. Life on the run must be difficult. So what brings the famous son of Andrei Asimov to my humble bath? Or should I say the infamous son of Andrei. May he rest in peace."

Max hadn't known what to expect. He'd only met Dmitry that once, twenty years ago, and that meeting had

been brief. He decided to play it straight; he had nothing
to lose.

"I need your help," Max started. "I'm looking for something, and I think you might be able to help me get it."

Dmitry was quiet a moment, nodding as if he'd
expected the statement. "You've made a dangerous gamble
coming here," he finally said. "You've put me in a tough
spot, Mikhail. The most wanted man in all of Russia.
Loathed by the FSB. Hunted by a private contractor. Shows
up in my bathhouse. Then asks for a favor."

Max was too surprised to remain impassive, and
wondered if he'd miscalculated.

"Yes, Mikhail. I'm aware of your troubles. Did you
know there is a hefty price on your head?"

Max recovered his composure. Of course the great
Dmitry Utkin would know that he was being hunted.
"Do you—?"

"No. I do not know who is trying to kill you, or who
killed your parents," Dmitry said.

Max didn't know whether to believe him. The old man's
face was passive, serene, as if he'd made peace with his
maker. In his time, Dmitry had held positions of power
within the military and the KGB under Khrushchev, Brezh-
nev, and Andropov. In a government that was run in the
back rooms and bathhouses of Moscow, Dmitry was one of
the Kremlin power brokers. Max thought it likely the old
man was lying.

"I'm running out of options," Max said. "I'll ask my
question and be on my way. If you see fit to help me, I'd be
ever indebted to you. If you don't, I'll never—"

Dmitry put his hand up. Water dripped from thin,
straight fingers. A thick gold chain hung from his wrist.
"Please," Dmitry said. "Do I look like a man who cares

about acquiring debts? By the time you get around to paying, I'll be dust in the earth."

Max was about to reply when the steamy haze was disturbed by a large woman wearing a kimono-style robe. Her face looked like it had been carved from a large piece of gelatin. Dmitry slid off the bench and floated toward the opposite bank. He stood and accepted a towel from the woman. Turning back to Max, he said, "Do you want to know the secret to eternal youth?"

Max stayed silent.

"A daily deep-tissue massage."

Max's heart sank. His bid to see Dmitry had been a last-ditch attempt at digging up information.

"Come," Dmitry said. "I'm sure we can find another table and another masseuse somewhere, eh, Greta? Let us partake in this daily ritual together. Then we can find some tea and talk some more. I'm sure you have many questions. Let us see if there are any answers to be had."

TWENTY-EIGHT

Moscow, Russia

The massage was superb. Greta summoned another woman twice her size dressed in an identical kimono, who proceeded to drill into his muscles with all her weight for over an hour. When they were done, Max's body was jelly and he was practically comatose. The two men dressed in robes and found their way to a tiny table where a tea service had been laid out.

"You're not worried about the FSB finding me here?" Max asked, after tea had been poured and they'd taken their first sips.

Dmitry chuckled. "They already know you're here."

Max paused with the tea cup halfway to his mouth, alarmed. "How—?"

"Relax, my friend. No harm will come to you in this place."

Max couldn't tell if he was telling the truth. Not for the first time, he questioned the wisdom of coming here.

"Maybe earlier you didn't ask me the right question," Dmitry said. "Maybe *who* isn't the right question."

"Ok," Max said. He thought for a moment. "Do you know *why* my father was killed?"

"Right. Now we're getting somewhere," Dmitry said. "I don't know the exact reason. But I can speculate."

Max sipped his tea and looked at Dmitry. "Are you going to give me the party line that he was killed by Chechen terrorists?"

Dmitry chuckled. "Standard propaganda. Right out of the manual. No, I believe the cause was much more compli-cated than that." The old man re-crossed his legs and poured more tea from the clay pot on the table. "To specu-late, you have to understand a little bit of Soviet history. Do you know why the Soviet Union dissolved back in 1991?"

To Max, this was an elemental question. The history had been much publicized. "When Gorbachev came to power in '85, the country was in bad shape," Max said. "Gor-bachev thought he could rescue the economy by reforming it – what he called *perestroika*. But rather than moving to a market economy, he tried to make socialism work better."

"The great Socialist failure," Dmitry said, nodding his head.

"Gorbachev also instituted a policy of openness, or freedom of speech called *glasnost*. When the reforms didn't work and it became clear that communism was a failed experiment and the economy was in severe stagnation, the non-Russian states such as the Baltics and Azerbaijan started Nationalist movements. The momentum moved to Georgia, Ukraine, and the others. Eventually, Gorbachev gave in to the pressure."

Dmitry's head was shaking. "You have the public

version mostly correct. People, especially in our country, conveniently forget one crucial event that occurred on August 19, 1991, just as the Soviet Union was crumbling. Our history books have erased this event from history. But the truth cannot be denied. Where were you in 1991?"

"On assignment in Germany," Max said.

Dmitry rose from the table and led Max back to the pool, where the old man resumed his history lesson.

"A small group of hard-line party members kidnapped Gorbachev and attempted a coup. They announced to the nation that Gorbachev was too ill to continue to govern, then called in the military. Massive demonstrations erupted. The military refused to fire on their fellow countrymen. Two days later, the coup ended and Gorbachev was reinstated. The Communist party was disbanded by Gorbachev a few days after the coup. Then it was only a matter of time before the Soviet Union was dissolved." Dmitry paused for effect. "What do you think happened to all those hard-line communists?"

"Jailed?" Max said.

"Some were. The leaders of the failed coup like Kryuchkov, Yazov, and Tizyakov. But many others simply vanished into the woodwork. Some converted their beliefs, found a place in Gorbachev's new government, and led normal lives. Some went into business for themselves and are now some of the wealthiest men in Russia. Some simply hid their beliefs, biding their time until the Party and the Soviet Union could be resurrected."

Suddenly Max thought he knew where Dmitry was going. "And my father?" Max asked. "What side of the fence did he fall on?" Just as when Max had opened a box belonging to his father in the basement of a butcher shop weeks ago, he got the feeling he was prying into an area of his father's life he'd rather leave buried.

Dmitry slid off the bench and floated off into the darkness and the steam. Eventually he returned, his white hair streaming out behind him like a fan on the still water. "Your father was a good man," Dmitry said. "He bled red, and if he'd wanted, he could have made quite a career for himself in the Russian KGB instead of the relative backwater of Minsk. But no one knew what side he was on, and he stayed in Belarus. When the coup happened, then quickly fizzled, your father was on the sidelines. At least publicly. He did a very good job of hiding his true feelings."

"Which were?" Max asked, growing tired of Dmitry's elusiveness.

"What makes you think I know?"

"I find it hard to believe there is much that happens in Russia that you don't know about," Max said.

Dmitry chuckled. "I in fact do not know," Dmitry said. "But I suspect, as have many others. And therein lies your father's problem. Or I should say *your* problem now."

Max's patience was growing thin, but he kept his annoyance in check, and willed himself to be patient. "And your suspicions?"

"To answer that, we have to agree on some more history. Would you like to join me for a light meal? A man of my age doesn't require much sustenance, but I still appreciate a fine meal."

"Of course," Max said. He'd agree to just about anything to keep Dmitry talking. The old man led Max out of the pool and down a hall to a small dining room. Max was guided to a comfortable but threadbare cushion on the floor next to a low table. Dmitry sprawled on several cushions at the head of the table. A young boy brought chilled vodka and pickled mushrooms.

When the boy had left, Dmitry said, "My grandson. I learned long ago to keep things in the family. Safer that way." Then he held up a glass of the cold liquid and said, "It's only when we're drunk that we Russians really trust anyone." He downed the liquid and refilled his own glass.

Recognizing the maxim, and deciding not to remind Dmitry that he was Belarusian, Max tipped back his glass and sucked the alcohol down.

"It's been twenty-some years since the fall of the Soviet Union," Dmitry said. "You know who runs our country now?"

Not understanding where Dmitry was going, Max gave the President's name.

Dmitry laughed. This time it was hearty, from his gut.

"You don't believe that, do you?"

"No," Max said.

"So who runs the country?"

"The FSB," Max said.

"That's a better answer. And if you'd said that five years ago, you'd have been right. You've been away for a while, no?"

Max nodded. "Paris. I was stationed there."

"Right," Dmitry said, nodding his head. "I remember. You were sent to Paris as a sleeper agent." He poured another round of the vodka.

"The FSB forgot about me," Max said. "I was operational until about five years ago." Suddenly Max made a connection, and his eyebrows raised. "So what happened five years ago?"

They were interrupted by the serving boy, who laid steaming platters of steak and vegetables on the table.

Dmitry waited until the boy had taken his leave, then lowered his voice to a conspiratorial whisper. "The correct answer to my question is that Russia is actually run by a secret group of twelve men who call themselves the Consortium."

Max's eyebrows went up. He wondered if the old man had gone senile.

Dmitry seemed to read the disbelief on his face. "Western media says Russia is run by the mafia. Some outsiders believe the country is run by the President as a puppet for the FSB. Most civilians believe the finely honed propaganda that the President is actually in charge. He's a well-loved man in this country. His approval ratings are the highest seen by any previous Soviet or Russian leader."

"False data," Max said.

"Maybe, but that's not the point," Dmitry said. "The President is a puppet. But he's the Consortium's puppet, not the FSB's."

Max digested that, then asked. "So what happened five years ago?"

"No one really knows," Dmitry said. "Or I should say that someone knows, but no one is saying. During the coup of 1991, Kryuchkov, who was the head of the KGB, disappeared and made off with fifty billion rubles that belonged to the Communist party. Whether he knew the party would be disbanded isn't known, but he funneled that money somewhere. The belief is that money was used by the Consortium to start buying up previously state-run assets, especially petroleum and natural gas production and refinery facilities. Remember, this was back in 1991 or 1992. Fast forward eighteen years. The FSB had been running things, but the Consortium had been growing more powerful, silently, behind the scenes."

"What about the mafia?" Max asked.

"The so-called Russian mafia is a side business tolerated by the Consortium," Dmitry said.

"So who are the members of this Consortium?"

"Don't get ahead of yourself," Dmitry said. He helped himself to a small piece of meat and a few pickled tomatoes. "Five years ago, there was a coup of sorts. Except this one was internal to the FSB. One night, the seven men who ran the FSB disappeared. Vanished."

"Vanished?"

"Yes. No trace of them has been found since."

"Even for Russia, that's surprising. To have seven high-profile men disappear all at once."

"I agree," Dmitry said. "The seven top posts were then reappointed in a secret session by the President. All the new posts were promoted from within the FSB."

"The new leaders of the FSB are puppets of the Consortium," Max said.

"Correct. Turns out that for years, the FSB was waging a war against the Consortium. The coup within the FSB five years ago was the culmination of the Consortium's plan. By taking control of the FSB, they had effective control of the country. They already controlled the presidency and the military."

"So who is in this Consortium?" Max said. "And what does it have to do with my father?"

"The membership is a mystery," Dmitry said. "Even I do not know. But I can speculate. Do you know how many billionaires there are in post-Soviet Russia?"

Max didn't. He shook his head.

"Eighty-five at last count," Dmitry said. "So you start with that list. From there, the next list you create is the men who control Russia's main industries. But those are only the known billionaires and industry heads. It's very possible there are former hard-liners in the Communist party, and perhaps a few former KGB heads, who are also in the Consortium. It's just impossible to know exactly who. They are very secretive."

Max nodded. "How do you know the Consortium is run by twelve men?"

"A guess. A rumor. I suspect the organization is much larger, with its tentacles in every major bit of Russian society. And probably extends to other countries as well."

"The whole thing sounds like a myth," Max said.

"Indeed," Dmitry replied.

Max let that sink in for a few moments. "So what about my father?" Max asked.

Just then, the doors to the dining room burst open and six men wearing dark suits rushed in. Max, lulled from the massage, the hot water, and the vodka, was slow to react. Before he could struggle to his feet, two pistols were shoved in his face. Max was jerked to his feet and his wrists secured. Max looked at Dmitry, then realized the old man had a gun pointed at his head. Dmitry had a pained look on his face.

With that, Max was yanked sideways, then pushed roughly down the hall. A minute later, he was rushed through the front hallway and into the entry room. As he was pushed through the front door, he saw Red Shirt grinning at him. Max was bundled into a waiting van. The vehicle's door slammed and he found himself flanked by two large Russians in dark suits. The van lurched and picked up speed. His worst fear had just come true. Max assumed they were heading to Lubyanka, the headquarters of the FSB.

TWENTY-NINE

Moscow, Russia

If his situation weren't so dire, Max might have found humor in the fact that he was ushered into Lubyanka, the infamous home of the feared and loathed FSB, wearing only a bathrobe. The ride from Dmitry's bathhouse to the hulking building was just over thirty minutes. In that time, no one spoke, and the van drove at breakneck speed, following a sedan through the quiet and rainy streets of Moscow. Max sat with his arms bent at an awkward angle, preventing him from sitting comfortably. Provoking his captors would be counterproductive, so he kept his mouth shut.

Wheels squealing, the vehicle turned into an underground garage where Max was hustled from the van and hurried through an underground passage, into a dank hallway and through a door to a row of holding cells. All the cells were empty. A man resembling a gorilla in a dark suit yanked open a barred door and Max was shoved into one of the cells. The door clanged shut, and a heavy metallic click sounded, locking Max in.

He tried to shake off the shock that came from his sudden incarceration. He stood in the center of his tiny cell for a moment, trying to gain his bearings. Three walls of the cell were solid concrete, while bars formed the fourth wall. The concrete was stained and chipped. The tile floor sloped to a small drain. A bucket stood in a corner, the room's sole item of furniture. A bare bulb hung from a socket high overhead. Even if he jumped, he couldn't reach the bulb, much less the ceiling.

Max reminded himself that he'd been in worse situations. Occupying his mind with busy work would help prevent the fear from setting in. He walked over and examined the door. The thick metal portal fit flush against the wall. No handle was evident. A small double-paned Plexiglas window was set in the center at eye height. Thick bars ran between the two panes of Plexiglas. Max looked out and saw nothing but a blank wall across from the door.

He turned back to the room and examined the drain, finding it screwed tightly in place. He knelt down and used a toe to test each floor tile, finding them all firmly in place, the grout intact. He rose and paced each wall, looking for anything out of place. The concrete was pockmarked and stained, but he could find no weakness or blemish that might give him an advantage. It looked like he was securely held in one of Lubyanka's infamous cells.

He sank down into a corner, forced himself to relax, and tried to think about his predicament. The most likely scenario was that Dmitry had given him up for the reward. Maybe Dmitry had told Red Shirt to wait a couple hours, then call the FSB. The thought made Max angry. It looked like Julia had been wrong. Or had she deliberately set him up? Max thought that unlikely. If Julia had wanted to turn him in, all she'd had to do was have the FSB waiting for him at Cafe Lucca.

He heard the sound of multiple leather soles on a gritty floor. A minute later, the door swung open and two uniformed guards burst in. They hauled Max up by his arms and frisked him, then ensured his plastic cuffs were still secure. Then they stood on either side of him as a third man entered the cell.

This man wore the uniform of a Russian officer, complete with full regalia on the breast and two stars on the shoulder. The officer towered over the other two men. A third guard stood in the hallway. Max was surprised to see someone with such a high rank standing in the middle of his cell.

"Mikhail Asimov, the famous traitor," the officer declared. His voice boomed in the tiny room.

Max shuffled his feet and tried to make his arms more comfortable. "You'll need to make an appointment," Max said. "I think my calendar is full for the next week."

"A comedian as well as a traitor," the officer said, his face impassive.

"How much did Dmitry make by turning me in?" Max said.

The solider laughed. "Poor old Dmitry. What makes you think he turned you in?" To the guards, he said, "Take him up to interrogation three, then soften him up a little. I'm not in the mood for any trouble." The officer turned on his heel and disappeared.

THIRTY

Moscow, Russia

The beating, when it came, was long, slow, and painful, just as he'd known it would be. The guards took their time working him over, first using a lead pipe on his torso, then using their fists on his face. When they were finally done, he could only see from one eye; the other was swollen shut. In true Russian fashion, they'd worked methodically, without emotion, and issued precise blows designed to elicit maximum pain without doing permanent damage. He knew they wanted him soft and compliant, not maimed. There would be plenty of time for maiming later.

By the time the officer arrived, Max was sitting limp on a wooden chair, naked, arms still tied behind him, drool dripping from his bloody mouth. The world around him was hazy, and the row of fluorescent lights above him were painful to look at. His head throbbed like it was in a vice.

"That's better," the officer said, standing in front of Max, his arms crossed.

Max spit blood onto the floor, but said nothing. Two guards stood behind him.

"Get him cleaned up and clothed," the officer ordered the guards. "And find him some coffee and cigarettes." He turned with a crisp movement and strode from the room.

Max was surprised when a painfully thin woman in a starched white uniform entered the room pushing a cart with medical supplies. She wiped his face with gauze, applied ointment, stitched up a gash in his cheek, and applied several bandages. One of the guards cut the bindings on his wrists. Max fell from the chair, finding it difficult to move his bruised body. Rough cotton clothes were tossed at him.

"Get dressed," one of the men ordered. A table was dragged over and a cup of coffee set down hard enough to make it slosh on the table. One of the guards tossed a pack of cigarettes onto the table next to a book of matches. Max took his time pulling on the clothes. Then he managed to get into the chair. With a quivering hand, he tried to light one of the smokes, and failed. Looking at the guard, he raised his eyebrows. With a grimace, the guard lit a match and held it to the end of Max's cigarette. Max breathed in deep, relishing the calming effect of the nicotine. He took a sip of the coffee, found it cold, and set it aside.

"Got any hot coffee?" he managed. The two guards ignored him.

Finally, the door swung open and the officer walked in. Max knew the two stars on his shoulder meant he was a lieutenant general, but he didn't recognize the man.

"Leave us," the officer ordered, and the men spun and disappeared. The officer closed the door and stood in front of it, several feet away from Max.

"This coffee is cold. Can I get a warm up?" Max asked. It hurt even to speak.

The officer regarded Max for a moment, then turned, opened the door, and barked an order. He stood in silence, watching Max with an amused look until a guard rushed in with two Styrofoam cups. Max could see steam rising from the top of each. This hospitality was not standard procedure for the FSB.

"I am Lieutenant General Spartak Rugov, Military Counterintelligence Directorate chief," the man said.

Max raised his coffee cup and said, "Nostrovia." Despite the pain in his head, his brain was spinning. Directorate Chief was a big deal. Those men were used to stalking the top floor of Lubyanka, doing backroom deals, and eating at the finest restaurants in Moscow. It was almost unheard of for such a man to be in the bowels of the FSB headquarters, consorting with prisoners.

And why was Military Counterintelligence even involved with Max's case? Normally the Control Service, the group that contained the Internal Security Directorate, would handle defections. He looked around the room and noticed no security cameras. There were no mirrors that might hide one-way windows. He sensed he was alone in this room with the officer.

Rugov strolled along the back wall of the interrogation room and sipped his coffee while he talked. He was keeping his distance. "I met your father once," Rugov said. "He was a great man. A man we all admired. What happened to bring your family to such disgrace?"

"I was hoping you could tell me that," Max said.

"Indeed. No one seems to know who killed your father," Rugov said. Max noticed Rugov's spit-shined shoes glinted in the fluorescent light.

"You mean who killed both my parents and my brother-in-law," Max said.

"Whatever," Rugov said.

"We may as well get this over with," Max said. "I don't know where my sister and nephew are. We purposefully hid them in a location I don't know of. So you might as well just kill me, or haul me off to the gulag. No interrogation technique can force me to tell you something I don't know."

Rugov looked at Max and sipped his coffee. He looked like the kind of man who never laughed. "That is not my concern," Rugov said.

Max kept his face passive, but he was confused. He'd assumed Dmitry had given Max up for the reward money offered by Max's pursuers. "Then why am I here?"

Rugov took another sip. Then he looked at Max and said, "I want the memory card."

Max stayed silent, working through the different scenarios in his head. Rugov wanted the memory card that had been stolen from the safe house. But if the FSB didn't have it, what had Dedov done with the card? And who had killed Dedov?

THIRTY-ONE

Moscow, Russia

"You don't know where it is?" Max asked, his coffee forgotten for the moment.

"I'm embarrassed to admit," Rugov said, "we don't."

"You didn't get it from Dedov before you killed him?" Max asked, taking a shot in the dark.

Rugov's stony face remained impassive. "What makes you think we killed him?"

"Who else would have?"

"The report I saw says he took his own life," Rugov said.

"Does Victor Dedov seem like the kind of man who would kill himself?"

Rugov shrugged. "Who knows what goes on in a man's life, behind closed doors."

Max decided to take a different tack. "Why is the FSB looking for the card?"

Rugov glanced away, but then looked back quickly.

Suddenly, Max knew the answer. "The FSB isn't looking for the memory card. You are."

Rugov didn't answer him, and instead said, "I need to know everything you know about where that card is. We can do it the hard way, or we can do it the easy way. Up to you."

Max put his cigarette out on the scarred wooden table. By now, the coffee and nicotine had settled the shaking in his hand and he was able to get another cigarette lit. He inhaled, then blew a plume of smoke at the ceiling. "How about we make a deal?" Max said.

Rugov didn't bat an eye. "You are not in a position to bargain."

"Obviously," Max said. "But let's approach this as civilized men instead of Neanderthals. You're probably going to kill me anyway. You won't leave me alive knowing that the Chief of Military Counterintelligence is running his own little operation outside the FSB's jurisdiction. Can we get some more coffee?"

Rugov seemed to consider the request. Then he stuck his head out the door and shouted a command. A moment later, two more Styrofoam cups appeared. Rugov shut the door behind the soldier. "Ok, talk."

Max bought himself a moment by taking a sip of the drink. "You call this coffee? This is shit. Ever been to France? Best damn coffee on the planet."

Rugov stared at him, silent.

Max thought quickly, going through the scenarios in his mind. His father, a former KGB Assistant Director in Belarus, had somehow caught wind of a group called the Consortium. Max guessed that his father had been investigating them when he found the memory card. Maybe it was the discovery of the card that had put their lives in jeopardy.

Or maybe Max's father had uncovered some encrypted communications containing information the Consortium had not wanted released. Now, there were multiple groups chasing after the memory card, all in an attempt to gain access to some mysterious information about the Consortium. That data must indeed be crucial information. Max wondered what side Rugov was on, guessing he was probably on his own side. Just like Dedov. He decided to start with the truth.

"I found it after our house had been bombed and my parents killed," Max said. "It was hidden in a photo frame in our barn, I assume by my father."

Rugov waved his hand impatiently. "I know all that. I know Dedov had it stolen from you. The question is, what did Dedov do with it?"

Max shrugged. "No idea. He wouldn't tell me. If I'd known what he did with it, I would have been chasing that lead instead of wasting my time with Dmitry."

Rugov nodded slowly, then took a sip from the Styrofoam cup. "You're right about this coffee," he said.

"I assume you traced Dedov's movements in the last week?" Max asked.

Rugov nodded yet again. "We did, and we're still chasing down others. Our best guess at this point is that he hid it somewhere, and was attempting to sell it to the highest bidder."

"You mean to the Consortium," Max said. He threw that word out on purpose, to gauge Rugov's reaction. Max caught the smallest, almost imperceptible tick in the corner of Rugov's mouth. It was enough to validate Dedov's claim that he had another buyer, likely the Consortium. Max had also just confirmed the existence of that organization. "Is that your plan, too? Find the list, sell it back, then retire somewhere the FSB can't find you?"

"Tell me about your meeting with Dedov," Rugov said, ignoring Max's question.

"We shared some bruschetta and he had fresh seafood farfalle and mozzarella stuffed with ham and vegetables. We reminisced about—"

"Enough," Rugov said. "I thought you wanted to do this the easy way."

Max figured he had nothing to lose. "He offered to sell me the card if I could outbid his other buyer."

Rugov's left eyebrow went up a fraction. "So he had the card?"

Max shrugged. "I assumed so. But I never confirmed it."

"And did you come to terms?"

"We did," Max said. "Although I have no way of knowing whether he intended to carry out his side of the bargain."

"What was the next step?"

"We were to meet back up in forty-eight hours. I was to bring the money, he was to bring the card."

"How much?"

"How much what?"

"How much did you agree to pay?"

"Ten million," Max said. He didn't see the point in holding anything back. Dedov was dead and the memory card had disappeared.

Rugov chuckled. "Ten million," Rugov said. "Dedov was playing you."

"How do you mean?"

"The memory card is worth much more than ten million dollars." Rugov looked as if he'd confirmed one of his suspicions. "You have no idea what is on that card, do you?"

Max stared at him. He was starting to get an idea, but he wasn't going to venture a guess. Rugov would just deny it.

Just then, there was a loud banging on the door followed by a muted voice talking rapidly in Russian. The voice was too faint for Max to hear.

For the first time, Rugov smiled. "Looks like our time is up. I wish you the best of luck, Mikhail. You're going to need it." Rugov opened the door and exited, slamming the door shut behind him. The deadbolt chunked into place.

Max lit another cigarette and stood up, stretching the sore muscles in his abdomen and back. He bent and touched his toes, grimacing in pain, then did some side bends. He wondered what his face looked like, then decided he'd rather not know. He stayed standing, leaning against the back wall of the room, going over everything he'd learned in the past few days. Some things were finally making sense. If this so-called Consortium really existed, and somehow his father had made an enemy of them, then Max's pursuers were indeed some of the most powerful men in Russia. But how did the memory card fit in? And was Rugov working for or against the Consortium?

He'd smoked two more cigarettes and drained the cup of coffee by the time the door banged open. Instead of the tall, pale, uniformed figure of Rugov, he was surprised to see a small, dark-haired woman with Asian features stride in like she had just bought the place. Neatly attired in a grey, tailored pant suit, she looked like she was about to wage a court battle with Alan Dershowitz. She was flanked by two Caucasian men in paramilitary clothing, both of whom had sidearms. She planted herself in front of Max, crossed her arms, and stuck out a hip.

"Hello, Mikhail."

Max had never seen the woman before. Her brow was furrowed and she stared at Max with eyes that could melt lead. Still, he couldn't help but be intrigued.

"Who the fuck are you?" Max asked.

"My name is Wing Octavia," she said. "You killed Nathan Abrams, and now I'm going to kill you."

THIRTY-TWO

Moscow, Russia

The small olive-skinned woman pulled a compact pistol from the shoulder harness under her jacket and pointed it at Max's head. He wondered how he had just gone from having a civilized conversation with Rugov to having a gun stuck in his face by an Asian woman in a suit.

"My life gets a lot easier if you are dead, so don't friggin' move," the woman said. She issued a command and the two paramilitary types moved around her, yanked Max up from the table, and slapped a pair of handcuffs on him. His world went dark as a black hood was shoved over his head. He stumbled forward when he was pushed hard in the back, then was half dragged, half pushed out of the room, down the hallway, and outside. He could feel rain patter on the hood before he was guided into the back seat of a vehicle. A moment later, the car was moving.

"How much did you pay Rugov for me?" Max asked.

"Too effing much," he heard the woman say. "Now keep quiet or we'll tape up your mouth."

"Why don't you just kill me here and now?" Max asked. "I have no idea where my sister and her son are, so you won't be able to torture it out of me."

Max felt a sudden, sharp blow to the side of his head. Stars shot through his vision, a brief blinding light in the dark mask, then he passed out.

———

Max awoke gradually. The first sensation he felt was pain in his head, especially on the side of his temple. Then he felt an ache over his entire body. He moved an arm, grimaced, then remembered the beating he'd sustained at the hands of the FSB guards. Max tried to force his eyes open and was reminded that one eye was forced shut by swelling. He opened his one good eye, and saw only darkness. A brief confusion took over, then he remembered the hood. Through the hood he could smell jet fuel and that oxygenized odor consistent with airplanes. He gave himself a moment to let his head clear, and realized he was sitting up in a comfortable chair. His arms had been re-secured in front of him. His mouth was dry to the point where he couldn't feel his tongue.

He strained to listen, hoping to hear something that might give him an edge. A murmur of voices came through the hood, but he couldn't make out the words or even the dialect. He decided to play possum. He regulated his breathing and listened. The voices came and went, obscured by a steady drone he assumed was from an airplane's engines.

To his right, he heard muted footsteps, something that

would have been imperceptible had his hearing not been sharpened by the darkness. Then he felt a sharp prick in his left shoulder and a warm sensation crawled over his body. The voices and the drone of the airplane faded away, and he fell into a deep slumber.

———

The next time he awoke, the first sensation he felt was cold. Not that sharp cold one felt when visiting Mount Elbrus in the winter, as he'd been forced to do during so many KGB training excursions. But a damp cold, like when the northeasterly winds visited Minsk in the middle of January, bringing moisture and causing the temperature to plummet. It was the kind of cold that sank into your bones and gave you a chill no matter how many layers you bundled in. Max was used to that kind of cold, and he forced it from his mind.

His head still hurt, but now it was a dull pounding, like he'd had too much vodka the previous evening. His mouth was bone dry and he had trouble moving his tongue. Gently, he flexed his arm muscles, felt they were sore, and realized his arms were unsecured. Off in the distance, he could hear the steady *plink, plink, plink* of water dripping. Moisture covered his skin and he guessed he was underground somewhere. Finally, he opened his good eye, then shut it again as a bright light pierced his skull like a pointed stick.

Gradually, he re-opened his eye, then shut it again, then cracked it a fraction of a millimeter, trying to get used to the light. The pain was so unbearable that, combined with the dry mouth, he guessed he'd been sedated. Gradually, he willed the eye to remain open and found himself staring at a single light bulb. He turned his head so he was looking into the shadows. The ceiling was made of hewn rock, held up by a stone wall and three walls of metal bars. The bars were tightly spaced, but would allow him to fit an arm through.

He was lying on a thin mattress positioned on a cot. He shifted his weight and felt the cot move underneath him. He sat up, fought off a wave of dizziness and nausea, and swung his legs down to the floor. He was still wearing the threadbare canvas shirt and dungarees given to him by Rugov's team. He could feel the cold radiating up through the stone floor and into his bare feet.

Through the hazy light coming from a string of bulbs hanging outside the tiny cell, he saw a small person sitting in a chair. He squinted, and saw it was the Asian woman. She had changed from the suit and was wearing a pair of jeans and a white collared blouse. On her lap was a compact pistol fitted with a silencer.

"Water," Max croaked. He gestured to his mouth.

She pointed at the floor next to his feet with the pistol. Max saw a large plastic bottle next to his cot. He took it and drank slowly, letting the liquid wet every crevice of his mouth. He set the bottle down with half the water remaining. As he did, he noticed a pool of dried rust-colored liquid on the stone floor. He looked closer, and noticed a spatter pattern of the same color continuing up the wall and onto the cot. While it didn't look fresh, it looked recent.

"Blood," the woman said. Her voice was an odd combination of melodic syllables and hard edges, like a cockney who had trained to be a singer. He guessed she was hiding a rough upbringing.

Max pulled up his feet and sat Indian-style on the cot. He forced his face to remain blank, despite feeling unsettled. This was clearly the woman who had been hired after Abrams to kill him on behalf of the Consortium.

"I'm not dead yet," he said. "So obviously you want something."

The woman stood up, and Max admired her from a distance. Her jet-black hair was cropped short and parted at the side, giving her a masculine look that wasn't softened by the abrupt lines of her jaw. Her jeans and blouse were fashionable. The boots were a riding style that went up to her knees and were made from black leather. She was a handsome woman, modern and steely eyed. He looked closely at her face and saw stress. Her eyes were dark and bloodshot, but she hid it with a stony expression devoid of emotion. She paced in front of the cell, throwing daggers at him with her eyes. Max could see no other people around, and no security cameras. When she spoke, it was a low hiss, laced with venom.

"Did you enjoy killing him, you son of a bitch?"

"Who?" Max asked.

"Who?" she spat. She continued pacing, and he could see her knuckles were white, clenched around the gun's handle. She was a powder keg about to go off. He decided to tread lightly.

"No, I didn't," he said. "But you have to understand. He killed my parents." When she didn't respond, he went on. "It easily could have gone the other way – he was this close to killing me." Max held up two fingers about a centimeter apart. "To the last, he did everything he could to protect you and his organization from being compromised."

To his surprise, he saw some of the tension disappear from her body. She turned and looked at him. "It's just business," she said, but it seemed to Max like she didn't mean it. Some of the fire had disappeared from her voice.

"One man's business is another's life," Max said. "You must have taken over where Abrams left off. Which is why we weren't able to recover much intel on Abrams' company. It was impressive the way you rolled up his operations so quickly."

If the compliment meant anything, it didn't show. She continued pacing.

After a few minutes, Max said something he thought might elicit a reaction. "I don't have the memory card, if that's what you're looking for."

She stopped and turned, her face blank. "What memory card?"

Either she was a remarkably good actress, or she didn't know about it.

"Is that what Rugov was interrogating you about?" she asked.

Max leaned back against the cold stone and remained silent. It was her move.

To his surprise, Wing lifted the gun, holding the compact pistol with two hands. The gun was steady, and Max saw determination on her face. She came toward the bars and pointed the gun at his kneecap. He fought the urge to move.

"I said, what memory card?"

Max didn't move, didn't speak. Would she really shoot him? Her eyes were darting back and forth, and some of the fire had returned. Her hand tightened on the pistol grip again. Still, she hadn't killed him yet. She obviously wanted something from him. He decided to hold out, and kept his mouth shut.

THIRTY-THREE

Undisclosed location outside Budapest

Wing kept the gun steady, fighting to stay in control. Her world was see-sawing between elation at having caught the man who was the source of her problems and the emotional reaction she'd had to the memory of Abrams. With Asimov in her clutches, she could buy herself enough time with her client to find the woman and child. While Asimov may not know where they were, he would certainly make good bait. Then when all three were buried, she'd agree to work for her client and bide her time until she had an opportunity to put a bullet in his skull. Then she could start her business over again.

Now her prisoner was playing games with her, trying to get into her head. She had no idea what he was talking about, but whatever it was might give her leverage with her client.

The prisoner seemed impassive, almost defiant, and that really irked her. She knew a bullet to the knee would go a long way toward relieving her pent-up frustration for Abrams' death. Could she get away with shooting him and still keep him alive as bait? Her finger applied tension to the trigger.

"What memory card, goddamn it?" she said through clenched teeth.

Her prisoner just stared at her, like a bruised and battered monk in lotus meditation. It galled her. How could he sit there in peace when she was in such turmoil? Why not shoot him in the head and be done with it? So many of her problems would disappear.

"Tell. Me. What. Memory. Card," she demanded. "Or I swear, I will shoot you in the knee. Do you know how painful that is?"

"I don't," he said. "I've been shot three times, but never in the knee."

His voice was calm, almost melodic, and it made her more frustrated. He wasn't reacting the way he was supposed to. Wing knew she wasn't much for inflicting the slow pain common with effective interrogation techniques. She'd tried it and found it distasteful. She relied on the single gunshot to an extremity, finding that the sudden and abrupt shock, pain, and terror of a destroyed joint generally got her the information she sought. It had worked before.

Her mind turned to her former mentor, the man who had been her surrogate father. The man who had rescued her from a hard life in the Indonesian slums. She summoned a picture of Abrams' face. The one man in the world who hadn't tried to take advantage of her, the one man she trusted. The one man she had loved. In front of her was the man who had killed him.

She pulled the trigger.

Max knew she was going to pull the trigger a split second before she actually did. He could see it in her eyes. They were the eyes of an angry woman. A woman who was acting from a deep place of emotion known only to her. Whatever pained her ran deep, and he was surprised to feel a moment of pity and concern for her.

He forced himself not to flinch. The gas expelled from the end of the silencer with a loud hiss, like a balloon suddenly deflating. The bullet clanged off the wall just to his right, sending rock chips flying, and ricocheted off into the darkness.

How she'd missed from such a short distance Max would never know. His best guess was that the woman was so distracted by her emotions that she flinched when she pulled the trigger, like a professional golfer shanking a short putt on the eighteenth green at Augusta National. The sound of the bullet clanging off the rock face woke her up. Her face showed instant surprise, either because she'd actually pulled the trigger or because she'd missed. She quickly regained her composure.

"Next time, I won't miss," she growled.

Max decided maybe she was right. "I found a tiny memory card in my father's possessions that I think is part of the reason he was killed. It's encrypted, so I can't read it. It was recently stolen from me. Others seem to be looking for it also, so I thought perhaps that's why you hadn't killed me yet."

Her face tightened for a split second before going passive again.

"What's on it?"

Max hesitated, unsure what he wanted to reveal.

Then he realized he had nothing to lose. "I don't know for sure, but I believe it contains the names and identities of a group of men known as the Consortium. And maybe some private communications between Consortium members."

She scrunched up her nose in a look that Max found oddly alluring.

"The Consortium?" she asked.

The fact that Wing didn't know the identity of her client wasn't surprising, but he wanted to rub it in a little.

"They're your client," he said, smiling.

Her face darkened. "My client is an old man in a wheelchair."

Max's memory went back to his discussion with Abrams, who had also mentioned an old man in a wheelchair. In an effort to build trust with his captor, Max told the woman what he'd learned from Dmitry about the group of twelve men called the Consortium. By the time he was finished, Wing had lowered the weapon. She sat back down in the chair and leaned forward.

"Do you know this man in the wheelchair?" she asked.

Max was surprised by the change in her demeanor. "I do not."

"He must be working for this Consortium," she said. "Or perhaps even be one of the twelve."

Max watched her face closely. As she mentioned the man in the wheelchair, he saw deep emotion in her eyes that he thought was either fear or anger. Or both. Maybe this was his opening.

"Tell me about your employer – this man in the wheelchair," Max said, keeping his voice soft. "Who is he?"

She bent forward and put her elbows on her hands. "I don't know who he is." She gave a brief description of his physical appearance, her encounters with the man, then explained how the man kept his identity a secret.

"You haven't uncovered his true identity?"

Her eyes narrowed. "Every time I try to investigate him, he's always one step ahead of me."

"He must have his tentacles everywhere," Max said. "Why do you work for him?"

She was silent for a few moments, and Max thought he'd pushed too far. Then she stood and turned her back on him, and he knew he was making progress. He decided to play another card.

"Whatever it is," Max said, "maybe I can help you."

She snorted a laugh and turned back to him. "You? Look at you. You're a wreck. You're barely alive, fighting a battle you'll never win. It's only a matter of time before you're planted in the ground. This guy has resources—" She broke off and turned away again.

Max shifted his legs to the floor, stood, and approached the bars. He leaned forward with his arms on one of the cross pieces. "Even if you do kill me, and manage to kill my sister and nephew, what makes you think this guy is going to release you from whatever hold he's got over you?"

She kept her back to him so he was prevented from seeing her face.

"What does he have over you?" Max asked.

She didn't reply.

"If you kill me and my family, he'll just lean on you to do other work for him. Who knows if you'll ever get out from under him," Max said.

He saw her hand clench on the pistol. Finally, she spun around and he saw fire and resolve in her eyes.

"It's not going to work," she said. "You can't talk your way out of this." She waved the pistol at him.

"Then why don't you just shoot me now?" Max asked. "I assume that would lighten the pressure on you considerably."

"In time," she said.

Max felt his opportunity slipping away. Oddly, he felt something for this woman. She had obviously been through a lot in her life, yet here she was, fighting to hold her own against powerful men like her client.

"At least hear me out," Max said. "I know I can help you, and we can get out of this mess together. I think we'd make a good team. What do you have to lose? Give it a chance. Give yourself a chance to earn back your independence. Is it better to be beholden to an overlord, or be your own woman?"

THIRTY-FOUR

Undisclosed location outside Budapest

The woman cocked her head and looked at him skeptically. The gun was still in her hand, pointed casually at the floor, but Max knew at any moment she might start shooting again. This time, she didn't reject him outright, so he pressed on.

"Hear me out. If you don't like the idea, you've lost nothing by listening."

A long moment passed while they stared at each other. Finally, she waved the pistol at him and said, "Let's hear it."

"You and I partner up and take out the man in the wheelchair." As soon as he said it, he knew it sounded crazy. It was a long shot that she might think was a desperate plea.

She laughed. "Forget it. There is no way I could trust you. Is that the best you've got?"

"Why would I kill you? The only reason you want me dead is because your client is holding something over your head."

"That's not the only reason. You killed Nathan. Besides, I never fail a client."

Max paused. This was the crux of her hesitation. It had to be. But if she hated him enough for killing Nathan, she'd have already shot him. "Is that your policy, or was that Abrams'?"

"Doesn't matter. It's important to my business. I can't be seen as turning on my clients."

Max knew he had to tread carefully here. "I respect that," he said. "But answer this. In a few weeks, would you rather have killed me and still be hunting for my sister and nephew, with your client breathing down your neck? Or would you rather be out from under him, free to gain a fresh start with your business? Besides, no future client is going to fault you for sticking up for yourself. In fact, seems to me that's the reputation you want."

She started pacing. The fact that she hadn't shot at him again was a good sign.

"I can help you find this guy," Max said. "Between my resources and your knowledge, we can root this guy out. Then we can kill him. Together."

"What resources?" she snorted. "The CIA?"

Max laughed. "Not the CIA. You've done a good job of infiltrating them and rendering them ineffective."

"Who then?"

"I've got someone who's pretty good at computers. Research, digital forensics, hacking."

"Pretty good?" she scoffed. "The last couple of *pretty good* hackers I hired ended up dead. Are you willing to risk that?"

"This person is more than pretty good. She routinely hacks into governments, including the FBI and—"

"That's nothing," she interrupted. "Even I can do that." She paused.

"This resource is different. That's all I can tell you."

She kept pacing, silent.

"How do you know she will help us?"

Max smiled to himself. She was already starting to use the word *us*. It meant he was getting through. "Let's just say she has my best interest at heart. This is where we start to talk about trust. You're going to have to trust me on this one."

"How do I know I can trust you? How do I know that if I release you, you won't just kill me, or escape, leaving me to deal with the consequences?"

"You know more about this guy than I do. I need your help and that information. He's my link to the Consortium. The only way I'm going to save my family's lives is by going on the offensive. I need your help to do that. Second, I'm a man of my word. I have no ill will toward you. If we partner up, you'll be effectively severing your contract with your client, which means I'll have no reason to kill you."

His captor stopped pacing and faced him, one hand on her hip, the other still holding the gun. She still looked skeptical. Just then, Max heard the sound of approaching footsteps. They grew in crescendo, shoes slapping on the cobblestones. The woman whirled, holding the gun at the ready. Max saw a young man hurtle into the room at full tilt, a heavy set of dreadlocks flying in the breeze. He wore a grey T-shirt with a band logo and his arms were covered in sleeves of tattoos. He was waving what looked like a file folder. She relaxed at the sight of him.

———

"Wing, I—" Enzo started, breathless from running the full length of the corridor.

"I thought I told you not to interrupt," Wing scolded. "You need to go. Now."

Enzo stood fast. His face showed excitement and he was waving a file folder in his hand. "I think you need to see this," he said.

She grabbed him by the arm and pushed him out of the room and into the hallway. Overhead, a dusty bulb cast a dim light and shadows flickered across the hewn rock walls and cobblestone floor. "Keep your voice down," she said. "Now what is so darned important?"

"I think I've figured out who the mole is," Enzo said, his voice now hushed.

"So? Out with it."

"Look at these," Enzo said. He shoved the folder at her. She took it and rifled through the papers. She saw lists of phone numbers with time stamps and duration. Many of them were highlighted. Some had blue ink marks next to them.

"What is this? I can't read your mind," she snapped, shoving the stack back at him.

"These are calls Walter made from his mobile phone, all in the last two months. I noticed a pattern, a lot of calls to the same number. So I traced it. The number is a mobile phone registered to a man with the name Horst Schmidt."

"Ok," Wing said, her irritation growing. "Who is Horst Schmidt?"

"Right. So I did some digging. At first, I was over-whelmed with all the possibilities. Horst Schmidt is a very popular German name—"

"Get on with it, Enzo. Give me the frigging punch line. Who is Horst Schmidt?"

Enzo looked shy for a moment. "Well, I don't know exactly—"

Wing's shoulders slumped. "You interrupted me to tell me this?"

"But I was able to link him to this picture—" He rifled to the bottom of the stack of papers and yanked out a black-and-white photo printed by a laser printer. He handed it to Wing.

One glance told her all she needed to know. The photo showed a man from medium distance standing next to a taxicab – the sort of old-style cab usually found in London. He was stooped slightly, as if he were about to get into the vehicle. The subject wore a suit, and although the picture was in black and white, Wing knew the suit was light grey. The man's close-cropped hair and chiseled nose could only be one person. She was looking at Mueller, her client's right-hand man.

Anger rose in her. "Where is that rat bastard? Where is Walter right now?"

"Upstairs at his machine, I think."

"Get him down here," Wing said, her anger flashing. Then she softened her voice and smiled. "Just tell him I need some help with the prisoner."

She watched Enzo turn and retreat back down the hall-way. For the first time in a long time, she let herself feel elation. Maybe things were finally going her way.

THIRTY-FIVE

Undisclosed location outside Budapest

From the cot where he'd sat down to await her return, Max watched the woman stride back into the room and pace in front of his cell. She looked distracted, and mildly pleased with herself. Max found himself admiring her figure as she walked.

"He's lying," Max said.

She whirled on him, looking like she'd just been slapped.

"What did you say?"

"I said, he's lying."

"How—"

"Your voices carried," Max said. "I could hear what you were saying." That was only partly true. Their voices had carried, but he could only make out a few of the words. He hoped it was enough to give him some leverage.

Her expression hardened. "Explain."

"First off, I could see it in his eyes and hear it in his

voice. He was cleverly disguising himself to appear earnest."
Max was guessing, taking shots in the dark based on his
intuition.

She looked skeptical, so Max made a calculated statement. Everything rode on this one moment. "You two are
sleeping together?"

Her mouth dropped open, and Max knew he'd scored.
"How the—" she stammered.

"It's pretty clear from the way you looked at him when
he came in," Max said. He stood and walked to the bars, and
again leaned on one of the cross pieces with his hands
clasped in front of him.

It only took a few seconds for her to regain her composure. "How do you know he's lying about the phone
numbers?"

"His tone was obvious, which I think he used to take
advantage of your affection, thus making you more likely to
believe him. Also, it's very unlikely that someone on your
staff would use a traceable phone. Perhaps Dreadlocks there
should explain how he matched the receiving phone
number to the picture. It's just too easy. And you fell for it
because you're sleeping with him. You wanted to believe
him."

She toyed with her lip, then turned away so Max
couldn't see her face. There was a chance he had her. Max
had no idea whether her employee was lying about the
phone numbers or not. He knew from long hours of interrogation training that the man had been hiding something,
though, and that was all Max needed.

Footsteps crunched on the grit of the cobblestone out in
the hallway. The gait was slow, unhurried. A few seconds
later, a burly man strode in. His oversized torso was
supported by skinny legs, making him look like he might

easily topple over. What was left of his reddish-brown hair was cropped short. He wore combat boots and had a sidearm strapped to his belt in a quick-draw holster. He looked capable and wary, and stopped just inside the room. Wing stood about ten feet away, halfway between the room's door and Max's cell.

"You called?" the man said. His voice had a nasal drawl to it.

The woman startled both men with the speed with which she pointed her gun at her employee. "Drop the sidearm, Walter."

Walter hesitated, his hands hanging loose at his sides. Max saw scorn on his face, like he was beneath being drawn on by a woman.

"NOW!" she said. "Slowly."

Max was impressed with the authority her voice commanded.

Walter's fatal mistake was likely borne from prejudice, or perhaps ego. The man slowly reached down as if to withdraw the pistol from its holster, but then gave himself away with his eyes as he tried to jerk the pistol up and quick-fire.

Her gun spat once and the bullet hit Walter in the right shoulder. He was spun by the impact of the slug, and his shot ricocheted off the far wall. Max crouched down to make himself as small as possible in case there was more gunfire. Walter sagged against the wall.

"Toss the weapon," she yelled, her gun held steady.

"You BITCH," Walter said. "You shot me."

"Toss the gun, or I'm going to shoot you again and then you'll be dead."

Walter's pistol clattered to the ground. Wing moved forward and kicked it away, then stood back. Walter slowly slid down the wall until he was in a sitting position. He reached up to try to staunch the blood flow from his chest. "Why did you shoot me?"

"Besides the fact that you drew on me?" she said.

Max stood up again in his cell. This was getting interesting.

"You've been giving our client information. You've violated my trust. You're our mole," the woman said.

Walter's eyebrows scrunched up. "That's bullshit," he said. "Who told you that? Enzo? That lying fuck. And you believe him? You guys fucking deserve each other."

Then the woman said something that surprised Max. "Not Enzo. Marisa picked up cellular traffic earlier this morning coming from our compound. She traced it to a burner phone."

"So what," Walter said. "That could have been anyone."

"Not anyone," she said. "There are only four of us working in this office. Marisa, Enzo, and I were in the operations room. The transmissions couldn't have been from us. You were the only one. Burner phones are against our policy unless you're in the field. Who were you calling?"

"It wasn't me," he said. "You've got no proof."

"Right now, you've got a gunshot wound to the shoulder. You need medical attention. If I put another bullet, say, in your thigh, then leave you here, you might bleed out."

"I'm telling you, it wasn't me," Walter said. He was pleading now.

To Max's utter surprise, she shot him again, this time aiming the gun downward, almost point-blank at his thigh. The gun spit and Walter howled, grabbing his leg. "Fuck! You BITCH!"

"Be thankful it's a flesh wound and I didn't destroy your knee."

Walter howled in pain. "Ok, ok. You're right. It was me on that burner phone. Just don't shoot me again."

Max's eyebrows raised. This he didn't expect. In a flash, he went over the scene with Enzo again in his head. The kid had definitely been lying about something. Suddenly, Max wasn't sure of anything, and it seemed the woman knew more than she was letting on.

"Who were you calling?" she demanded.

Walter's face had broken out in sweat and he rocked back and forth in pain. The leg with the gunshot wound was stretched out in front of him, and there was a ragged hole in his pants at about mid-thigh. Blood had seeped out and spread to a stain on his leg the size of a dinner plate.

"He's going into shock," Max said.

The Asian woman ignored him. "Tell me who you were calling and we'll get you some medical attention."

Walter said nothing.

Wing kicked out a booted foot and connected squarely with Walter's wounded thigh. Walter screamed in pain.

"Mueller!" he yelled. "It was Mueller."

Wing turned around and looked at Max smugly. "Looks like Enzo is innocent after all."

"No, he isn't," Walter managed.

She whirled back around. "What did you say?" She had the gun pointed at Walter's head.

Walter smiled. He rolled his head back against the wall, looking like a man who had just played his last ace.

"He was in on it too," Walter said.

"Prove it," she said, her voice cracking.

"I need assurances you won't kill me," Walter said. "Do whatever you want. I just don't want to die. I've got a son—"

"Tell me or I'm going to kick you again in the leg, and keep kicking until you pass out. Then I'm going to bind up your wounds, strap you to the board, and slowly take you apart until you tell me what I want to know. Tell me fast, and I may let you live."

Max grimaced at the woman's viciousness. She kicked Walter's leg again, sending him into howls of pain.

"Out with it, Walter," she said. Her voice was a low growl.

"It was all him," Walter said. "Enzo set the whole thing up. He said you were going down, that this operation wasn't going to last. He said all we have to do is—"

"Proof," she demanded. "I need proof."

Walter seemed to cast about, thinking. Max could see the wheels turning, and found himself rooting for him. *Come on, Walter. You're my ticket out of here.*

Suddenly Walter's face lit up. "Check the firewall. He's got a white-listed IP address in there for Mueller. It's hidden behind a proxy, so you or Marisa wouldn't find it. I think it's 66.147.244.80."

The woman turned, her eyes flashing in anger. She stooped and picked up Walter's pistol and shoved it into her waistband. She walked over and used a set of keys to open Max's cell. Holding the gun on him, she said, "Drag him into your cell. Do it."

Max left the cage and walked over to Walter. The man's skin was soaked with perspiration and his face had lost all its color. Max reached down and put his arm under Walter's shoulders. "You've got to help me, Walter. On the count of three," Max said.

On three, he heaved and managed to get Walter to his feet. He half carried, half dragged the man into the tiny cell, where he laid him on the cot. The door clanged shut and he heard the woman lock it behind him. She turned and stalked out of the room.

THIRTY-SIX

Undisclosed location outside Budapest

Max heard Wing's boots marching away down the corridor. Eventually they faded, leaving him with the sounds of Walter's ragged breathing.

"Help me," Walter muttered, his voice feeble. Max turned back and looked at him. Walter's chest was heaving and his face dripped with perspiration. Max yanked the man's shirt open and wrestled it from his body. The shoulder wound was high up on his deltoid, away from major arteries and organs. He ripped Walter's shirt into strips, then pressed a piece of the material onto the shoulder wound. If Walter were to live, the bullets would need to be removed to prevent infection and sepsis, but the first order of business was to staunch the blood flow.

"This is going to hurt," he told Walter. "So bear down." Max gripped Walter's pant leg and ripped the material length-wise down Walter's leg. Walter gasped when Max touched the wound. Max examined the injury and confirmed this one too was just a flesh wound. Walter was lucky, if he managed to stay alive.

Max ripped another strip of material from Walter's shirt, then tied it tight around the gunshot wound on his thigh. Then he folded the end of the mattress under him so the man's feet were elevated, to force more blood into Walter's torso to combat the shock. Without medical equipment, there wasn't much else Max could do for him.

"Is what you said about Enzo true?" Max asked.

Walter didn't answer.

Max considered the woman's trigger-happy brand of torture, and wondered how effective it actually was. "Did you just say that to make her stop shooting?"

Walter turned his head, and Max could see his eyes had taken on a glassy stare. Max slapped him.

"Is what you said true?" Max demanded. He grabbed the man's face and pinched hard. "Don't pass out on me, goddammit."

It was all for nothing. Walter faded out of consciousness.

Max patted him down. In the man's front pocket, he found a wad of papers and money secured with a rubber band. In the stack was an Australian passport with the name Walter Thomas. There was also the equivalent of several thousand US dollars in various currencies. Max put the wad of papers and the currency back in Walter's pocket. He also found a smartphone. Tapping the button at the top, the screen flashed and asked for a four-digit code. Max tried several combinations until the phone locked him out. He shoved it back into Walter's pocket. Then he sat down to wait, his back to the stone wall.

———

He didn't have to wait long. Soon he heard hurried footsteps on the cobblestone outside the room. A quick check of Walter revealed the man hadn't woken. Max stood and watched the entryway.

Three people barged into the room. The first to enter was Enzo, looking harried and fearful. Wing followed with her gun extended, pointed at Enzo's head. Her face was a mask of fury. Following her was a tall, out-of-shape woman Max placed at about forty. A few lines of grey shot through her dark hair and her eyes looked haunted. She also held a gun trained on Enzo, but her gun hand wavered and she looked uncomfortable holding the weapon. Max guessed she was Marisa, the assistant Wing had mentioned earlier.

Max's captor tossed a set of keys to Marisa. "Open the cell two down from them."

Marisa fumbled with the keys, finally managing to get the cell open. Wing shoved Enzo from behind, and he stumbled into the tiny room. Marisa swung the door shut and locked it, tossing the keys back to Wing.

Wing walked over to Max's cell.

"Looks like both you and Walter were right," Wing said.

"Walter's innocent?" Max asked.

"Walter is definitely not innocent. They were in this together."

"So now what?" Max asked. "Kill all three of us?"

Wing started pacing. If Max were in her shoes, he might just kill all three of them, then burn the place down. Start over fresh. He hoped she wasn't that impulsive.

She stopped walking and turned to look at him. "Remind me why you won't just kill me if I let you out? Or why you won't disappear?"

Silently, Max breathed a sigh of relief. "I have no reason to," he said. "When you release me, you'll demonstrate trust and you'll effectively sever your contract with your client. At that point, I'll have no reason to kill you because you'll have given up your reason to kill me."

"And you won't just leave?"

"I need to find your client. You can help me. We'll make a great team."

"I'm still not sure I can trust you," she said.

"That's the choice you have to make right now. I was right about Enzo. And together, we're stronger than you are on your own. Kill me, and your client still controls your life. Partner with me, and we go after him together. I'm your best bet at getting your freedom back."

She wavered. At one point, she glanced at Marisa, but the older woman's face was impassive.

Finally, Wing used her keys to open Max's cell door. She pointed her gun at Walter's head and pulled the trigger. Walter's torso jumped slightly and a spray of blood and brain matter radiated out onto the cot and the walls. She turned and Max braced himself.

She reached into her waistband with her free hand and retrieved Walter's pistol.

Looking at Marisa, Wing said, "This is what Nathan would have done."

Marisa gave Wing a brief nod, and Wing handed Max the pistol, butt first. Then she turned and walked over to the cell holding Enzo.

Max checked the action on the gun. Walter had chosen well. The weapon was a SIG Sauer P229, a compact version of the weapon popular with elite special forces units, and one of Max's favorites. This one was silver plated with a brown handle. He dropped out the mag and found the nineteen-shot magazine one bullet shy. He racked the slide, then caught the bullet that flew out and shoved it into the top of the mag. He slammed the magazine back in and re-racked the slide, and stuck the gun in his waistband.

Turning, he saw Wing pointing her pistol at Enzo, her face full of fury and sadness. Marisa's head was turned.

"Wait," Max yelled. "Don't kill him! For fuck sake, don't shoot him."

THIRTY-SEVEN

Langley, Virginia

Kate snatched the latte from her assistant's hand without even a thank you, barely pausing as she stalked out of her office and into the hallway. The coffee was her third of the day, and she was wired. She didn't care – she'd stay caffeinated all day if she had to. She could feel her carefully crafted world crumbling around her and she'd be damned if she was going down without a fight.

The meeting request from the Director's office that popped up in her email had been the catalyst to send her running from her office. The meeting wasn't scheduled for another forty-eight hours, but she knew it might be the death knell for her and Max, and she only had a short time to save both their hides. Her biggest problem was she didn't know where the fuck Max was.

Her heels clicked on the hard linoleum. She sent a group of dark-suited men scattering and almost took out a mailroom cart before she stopped in front of a door and

swiped her card. The entryway opened with a hiss. She
stalked down another hallway and through another security
door. Each door she went through took her further away
from the nerve center of Langley. She swiped at a final door
and stepped into a small, hot room.

The room's former contents had been pushed against
one wall – mops, brooms, cleaning supplies, and huge boxes
of toilet paper. Along the opposite wall, several folding
tables had been crammed together in a u-shape. A row of
monitors were set up on the tables, and in the center of the
makeshift command center stood Kaamil. Normally impeccably groomed, Kaamil looked as disheveled as Kate felt.
His shirt sleeves were rolled up and stains showed under his
armpits. His brown face glistened with a sheen of sweat,
and his tie, Kaamil's signature article of clothing, was
nowhere to be seen. When he turned, Kate's heart sank. She
could see defeat written on his face.

"Update," she ordered.

He kicked an empty pizza box out of the way and
leaned back on a table, knocking over a half-full bottle of
soda. He seemed not to notice. "He's a total fucking ghost,"
Kaamil said. "There is no trace of him."

"Fuck," Kate said. She planted her feet and crossed her
arms. "European immigration?"

"Nothing. I used a database search spider that could
also crawl photo descriptions. Hundreds of guys in their
mid-forties with shaved heads entering Heathrow, de
Gaulle in Paris, Frankfurt. But no way to know if any
are him."

Kate thought for a second. Kaamil was a well-rounded
operative, and his vast skills included computer forensics,
but she thought his hacking skills were mediocre. She'd
provided him with access to the immigration databases, but

expected he'd have to search by hand. She was impressed by the implementation of the spider. "You're doing this alone, right? No outside contractors?"

"Of course," he answered promptly, staring at her directly.

"Can you start a trace on each of the identity leads?"

"Already in progress, although it's going to take a while. There are a lot of men in their forties over six feet tall with shaved heads going through European immigration in the last week. And he could have been in disguise."

"Did you try Moscow? And Minsk?"

"You really think he'd dare to go back to Russia?"

"I think he's crazy enough to do anything that he thinks might save his family," Kate said. "Check Moscow. And check Minsk."

"Will do," Kaamil said with a sigh. He looked exhausted. Kate knew he'd been pulling long nights in this dank room, taking only cat naps on the floor since she'd decided to confide in him. She was slowly being dragged down, and she needed someone's help. Kaamil was her most loyal officer. He was descended from a family of sheiks in the UAE and didn't need money. As far as she could tell, he'd have no reason to be the mole. If she couldn't trust him, she figured she might as well hang up her spurs. "You want to take a break? Go home? Take a shower?"

Kaamil's brow narrowed. "No fucking way. This is important, right?"

"In forty-eight hours, I'm pretty sure the Director is going to shut Max down. She's got a hard-on for her drone program and thinks human assassins are cumbersome, dangerous, and unpredictable. Unfortunately, Max isn't doing himself, or me, any favors by disappearing. In her sample size of one, so far she's right."

"Got it," Kaamil said. "In that case, I'll keep after it."

Kate's face softened. In the mess that was her world, Kaamil's loyalty was a bright spot. "Thank you."

"Don't mention it. Some air conditioning would be helpful."

"I'll see what I can do. Call me the minute you have something." She turned to go.

"Oh, there is something else."

She turned back.

"I've also been monitoring the intelligence chatter. FSB, MI6, Mossad—"

"How have you been doing that?" Kate demanded.

Kaamil looked uncomfortable. "You probably don't want to know."

"Kaamil!"

"I have a connection at the NSA."

"Christ. You said you were working alone."

"My connection is only providing me with the raw feeds. They don't know what I'm looking for."

"Ok, fine. Let's keep it that way. Must be a good connection," Kate said. The NSA was notoriously secretive, even with their peers at the CIA and FBI. "And?"

"There seems to have been some kind of operation in Istanbul two nights ago. An attack on a restaurant in the outskirts of the Old City. Four confirmed dead."

Kate's heart raced for a second, but she remained calm. "How do you know it was an intelligence operation and not a turf battle between gangs?"

"Because there were no reports of the conflict in the news media. And because the NSA intercepted this." Kaamil turned and tapped on a keyboard. One of the screens came to life. Kate stepped forward and read the message.

"How did the NSA intercept this, much less read it?" she asked.

"My contact isn't saying. But she alluded that they have the ability to decrypt some of the FSB's secure transmissions."

Kate turned to look at him. "She?"

Kaamil instantly blushed.

Kate turned back to the screen and read the message a second time.

Target anticipated attack, escaped. Four deceased. Returning to Moscow.

"Who sent this, and who received it?"

Kaamil tapped a few keys. "Sent by a lieutenant Chazov. Recipient was a Lieutenant General Spartak Rugov."

Kate searched her memory. She had an encyclopedic knowledge of the Russian chain of command, having once been the CIA's Moscow station chief. "Rugov is a big deal. He runs Military Counterintelligence at the FSB. He's the Directorate chief."

"Right," Kaamil said.

"Why would military counterintelligence be chasing after Max?"

"If the target was even Max," Kaamil said.

"Right," Kate said. Her instincts told her it had been Max, or maybe she just wanted to believe they'd stumbled onto a lead. Maybe she was grasping at straws. "Why would Max be in Turkey?" she mused, almost to herself. "Did you look through immigration at Ataturk?"

"Yes. Thirty-eight men who matched Max's description came through Ataturk in the past three days."

"Crap."

"Right. With the shaved head and some facial stubble and skin that easily tans, he could pass for a Turk pretty easily. I'm in the middle of chasing them all down now."

"Good," Kate said absently. Her mind was accessing a map of Turkey, the Caucasus, and the Black Sea. The geography was etched permanently into her mind. "If you were trying to get into Russia, but didn't want to fly into Moscow, how would you go?"

Kaamil shrugged. "Maybe fly to Kiev, then over the border? Take advantage of the conflict."

"Think again," Kate said. "That border is actually pretty tight. Lined with the Russian troop buildup."

"Fly into Estonia. Drive over the border to St. Petersburg. Then fly domestic to Moscow?"

"Maybe. That's not bad. But what about a boat across the Black Sea from Istanbul to Rostov? Then either a domestic flight or vehicle from Rostov to Moscow?"

"That might explain Max's trip to Istanbul."

"Fuck," Kate said. "I can't believe he's heading into Russia."

Kaamil was silent.

"Get anything else from your contact over at the NSA?" She winked when she said the word *contact*.

"Very funny," Kaamil said. "And no. Nothing else."

"Ok. Stay on it. I think this Istanbul thing is real. Find him. We have two days, otherwise our lights are going out."

She turned and strode from the room.

THIRTY-EIGHT

Undisclosed location outside Budapest

Bokun took one last look at the detailed plans for the underground tunnel system he'd loaded on his smartphone. He didn't like being out in the open. Around him were nothing but fields, farmhouses, and the occasional barn, as far as his eye could see. Trees lined the roads, but otherwise the land was flat. He knew he needed to move quickly, before the woman killed his prize. But he also knew caution and patience ruled the day in his line of work. Still, he urged himself forward. The thought of losing his prey made his stomach ill.

He checked and rechecked his weapons and gear before closing the van's doors. The assassin carried a silenced Sig Sauer 9mm pistol with a seventeen-round magazine. Two more mags were in pockets of his tactical vest. He also carried an IWI Tavor, an Israeli-made, compact, semi-automatic assault rifle known as a *bullpup*. Each magazine carried thirty 5.56 x 45mm rounds. He had two more of those mags in his pocket. He wore a set of compact night-vision goggles pushed up on his forehead.

With the bullpup slung over his back, the assassin set off through a field on a diagonal path from the van's location. His destination was an outbuilding at the corner of the field. He was moving fast, confidence bolstered by the knowledge that the woman's perimeter defenses were limited. He was perspiring freely when he reached the small building. He stopped with his back against the wooden exterior and waited. He sensed no movement; heard no sounds save for the calls of a black crow that was bothered by the assassin's appearance.

Bokun ducked around the building and found the door. The weather-beaten wood seemed like it would give way to a shove. A shiny metal padlock hung from the latch, contrasting with the old structure. He produced a thin piece of metal, and in seconds had the lock opened.

Inside, underneath some boxes in the corner, Bokun found the trapdoor he knew was there. He used the recessed handle to pull up the door, glanced into the hole, and found a crude ladder leading down to a tunnel. He tested the first rung of the ladder and, finding it solid, quickly descended to the dirt floor. He lowered the night-vision goggles over his eyes.

Keeping his head bent to avoid the exposed beams, he started off at a slow jog. As he ran, he felt the anticipation of finishing the job he'd set out to do. He knew he'd been lucky that the FSB had seen fit to turn Asimov over to the woman. Asimov could easily have disappeared into the Russians' gulag, never to be seen again. Even with Bokun's long reach, he would have difficulty finding Asimov and killing him in the byzantine and dangerous prison system. With a new burst of energy, Bokun began to sprint.

When he came to the end of the tunnel, he found a similar ladder made from crumbling wood. Above, he saw another trapdoor. At the top of the ladder, he paused to listen. Straining his ears, he picked up no sounds other than the faraway cadence of dripping water. He pushed the door open a crack and looked out through the night-vision goggles. The room was filled with storage containers and boxes piled to the ceiling. Bokun pushed himself out and onto his knees in a tactical position, the Tavor ready. Nothing stirred.

He moved to the door, cracked it open, and glanced out. He found a hallway lit with a string of low-hanging bare bulbs, but saw no movement. He knew from the plans that to the right was a freight elevator that would take him up to the main offices. To the left were interrogation rooms and a row of cells for keeping prisoners. He guessed this was where his target would be.

The Tavor in hand, he started moving. At the end of the hallway, he saw a faint light. As he went, he glanced into the rooms he encountered. He saw no one.

Despite the grit underneath his feet, the assassin walked silently, a skill borne from years of practice and an uncanny ability to know exactly where to put each foot. Hugging the wall, he stole down the passageway, death in a shadow.

Halfway down the corridor, he paused. Voices came from the lit room up ahead. Straining his ears, he thought he could pick out at least two, a male and a female. He hoped he wasn't too late; he had a score to settle. His head began to pound, the familiar pain that pierced his forehead like a cleaver. Bokun picked up the pace, his need to kill overtaking his caution.

A few steps later, he could hear the voices more clearly. Then he heard a male voice shout out.

"Wait," the voice yelled. "Don't kill him! For fuck sake, don't shoot him."

The assassin moved faster.

———————

Wing turned her head toward him, and Max saw determination etched on her face. The woman had been betrayed, and she'd have her vengeance. Max moved out of his cell and came to stand by her. Enzo was crouched down, an arm over his head as if trying to ward off a blow. Max placed his palm on top of her hand that held the pistol and gently pushed downward.

"We need him," Max said. "He's our link to your client. Enzo can guide us to him."

Wing resisted the pressure, and he saw her put tension on the trigger. Max was surprised by the strength in her tiny arm.

"We can do it without him," Wing said. "He's just baggage we don't need."

"Don't throw away the opportunity," Max said. "I bet he'll cooperate with us."

The strength in her arm wavered, and Max saw the tension on the trigger lessen. He pushed her arm down and she let the gun fall to her side.

Just then, Max heard a sound that came from beyond the door to the room. It was a slight grinding noise, like sandpaper on wood. Max's senses had been tuned to pick up even the smallest disturbance in the space around him. He whirled toward the door and brought his pistol up. Wing, who must have sensed the same noise, also turned.

"Is there anyone else here?" Max whispered.

She shook her head.

Suddenly, the silence in the room was shattered by the deafening chatter of a semi-automatic weapon. In a matter of seconds, the scene in the room turned chaotic as bullets pinged off the floor and the room's rock walls. Instinctively, Max registered the distinctive sound of the gunfire as coming from a bullpup-style weapon, most likely an Israeli Tavor.

The gunfire came from just beyond the doorjamb, and Max could see a gloved hand and black-clad arm holding a compact submachine gun.

The attacker had the benefit of surprise, but had also elected to stay behind cover, thus impeding his angle of fire. Marisa, who had been slow to react, was the first casualty of the semi-automatic rounds. Three large-caliber bullets ripped into her chest and she screamed and fell, propelled backward by the impact. Her gun clattered to the ground.

Max started firing using a two-handed grip. Un-silenced, his pistol popped loudly in the small room, adding to the din of the battle. He squeezed off three rounds, hitting the wall near where the bullpup was chattering. Max saw Wing execute a perfect roll to her left, away from the angle of fire, and come up shooting. Her silenced pistol chewed holes in the wall near the attacker's arm. The bullets from the bullpup kept coming.

Enzo was the next victim. Rounds careened off the cobblestone floor as the line of fire swept toward the row of cells. Four rounds found Enzo, two impacting him in the head and two in the torso. He was dead before his body hit the ground.

The attacker's rounds arced toward Max. Max squeezed off three more rounds and took chips of stone off the corner near where the bullpup extended.

The Tavor's gunfire paused.

"Bokun, is that you?" Wing's voice rang out.

Max's eyes narrowed at the sound of the assassin's name.

"Stop shooting," Wing yelled. "I'm ending the contract on Asimov. He's no longer your target."

As if in answer, the bullpup appeared around the corner and started shooting blindly in the direction of Wing's voice. The shooter's one-handed grip made the weapon unstable, and bullets flew wildly around them.

"Bokun! Stop shooting!" Wing bellowed. "The contract is ended." The bullpup chattered again, its operator spraying bullets wildly around the small room. Max knew it would only be a short time before they both were hit.

Max signaled to Wing for covering fire. She started putting bullets into the wall near the shooter's arm. The Tavor retracted. Max ducked and rolled to his left under the covering fire, and ended up next to the room's front wall. He edged closer to the door, holding his gun extended. Wing let up the fire. A moment later, the bullpup reappeared. Max fired twice, hitting the gun with both shots.

The owner reacted by dropping the gun. Max darted forward, closing the distance between him and the doorway in an instant, and kicked away the Tavor. He paused at the doorjamb, ready for another weapon to emerge. Instead, he heard footsteps moving away from the doorway in a hurry. Staying low, Max put his head and arm around the doorjamb and started firing. He could see the outline of a tall figure retreating down the corridor. Between the darkness and his hurried aim, Max's shots went wide. Then bullets started hitting the wall and floor around him. Max pulled back, and the fleeing intruder disappeared.

THIRTY-NINE

Undisclosed location outside Budapest

"We need to go after him," Max urged. He jammed a new magazine into his SIG and examined the Tavor. There were only a few rounds left, so he tossed it aside.

"Hold on," Wing demanded. She was moving from body to body, feeling each for a pulse. Finally she joined him, a determined look on her face. Max watched her drop the mag out of her pistol and slam in a new one. "He meant to kill all of us," she said.

"Are you surprised?" Max asked.

"Yes. As of five minutes ago, he was working for me."

Max stuck his head around the corner. The hallway was empty. He knew the attacker could be waiting for them in one of the rooms down the hall.

"What's the best way out of here?"

"The only way I know is up the elevator."

"Either he's gone or he's waiting to pick us off as we leave. Here is how we'll do it." He told her his plan.

Max started out, hugging the left wall, his pistol out in front as he moved down the hallway. Wing hugged the right wall moving more slowly, her own pistol out. Max found the first door and went in fast and low. He found the room empty. He covered Wing from the door while she darted into the room. They moved down the hallway in this fashion, searching the half-dozen rooms and finding nothing, until they reached the elevator. The freight elevator's car was resting on the ground.

"If Bokun had left via the elevator, wouldn't it be at the top floor?" he asked.

"Unless he wanted to confuse us," Wing said.

"Or maybe it's a trap. You sure there is no other way out of here?" Max asked.

"Anything's possible," Wing said. "This building used to be owned by the Hungarian Secret Police. Who knows what kind of labyrinth they created down here."

"We're in Hungary?" Max asked, looking at her.

"Yes, just outside Budapest."

"What's our vehicle situation?"

"There will be several in the parking garage. Mine, Marisa's, and probably Enzo's. Oh, and Walter's."

"Anything you need to grab? This place is probably blown. We shouldn't come back here."

Max saw the wheels spinning in her head and momentarily felt for her. Her team had been destroyed, and now it was only her. The assassin she'd hired was now trying to kill her. And she was stuck with him, her former enemy. Most people would have probably sat down in a corner and cried. He was impressed with her resilience.

"My laptop would be helpful."

"Ok. Cover me," Max said. He felt like they'd missed something. He turned and retraced his steps. The room nearest to the elevator contained a metal chair, bucket, and a stained wooden rack Max assumed was used for interrogations. Nothing else. The second room he examined was a storage room. Crates were piled high and he saw stacks of empty boxes with electronics brand names emblazoned on the sides. The boxes were stacked high.

He paused to listen. The only sound was the *drip, drip, drip* of water somewhere behind him. An earthy smell permeated the basement, reminding him of rotting vegetation. He turned and waved Wing over, holding his finger to his lips. He pointed at the boxes. She used the doorjamb for cover and pointed her pistol into the room.

Max stepped inside, his footsteps soft and silent, gun held out. The boxes and crates loomed in the darkness. He skirted them to his left, then suddenly pushed at the top box with his left hand and sent it tumbling backward. He heard it fall to the ground, the hollow sound of cardboard bouncing on stone. He heard nothing else. He pushed another box, and heard nothing but the bouncing box. Finally, he peered around the stack of boxes, gun held in front of him.

The two boxes he'd pushed over were resting at odd angles on the floor. Next to one was an open trapdoor. He waved Wing over.

"On the count of three," he whispered. Wing held her gun at the ready. On three, they both approached the trapdoor, guns out. In the inky darkness below, he saw a rickety ladder that disappeared into a dark tunnel.

Max looked at Wing. "Did you know about this?" he whispered.

"Negative," Wing whispered. "We'll be sitting ducks down there."

"Agreed. I'm betting he's gone, though."

"Why?"

"The tunnel is a trap for us, but it would also be a trap for him."

"He could be outside the other end of the tunnel, waiting for us to pop up."

"He could. But he's also an assassin. Most assassins are very cautious by nature. We like things to be well planned, and we like the element of surprise. Stealth is our friend. We don't like face-to-face battles, especially when we're outnumbered." Max shut the trapdoor. "We gain nothing by going down that tunnel. Best case is he's gone, worst case is he's left some kind of booby trap. We should go up the elevator."

Just then, they were both jolted by a loud explosion. The ground moved under Max's feet and he fought to keep his balance. Rock and debris fell from the ceiling and the boxes and crates shifted. Wing had to steady herself against the wall.

"What the—?"

He turned and saw a plume of dust in the hallway. Wing behind him, he stepped out of the storage room, waving at the dust. As the air cleared, he saw that the space where the elevator had been was now a pile of rubble. The elevator car itself was mangled beyond use and was half covered by a pile of rocks and dirt. The severed end of the elevator cable lay on the ground.

"He's flushing us into a trap," Wing said grimly.

"Looks that way, doesn't it?" Max said.

Max turned back to the storeroom and contemplated the hole with the ladder. The jolt of the explosion had caused the trapdoor to slam shut.

"Hold on," Wing said. She removed her smartphone and tapped a few times on the screen. Max looked at her.

"Good. The Wi-Fi is still up." She tapped some more. "There. I just activated a self-destruct program," she said. "I erased all the workstations, file servers, firewalls, and the rest of our data center. If anyone gets into our offices upstairs, they'll find a bunch of gear, but no data."

Max was impressed. "Shame," he said.

"I have everything backed up," she said, with a wink. The unexpected levity took Max by surprise. For a woman with everything seemingly crumbling around her, she was taking it all in stride.

"Of course you do," he said. "You ready?"

Wing indicated with her pistol that she'd cover him while he opened the trapdoor.

"On three," he said. When he said *three*, he yanked open the door and Wing pointed her gun into the hole. Max heard nothing. The vegetative smell was stronger now. He eyed the rickety ladder. A few weeks ago, he'd been in a tunnel that turned out to be a trap, and it had almost gotten him killed. He swallowed back the fear. "You got a torch or a light around here?"

Wing pulled out her mobile phone, tapped a button, and a bright light emitted from the phone's built-in flashlight.

Max smiled at her, and caught her eye when she returned it with a rueful grin.

"I'll go first," Wing said, breaking the moment, and handed Max the light. He directed the beam down into the tunnel. With one hand holding her gun, Wing swung her legs onto the ladder and climbed down. Max handed down the phone. He joined her a moment later and found her crouched, gun pointed down the tunnel.

The floor was hewn from dirt and rock and the ceiling was held up with wooden beams spaced every few meters.

Wing's light illuminated only a few paces in front of them. The tunnel sloped up and disappeared into the darkness.

With a backward glance, Wing started off. Max followed, stooping to keep from hitting his head on the beams.

At fifteen paces, Wing stopped, crouched, and surveyed the ground. They'd have a hard time seeing a thin filament line strung at knee level. Thankfully, the walls on both sides of the tunnel were smooth. There was nowhere to hide a small explosive device. Wing stood and moved forward.

While he walked, Max tried to put himself in the assassin's head. Wing had attempted to cancel the contract while the attacker was in mid-operation. Obviously something had changed with the assassin's operating arrangement, and Bokun was now after both of them. Perhaps someone had outbid Wing's contract amount.

He followed Wing up the sloping tunnel, both of them stopping every few meters to survey the floor, walls, and ceiling. Max knew if the assassin was waiting at the end of the tunnel with a gun, they were sitting ducks with the light. But he didn't see any way around it. He half expected to hear the sound of a grenade bouncing along the dirt floor toward them.

Max found it odd that the attack had been so crude. He knew Bokun was a calculating and effective killer. The only explanation was that the man had acted out of haste and desperation. Desperate men made mistakes.

He followed Wing for another ten minutes, his heart in his throat. When they reached the end of the tunnel, Max breathed a sigh of relief. Another ladder led up to an open trapdoor. Max took a few seconds to survey the ladder, and declared it free from traps. He climbed up first, stuck his head out, and swept his pistol around. Seeing no movement, he surveyed the room. It looked to be a small storage building. Dust floated in daylight that streamed from wooden slats making up the building's walls. A door stood in one wall. He saw no one. He jumped out of the hole, landed in a crouch, and spun around, covering Wing as she climbed out.

They looked at each other, and Max shrugged. The room was empty, and he saw no evident danger. He walked to the door and examined it. His first thought was that a C-4 explosive device had been placed on the outside of the door, set to go off if the door opened. It's how he would have done it.

Max turned from the door and walked to the wall, where he could see daylight streaming through several holes in the wood. Testing a slat with his hand, he found it brittle and flexible. He looked out one of the holes and saw a field extending about a kilometer to a tree line. He saw no movement.

"Cover me," Max said. He put his pistol in his waistband and grabbed a wooden slat and yanked. The rotten wood came free. He pulled on two more slats and created a narrow hole in the side of the building. Wing kept the gun pointed out the hole as he removed enough slats to create a space large enough for her to crawl through.

Max covered Wing as she slipped through the slats and out into the sunlight. Suddenly, Max heard the telltale crack of a rifle shot.

FORTY

Undisclosed location outside Budapest

He heard Wing hit the ground, then movement, as if she were scrambling in the grass on all fours.

"You hit?" Max asked.

"No." Her voice came from his right, outside the door. "Shooter to your left. Five hundred meters. The door is rigged with an explosive."

Max found himself appreciating the artistry of the assassin's trap. The destroyed elevator. The booby-trapped door. The position of the sniper. The only weak spot in the setup was the sniper's distance. Still, five hundred meters would be easy for a man like Bokun. "Can you disarm the bomb?"

"Negative. Not in my skill set." Wing said. "It looks like a lot of C-4. There's a wire running from the bomb to the doorknob."

"It's set to go off if the door opens," Max said.

He looked above his head. The roof was pitched at an

angle, supported by dilapidated trusses. Cobwebs and birds' nests covered the rafter's interior.

Suddenly he heard wood splinter and felt a projectile fly by his head. Another followed that narrowly missed his kneecap. Then another. Bullets careened as they punctured the walls. The assassin was firing into the building blind, in the hopes of catching one of them with a lucky shot.

Max shoved the pistol into his waistband and jumped, catching a rafter with both hands. Another bullet flew by as he swung his legs and pulled himself up onto the beam. Another bullet sent wood splinters flying and another flew through the space where he had just been standing. The wall to Max's left now had jagged holes in the wood. The air was thick with dust and wood particles.

Max was counting the bullets, a habit ingrained in him by his father. Most modern long-range rifles used thirty-slug magazines. The count was in the high teens by the time he reached the rafters. He jumped from beam to beam, holding onto the trusses, and headed for a corner of the building where he saw light streaming through a hole in the roof.

"Can you return fire?" Max yelled.

"Negative," came the reply from Wing. "Too far."

"Can you spot him?"

"Hold on." He heard her moving in the grass. "He's lying on top of a white van across the field."

Max reached the corner of the building, grabbed a rafter with two hands, and started kicking at the spot where the roof had rotted. Soon he had a hole large enough to climb through. He stuck a leg out, gripped the opening with both hands, and swung his body out the hole. He let himself drop, then rolled as his legs hit the ground. Bullets started chewing up the ground where he landed. He propelled himself to his right and came to rest behind the corner of the building farthest from the shooter's position, on his stomach, next to where Wing lay. He glanced up to see a medium-sized charge made from C-4 attached to the outside of the door. The crack of a bullet careening through the wood slats caused him to duck.

Max had counted twenty-six bullets. He waited, lying still for a few moments. The shooting had stopped, and Max guessed Bokun was jamming in a fresh magazine. Staying crouched, Max looked around. Fifty meters behind them ran a tree line, which meant relative safety. "How are your military crawling skills?"

"I practice nightly," Wing said.

"Great. That'll come in handy later," Max said.

"Are you getting fresh with me already?" Wing said, her face a mask of incredulity.

"You started it."

"You're delusional."

"If this budding relationship is going to move to the next level, first we have to survive," Max said, grinning at her. "We can out-wait him. At some point, he'll get uncomfortable with being exposed. All it would take is for a farmer to come by with a tractor. Or we can retreat, keeping the building between us and him—" Suddenly, something registered in his mind. He looked back up at the explosive device and saw something attached to it. Something he'd missed because of the distraction of the flying bullets.

"What is it?" Wing asked.

"We need to go. Now!"

"What is it?"

"Run!" Max yelled. He grabbed her arm and propelled her up onto her feet. He started sprinting through the field, doing his best to keep the building between him and the sniper. Wing was right on his heels. He cut to his left a step.

As he did so, he felt the air displace next to his ear as a bullet sang by. Then a heat wave hit him in the back like a gigantic hand, propelling him forward and off his feet. The sound wave hit next, temporarily deafening him. His world went quiet as wood splinters rained down on them.

Max lay on the ground, temporarily stunned. Everything seemed to move in slow motion. He lifted his head and looked around. Wing was sprawled to his left. Max turned his head, feeling like he was moving in quicksand. The building behind them had completely disintegrated. They were sitting ducks. Through the smoky haze, he could see a tiny white fleck in the distance. He turned his head back, willing himself to get up. He looked at Wing. She was slowly stirring, looking like she was trying to clear cobwebs from her head. She looked up and turned toward him. Her eyes were glazed over.

Just then, Max saw a spurt of dirt leap up next to her arm and realized she'd just come a few inches from being killed. His body leapt into action and he grabbed her arm, heaving them both to their feet. "Run!" he yelled.

They took off at a sprint. Max forced himself to weave, his legs pumping hard, heart pounding. Any moment, he expected a projectile to rip into the back of his head. A bullet flew by. Then he felt a searing fire in his left shoulder. He ignored the pain and kept moving. Wing was beside him, her black hair plastered to her forehead by sweat. A moment later, they both entered the relative safety of the trees and slid to a stop in a shallow ditch. They both lay there for a moment, panting. Max's left arm felt wet.

"You hit?" he asked.

"I don't think so." Then he saw Wing's face hovering near his. "Max! Your shoulder is covered in blood."

Max flexed his arm and pain shot through his deltoid.

Wing ripped away the arm of Max's shirt and used it to wipe away the blood. Then she fell back, laughing.

"What is it?" Max asked.

"It's just a graze," she said. "You have an inch-long furrow in your shoulder, you lucky son of a gun."

———

Their exodus from Hungary was quick and painless. After Wing had tenderly placed a makeshift bandage on Max's shoulder, a quick reconnoiter told them the white van was gone. They backtracked through the fields to Wing's office, where she grabbed a small laptop computer and a go-bag with cash and two new, unused identities. Then they hopped into Enzo's beat-up pickup truck and made for Bratislava, Slovakia, in case the airport in Budapest was being watched by the assassin.

They ditched the pickup truck in the airport parking lot and jumped on the first available flight – a regional jump to Zagreb, Croatia. From there, they flew to Brussels. Max's intention was to make the 300-kilometer drive south to Paris in a car, but they were both so exhausted by the time they arrived in Brussels that they decided to take a room and get some much needed sleep. Hotel after hotel was booked, and Max was about to give up when he found a single room in a boarding house near the Rue du Marché au Charbon. He was about to dismiss it and keep looking when Wing grabbed his arm and said, "Let's just take it."

Max paid cash and gave the man behind the desk an extra 100-euro note to keep their names off the registry, winking when the man gave him a knowing look. Max figured the man assumed they were lovers attempting to keep their affair private from their respective spouses. They tossed their bags and, despite their fatigue, did a lengthy Surveillance Detection Route through Brussels. Sure they weren't being followed, they managed to grab an empty table in the back of Au Soleil, an ultra-hip cafe trendy with the gay crowd.

They both ordered beer – Max a St. Feuillien Blonde in a squat bottle and Wing a Westmalle Tripel that came in a goblet – and settled into a comfortable silence. Wing toyed with a small locket around her neck while Max scanned the crowd, still unable to relax. When the waiter returned, Wing ordered a charcuterie of meats, along with some cheese and a small salad. Famished, Max ordered a moules et frites – a plate of mussels steamed with onions served with fries and a beef stew made with beer. When the food came, Wing toyed with hers while Max ate with gusto.

When the dishes had been cleared and more beer was served, Max finally broke the silence. "You haven't told me what he's got over you," Max said gently, referring to her former client.

Wing looked away, her gaze following the crowd for a long moment. At first, Max thought she wasn't going to answer. Finally, without looking at him, she said, "He's got my father."

Max was stunned, understanding immediately the implications of the choice Wing had made to abandon her client and join forces with Max.

"I didn't know him well," Wing continued. "He and my birth mother gave me up for adoption when I was an infant. When I first joined Nathan's organization, I used our resources to track down my birth parents. My mother passed away from cancer many years ago, but my father lived in the slums outside Jakarta – the same slums I grew up in. I was resentful for so long, and couldn't understand why they abandoned me. Finally, I got the courage to meet him, and we bonded instantly. He told me that my mother had always been sick, and that the burden of caring for me was just too great. Anyway, I assume he's dead by now."

Max took her hand in his. "I'm so sorry, Wing. I had no idea."

"It's ok," she said, squeezing his hand. She pulled her hand away and reached down the front of her shirt, producing the locket. Taking if off, she handed it to Max. "Open it."

Max snapped it open. On one side he saw a picture of what he assumed was Wing as a younger woman. The other side held a photo of a deeply wrinkled man with a full head of white hair.

"You look just like him," Max said, smiling.

She gave him a wan smile in return, accepted back the locket, and secured it around her neck.

———

When they returned to the boarding house, they both stared awkwardly at the single bed for moment before Max said, "I'll take the couch." He grabbed a pillow, found a blanket in the closet, and settled in, watching Wing in the dim light as she immodestly stripped to her underwear and slid between the sheets. She turned her back to him and pulled the covers up over her shoulder.

Max stayed awake a while longer, trying to make sense of his feelings for his new partner and trying to guess at hers. They clearly had a comfortable attraction for each other. The flirting and banter came easy. The physical connection was a bit more stilted, as if they were both damaged goods hesitant to test the waters. Max was empathetic to the stress and turmoil he knew she must be feeling from the disintegration of her life and business, and the decision to partner with him. He was treading lightly, despite the strong attraction he felt for her. Part of him wanted to save her, part of him wanted to make her feel better. He fell asleep wondering if they could ever carve out some kind of future together or whether they were both destined to grow old surrounded by the loneliness of their profession.

———

Max awoke to a ray of sunshine in his eyes and the small form of Wing in his arms. During the night, he realized she must have come to the couch from her bed. His arm was around her waist, and their hands were intertwined. He savored the feeling of his skin against hers, until she stirred. She gently moved his arm, got up from the couch, and went into the bathroom. When she emerged, she was fully dressed.

"I'm going to get coffee." She walked out the door without a backward glance.

FORTY-ONE

Langley, Virginia

Kate had fought nausea all afternoon with a bottle of Pepto-Bismol. Maybe it was the coffee she had subsisted on all day or the vodka hangover from the previous night, but she doubted it. In the fifteen years of her CIA career, she'd put men's lives at risk, lost agents she'd cared about, and directed missions with life-and-death consequences, all while maintaining an iron constitution. She cursed the weakness she felt in advance of her meeting with the Director. Kate knew she had only herself to blame. She was kicking herself for agreeing to Max's scheme and for failing to predict the political consequences of covering for him.

The Director's assistant, a tall effeminate man the Director had brought with her from her time in the Senate, regarded Kate with a cool stare. He hadn't offered coffee or water, and she'd refused to sit, preferring to stand and pace.

At four p.m., she heard a faint buzz on the assistant's desk. He stood and said, "You may go in now, Ms. Shaw."

Kate took a breath and flung open the door to Director Montgomery's inner sanctum. If Kate's stomach had been doing flips while she'd been waiting, it was whirling like a Tasmanian devil now. Seated around the Director's conference table were eight men in dark suits, each with a notebook on the table in front of them. The Director sat in her usual place at the head, facing the door, resplendent in a white blazer-blouse combination. A pair of reading glasses were perched on her nose. Bottles of water and coffee cups littered the conference table. Kate looked around and saw no available chairs.

"Kate," the Director said. "Thanks for joining us."

"My pleasure," Kate said. She remained standing with eight pairs of eyes staring at her from the table. She saw Charles Tedford III sitting along one side of the table, looking pleased. She tried to find Bill's eyes, but his were the only ones looking away. He was jotting some notes on a legal pad.

I'll remember this, Bill, she thought.

"How goes the search for your wayward agent?" the Director asked.

Kate fought to keep her composure. Besides Bill and Charles, she recognized four of the other men around the table. They were the heads of other departments: Analysis, Cyber, Support, and Operations. The two other men she didn't recognize. They were each in their late forties or early fifties, with the same swarthy skin and weathered look as Bill, making Kate guess they came from the operational side. "Progressing," she said.

"So no sign of him," stated the Director.

"We have some leads."

"And our target?"

Kate bristled. The Director knew full well that the target was still alive.

"No change in status, ma'am."

"And why is that, Agent Shaw?"

"Ma'am, we discussed—"

"I'm aware of what we discussed," the Director said. "Repeat it for these men."

Kate bit her tongue and began. "The target, one Victor Volkov, is a well-known Russian mob boss. Some say he's the wealthiest mobster in Russia, and one of the wealthiest men in the world. He's known for railing publicly against *Forbes* magazine for not including him in its annual Forbes 400 list. He runs operations across Western Russia, Moscow, Belarus, and the Ukraine. Gambling, prostitution, as well as many semi-legitimate businesses in oil and gas."

From the blank stares she was getting, she assumed everyone in the room knew this. Still, the Director didn't interrupt. Kate guessed Director Montgomery was simply handing her a long length of rope with which to hang herself.

"The CIA has obtained intelligence that Volkov has been instrumental in funneling weapons, spare parts, and supplies like uniforms and food items, to the pro-Russian rebels in Eastern Ukraine. He is acting as the Russian president's right-hand man in the Russian government's quest to prolong the conflict, while giving the president plausible deniability. Volkov effectively controls the border along Eastern Ukraine using a small paramilitary army comprised of Red Army soldiers and hired contractors.

"We believe that taking out Volkov will achieve two strategic aims," Kate continued. "Along with a coordinated surge by the Ukrainian military, the first objective is to interrupt the supply chain and give the Ukrainians an advantage. The second objective is to send a message to Russia that they need to stay out of Ukraine."

Kate glanced around the table. Several of the men were either staring into space or doodling on tablets. Bill was looking at his smartphone. She smelled a setup, and reminded herself to tread carefully.

"Well summarized, Agent Shaw," the Director said. "Please walk through the operational plan to achieve those objectives."

"Volkov is well guarded, as you can imagine," Kate said. Her instinct was to pace, but she kept her arms at her sides and stood her ground. "He operates out of a compound in Rostov, a large port city on the Black Sea in southern Russia. He takes periodic trips to Moscow, where he has a permanent seat at the Russian President's table. We have intelligence on Volkov's movements and security details from a source internal to his organization that we've cultivated over the past twelve months. This source has revealed that Volkov takes periodic trips, undercover, to Donetsk, the city in Eastern Ukraine that serves as the pro-Russian rebels' stronghold. We have a detailed plan to assassinate Volkov during one of these trips using a strategically placed explosive device."

"And when do we expect that plan to operationalize?" the Director said, leaning into the table. Kate found her toothy smile irritating, and it distracted her long enough to make a misstep.

"We're waiting for our on-the-ground asset to become available," Kate said. She instantly regretted her words.

"Really," Montgomery said, as though she'd caught Kate in a lie. "You make it sound as if your asset is off on another assignment or vacationing at his summer cottage. Isn't it true, Agent Shaw, that you've lost control of this asset and you actually have no idea where he is?"

Kate flushed, and tried to make her dry throat work. "That is an accurate statement, ma'am."

The Director sat back in her chair and crossed her legs. "And where are we on plan B?"

The trap had been sprung. Kate had walked into it, fully knowing it was there, yet unable to do anything about it. "We're not, sir, er, ma'am." To cover her mistake, she pressed on. "We do not believe a drone strike is a viable alternative to the human asset on the ground. Nothing in our intelligence suggests Volkov is ever in a remote-enough location to eliminate the risk of civilian deaths that may result from a drone strike."

The Director's face darkened and she grew animated, clearly relishing both the trap she was springing and her proximity to the details of the operation. "And what does your intelligence say about how Volkov gets from his compound in Rostov to Donetsk?"

Kate knew where she was going, yet was powerless to stop it. "By vehicle, ma'am."

"And we all agree," the Director swept her arm around the table, "that a drone strike on sovereign Russian soil would be a diplomatic nightmare of epic proportions, do we not?" Heads nodded all around the table. "Tell us, Agent Shaw, how many kilometers it is from the Russian border to Donetsk."

"Ninety, ma'am."

"Are those ninety kilometers all through densely populated civilian areas?"

"No, ma'am."

"There are long stretches of open fields, pastures, and forested areas, are there not?"

"Yes, ma'am."

"We have an insider who can alert us as to when the target departs for Donetsk. And we have satellites that can track the movement of his convoy. And we can get permission from the Ukrainians to fire a drone on their soil, correct?"

Kate kept silent. They were rhetorical questions. The director spread her arms. "Seems like the use of a drone to eliminate Mr. Volkov is a slam dunk."

Kate cringed. It was well-known among operators in the field that there were no *slam dunks*. It was a phrase used by bureaucrats. "No, ma'am." Her voice sounded quiet and weak.

"Pardon me?" the Director asked, her voice ringing out over the room.

"No, ma'am," Kate said more loudly, figuring her career at the CIA was already in jeopardy. "It's not a slam dunk. Volkov has made it a practice to bring his family along for the trip. On more than one occasion, either his mistress and her infant, or his wife and their two little girls, have accompanied him."

The director paused for emphasis before speaking. "And therein lies the problem, Agent Shaw. Your philosophies and those of this department differ. Would you not sacrifice a few lives to save the lives of thousands?"

Kate felt like a drowning woman reaching for a rope, only to have it jerked away. "You mean to serve the goals of the United States by controlling the pipelines of natural gas flowing through Ukraine?" she blurted. Her head was swimming. "I mean, don't kid yourself," she continued. "You're not saving thousands of lives. The Ukrainians will sweep in and kill the majority of the rebels, most of whom are simply Russian-speaking Ukrainian civilians."

"Enough," the Director said, standing. Her tall, lanky frame towered over the table. Despite Kate's intense dislike of the woman's policies, she had a brief moment of pride that a woman was turning the former men's club of the CIA on its head. That feeling was fleeting, however, as Kate listened to the Director's next words.

"I'm making an organizational change, Agent Shaw, effective immediately. The drone program is no longer under your jurisdiction." She pointed at one of the men Kate didn't know. "Mike Gallagher will take over. He's been read in and will be ready to take out Volkov on the target's next trip to Donetsk. Operational details have already been shared with the Ukrainians and they are in full support. Gallagher will report to Bill. Kate, you're to turn over all operational control and staff of the drone group to Mike by end of the day."

Kate fought hard to keep her mouth from falling open. She'd expected a reprimand, and even expected to be ordered to execute Volkov using the drone program. But she hadn't expected this.

"Also, effective immediately, your new official title will be Special Agent in Charge of Special Operations. Your scope of duty will be limited to managing our fleet of human assets." Kate felt like she'd been punched in the solar plexus. Director Montgomery had just knocked her down two grade levels.

"Lastly, your first assignment will be to disband the Human Asset team. I want a plan on my desk by the end of next week, and you have three months to shut down your own department. The CIA will no longer be conducting assassinations using human assets."

The world in front of Kate seemed to blur. Everything she'd worked for in the past five years had just disintegrated into thin air. The table and the men and the credenza and the Director all seemed to swirl together. She felt vertigo, like her head was in a whirlpool. With a herculean effort, she steadied herself and managed to keep from crumbling to the ground.

"One last thing, Agent Shaw. When you do find your Russian, bring him in. I want him properly interrogated. I'm sure there is a ton of useful information in his head."

"Belarusian," Kate muttered.

"What was that? The Director asked.

"He's Belarusian," Kate said more loudly. "Not Russian."

"Whatever," the Director said. "You're excused."

FORTY-TWO

Paris, France

"What is this place?" Wing asked as they approached the double doors of what looked like a night club. The building's gilded exterior promised something special, and she could hear the thumping of a bass drum and the tinkle of a piano inside. The odor of stale cigarette smoke and day old beer hit her nostrils as she followed Max through the doors. The entryway's walls were covered with black-and-white photographs of various musicians, some with signatures scrawled across their faces. Wing did a double-take as she saw one semi-legible inscription that read, *To Max. Keep on jammin'*.

"Just a jazz club," Max said.

"Yours?" Wing asked.

"Not anymore," Max said. She thought she heard sadness in his voice. The music became louder as they made their way down the short hall, and she heard female vocals, low and soulful. They entered the main room where a jazz band was in full swing. A tall, painfully lean woman with bright white hair to her waist stood next to the piano, belting out lyrics.

Max led Wing through the crowded main room to the end of a bar along the back wall. The room was filled with a well-heeled crowd of mostly older Parisians out on dates with their spouses. She scanned the room, looking for threats, as Max stood at the bar gesturing to the bartender.

During their long trip to Paris from Budapest, Max wouldn't be specific about their destination. *Trust me*, he'd said. For the second time. She had, but couldn't help second guessing herself. Was she doing the right thing, putting her trust in a man she hardly knew?

Suddenly, she saw Max accosted by a rotund woman with glistening black skin.

"Oh my gawd," the black woman gasped with a Creole accent. She wrapped her meaty arms around Max in a bear hug, then let go and led him toward the service entrance. Max signaled to Wing, and she followed them into the cramped kitchen where a man in a hairnet was washing pots and pans.

Max offered introductions. "Della, this is an associate of mine. You can call her Jane." Wing took the woman's hand in her own. "Jane, this is Della, proud owner and manager of this fine establishment."

Della pumped her hand once, beaming. "Only because Max here, the little devil, gave me the club, bless his heart." Then she winked.

Max shushed her. "I need to borrow the apartment upstairs for a quick meeting. If it's not too much trouble, we could also use a place to stay."

"Of course, *zanmi*," she replied. "The place is the same as you found it. I knew you'd be back one day." Her face crinkled into a smile. "Do you require anything to drink?" she asked.

Max declined, kissed Della on the cheek, and led Wing up the stairs and through a door at the top. She found a small but sumptuous apartment consisting of a tiny kitchen, a sitting room furnished in leather, and a nook with a butcher-block table.

Wing took a seat at the table and watched him fuss over a kettle and a coffee maker. She admired his broad shoulders and narrow hips, wondering briefly if she'd ever give into him fully. The aroma of fresh ground coffee filled the room, and a few minutes later, he set a steaming mug of light brown liquid in front of her. Wing smiled inwardly, realizing he remembered how she liked her coffee.

She sipped the hot drink and looked around. The space was small and comfortable, with just enough patina about it to make it warm. She could hear a hint of the bass from downstairs, but not enough to be disruptive. She felt at home here. "You used to live in this apartment?"

"Most of the time," Max said smiling at her. "I also kept a flat a few blocks away, but I spent all my time here."

"Do you miss it?" she asked.

Max poured a cup of coffee for himself and sat down at the table. "Every day," he replied.

Footsteps sounded on the stairs, making her tense. Max indicated with his hand that it was alright. A moment later, the lounge singer flowed into the room, apparition-like and graceful. Her long hair shimmered white in the dim light of the room, and her arms, encased in a swirl of silk, floated about her as she walked. The woman went over to Max, gave him a peck on the cheek, and put a box on the table in front of him. Then she turned and looked at Wing as though she were a half-eaten mouse the cat had deposited on her doorstep.

"Consorting with the enemy, are we, Max?"

"The enemy of my enemy is my friend." Max said, opening the box. He removed a new Blackphone and held it up for Wing to see.

"Mmm," the woman said. "I don't like it."

"And yet, here you are," Max said. Turning to Wing, he said, "Meet our hacker. We'll keep names out of it until we get a little more friendly."

"Good idea," Wing said, focusing on her coffee. The lounge singer looked like a recovering heroin addict. Intricate tattoos covered both of her arms and a tiny, silver spike was lodged in one earlobe. For the first time, Wing started having misgivings about her new partnership with Max.

"Charmed, I'm sure," the singer said. "I prefer computer scientist. When I hear *hacker*, I think of zit-faced teens in their parents' basement breaking into their school's server to change their grades." She perched herself on one of the chairs, sitting with her legs pulled to her chest. She looked like a bird.

"I told you," Max said, talking to Wing. "She can't refuse a challenge."

"The last two hackers who tried to help ended up dead," Wing said, looking right at the woman. "Maybe you should try to help us after all."

The woman smiled and put a hand on Wing's forearm. Wing thought she could feel tentacles of ice flowing from the woman's thin fingers, and fought the urge to pull her arm away. "Darling, don't you worry your pretty little head about me. I'm not scared of any little old man in a wheelchair. I eat men like him for dinner." She flicked a long tongue over her lips like a lizard.

"Cut the shit, you two," Max said. To the woman, he said, "Do you have anything for us?"

With a flourish, the lounge singer removed an envelope from somewhere in the silk shawl that covered her bony shoulders, and set it on the table. Then she flicked it at Wing with a long, white nail. "This who you're looking for, hon?"

The envelope slid into the base of Wing's coffee cup and she had to snatch the manila package before coffee sloshed onto the table. She shot Goshawk an irritated look, but the woman was smiling at Max in a way that made Wing think their relationship was more than strictly business. Wing forced her gaze back to the envelope, unwound its closure-string, and dumped the contents onto the table.

What she saw surprised her. Three glossy photographs were spread on the table. She picked up the first. It was a surveillance shot of an old man in a wheelchair. He was being levered down from a specially made door in the side of a private jet using a mechanized lift. The cameraman had been at a distance, and the light was dim, but she had no trouble making out the wizened face of her client. The second photo, also taken with a telephoto lens, showed the same man being wheeled into the rear of a black sprinter van. The third showed him in what looked like an auction hall, and seemed to have been taken with a hidden camera.

"Your mouth is hanging open," the singer said.

Wing closed it. "How did you—?"

"You don't need to know my methods, darling," Goshawk said.

"I called her from the airport and asked her to get started," Max explained, picking up the photos and examining each with care.

"Who is he?" Wing asked. It galled her to be outdone by this offensive woman, but she had to admit she'd gotten results where others had failed.

"That's where things get murky," the singer said, the smug look disappearing from her face. "I don't have a name, yet. I can tell you who I think he used to be, but not sure it will help you find him."

"So tell," Wing said.

The woman turned so she was talking only to Max. "There seems to be some evidence that he's a former high-ranking officer in the Wehrmacht."

"Hitler's army," Wing said.

The singer turned toward her. "Correct."

"But that would make him—"

"In his nineties," the tattooed woman finished. "If he was eighteen in 1943, he'd be ninety-three today."

"Ok, so why does he not have a name? And how do you know he was in the German army?"

Goshawk's smug look had returned. "My main sources of information are databases from the CIA, Interpol, MI6, and other intelligence agencies. One of my favorites is Mossad's. It's a little trickier to get into, but that agency is meticulous about their intel, and their database is well struc-tured. Unlike the CIA's, which is a mess," she said, rolling her eyes. "Max asked me to find the identity of a super-wealthy old man in a wheelchair. Not much to go on, but I scored a hit in the Mossad database. The Mossad, as you know, keeps extensive records on their hunt to find German officers who perpetrated war crimes at Auschwitz and other concentration camps."

Wing pointed at one of the photos. "This man was at Auschwitz?"

"The Israelis have no direct evidence, at least none that I could find. But he's suspected of being at Treblinka."

"Poland," Wing said. "What do they base their evidence on?"

"Facial recognition. The Israelis have some of the best technology on the planet. They're using large networks of computers to compare current images of suspected Nazis to vintage photos of young German officers."

"And?" Wing said.

"According to their database, the old man in the wheel-chair has a 76.5 percent chance of matching up to a young German officer named Wilbur Lynch."

"And where is this Lynch?" Max asked, intrigued.

"Disappeared," the lounge singer said. "According to both the Mossad's database and Germany's military, there are records on Lynch until 1945. Then, he simply vanished."

"Killed in action?" Max asked.

"Nope. No record at all. No death certificate. No tax records. No marriage license. It's as if all records on the man after 1945 were erased."

Wing contemplated that for a moment. "So we're really no closer to finding him," she stated.

"Not true, but don't get your panties all twisted up, my dear. I'm just getting started. I'll be in touch when I know more." The lounge singer stood from her chair in one fluid motion and planted a wet kiss on Wing's cheek, then turned and stroked Max's jaw. "Now you two behave yourselves," she said with a smirk. "Don't do anything I wouldn't do."

Wing thought she saw her slip something into Max's

hand before disappearing. The door banged shut, and they were left with a lingering scent of vanilla.

"I think she likes you," Max said with a wink.

Wing sipped her cold coffee and ignored his comment. "Now what?" She noticed that whatever the singer had slipped into Max's hand had disappeared.

Max looked up. "Indeed," he said. "That is the question."

FORTY-THREE

Vienna, Austria

The man formerly known as Wilbur Lynch nudged the joystick of his wheelchair and moved closer to the conference table. A star-phone's green light was lit, indicating it was on and connected. Next to the green light was a blinking red light, indicating the call was not yet secure.

"What's taking so long?" Lynch growled. So far, despite his best efforts, the three remaining members of the Asimov family still lived. Lynch wasn't used to failure, and to this point, every resource he'd thrown at them had failed. The bomb maker and Nathan Abrams had both been killed. Wing Octavia, Nathan's so-called protégé, was as inept as a pubescent teenager, and seemed to have disappeared from the grid. The psychopathic and unpredictable assassin, Alexander Bokun, whose fee Lynch had doubled, was Lynch's latest strategy. He sipped scotch from a crystal Old Fashioned glass, hoping the smoky warmth of the brown liquid would soothe his irritation.

"If you want something done right, you have to do it yourself," Lynch grumbled to himself.

"What was that, sir?" Opposite him stood his trusted assistant Mueller, a constant source of comfort. Lynch prized the man's ruthless resourcefulness and undying loyalty. Those values were rare in this world, and Lynch took none of it for granted. Lynch had made Mueller a wealthy man.

"Nothing," Lynch said.

"The call is bouncing around several servers, sir," Mueller said.

"Used to be we didn't need this kind of nonsense," Lynch grumbled.

Finally, the red light shone steady, and a series of clicks emanated from the star-phone's speaker. A scratchy voice came over the line, mixed with static.

"Confound it," Lynch muttered. "We can put a man on the fucking moon, but we can't make clear cell phone connection."

"Yes?" the voice said.

Lynch bristled at the insolence in the man's tone. "Report," Lynch growled.

"Nothing," replied Bokun.

"Goddammit," Lynch growled. "You had all the intel. Even a child could have killed him with the information I gave you."

There was silence on the other end of the line.

"I don't know who you think—" Lynch fumed.

"They're working together now," Bokun said.

"What do you mean they're—?"

"Asimov and the woman. They escaped together."

Lynch contemplated that bit of news. He looked at Mueller, who just shrugged.

"I suppose—"

"I'll find them," Bokun said, interrupting again. "Then I'll kill 'em both. I'll include the woman free of charge."

Then the line went dead. Lynch hurled his water glass at the wall, where it shattered into millions of tiny crystal fragments.

The act seemed to settle his blood pressure, and he looked at Mueller. "Hypothesis?"

"Someone tipped them off?"

Lynch forced himself to breathe. He'd been given this assignment as a test, and he had no intention of failing. He motored his chair over to the floor-to-ceiling window that overlooked the Danube River. His was the tallest building in all of Vienna, and the view of the city usually calmed him. But this time the twinkling lights did nothing to tame his anger. He was failing the test. He knew it, and the Consortium knew it. Perhaps this was some kind of a diabolical force of nature to keep the Council at twelve members. Maybe the number twelve was sacrosanct. The number of apostles. The number of months in a year. The manifestation of the trinity to the four corners of the horizon. The twelve-year cycle in Asia. The twelve names of the sun in Sanskrit. The twelve tribes of Israel. Lynch banged his fist down on the arm of his chair. He'd be damned if he'd let that kind of mumbo-jumbo get in his way. He would kill the Asimov family, and finally be accepted into the Consortium as its thirteenth member. The number thirteen wasn't without significance, he reminded himself. If nothing else, it was inspired by Satan.

"Get Bluefish on the phone," Lynch said, still looking out the window.

"Sir, it's 3:30 a.m. over there."

"I don't give a fuck what time it is," Lynch growled. "Get him on the phone."

He heard Mueller dialing a long string of digits. Finally, Mueller announced, "Bluefish, sir."

Lynch whirled the chair around and approached the table where the phone's green and red lights shown steady.

"Odd. I was just about to call you," the metallic voice from the speaker said. Lynch knew both voices were being run through software designed to disguise their identities. The measures Lynch had to go through just to talk with the man impressed even him. Given Bluefish's position, Lynch was willing to do whatever it took, including pay through the nose to any of the various numbered bank accounts the man, or woman, maintained.

"What about?" Lynch said.

"I got a lead on another hacker trying to dig up information on you," Bluefish said. "You're a popular man these days. I haven't identified him yet, but I will. This one is a little more elusive than the previous ones."

"Don't fail me," Lynch said, his interest piqued.

"Wouldn't dream of it. How'd the operation in Budapest go?"

"Not well," Lynch growled at the phone.

A pause at the other end.

"We'll get him, don't worry. I've got my best team on it." He glanced at Mueller.

Another pause on the other end. "This is taking longer than we'd all like."

"Tell me about it," Lynch said. "I need you to keep watching."

"Of course," the voice said.

Lynch's finger was about to jab at the button to sever the

connection when the voice on the other end said, "I've got something else you might find interesting."

Lynch's finger stopped in mid-air.

"I got a hit on someone on your list."

"Tell me," Lynch said. He dared get his hopes up. Lynch maintained a list of people he was looking for on a secret server he shared with Bluefish. His contact would alert him if any of the names popped up in various places, such as a banking system, immigration, or a cellular network. Each hit generated by Bluefish resulted in a hefty payment to one of the off-shore accounts.

"The name is Wing Octavia."

Lynch smiled. Fate taketh away, and fate giveth.

"Where?"

"Outside Washington, D.C.," said Bluefish. "Her face was picked up on a surveillance camera in downtown Alexandria. One of my algorithms matched her face with the image you provided."

"Excellent," Lynch said.

"My standard fee applies," Bluefish said. "I'll send you the details."

"Money well spent," Lynch said, but the line was already dead.

Lynch looked at Mueller.

"The National Security Agency of the United States is a helpful ally, no?" Mueller asked.

Lynch moved his chair back over to the window and gazed out. "Get Cezar on the phone. We need to tighten the screws on our old friend Wing. Then get me Yuri Aristov. It's time to put him in play."

Suddenly, Lynch felt back on his game.

FORTY-FOUR

Alexandria, Virginia

Max pulled the ball cap tighter on his head and slipped on a pair of clear, thick-rimmed glasses. He'd purchased a black zip-up hoodie at the airport and wore that over a black T-shirt and jeans. A compact pistol was in a holster hidden by the hoodie. He'd been watching the building across the street for several hours from a rented white SUV, and knew the apartment was empty. He'd seen its sole occupant leave twenty minutes ago and head down the street on foot.

The apartment building was one of those gentrified, renovated warehouses that had been converted to loft-style condominiums. It was four stories high, with floor-to-ceiling windows in each unit. Tiny, narrow balconies lined the front, and Max wondered why any architect would design such a small space. There wasn't even room to enjoy a cigarette.

Reconnaissance earlier that day indicated the rear of the building was lined with fire-escape ladders and platforms, and backed up to an alley. The first floor had a restaurant-bar combination that looked to be popular with the younger set, and a dog-grooming shop was next to that, closed and dark. It was a populated and busy area, so Max decided on a direct, frontal approach instead of taking the risk he'd be spotted on the fire escape. He stepped out of the SUV and headed toward the building.

The front doors led to a small vestibule containing a set of doorbells with names printed next to them. Max put his hand in his pocket and palmed a thin strip of metal. Assuming he was on camera, he hunched over the lock and made like he was using a key. He slipped the strip of metal into the lock, obscuring it from the camera's view with his hands. He lightly jiggled the strip of metal up and down until the tumblers gave way and the door opened. Max used the stairwell and took the stairs two at a time to the third floor. He stepped onto the plush carpet, seeing no one. At the third door on the right, he stopped and did the same trick with the strip of metal on that lock. A few seconds later, he was in.

He stepped into an open floor plan with a wide living room/kitchen combination. The couch and chairs were separated from the kitchen area by a long center island topped with granite. Silver appliances gleamed in the neon lights coming through the front windows. The furniture was Scandinavian, made from teak-colored woods and dark leathers. A wide-screen television sat on a low table. He saw no family photos, no keepsakes from travel. The place looked un-lived-in except for a half-empty bottle of vodka on the kitchen island, its cap off. A door off the living room led to a single bedroom with an unmade king-sized bed covered with white sheets. Max did a quick search of the unit and found it empty. He helped himself to a glass of the vodka with ice, grabbed the TV remote, and pulled a leather chair into the shadows and sat. He turned the television on to a news channel and left the sound off. He sipped the vodka and resisted the urge to smoke, absently watching the images scrolling by on the television. He absently toyed with the pistol on his lap.

He didn't have to wait long. Soon, he heard scratching at the front door, like someone was trying to use a key. The door opened and he saw Kate enter the room. Or rather, he saw her stumble into the room, pulling a man behind her. Her curly hair flew wild and she was having trouble staying upright on tall heels.

Max sized up the man from his spot in the shadows. Kate's date was average height and build and wore a suit with a red tie undone at the neck. He was handsome but boyish, and looked to Max like a stockbroker, or maybe a lawyer.

Kate dropped her purse on the floor, spun around, and shut the door. The man tracked her with his eyes, swaying slightly, and dropped his suit jacket next to her purse. As the door shut, the stockbroker tried to kiss her. She wiggled free and moved into the bedroom, the man close on her heels.

Max set his glass on the floor, stood, and moved quickly to the bedroom's doorway, gun in hand. His shoes were silent on the wood floor. He peeked in, seeing Kate disappear into the bathroom. The man's back was to the door, and he was unbuttoning his shirt.

Max reversed his grip on the pistol, took a quiet step into the room, and hit the man in the temple with the butt of the gun. The man's knees crumpled and he went down. Just then, the door to the bathroom opened and Kate emerged, wiping her hands on a towel.

"I think—" She froze in mid-stride.

Max put the index finger of his free hand to his lips, then pulled off the hat and glasses.

"What the fuck, Max?" She wasn't smiling, and with the light from the bathroom, he could see dark circles under her eyes.

Max put the gun in his waistband. "Help me drag this guy out of here," he said.

"Fuck you," Kate said. "You clocked him. You drag him outta here." She left the bedroom.

Max grabbed the guy by the armpits and pulled him out of the bedroom and through the living room. Kate tossed the man's jacket onto his stomach and held the door. Max dragged the guy down the hall and manhandled him into the stairwell, where he left him propped against the wall. He figured the man would wake up with an enormous headache, wonder how he'd gotten there, then simply go home and sleep it off.

"Who's the guy?" Max asked when he returned to Kate's apartment.

"You've got a lot of nerve," Kate said. Her eyes flashed. She looked as angry as Max had ever seen her. She was starting a kettle on the stove.

"Come on," Max said, smiling. "I just saved you from bad sex and an awkward morning. What are you doing dragging home some random stockbroker anyway?"

She looked away. "How do you know he's a stockbroker?"

"Am I right?"

"Don't know, actually." She fussed with a can of instant coffee, keeping her back to Max.

"What's his name?" Max asked.

"Fuck you," she said.

Kate turned and handed him a cup of watery brown liquid. He inhaled, then wrinkled his nose. He hadn't had a good cup of coffee since he'd been in Turkey, and it looked like he was going to have to wait a while longer. Kate walked over and sat on the couch. She reclined and pulled an afghan over herself, glancing absently at the television. An attractive blonde was animatedly gesturing at a colorful map of the metro area, pointing to a large cold front positioned to the west. Max pulled the leather chair into its old position and sat down.

"Where the fuck have you been?" Kate asked. "Do you know what I've been through because of you? And why are you here, anyway?"

"It was the only way I could think of to talk privately. I don't trust your friends at the CIA."

"You couldn't just meet me at a park bench like everyone else who doesn't trust the CIA?"

"Not my style," Max said. He reached into a pocket and took out a piece of paper, unfolded it, and set it on the coffee table. "Printed this out this morning. Was this you guys?"

Kate leaned forward and glanced at it. "I don't read Ukrainian," she said, sitting back.

He recited the headline from memory. "Russian mob boss, Victor Volkov, condemns the killing of his family."

Kate sat up straight and looked at him. "What did you say?"

"A drone strike in Eastern Ukraine took out Volkov's family, but missed him," Max explained. "By quite a margin, it seems. He had sent his family on to Donetsk ahead of him. He planned to follow the next day. But Volkov was a hundred kilometers away when the missile hit. It took out fifteen people, including his wife, two daughters, one of his lieutenants, a handful of his foot soldiers, and several civilians."

Kate looked more sober now.

"I didn't see any word of this in the US news media," Max said.

"Not surprised," she said.

"I take it you knew nothing about this?"

"Thanks to you, I no longer operate that group," she said. "I'm totally out of the loop."

Max sat back. That explained at least part of her anger. "What happened?"

Kate peered into her coffee and didn't speak for a long time. When she finally did, she kept her gaze locked on her cup. She told him how the Director had demoted her and was shutting down the CIA's human asset program.

The fact that the CIA was no longer going to protect him and his family was not a shock. Because of the leaks within Kate's team, the arrangement hadn't offered them much protection anyway. There might be longer-term implications if they could ever unearth the mole. A CIA-sponsored witness protection plan offered them some perks Max couldn't get elsewhere, like official new US identities. It also meant he was going to lose the income Kate had promised him. On the positive side, now he didn't have to work for her and he could focus on his family's safety without interruption. Max was not, however, so obtuse that he didn't realize Kate's career had just been ruined.

"Would it help you if I went and took out Volkov?"

Kate threw up her hands and let out an exasperated moan. "I don't know, Max. Maybe. I'm not sure I care anymore."

"I realize I may have been the lightning rod for this,"

Max said. "But it sounds like the Director had already made up her mind and was going to shut us down anyway."

"Maybe you're right, Kate said. She sipped her coffee. "Why are you—?"

Max held his hand up, distracted by something on the television. The station had switched from the blond weather woman to a tall man in a windbreaker reporting live. He stood next to a yellow police line, and several rescue vehicles and police cars, their lights flashing, were parked haphazardly around him. In the background stood a two-story motel, its exterior second-floor walkway lined with gawkers.

"What is it?" Kate asked, following his gaze to the television.

"Hold on." He grabbed the remote and punched the volume button. The reporter's voice came through the TV's speakers.

"—where police are saying at least two men are dead after what appears to be a shootout between several gunmen. Details are scarce, but eyewitnesses are reporting that a black SUV entered the parking lot and started shooting automatic gunfire at the motel. Then several men jumped out – some people are saying two men, some are saying three. They used a battering ram to break down a door, then entered the room with guns drawn. People heard more gunshots. A few moment later, the SUV left the parking lot and disappeared."

"Max! What is this about?"

Max jumped to his feet. "That's the hotel where I left Wing."

FORTY-FIVE

Alexandria, Virginia

Max punched the gas and spun the wheel, causing the tires to screech as they exited the parking garage in Kate's Audi. Max drove with one hand, hitting a speed-dial button on his phone with his other.

"You might want to keep to the speed limit so we don't get pulled over," Kate said, fumbling for her seatbelt.

Max ignored her. The phone was ringing with no answer. He ended the connection, then redialed. The number was to a disposable burner phone Wing had purchased at a convenience store for cash when they'd arrived in Alexandria the previous evening.

"Can you explain to me how you came to be traveling with your mortal enemy?" Kate asked.

Max ignored her, distracted, listening to the drone of the ringing. Dread was settling into his belly. He was pinning his hopes on the fact that the reporter hadn't mentioned anything about a dead woman.

Max ended the call and pushed the accelerator down. His other hope was that perhaps the altercation at the hotel hadn't been centered around Wing. She'd grown more reserved since their meeting with Goshawk, and perhaps she'd decided against their partnership after all. Before leaving France, they'd argued about tactics, with her advocating a trip to Germany to track down leads she had with the German Secret Service and Max making a case to go to the US to connect with Kate. Maybe Wing was on her way back to Europe.

"Max!"

He looked over, startled. "Right, sorry."

In as few words as possible, he filled Kate in, omitting his conversation with Dmitry, but telling her about Rugov and his brief stay in Lubyanka, and then his incarceration at Wing's operational headquarters. He finished with the story of their escape. "She's probably on her way back to Europe."

"Holy crap, Max."

"Tell me about it."

"What made you trust her?" Kate was looking at Max, surprised.

"It was my only option." He cranked the wheel hard and the Audi leaned into a right turn. The motel where he'd left Wing was a few blocks up.

Suddenly, he jammed on the brakes and brought the sedan to a halt next to a curb.

"What are you doing?" Kate asked.

Max pointed up ahead. A block away were a half-dozen squad cars marked with the words *Alexandria Police Department*, their red and blue lights flashing, parked in a semi-circle around a motel parking lot. Several white-shirted paramedics stood talking in a circle near three idle ambulances, their rear doors open. Yellow crime-scene tape encircled the parking lot. A group of men were setting up portable flood lights. Several of the motel's occupants stood on the second floor's open walkway, watching the action.

"I'll find out what's going on," Kate said. She pulled out her CIA credentials. She stepped out of the car and walked toward the motel.

Max kept his eye on the rearview mirror and the two side mirrors as he sat idle. He eased the pistol onto his lap and absently ran a finger along the barrel. The cold metal felt reassuring.

Things were starting to slip out of control. His CIA protection was gone. The memory card had disappeared, and he had no leads on its whereabouts. Wing's client, a man who presumably might have information on his parents' killer, was a ghost. And now it looked as if Wing had somehow been compromised, and was possibly dead.

His heart skipped a beat at the thought. Max had felt drawn to Wing, perhaps from a shared connection over their occupations and background. The feeling was a little foreign to him, and he wasn't sure he liked it. He knew his first priority was to his family, but he couldn't help his feelings for Wing.

If you're going through hell, son, you might as well keep going, his father would often quip. Later, Max learned that quote was attributed to Winston Churchill.

Kate stood at the edge of the police line talking with a stooped man wearing a sport coat. He looked haggard and irritated, but seemed to be answering Kate's questions.

Max's smartphone rang. He glanced at the screen and saw *unknown caller*. Thinking it might be Wing, he stabbed at the answer button. Instead of her voice, he heard a series of clicks, then words that were distorted by the metallic sound of security software.

"Max, I need you to listen. I only have a second." It was Goshawk. He could hear rapid typing in the background.

"What is it?"

"I've been asked to relay a message to you."

Max picked up stress in her voice. "Is everything alright?"

"Just listen." Then she recited as if reading a prepared statement. "If you want to see Wing Octavia alive, the pleasure of your company is requested at 40°56'32.0" north, 75°43'51.9."

"Who sent—?" Max started to ask. But Goshawk had already ended the call.

Max wasted no time in typing the GPS coordinates into a mapping app on his phone. While the map loaded, he considered the phone call. Goshawk's brusqueness was uncharacteristic, even for her. He hoped everything was alright. The last thing he needed was to have someone else to worry about. The most alarming thing was that whoever had taken Wing seemed to also have figured out how to contact him through Goshawk. Max could think of only one person who had that kind of power.

Max looked at his phone. The map had come into focus and showed a small blue dot in an area colored in green. Max scaled the map down and saw that the blue dot was located somewhere in Eastern Pennsylvania. He tapped on the *directions* icon, and a second later, the app informed him that he was 213 miles from the location of the blue dot.

The passenger door opened and Kate slid in. Max handed her his phone, put the car in gear, pulled out of the spot, and performed a u-turn with screeching tires.

"Where are we going?" Kate asked, looking at the screen of his phone.

Max relayed the brief conversation he'd had with Goshawk.

"I guess you got more intel than I did," Kate said. "According to the detective in charge of the scene, hotel residents reported hearing gunshots at about one a.m. The occasional gunshot is normal for that neighborhood, but someone called the cops after what they described as 'a hail of bullets from automatic weapons' directed at a room on the first level."

"What room number?"

"121," Kate said.

"That was our room," Max said.

"The room was shot to pieces," Kate continued. "Witnesses reported seeing a large, dark-colored SUV pull up just before the shooting started."

"What about casualties?" Max asked.

"According to witnesses, the automatic gunfire finally ceased. A few minutes later, more gunfire was reported. This one was described as sounding more like pops, and more sporadic."

"A pistol," Max said. "Casualties?" he repeated.

"Or several pistols," Kate said. "Cops arrived only a few minutes after the final volley of shots, which is impressive in this town."

"Goddammit, Kate. Any casualties?"

"Police found no sign of a black SUV. In room 121, they found two bodies, both male, Caucasian, of Slavic or Eastern European descent."

"No body of a small Asian woman?"

"Negative. I asked specifically, which of course made the detective curious."

"So they shoot up the room," Max said. "Wing somehow survives the initial barrage. Then they storm the place and she manages to take out two of them before being overwhelmed and taken hostage."

"Right. Or, she was killed and they took her body to cover up that fact."

"Right," Max said. "Either way, our only lead is these GPS coordinates." He made a left turn onto the George Washington Parkway, then pushed the Audi up to ninety mph, about as fast as he dared on the vacant but narrow and curvy road out of DC.

FORTY-SIX

Eastern Pennsylvania, near the town of Jim Thorpe

The Audi bumped along a washed-out dirt road. Periodically the bottom of the car would scrape on a rock, causing Kate to grimace. Their journey had gone from the interstate to a main street through the small town of Jim Thorpe, to a winding paved road that followed a river, to the rutted, hilly two-track they were now on. Kate was navigating using the mapping application on Max's phone.

As they drove, a morning sky with a red glow gave way to low, dark clouds. The occasional rumble of thunder could be heard somewhere in the distance. The Audi's in-dash clock read 7:45.

During the drive, Kate had called Kaamil and inquired about the scene in Alexandria and any possible police action near Jim Thorpe, Pennsylvania, the only town near the coordinates Max had been given. Kaamil had said details were still sketchy on the scene in Alexandria, and that there were no reports of any police activity near Jim

Thorpe. He'd keep them informed on any new developments.

Max turned onto a narrow track with branches that scraped the sides of the sedan. "We're probably two hundred yards from the location indicated by the coordinates," Kate said, looking down at the screen. Max found a place to turn the car off the road. He executed a three-point turn with the Audi, scraping the bottom twice on the raised center of the dirt track. He parked in a turnoff facing the way they'd come.

"Let's go on foot from here," Max said. He opened the car door and stepped out, breathing in the fresh scent of pine needles. The odor reminded him of operations he'd performed in the Caucasus Mountains of Georgia, near southern Russia. He shuddered at the memory of what he'd had to do, and put it out of his mind. It made him sad that such a pleasing scent was associated with those terrible memories.

Kate rummaged in the trunk, then emerged and handed him a shotgun. He was pleased to find the gun was a semi-automatic, which offered obvious benefits over its pump-action cousin. He ensured the weapon was loaded and accepted a handful of shells from Kate, which he stuffed in his pocket.

"We're not exactly heavily armed," Max said. They had two pistols and a shotgun between them. "Anything else in there?"

"This will have to do." Kate slammed the trunk, then turned and sniffed. "Do you smell smoke?"

Max sniffed the air again. The wind had shifted, and he caught a tinge of burning wood. "Yes. Come on."

With Max in front, they set off at a cautious pace up the gently sloping road. He held the shotgun at the ready, and

Kate held her pistol down by her leg. The wind picked up and the tree branches swayed and rustled. As they walked, the smell of smoke grew stronger. Periodically, Max stopped to listen. He heard nothing but the sounds of the forest.

Finally, the road turned into an even narrower drive and Max saw a mailbox off to the left. A drop of rain hit him as he walked. After a quick hike, they emerged into a clearing that contained a large, new-looking log cabin. The home had an A-frame cathedral-style roof with expansive windows looking out over a tree-lined valley. A gravel driveway led to a two-car garage, and a small manicured lawn surrounded by a freshly tended flowerbed greeted visitors at the front door. The home was impeccably kept, and looked like it could be featured in *Home & Garden*.

Max smelled smoke again. He glanced around, looking for the source. Everything was silent, still. Then he looked at the apex of the roof and noticed a small chimney hidden from view by the crown of the roof. A thin thread of smoke curled out from under the chimney cap.

FORTY-SEVEN

Eastern Pennsylvania, near the town of Jim Thorpe

Perplexed, Max looked back at Kate. She shrugged her shoulders. He had expected to find guards, or some kind of trap. He sure didn't think he'd be walking into an idyllic setting in the woods. He led Kate back down the road and out of sight of the cabin. "Are you sure we have the right GPS coordinates?"

Kate fiddled with the phone. "Yes, I'm sure." She showed the screen to Max. He looked closely and saw the numbers as they'd been reported from Goshawk. "It's not like these houses are close together," Kate said. "The next one looks to be half a mile away, so this has to be it."

Max nodded, then looked around. Another raindrop hit him on the top of the head. The scene felt odd to him, like it was just a normal log cabin in the woods. He pictured someone curled up in front of the fire, cup of hot chocolate in hand, dog at their feet, reading a novel.

"Let's recon the house," Max said. "I bet we have the

wrong property. Maybe Goshawk transposed a number. She did seem awfully distracted. You take the left side, I'll take the right. Meet back here in ten minutes. Let's sync watches."

"No watch," Kate said, waving his phone in the air.

"Fine. Can I have my phone back?"

She tossed it to him, turned, and disappeared into the woods. Max kept the shotgun angled down and hiked back to the clearing. Smoke still wafted from the chimney. He didn't like doing this in the daylight, but wasn't going to wait until nighttime. He followed the tree line to the right, walked past a horseshoe pitch, and came around to the side of the house. He darted across the neatly cut yard and put his back to the wall next to a door on the side of the garage. He tried the knob, and was surprised to find it unlocked. A glance through the door's window ensured the garage was empty. He opened the door, ducked in, and found various lawn tools, a riding mower, and some sporting equipment. Parked nose-out was a forest-green, four-door Jeep with oversized tires. He put his hand on the hood, and found it cold. He opened the driver's side door and searched the interior. Under the rubber floor mat, he found a key with *Jeep* emblazoned on it. He pocketed the key.

Max left the garage, shutting the door behind him, and moved around to the back of the house. He found himself below a deck that ran the length of the house, a row of sliding glass doors giving him access to the ground level. He chanced a glance in and saw a family room, complete with a large sectional couch, an enormous television, and a coffee table. A piece of exercise equipment stood behind the sectional facing the TV. The room was unoccupied. He tried the sliding door and found it locked. Glancing at his watch, he turned away from the house. More raindrops hit him as he dashed across the lawn, disappeared into the trees, and found his way back to the road.

"Over here," Kate hissed.

He found her crouched down next to a tree, pistol in her hand.

"Report," Max said.

"Bedrooms on the left side of the house. Beds made. No clothing or bags visible. Nothing remarkable. Couldn't see into the main level without getting up on the deck. Too risky."

"Agreed," Max said. He reported his findings. "Something's not right with this scene."

"I say we just knock on the door," Kate said. "Any more of this skulking around and someone is going to call the cops. Or we'll get a shotgun blast to the head."

Max nodded. It hadn't occurred to him to simply knock on the door. He was getting mentally prepared to storm the house through the basement. "Good idea," he said. "We don't need to be terrorizing ordinary citizens. I'd feel better if one of us stayed behind to keep watch on the road."

Kate grabbed the shotgun from his hand. "I'll stay, you go. But if Granny offers you a mimosa, come get me." She winked at him.

He set off down the drive, leaving Kate hidden among the trees. Max had the pistol in its holster, concealed by his sweatshirt. As he crossed the clearing in front of the house, Max saw lightning flash and heard thunder directly overhead. Then the skies opened and water began to pour down in buckets. He dashed across the circle drive and up the two steps to the front porch. Two green Adirondack chairs stood to one side of the front door. He glanced behind him and saw no one, then knocked hard on the door.

In response to his knock, Max heard a dog barking

somewhere deep within the house. He was just about to bang his fist on the door again when it swung inward. Max had his hand cocked to yank out his pistol, but hesitated when he saw the house's occupant. A stooped old man stood in front of him wearing a dirty apron over a red flannel shirt. Suspenders held up baggy dungarees and shearling stuck out the tops of red flannel slippers. The old man removed a pipe from his mouth and in a loud voice, said, "Help ya?" Next to the man sat a docile-looking yellow-haired dog.

Surprised, Max hesitated. Before he could say anything, the old man growled, "Whatever yar sellin' son, I a'int buyin', so be off wit' ya."

Something about the man's voice sounded vaguely familiar. It had a hard edge to it, like he might be from Eastern Europe but was trying to disguise it with an American accent. Max looked hard at the man's craggy face, but recognition didn't come. He suddenly felt silly.

"I'm sorry, sir. I must have the wrong house," Max said. Then the dog barked.

With surprising agility, the old man withdrew a pair of thick glasses from his breast pocket and shoved them on his face, then leaned forward, peering through the spectacles.

"Ah, yes," the man said. "You must be Mikhail Asimov."

Shocked, Max's hand instinctively moved for his pistol.

The old man was talking before Max's gun was out. "No need for that, Mikhail. There's no danger here for you."

Max brought the gun out, but held it pointed to the side. The dog growled, showing its fangs.

"Who are you?" Max demanded. "Why are you here? Where is Wing Octavia?"

The old man turned, stooped to pet the dog's head, and

started walking back into the house. The dog gave one final snarl, then turned and followed the old man. The front door was still open.

"Come on in," the old man called out. "And invite your lady friend in before she catches pneumonia out there in the rain."

FORTY-EIGHT

Eastern Pennsylvania, near the town of Jim Thorpe

Max turned and signaled Kate to join him. She ran up to the porch, hair plastered to her forehead from the rain, a quizzical look on her face.

"Stand guard in the living room, where you can see the driveway," Max said. "Fill you in later."

Max stepped through the cabin's front door and saw an odd mixture of rustic log cabin bric-a-brac combined with modern technical gear. The log walls of the home were covered with fishing tackle, stuffed and mounted fish, and hunting paraphernalia. Over a deep leather couch, mounted on the wall, was the head of an elk with an impressive rack of antlers. He also noticed a fish-eye security camera on the ceiling of the hallway and a large-screen television opposite the couch. He assumed someone was watching through the security camera. Pistol still out, Max followed the dog into the kitchen, where the old man stood at a massive, wrought-iron stove.

The cabin's interior smelled like baked goods and ginger, and the counters were filled with all manner of cooking supplies. The stove held a large teapot, and three mugs were set out on a tray. A large-screen monitor was set on the kitchen table, a small webcam mounted on top. The old man was at the stove, fussing with the teapot.

The wall opposite the kitchen's entryway was two stories high and comprised of floor-to-ceiling windows that showed a stunning view of the green valley below. A blue tentacle of a lake was visible at the bottom of the valley. He moved away from the window, not wishing to be exposed.

"That's Black Moshannon Lake," the old man said. "Odd names for things in this country, don't you think, Mikhail? Not like home, where things are named like you'd expect."

Max turned and looked hard at the old man. His face was weather beaten, with deep wrinkles and a bulbous nose. He had grey stubble that gave him the look of a drunk the morning after a bender. A few tufts of white hair stuck out from under a small, black watch cap.

"Do I know you?" Max asked. The man fussed at the stove, ignoring Max's question.

The old man turned toward Max with two mugs. He handed one to Max, who could smell the deep, rich scent of black Darjeeling tea. Then the old man hobbled through a large archway that led from the kitchen into the living room. Max heard Kate thank him for the tea.

When he returned, the old man reached into the oven with a towel, and emerged with a tray of light brown cookies. The smell of ginger was stronger now, and Max was reminded of his childhood.

"They're not from Tula," the old man said, naming the

town in western Russia famous for its gingerbread, "but they are my mother's recipe. I think you'll enjoy them."

Despite the pull of the traditional Russian treat, Max hesitated.

The old man grabbed one and took a bite. "Not poisoned, Mikhail," he mumbled through the mouthful.

Max took one for himself and sniffed it, inhaling the pungent aroma of ginger.

The old man walked over to a kitchen table that looked homemade, hewn from rough logs, and set down a tray of cookies and a teapot. He poured himself a cup and fell heavily into a chair. The dog, who had followed the man everywhere, lay down at his feet.

"Come," he said to Max. "Sit. Let's talk."

Max glanced through the tall windows and took note of the stand of trees to the left of the chasm that opened down to the lake. If he sat at the table, he'd be in the direct line of fire of anyone hidden in the woods with a sniper rifle. He remained standing.

"Fine. Suit yourself," the old man said, taking another cookie. "It's the little things from the homeland you start to miss, you know. The vodka is watered down. The cigarettes are bland. The tea is bitter. The women are not as adventurous. This is my way of staying connected."

Max took a bite of his cookie, relishing the treat's soft center. The strong flavor of ginger spread through his mouth, bringing him instantly back to his childhood in his mother's kitchen. Each weekend, she'd bake a large batch of the cookies, and he'd take two of them to school along with the rest of his lunch.

"Where's Wing?" Max asked, getting antsy. "And who are you, and why are you here? And how do you know my name?"

The man gazed out the window, slowly nodding his head. "The stuff I've seen in my lifetime, Mikhail. One comes to know a lot."

"You talk in riddles while Wing is missing. Can we get to the point?"

The old man turned back to him. "Yes, I understand. We sit, enjoying cookies and tea from the homeland, while she blows in the wind."

Then Max heard Kate gasp. She'd stuck her head in the kitchen, and was staring at the old man. "You're Yuri Aristov, aren't you? How the fuck—?"

The old man turned to Kate. "I was wondering how long it would take you to figure it out. I suspect I'm famous in your circles. Or maybe I should say, *infamous*."

Max instantly recognized the name as the KGB's most famous defector. Yuri Aristov had been a Russian general who disappeared in 1982. Everyone assumed he'd defected to the United States, but there had been no direct evidence.

"So the rumors are true?" Max asked.

The old man took a sip of his tea with a shaky hand and set the mug down on the table with a *thunk*.

"Yes, Mikhail. The rumors are true. Every day is a blessing for me now, so it doesn't matter who knows. On September 15, 1982, I walked into the US embassy in West Berlin and disappeared. I've been living in Florida ever since. The Americans keep waiting for me to die, but inconveniently, I keep hanging on. I think it's the cigarettes and the vodka, but my doctor says it's just my genes." He laughed, sending a spray of crumbs from his mouth.

Max caught Kate's eye. "That true?" Max asked.

Kate nodded. "His story is legend at the CIA. One of the greatest coups of the CIA's actions during the Cold War. He spied for us for years, until things got too hot and they had to pull him out." She looked at Aristov. "You gave us the details of the Soviet Union's chemical weapons program."

Aristov nodded. "That's why I defected. Later I found out the US had used that information to bolster their own secret chemical weapons program. But by that time, I was stuck. I was a dead man if I stuck my head up anywhere, so I disappeared into the CIA's protection program and spent my days walking the beaches of southern Florida."

"The US doesn't have a chemical weapons program," Kate said. "Nixon renounced their use in '69."

Aristov cocked his head at her. "Don't they?"

Kate looked angry. "Yes. There is no record of us even deploying chemical weapons since World War II."

"That doesn't mean the weapons aren't stockpiled," Aristov said.

Kate leaned back against the counter and crossed her arms, looking miffed.

"Why are you here right now?" Max asked.

The old man looked back at him. "Any idea what it took for this old man to carry all this gear and cooking equipment in from the car? I'm not as spry as I used to be, you know."

Max was growing impatient, but he also wanted to humor the old man. Yuri Aristov was a legend, and now a kindred spirit. He was another man who had defied the KGB and lived to tell about it. Max was torn between wanting to know what was in the man's head and the urgency of finding Wing. He forced himself to keep his mouth shut.

The old man sighed. "I've been asked to be an emissary."

"By whom?" Max prompted.

Aristov took a long sip of his tea, then refilled his cup

from the pot. He removed a watch from the pocket of his apron. With shaking hands, he managed to get it open, muttering to himself while he studied the watch face. Then he said, "Ms. Shaw, will you please excuse Mikhail and me?"

Kate looked at Max expectantly. "What you have to say you can say in front of her," Max said.

"I'm sorry," Aristov said. "I can't permit it. I'm under strict instructions. What we're about to do is for your eyes only."

"Do you mind standing guard on the porch?" Max asked. "I'll keep this as brief as possible."

Kate hesitated, then she strode from the room. A minute later, he heard the front door open, then slam. He looked at Aristov expectantly.

The old man reached over and switched on the monitor.

"Before we start, Mikhail, how do you say – please don't blame the messenger."

"I believe it's please don't *shoot* the messenger," Max said.

"Yes, that's it," Aristov said. "Please don't shoot me."

The monitor had warmed up and now Max could see a vast and ornate room depicted on the screen. Rows of artwork hung along both walls of what looked like the nave of a massive cathedral. Warm light spilled from narrow stained glass windows. Where he expected to see rows of church pews, there were several leather-clad benches sitting parallel to the walls. Velvet ropes stood in front of each work of art, giving the impression of a museum.

The old man tapped on the screen of the small tablet. "We're muted now," he said, then added, "I'm doing this as a favor to Wilbur Lynch."

At the sound of the name, Max tensed. "How do you—?"

The old man held up a hand, palm out. His fingers were misshapen and bent with age. "In our world," Aristov said, pointing first at himself, then at Max. "You're either a friend of Wilbur Lynch, or you're an enemy. Friends prosper. Enemies suffer, and most die."

"Is he holding Wing?" Max asked, his brow furrowed and his voice low.

Yuri Aristov shrugged. "I know nothing, Mikhail. You must approach the monitor, otherwise he will not be able to see you."

Max glanced out the window. The clouds had moved lower, and a layer of heavy dark fog prevented him from seeing the tree line. All that was visible was a plunging crevasse leading to the lake below.

"Your caution is warranted," Aristov said. The old man rose from the table, and with an effort, moved to the stove and set the kettle on a flame. Max got an idea and grasped the edge of the table and pulled, scraping it across the wood floor several feet toward the center of the kitchen. Then he moved a chair to the table and sat down in front of the monitor. Now, he was sheltered from a possible sniper.

Aristov watched, seemingly amused. "There will come a time, my friend, when you'll grow weary of looking over your shoulder. Then you'll find yourself wishing for someone to come and end it all."

"I'm already weary," Max grumbled. "But I'll not rest until my nephew is grown and safe and able to take care of himself."

"How paternal of you," the old man said. "I guess maybe you did inherit that gene from your father after all." Glancing at his watch, Aristov said, "Two minutes."

FORTY-NINE

Eastern Pennsylvania, near the town of Jim Thorpe

Max's nerves were taut as he peered into the monitor, waiting for something to happen. He felt exposed, like he'd been lured into complacency by a relic from Russia's past and memories of his own childhood. He felt better knowing Kate was outside on patrol with the shotgun. He couldn't think of any other move than to let it play out.

Max looked over at Aristov. "Assuming Lynch is the man who has been trying to kill my family, and assuming he knew where I'd be, why isn't he sending an attack team to take me out?"

"I wondered the same thing," Aristov said. "Lynch is a shrewd man. He must think there is some up side to keeping you alive."

"By now, I doubt he thinks I'm an easy mark," Max said.

"So maybe he wants to make a deal."

Max pondered that. "How do you know him? And why,

if you're in the protection of the CIA, are you even in contact with him?"

Just then, Max heard a faint mechanical whir come through the monitor. He tensed. Nothing moved in the large room on the screen. The noise grew louder, until finally the image of a man in a wheelchair appeared in front of the camera. Max realized the sound had come from the wheelchair's motor, and that he had approached the screen from behind the video camera. The man was moving his mouth, but Max couldn't hear any words. Then he remembered to un-mute the sound, and a high-pitched voice come through the monitor.

"—you come face to face with your mortal enemy, is it, Mikhail? Or should I call you Max Austin?"

Max stayed silent and took in the man on the other side of the camera. He looked like a skeleton, an apparition from some other plane. His skin was pale yellow, almost tinged with green. The man's cheeks were sunken in so far that the shadows made it look as though he had holes in his face. He had a habit of finishing his sentences with a wet, wicked-looking grin. Wisps of white hair floated around his head like they were charged with static. When he talked, long, bony fingers toyed with the controls of his wheelchair. The man's eyes blazed at Max through the monitor, and showed a strength that was unsettling; a reminder that his adversary was truly a dangerous man. Max said nothing, and waited.

"Thank you for agreeing to meet with me," said the old man in the wheelchair. "Yuri, our mutual friend there, can be quite convincing, can he not?"

Again, Max said nothing.

"You and Yuri share some history, you know. You should—"

Tired of the game, Max interrupted. "Wilbur Lynch, if I'm not mistaken?"

A brief flash of annoyance crossed the man's face but was gone in an instant, replaced by an eerie grin. Lynch flicked a tongue over his lips before speaking.

"Yes, yes," he said. "I understand your friend – what is her name? Goshawk? Yes, Goshawk managed to penetrate some of my defenses."

When he said Goshawk's name, Max's blood chilled.

"Don't worry," the old man continued. "We'll find her. And when we do, we'll make an example of her just like we do anyone who tries to determine my identity. We'll let her run for a while, like a marlin on the end of a line. She'll wear herself out, then she'll make a mistake. When she does, we'll put an end to her amateur singing career."

"You'll never find her," Max said, even though his confidence wavered. "She's too good for you."

Lynch cackled with laughter. His head tipped back and Max saw spittle fly from his mouth. His body shook in the oversized suit like a bag of bones. Finally, he calmed down enough to talk. "Even you don't believe that, Max Austin," Lynch said. "Max Austin. I like that name. It's got a certain ring to it. Like you should be wearing cowboy boots and driving a pickup truck. Very American."

"You set this meeting. What do you want in exchange for Wing? If it's me you want, let's discuss a trade."

"Ah, a man after my own heart. No beating around the bush." Lynch flicked the joystick on his wheelchair and moved a little closer to the video camera. "First, let me congratulate you. You've proven far more resilient than I thought possible. Poor old Nathan. I'm disappointed you dispatched him so easily. He was very useful. Then, somehow, you managed to convince the beautiful Wing Octavia to switch teams. Maybe she gazed into your eyes and was smitten, who knows. You've even eluded my new friend Aleksander Bokun—"

"Get on with it, Lynch," Max broke in. "You're wasting time."

Lynch's smile faded. He hunched his frail body and tried to get even closer to the camera. "Did your mother teach you no manners, Mikhail? When someone is paying you a compliment, you're supposed to—"

"I'm five seconds away from shutting this camera down," Max said. "For all I know, you've got a team en route and you're just killing time until they arrive."

Lynch sat back, and let out an audible sigh. "I'm here to acknowledge we've reached a stalemate. I'm admitting I underestimated your abilities. Rather than continuing to throw my forces at you like the Persians at Thermopylae, I thought perhaps we could discuss an agreement, like mature adversaries."

Max let out a snort. "I think you must have misread my intentions. I'm not in the business of giving my enemies any quarter. You've made it clear that my family will only be safe when everyone who wants us dead is removed from the face of the earth. You started this thing, but I'm going to finish it. I'm coming for you, Lynch."

Lynch's smile faded, and his fingers drummed a pattern on the wheelchair's arm, then moved to toy with the chair's joystick. "There is a major flaw in your assumptions," he finally said, letting that statement hang in the air.

Max was getting agitated, but he knew he needed to let this play out. The more information he had on Lynch, the better chance he had of finding him. He wanted to keep the man talking. "What flaw is that?"

"You were trained for one thing, Mikhail. I know, I've

seen the file. I know all about you. I know your father taught you to follow in his footsteps. I know he and the KGB molded you into a killer, a cold-blooded machine capable of one thing, and one thing only. Killing." Lynch paused to let that sink in.

"Your solution to every problem is to fall back on the one thing that you know," Lynch continued. "It's a base way of thinking. The animals who rely on killing their prey as their only solution typically have the smallest brains in the animal kingdom."

Max fought hard to control his reactions. He desperately wanted to end the call and get away from the cabin. Instead, he leaned back and crossed his arms over his chest.

"What if killing scores of people won't make your problem go away?" Lynch asked.

"Explain to me how that would be possible," Max replied.

A smug look came over Lynch's face. "What if you simply couldn't kill enough people to end the threat to your family? If that were the case, wouldn't it make sense to negotiate a truce?"

Max leaned forward. "You're talking about the Consortium."

Lynch's brow furrowed. "I see Dmitry has been running his mouth."

"It was Goshawk," Max said. "She uncovered—"

"Bullshit," Lynch spat. "That would be impossible. Regardless, it doesn't matter."

"Tell me about the Consortium," Max said. "Are you a member, Lynch?"

Lynch's eyes flashed for a moment, and Max knew he'd scored a hit. Lynch was not a member, and that made the old man angry. "My death is your ticket to entry, isn't it?" Max said.

"It's important for you to understand something," Lynch said. "The Consortium is not a physical entity. It's not—"

"It's a secret council of men," Max interrupted. "Sort of like the Freemasons or the Illuminati."

"You're wrong," Lynch said. "The Consortium is much more than just a secret society. The Consortium is a way of life. It's integrated deep into the fabric of our society—"

"So it's a religion?" Max asked, wanting to keep him talking.

Lynch got a look on his face like he'd just eaten a lime. "Religion," he spat. "A device used to control vast swaths of populations since the dawn of time, yes. But crudely implemented. Think of the overhead, for God's sake."

"So what, then?" Max asked. "They've created something no one else has thought of before? Come on, Lynch," he mocked.

"I've said enough," Lynch said. "Suffice to say that your little plan of killing every member of the Consortium won't do you any good. You cannot simply lop off the head of the snake to kill its body. Think of the Consortium as a Hydra. You cut off a head, and two grow back. You kill me, someone else will just take my place."

"Assume I believe you. What's your offer?"

"Finally, we get to brass tacks," Lynch said. "We both have something the other wants. You have your life, and the lives of your sister and nephew. I have a contract that stipulates your deaths." Lynch paused for effect. "Perhaps there is some happy medium that will allow us to put this ugly affair behind us."

"You obviously have a proposal," Max said.

"I think we can both agree that the best outcome is for little Alex to enjoy a normal life, preserve the Asimov DNA, and restart your family line, am I correct?"

"Stop fucking around, Lynch. What's your offer?"

Lynch sighed. "It's simple. Come work for me. I need someone with your skills. I will make you a wealthy man, and your family will be protected."

Lynch sat back, as if he'd finished delivering a sermon.

"You must be—"

"Before you jump to a hasty answer," Lynch said, "let me sweeten the deal a little." He leaned forward and touched something on the table in front of him. The video feed on Max's screen flickered, and the view of the hall full of paintings was replaced with a picture of a small room. The camera was slightly out of focus, but Max could make out a chair with someone sitting in it. Max leaned forward and squinted, trying to make out the occupant.

Then the video feed focused slightly, and Max could see it was a woman. Her naked body glistened with blood and sweat, and there were lash marks across her chest and abdomen, as if from a whip. A black hood covered her head. Her arms were pulled back and fastened behind her. Her chest heaved, in what looked like panic. And pain.

Despite the hood and camera's focus, Max had no doubt who occupied the chair. The woman was Wing.

FIFTY

Eastern Pennsylvania, near the town of Jim Thorpe

Max forced himself to breathe. The hood was pulled away and a familiar face stared back at him, confirming his fears. It was Wing.

Or at least a vague resemblance of Wing. To his horror, it looked like someone had gone to work on her face with a whip. Deep red welts covered her cheeks, nose, and forehead. Her eyes were swollen to the point of being unable to open. Blood dripped freely from her chin and nose. Anger rose in him like a volcano.

The view of the tiny room was replaced by Lynch, leaning into the camera. Max was too angry to find words.

"That's the trade, Mikhail," Lynch said. "Come work for me and I'll let Wing Octavia go. And I'll guarantee the safety of your sister and nephew. I'll be back in ten minutes to hear your answer."

The screen went black.

—————

Max pushed away from the table and walked out of the kitchen, trying to control his anger. He heard Aristov calling, but ignored him. Despite Max's knowledge that Wing had been captured, seeing her in that much pain hit him hard. He walked up and down the length of the living room, fighting for control of his emotions. To focus himself, he centered his mind on solving the problem.

As he paced, something Lynch had said in passing rose to mind. Something that made him wonder exactly how he'd come to be standing in this cabin. Max strode back into the kitchen.

"What does he mean, we share a history?" he asked Aristov.

The old man was still sitting at the table, sipping his tea and staring out the window. The rain clouds had partially lifted, and a few rays of sunlight broke through from an opening in the clouds, illuminating the hazy outline of the forest. He scanned the trees, looking for glints of reflections that might indicate a rifle scope or binoculars. He saw nothing.

Aristov emitted a long sigh and leaned back in his chair. He removed his pipe from his pocket along with a leather pouch and started to fill the bowl with a pungent tobacco.

"With all due respect, Mr. Aristov, the clock is ticking. If there is any information that would be helpful, now would be the time to—"

"I take it your answer to Wilbur is *no*?"

"He can go fuck himself," Max said. Thunder sounded in the distance, then a crack of lightning.

Yuri held a Zippo lighter to his pipe with shaky fingers. He inhaled deeply, blowing out a plume of sweet-smelling smoke. "You'll work for the KGB," he said. "A morally reprehensible organization if one ever existed. And the CIA, a similarly repugnant group. But you draw the line at working for Lynch to save your family's life?"

"It's a trap," Max said. "There is no way I can trust him. He's motivated by power, and will stop at nothing to be accepted into this Consortium, whatever the hell that is."

Yuri nodded and took a puff on the pipe. A cloud of grey smoke drifted from his lips. "Better men than you have sold their soul to that devil and lived to tell about it."

"Make that mistake once, shame on them," Max said. "Make that mistake twice, shame on me."

"The CIA fucked you over, so why wouldn't Lynch fuck you over, too?"

"Precisely."

"Lynch is actually a principled man in some respects. Honor among thieves and all that."

Outside, the weather had turned again. Rain started coming down in sheets, pounding against the window in gusty bursts.

"Do you think the world would be a better place without Lynch in it?" Max asked.

Instead of answering, Aristov said, "Sometimes, Mikhail, it's better to lose the battle to win the war. 'He who is prudent and lies in wait for an enemy who is not, will be victorious.'"

"You're quoting Sun Tzu at me?" Max asked.

"'He will win who, prepared himself, waits to take the enemy unprepared.'"

"Enough," Max said. "I can't trust Lynch. It's a death sentence."

The old man re-crossed his legs and blew out another

plume of smoke. "What if there was a way you could trust him?"

Max paused. "How do you mean?"

"What if you had something he wanted. Something that by its possession, guarantees he wouldn't harm you. Some collateral."

"Like what?" Then it dawned on him.

Aristov shook his head. "Not the memory card," he said, as if reading Max's mind.

"Wait," Max said. "How do you know about the memory card?"

At this, Aristov rose and hobbled over to the stove. "This rainy weather makes my joints ache," he muttered. Louder, he said, "To answer that requires a story."

Max groaned. He glanced at his watch. Only a few minutes had passed, and he wondered at the implications of not showing up to meet Lynch at the appointed time.

"You're going to want to hear this story," Aristov said. Max turned to see him pouring hot water into two mugs.

The old man plopped back into his chair and began fussing with his pipe. He banged it against the table, then filled the bowl with a new stash and held the lighter to the tobacco. As he flicked the Zippo closed, Max caught a glimpse of a logo embossed on the side of the metal casing.

"Wait a minute," Max said. "Let me see that." He took a step toward the table.

Aristov toyed with the lighter, flipping it over and over with amazing dexterity for a man whose hands were disfigured from arthritis. He looked at Max with a glint in his eye, then handed it over.

Max examined the silver lighter. It was nicked and scraped, and had a small dent in the lid. The side facing Max was blank. He flipped it over and examined the mark that had caught his eye. It was a raised etching of a small flag. The flag had three evenly spaced bars running horizontally and no other markings. The top and bottom bars were white, the middle bar red. The colors had faded over time so the whites had a patina that made them look beige. The red had faded to orange. But Max would recognize the flag anywhere.

"This is the old Belarusian flag," Max said, looking at Aristov curiously.

The old man smiled. "I told you you're going to want to hear this story."

Max was confused. The Yuri Aristov who had defected to the CIA had come from a town east of Moscow, and had been proudly Russian.

"It's time for the story to come out," Yuri said. "I've been living a lie for too long." He paused to take a puff on his pipe. "My real name is not Yuri Aristov. It's Mikhail Asimov."

———

Max was stunned. "How is that possible?"

"Did you ever wonder what happened to your grandfather?" Aristov asked.

As soon as the old man said it, Max saw the resemblance to his father. The nose was the same, the pronounced forehead similar. He was surprised that he hadn't noticed it until now. "I was told he'd been killed before I was born."

Yuri shook his head. "He wasn't." He took another puff of his pipe. "You might want to sit down for this."

Max remained standing.

"Suit yourself," Aristov said, beginning his story.

"It was World War II. I was a young private in the Red Army, assigned to the front in Poland. By that time, Poland had already been divided between Germany and the Soviet Union, and I was on the front lines. It was an ugly place to be." He puffed, lost in thought.

"One night, I was out on patrol with my sergeant. I remember it was so cold, I couldn't feel my pecker. Snowing. Blowing. Dark. Well, the Sarge and I got separated in the snowstorm. Like an idiot, I wandered too far across enemy lines. Next thing I knew, I was looking down the barrel of a German MP40. That was the last time anyone saw or heard of Mikhail Asimov. Until you were born, of course, and Andrei saw fit to name you after me." He took another puff on his pipe. "A bittersweet moment for me, you can be sure."

Max said nothing.

"I spent two years as a German prisoner of war," Aristov said. "It was two long, miserable years. During that time, I came to know one of my German guards. He and I bonded over our love of gin rummy. We would play for hours just to pass the time. Anyway, the Germans, who were excellent record keepers, somehow managed to mix up my name. Asimov is very similar to Aristov. I didn't know the records were mixed up until I escaped."

"You escaped?" Max asked.

"With the help of the German guard. We made a plan over months of cards. He got me to the edge of camp, then slipped me some papers as he held the wire up for me to climb through. I didn't think much of it until I got back to the Russian side. I was delirious from dehydration and hunger and cold, and was sent to the infirmary. The orderlies found the papers on me, and assumed the name on the papers was mine. Yuri Aristov. I didn't realize the mistake until a member of Yuri Aristov's family showed up to visit me at the infirmary."

"Wait a minute. How come the family didn't recognize the mistake?"

"I didn't know at the time," Aristov said. "But a few months later, I found some pictures of the real Yuri Aristov. The resemblance was uncanny."

"Why didn't you just correct the mistake when the family showed up?" Max asked.

The old man looked embarrassed. "Turns out Yuri Aristov's father was—"

"General Bogden Aristov," Max finished.

"Exactly," Yuri said. "I went from being a poor peasant soldier to a military hero and the son of a powerful general in two years."

"So how did you—?" Max asked.

"Amnesia," Yuri said. "I faked it, and pretended to gradually recover. I went on to have a stellar military career, enabled by being in the right family. All these years, I've been living a lie."

Max sat back. "Ok. How is this relevant?"

Aristov puffed on his pipe. The dog got up, stretched, circled, then lay down again.

Max finally got it. "The German soldier's name was Wilbur Lynch."

Aristov nodded. "That's right."

Max was stunned. His parents had rarely talked about his grandfather. Everyone just said he'd been killed in the war. The truth was shocking.

"What happened to the real Yuri Aristov?" Max asked.

"That's what makes this story so remarkable. My biggest fear was that he'd show up one day, and my ruse would be blown. About a year after my escape, I received a package.

In it was a picture of the real Yuri Aristov, a bullet hole in his forehead, dead. On the back of the picture, the word *gin* was scrawled in ink."

"Lynch had orchestrated the whole thing?"

Aristov nodded. "Even back then, he was a master at making investments that would pay off later. I've been in his back pocket ever since. He became a shipping tycoon, while I went on to prominence in the Red Army. When he called, I'd do what he asked. We made a lot of money funneling Soviet weapons into the hands of rebels and anarchists."

Max looked at him.

Yuri shrugged. "I owed him, and there was always the subtle threat that if I didn't do what he asked, I'd wind up dead."

Max let it go. "Can you tell me where he lives?"

Yuri sat back and tamped his pipe down, then reached for his pouch. The kitchen was already sickly sweet with the smell of the tobacco, but he jammed more of the leaves into the bowl and held the lighter to it. When a big plume of smoke blew from his mouth, he said, "This is a dangerous game, Mikhail. I can't say I recommend that course of action."

"We're blood, Yuri."

"I realize that. Your father didn't heed my warnings, and look what it's led to."

"You talked about this with my father?"

"Yes," the old man nodded, puffing thoughtfully on his pipe. "Wilbur appealed to me to intervene, just like he appealed to me to intervene with you. Your father didn't listen, either."

Max felt proud. His father hadn't backed down, and Max didn't intend to either. "I'm going after him, whether you help me or not."

Yuri nodded. "I figured you'd say that. You're just like your old man. Smart and obstinate. Too smart for your own good, I'm afraid." He dug into the pocket of his flannel shirt and tossed the lighter at Max. Max caught it, with a questioning look on his face.

"Open the bottom," Aristov said.

Familiar with the workings of a Zippo, Max slid the inside piece from the lighter's outer casing.

"Pry up the felt pad," Aristov said.

Max did as instructed and pulled up the felt pad used to refill the Zippo with lighter fluid. A tiny metal box fell into his palm.

"Open it."

Max pried open the box with his fingernail. Inside, he found a tiny memory card. He dumped the chip into his hand and examined it. It was identical to the one he'd been looking for, except this memory card had a red label. The memory card that had been stolen from him had had a gold label. "What's this?"

"The encryption keys you're looking for," Yuri said.

"Where—?"

"Your father gave it to me for safe keeping."

"My father trusted you with it?"

"Blood trumps all, Mikhail. Always remember that."

Suddenly, the dog sat up and barked. Then Max heard the distinctive blast of a shotgun coming from somewhere outside the cabin.

FIFTY-ONE

Eastern Pennsylvania, near the town of Jim Thorpe

All hell broke loose. An explosion sounded from the direction of the front door. He was jolted off his feet and fought to steady himself. Max's hearing disappeared for a moment, then it returned in time for him to hear the sprinkle of debris on the wooden floor. The kitchen's large windows had burst outward, and rain started pouring in. Max had been standing near the stove, protected from the force of the explosion by the wall between the living room and the kitchen. Yuri, however, had been at the kitchen table, which had a direct line of sight down the hallway to the front door. The concussion of the detonation pushed the kitchen table toward the window and blew Yuri's chair over, with him in it.

Instinctively, Max shoved the memory chip into his pocket and yanked the pistol from his waistband. It looked like his fears about Lynch setting him up were coming true. He pictured the house surrounded by commandos, and thought wildly about how to escape the onslaught. A moment later, the sound of automatic gunfire filled the house, and bullets started chewing up the kitchen table and the wooden floor.

Yuri wasn't moving from where he'd fallen. The barrage of gunfire prevented Max from getting to him. Max moved to the doorway and put his back to the wall, holding the pistol in a two-handed grip. Another hail of bullets filled the kitchen, and to Max's horror, he saw Yuri's torso jolt from the impact of several rounds. He heard the sound of something metallic bouncing on the wood floor and hurled himself to his left, into the kitchen.

He hit the floor on his shoulder, felt a jolting pain along his left side, then rolled, holding onto the gun. The grenade exploded, showering Max with bits of wood from the table and spatters of something wet. It took a second to register that it was Yuri's blood.

Max expected to hear gunfire from multiple directions that might signal several intruders. Instead, he heard the shotgun fire again. At least Kate was still alive.

He considered making a dash for the blown-out window to escape by climbing down the chasm toward the lake. He suspected the attack team wouldn't be covering that route because of the steepness of the cliff. That would mean leaving Kate behind, so he rejected that option.

Instead, pistol at the ready, Max moved through the arched entryway that led from the kitchen into the living room. He saw a large hole blown out of the side of the cabin where the front door had been. He had his gun pointed forward, ready to shoot, but he saw no one. Surprised, he looked around. There was no onslaught of commandos. Feeling like a sitting duck, he tipped over a coffee table made from hewn logs, took cover, and waited for the intruder to make his way through the kitchen and around to the living room. He checked his pocket to make sure the chip was still there, and felt the Jeep key he'd grabbed earlier.

Max heard footsteps crunching on the front porch, and he spun toward the sound with his pistol. He saw a wild mass of curly hair and the tall form of Kate materialized out of the swirling mist with the shotgun at her shoulder. She entered the house, gun pointed down the hall, and saw Max. She briefly held up a hand with one finger extended, then replaced her hand on the gun's barrel. The signal meant there was a single intruder. That meant he and Kate had numbers, and Max rejected the idea of retreat. The intruder had to be Bokun. But how had he found them?

Max heard the sound of another grenade bouncing on the floor, straight at him.

He knew it was a trap. Bokun was using the grenade as cover before he made his move. Max flung himself to his right, away from the grenade and toward the front door, simultaneously firing his weapon toward the kitchen. He scrambled until he was behind a chair. The form of a man, clad all in black, retreated back into the kitchen as Max's bullets plunked into the woodwork surrounding the door. The grenade exploded, shredding the coffee table and driving slivers of wood into Max's skin. He held his position, knowing he and Kate had the gunman trapped.

The shotgun roared, followed by the chatter of the assault rifle, then Kate screamed. Max dashed down the hallway and almost ran into Kate running toward him, holding her left shoulder. Blood covered her hand and shirt, while the shotgun hung lifeless from her left hand.

"Flesh wound," Kate said.

"Ok, keep moving," Max said. With Kate injured and

the attacker armed to the gills, they were now out-gunned. He pressed the Jeep key into her hand. "I'll keep him occupied. You get the Jeep started." He stowed his pistol and took the shotgun from her. He heard her retreating down the hallway. An arm and a weapon appeared around the dining area doorway and Max fired, blowing a hole in the wall and sending wood splinters flying. The arm retreated, then reappeared, tossing another grenade.

Max almost stumbled as he backed through the front door onto the porch. He jumped onto the front walk and moved toward the garage. The grenade exploded just inside the door. A flurry of gunfire erupted, and bullets plunked into the ground. Max fired the shotgun blindly into the house, silencing the automatic gunfire.

From his left, he heard the wrenching and scraping of metal and the Jeep came crashing through the closed garage door. It ground to a halt in the gravel next to Max. He flung the rear door open and crawled in.

"Go!"

The tires churned in the gravel and caught, and the Jeep lurched forward.

———

Rain pounded against the Jeep's hardtop. Kate spun the wheel and the vehicle slid in the mud before its knobby tires found purchase. Max righted himself and got up on his knees in the back seat, pointing the shotgun toward the rear.

A round of gunfire hit, causing the back window of the Jeep to spider web. Max glimpsed a lone figure standing in the gaping hole that used to be the cabin's front door, pointing a semi-automatic rifle at the retreating Jeep. Dressed all in black, the man was tall and painfully thin. A scraggly beard covered his face, a black watch cap on his head. The man started sprinting after the car, firing the rifle as he went.

"It's Bokun," Max yelled.

"Who?" Kate was wrestling with the wheel. Bullets plinked into the rear of the Jeep.

Max aimed the shotgun at the back window and fired. The *BOOM* of the gun filled the interior of the vehicle and the window disappeared from the spray of buckshot.

"Fuck!" Kate yelled.

"Sorry," Max said. He aimed the gun at the running figure. The Jeep hurtled forward toward the surrounding woods. The man was gaining on them, moving at a pace Max didn't think possible. He pulled the trigger and another *BOOM* filled the Jeep. Bokun faltered slightly. Max pulled the trigger again and heard a click. He cursed as he tossed the shotgun aside and pulled out his pistol. The man was still coming, holding the assault rifle up. The attacker was moving too fast to aim accurately, and the shots flew wide.

Max squeezed off two rounds from his pistol as the Jeep passed the tree line and entered the darkness of the forest canopy. Both shots went wide as the Jeep jounced over ruts in the dirt track. He saw the man slow down and toss the automatic rifle to the ground, then Kate rounded a curve and Max lost sight of Bokun.

"Stop the Jeep," Max yelled.

"Are you crazy?"

"It's time to put this guy down. He's chased me all over the world. There is no way I can go after Wing with this asshole on my tail. I think I wounded him, it's time to end it."

"No way," Kate said, keeping the accelerator down.

"What if there are more men?" The Jeep took a jarring bounce and tree branches scraped at the vehicle's sides.

"He operates alone," Max said.

"How do you know?"

"Because he and I were trained by the same people. He's just like me. Now stop the fucking car or I'm going to jump out."

Kate jammed on the brakes and the Jeep ground to a halt. "I'm coming, then."

"Negative. You need to get that wound treated. You being injured will do me more harm than good. Plus, the Jeep needs to keep moving so I gain some element of surprise."

He shoved open the door and jumped into the rain, then disappeared into the thick forest.

FIFTY-TWO

Just outside Jim Thorpe, Pennsylvania

Max crept through the trees, his clothes becoming soaked from the rain. He couldn't make the house out through the fog and the foliage. A dank mist clung to the tree branches and reduced visibility to a few feet. Keeping the location of the house to his left, he began circling, moving as fast as he dared. His pistol was held out in front of him.

Max put himself in the assassin's mind. If it were him, the first thing Max would do was watch to ensure the Jeep didn't return. He would position himself with the best possible range of sight. After that, he'd clear the house and check to ensure each victim was truly dead. Then, he'd leave the scene as quickly as possible.

He visualized the house and the clearing in his mind, trying to determine the assassin's most likely exit point. Max's mind went immediately to the sharply sloping cliff off the front of the cabin. This was where Max would make his exit; he assumed Bokun would do the same.

Then he stopped, realizing Bokun would be doing the same thing – putting himself in Max's mind. Which meant the assassin was ready for him. Max braced himself.

The attack materialized out of the mist like an apparition. A hand chopped down on Max's forearm, causing a bolt of pain to radiate to his spine. Max dropped the pistol just as Bokun's fist hit him in the side of the head.

Another fist hit Max square on the jaw and rocked him, sending pain through his face and into his neck, and shooting stars across his vision. It wasn't the first time Max had been hit hard in hand-to-hand combat, and his instincts kicked in. He fell with the momentum of the punch and rolled to his left, buying time to clear his head. When he came to his feet, the assailant had vanished into the mist.

Ahead of him, he saw a stand of hemlocks waving gently in the breeze, their spiny needles rustling against each other. He saw no other movement.

Max let his ears do the work, and heard only silence. The trees stopped swaying as the wind died. A minute ticked by. Max glanced down. The earth was covered by a mixture of loamy soil, fallen pine needles, branches, and the occasional green maple leaf. His keen hearing would pick up even the quietest boot step on pine needles. He heard nothing as he turned slowly, scanning the woods around him. Two meters away, he could see the dark outline of his pistol where it had fallen next to a tree. He edged toward it, moving from tree to tree for cover.

Max wondered why the assassin hadn't simply shot him. Then it dawned on him. This had become personal. The assassin needed the satisfaction of taking Max down using his own two hands. Max didn't have the same need. He'd shoot Bokun on sight and be done with it.

"Come on out, Bokun," Max called. "Let's end it right now."

He crept slowly toward the gun.

"I know what this is all about," Max said. "You're still pissed off that you always came in second at the Institute. Couldn't beat me then, and you can't beat me now."

The forest answered back with silence.

Max crouched with his shoulder to a tree trunk and reached down to pick up the gun, keeping his head up. As he straightened, he felt a searing pain in his left quad. He looked down and saw the handle of a throwing knife sticking out from his leg. He sucked in his breath and fought the urge to pull the knife out. He calculated the trajectory of the throw and squeezed off two rounds. The shots echoed among the trees, then faded.

Max moved to his right, favoring his left leg, and put a few trees between himself and the direction the knife had come from. The pain in his leg was excruciating, but as much as he wanted to remove the knife, he knew he needed to leave it until he could tend to the resulting wound, or he might bleed out.

Once again he listened. He heard only silence.

Then, he heard the faint tell of a snapping pine needle, and he reacted as quickly as his leg would allow, shuffling to his left. Another throwing knife embedded itself in the tree, neck-high, where Max had just been standing. Max fired three shots in the direction of the throw, the pop of the gun echoing through the forest. Silence descended on him once again.

He heard the flapping wings of a bird taking flight, then the scurry of an animal through the underbrush. He tracked the sound with his pistol but held his fire.

Max felt his blood mixing with the cold rainwater that

soaked his pant leg, and forced the thought from his mind. Water ran freely down his forehead, but he blinked through it, the mist swirling as the wind picked up.

Max figured the assassin's game would be to slowly wear him down, weaken him, then pounce once he was sufficiently fatigued from pain. He moved to his left, toward the house.

He felt motion in the air as another knife flew by his ear and thunked off a branch. This time, he held his fire and forced his injured leg to move faster. He wanted to get to the house, where he might have a better chance at defense.

Suddenly, the blur of a form sprung from the trees and launched itself at Max, driving its shoulder into his abdomen. The two men went down in a tangle of swinging arms and kicking legs, and Max's wind was knocked from him. Both men rolled on the ground, and Max tried to bring the pistol to bear on the other man.

The attacker was fast, strong, and had the element of surprise. He ended up straddling Max, and struck two swift blows with his elbows, then managed to knock Max's weapon from his hand before Max could get off a shot.

Blows rained down on Max's face as the attacker leaned in. Max caught a glimpse of his bearded face, eyes flashing with pure hatred and blind madness. He could see the scars that had disfigured one side of Bokun's head from the bomb back in Croatia. Max covered his face with his arms, the way a boxer would protect himself from a stronger opponent.

Max tried to buck the wiry man off, but the assailant held fast, fueled by fury. Max could feel himself succumbing to the blows, and knew that any second, the assassin might stun him to the point where the fight would be over. Max started working his legs at the soil, trying to gain purchase. His right hand scrabbled beneath him, looking for a rock or a branch or any kind of weapon he could use to dislodge the attacker.

His hand found nothing. In his wild flailing, his right hand brushed against the hilt of the knife embedded in his thigh. He grabbed the handle and yanked it out. He swung, jamming the blade into the side of the assassin's neck.

The blows stopped. Bokun put his hands to his throat. Blood gurgled from the assassin's mouth as he tried to say something, the words failing him. Max pulled, and the knife came free. He swung and swiped the blade across Bokun's throat. Blood gushed from the man's neck, covering Max in the warm, silky liquid. The assassin clutched, gave one last gurgle, then fell sideways, lifeless.

FIFTY-THREE

Just outside Jim Thorpe, Pennsylvania

Kate wrestled with the wheel of the Jeep as it bounced along the track, slipping in the mud and splashing through puddles. The swirling fog cut her visibility, but she urged the vehicle forward as fast as she dared. Her shoulder burned as she wrenched the steering wheel back and forth. Her conscience screamed at her. Her first instinct had been to agree with Max – she was no use to him injured. Now, however, she realized she couldn't abandon him.

She jammed the brake pedal down and the Jeep slid to a stop in the slick muck. Hemlock needles scraped at the car's paint. She ripped off the sleeve of her blouse and examined the wound, prodding at it with her fingers. A deep furrow had cut across her bicep and her arm was slick with blood, but the bleeding itself had slowed. Kate used the material to secure a bandage tight around her arm.

She slammed the Jeep in reverse and bounced over ruts as she did a three-point turn. She hit the accelerator, and the Jeep's wheels spun for a moment, then the tires caught and she lurched forward. Kate yanked her phone from her pocket, jammed in an earbud, and hit a speed-dial button. A moment later, Kaamil answered.

"I couldn't trace the video feed," he said. "They had it bouncing everywhere, and then it disappeared through a firewall that I couldn't get through."

Kate thought he sounded distracted. His voice was hollow, and he wasn't speaking with his usual pep. "What's wrong, Kaamil?"

"Um, well—" he stammered.

Now Kate was alarmed. Her most trusted agent never stammered. "Out with it," she demanded. The Jeep bounced, and she yanked on the wheel to keep from sideswiping a tree.

"Well, the firewall I ran into," he said. "It's, um—"

"Tell me, goddammit. I'm sitting here wounded, and Max is tangling with Bokun. I don't have time to fuck around."

"I think it's an NSA firewall," he said quietly.

"What?" she asked, shocked. "The video feed from Wilbur Lynch was running through an NSA firewall?"

"I'm pretty sure," Kaamil said. "I was just about to reach out to my contact there to make sure—"

"Don't do that," Kate said. "Sit tight and I'll get back to you."

Just then, a blurry apparition loomed out of the mist in front of the Jeep, standing in the middle of the track. The figure was covered in mud and soaked through to the skin. Kate let out a yelp and jammed on the brakes, grappling for the gun next to her leg. The Jeep skidded sideways and ground to a halt. Kate brought the gun around and pointed it out the side window. The figure held up its arms, and

Kate sighed with relief, recognizing Max's eyes through the mud and blood.

———

"Holy crap, are you ok?" Kate asked as Max climbed into the passenger seat.

He tried not to put any pressure on the leg with the knife wound. After climbing out from under the lifeless body of Aleksander Bokun, he had ripped apart the man's shirt and used it to tie a tourniquet around his upper leg in an effort to staunch the bleeding. But it was hard to walk, and he felt dizzy. He leaned the seat back, trying to keep the leg straight.

"I'm better than he is," Max said, grimacing.

"Dead?" Kate asked.

"Dead," Max said.

"I'd hug you if you weren't covered in blood and mud and stuff," she said, looking relieved.

Max shot her a wan smile. He turned and rummaged in the back seat, and came up with a wool blanket. He tried to use a corner to wipe his face clean, but was only moderately successful.

They heard a single bark come from outside the Jeep. Max's hazy mind immediately went to his nephew and his new puppy Spike, and he opened the door, looking for the tow-headed ten year-old. He saw nothing but mist swirling among the trees. He realized his pain and fatigue-addled brain were playing tricks on him.

Then there were three rapid barks in succession, and a yellow furry mass launched itself, landing on his lap. Pain shot through his leg, then the dog bounded into the back seat, turned, and sat expectantly, tongue hanging from its mouth. It was Yuri's dog from the cabin.

Kate examined the tag around the dog's neck. "Charlie," she said, giving the dog a pat on the head. She turned back and put the jeep in gear. "Can't leave him out here all alone."

A deep fatigue threatened to overwhelm Max. He didn't know if it was the loss of blood from his leg wound, the beatings he'd sustained over the past week, or the days without sleep or nourishment. He was at a loss as to what to do next, and just wanted a hot shower, a meal, and a long sleep. He reclined the chair even more and felt a deep relaxation wash over him, punctuated only by the dull throb in his thigh and the jolting of the vehicle as it moved over the rough trail.

Through the haze in his mind, he heard Kate speak. She sounded far away. "Max, are you alright? Maybe we should get you looked at."

Instead of answering, he dug in his pocket and removed a small baggie. It was the packet that Goshawk had slipped him back at the club in Paris. He dumped a couple of oblong white pills into his hand and popped them into his mouth, swallowing them dry.

"Is that more Vicodin?" a distant voice asked. "Christ, that's it. We're getting help."

Max drifted off into an opioid-induced fog. The image of Wing in the video feed, bound and gagged, surfaced in his mind. In his vision, she sat in a wood-paneled room. He could see the pain in her eyes, her mouth contorted in terror. He could see the lash marks from the whip covering her chest and arms, the welts raised on her skin in bas-relief. Blood covered her body, and her eyes were swollen almost shut. Her chest heaved, and she breathed in short bursts, like she was hyperventilating. Max felt Wing's panic in his own chest, as though he were her twin, connected through some unseen tether. He wanted to breathe for her. He wanted to untie her and wrap her in his arms, tell her she was safe. He wanted to pick her up and carry her from the room, nurse her wounds, place her in silk sheets and give her time to heal. Restless, tormented, he cried out even as he slept.

———

Kate looked up, startled by Max's cry. His head lolled back and forth as the Jeep traveled over the rough road. It wasn't the first time she'd seen him popping pills recently. She also didn't know if he was just resting or if he'd passed out. The amount of blood on him was alarming – how much of it was his and how much of it was Bokun's, she didn't know. If he was comatose from loss of blood, she needed to get him to a doctor. She punched the gas and the Jeep jumped forward.

The dirt track came to an end and she wrenched the wheel and skidded out onto a blacktop road, teetering up on two wheels. Kate fought with the steering wheel and the Jeep evened out. She drove with one hand on the wheel. With the other, she fished through Max's pockets until she found the baggie. She peered at the pills and saw the word 'Vicodin' stamped on one. She put the baggie in her pocket.

Max moaned again. Looking over, she saw his breathing had quickened. With her free hand, she brought out her phone and stabbed at the screen to dial a number. A moment later, Kaamil picked up.

"I was just about to call you," he said. Kate noticed his voice was brighter, and had more energy.

"I need you to do something for me," Kate barked. "I

need a medic to meet me at the Newark black ops site. I'll be there in ninety minutes. Less if the traffic doesn't fuck me."

"I'm on it," Kaamil said. "Are you ok?"

"Yes. Why were you calling me?"

"I talked with my NSA contact—"

"I thought I told you not to call her."

"She called me," Kaamil said. "I figured I should at least hear what she had to say."

"And?"

"It looks like that firewall routing was sanctioned from very high up in the NSA. She wasn't specific, but she sounded scared. From the limited info she told me, I'm guessing it's at a Directorate level."

"Did she mention which Directorate?"

"Negative."

Kate hung up, her mind reeling. The fact that Lynch had access to that much power was alarming. How deep did this conspiracy go?

————

The water was scalding hot, but Max didn't care. He cradled Wing's broken body under the shower and tried to wash away the blood. Then he was back in the tiny room with walls made of wood. His vision was foggy, like the mist from the forest had entered the room, or the camera was unfocused. Wing sat in a chair, the hood back in place. She rocked back and forth, as much as her bindings would allow. He watched as a drop of blood fell from beneath the hood, joined a rivulet of water, and ran down her breast until it fell into her lap.

The fog cleared for a moment and Max was standing in

front of her. The room around him was cramped, and he
caught the smell of cedar and hay, and something else.
Something more pungent. Like the smell of animal dung.

He reached out and touched the wall. The timbers were
rough-hewn, like they'd been cut by hand. He drew his
fingers upward, tracing over the ridged and pockmarked
surface until he touched a small indentation in the wood.
Something had been carved there. He traced the lines of the
carving with a finger. Then his hand continued up until the
wall ended at shoulder height and his fingers fell away into
darkness. Max moved his hand to the left and brushed up
against something metal. It was a bar, running from where
the wooden wall ended up above his head. He moved his
hand sideways, encountering more metal bars spaced every
few inches.

He looked back at Wing, who was helpless, incapaci-
tated. He tried to move forward, to free her, but his torso
was frozen, as if his waist was tied down by invisible guy
lines. He strained, flexing the muscles in his legs, but he
couldn't free himself. Somewhere in the distance, a laugh
emerged through the mist. It was a high-pitched cackle that
echoed and reverberated around the tiny room, causing
Max to fight even harder to get free.

Then it came to him. From somewhere deep in his
subconscious, freed by the pharmaceuticals, dug up from
recent memories, the answer emerged. The dung-like
animal smell was horse manure. Mixed with the grainy
smell of hay, the odors brought him back to his childhood in
his father's barn. And it brought him somewhere else.

Suddenly, he knew.

Max's eyes popped open and he had to shield his gaze
from the bright sunlight coming through the Jeep's wind-
shield. Streams of traffic were speeding on a four-lane

highway and row after row of smokestacks billowed grey fumes into the air. A commuter train raced alongside their car in the highway's median. Kate stared at him from the driver's seat of the Jeep.

"I know where Wing is being held," he announced. Then he felt the world spin around him and he slipped back into unconsciousness. This time, it was pure darkness.

FIFTY-FOUR

Newark, New Jersey

Max felt motion, then he was jolted and pushed against some kind of strap that held him down. He opened his eyes, but the bright light pierced his brain like a spear, so he clamped them shut again. The motion stopped, and he cracked an eye. There was a dark opening in front of him. He wondered for a moment if he was dead. Then the motion started again, and the darkness swallowed him. A light came on somewhere and he heard voices, although he couldn't make out the words. A female's voice, urgent and commanding. Then a male, calmer and reassuring.

Hands jostled him. Then, he was moving at a rapid clip. He winced as something sharp jabbed his arm. A bright light flicked on directly over his face and he clamped his eyes shut again. He felt himself slipping into another hazy dream.

This time, he was lying naked on his back in a bed, partially covered by a soft, white sheet. A woman lay on her stomach next to him, one leg thrown over his. A black orchid was tattooed on her shoulder blade. Her wavy, auburn hair was spread out on the bed next to her, and he caught the scent of orange-blossom. It wasn't Wing – he didn't immediately recognize her, but seeing her filled him with comfort.

She rose on one elbow and looked at him through dark, almond-shaped eyes. Max saw confusion on her face, and he realized she didn't recognize him either. Deep sadness overcame him as the woman stood from the bed and walked away into the darkness. Max wanted to follow her, to try to explain. But no words came, and he drifted back into the black.

———

Max jolted awake as ammonium carbonate coursed through his nostrils and into his brain. The smelling salts forced him into instant consciousness. Kate stood in front of him, her curly hair wild and untamed. Next to him stood a handsome man in a pink golf shirt and white trousers. His rugged face was deeply tanned, and a gold watch glittered on his wrist in the harsh light from overhead. The pain in Max's head almost overwhelmed him, but he fought to keep his eyes open.

"Max, thank God. How do you feel?" Kate said. She attempted to tame her hair, but ended up just twisting it in her hand.

Max saw an IV in his left arm. He followed the tube up over his head, where a half-full bag of blood hung from a metal stand. He looked forward again and saw that his pant leg had been cut away. A thick, white bandage was wrapped around his right thigh. His leg hurt like a fire brand was stuck to his bare flesh.

"Water?" he croaked.

The man in the pink shirt handed him a cup with a straw. Max drank the entire cup and handed it back.

"I thought we'd lost you," Kate said, her eyes narrow with concern.

"Who's your friend?" Max asked, nodding his head at the man.

"A local ER doc we have on call," Kate said. "We interrupted his golf game."

"I was shanking it left and right today, so I don't mind," the man said. His voice was low and smooth, like a radio actor's. "Fifteen stitches in your leg to close the wound. The blade missed anything critical, which is lucky, given how deep it went. You lost a lot of blood. We put two bags back in you, this is the third. You're going to need to rest for a while before you start jogging on that thing again. Oh, and we went light on the pain meds, on Kate's instructions," the doctor said, as if apologetic.

Max looked at Kate, who shrugged and said, "I didn't think you'd want your mind clouded by medication."

"Right," Max said. "Thanks, Doc."

"Happy to help. If there's nothing else—"

Kate shook the man's hand and escorted him out of the room. Max watched them go, then looked up at the bag. It was almost empty. He grasped the IV needle and yanked it out of his arm, letting it fall to the floor. He swung his legs off the gurney and tried to stand, swayed from sudden dizziness, and sat back down. He took three deep breaths, and willed the wooziness to go away.

He stood again, wobbled, and fell. A pair of arms caught

him, and he smelled the faint scent of lilac as Kate eased him back to a sitting position on the bed.

"What the fuck, Max?"

"We have to go. I know where she is."

Kate knelt down to the floor and started retrieving the items she'd dropped in order to catch his fall. She gathered up a pair of pants, a T-shirt, and other clothing items, and set them on the bed next to him.

"You need to rest, Max. For fuck's sake, you can barely walk."

"Did you hear me? I know where she's being held. We have to move."

"Yes, I heard you," Kate said. "I also heard you in the car. You were coming in and out of consciousness babbling about knowing where she was, but you never gave the location. So where is she?"

"Upstate New York. At the Secret Service compound where we were staying."

Kate frowned. "Are you sure? That seems unlikely."

"I recognized the location from the video feed. She's being held in one of the horse stalls in the compound's barn."

"Max, how could you know that?"

"Because Alex carved his initials into the wall of one of the stalls. *AA*. I remember because I was angry that he'd defaced something that didn't belong to him, but the damage was already done."

"Max!"

"Right. So when Lynch cut over to the video feed showing Wing held captive, I saw the walls of the horse stall had the same initials carved into them. It didn't register at the time, but my unconscious mind must have caught it. When I was out and hallucinating, it resurfaced. I'm sure of it, Kate. That horse stall is the same one that's in the compound up in New York."

———

Cezar paced the length of the barn, his boot heels clicking on the wood planks. He absently touched the gun at the small of his back as he walked. The smell of the barn was getting to him. Since the Asimov family had fled the compound, it looked like no one had cleaned the stalls. When they'd first arrived, he'd dispatched one of his men to muck them out. The man had refused, complaining bitterly. Cezar had threatened him with a pistol shot to the kneecap, but the man had called his bluff, knowing Cezar needed him healthy. Now the overpowering smell of horse manure clung to Cezar like the gaudy perfume of his favorite call girl.

As he walked, he threw glances into the stall where he'd tied up the woman. It wasn't too long ago that Cezar had taken orders from her. When Abrams had been killed, Cezar had gone looking for a new employer. A tall German named Mueller had been top bidder. Cezar figured it was just one of life's ironies that found him holding his old employer captive. His loyalties went to the highest bidder, and Mueller's hefty payments ensured Cezar would do anything the man asked.

This time, he stopped in front of her. The captive's head hung forward, still hooded, and her small body was held up only by the rope binding her to the chair. Blood pooled among the horse manure and turned the hay on the floor maroon. A small video camera was set on a tripod in front of her.

More than once, he'd entered the stall to ensure she still

had a pulse. The tall German had been clear that under no circumstances was Cezar to kill the woman. Not until he, Mueller, gave the order. There'd be dire consequences, Mueller had promised, if Cezar happened to kill her by mistake.

He had taken that to heart, and forced restraint as he'd stripped off the woman's clothes, tied her to the chair, and beat her. Instead of a lead pipe, his favorite weapon for this particular job, Cezar had used a thin bamboo cane. Still, she'd gone in and out of consciousness since he'd started the beating, so in between hits with the cane, he'd fed her water.

Cezar stared at the mobile phone in his hand, willing it to ring. Despite Mueller's assurances, he felt exposed out here with only two men. The German had said the facility had been temporarily removed from the Secret Service's rotation, pending completion of an ongoing investigation.

Despite staring at the phone, he was startled to see it buzz with an incoming call. He hit the receive button and held it to his ear.

"Hello?"

"Reinforcements are on the way," came the voice through the earpiece. It was Mueller.

"When? How many?" Cezar replied.

"Soon. Four men. But they're good."

Cezar instantly felt better.

"I made it clear they report to you."

"Thank you," Cezar said. "What about the—"

"Is she still alive?"

"Of course," Cezar said.

"Do nothing with her, until instructed otherwise," Mueller said, his voice hardening.

"Of course not—"

"If she dies, you die."

"Absolutely," Cezar said. "What's the plan? How—"

The phone went dead. Cezar shoved it into his pocket and ran into the stall where the woman sat. He wiped away the drying blood and touched her neck, just under her jaw, over her carotid artery. Panic flooded his chest as he groped, not finding a heartbeat. Then he breathed out in relief when he felt a faint pulse.

"Don't die on me, bitch," he muttered as he strode out of the barn, into the fresh air to await reinforcements.

FIFTY-FIVE

Wilmington, New York

Max crept through the forest on the north side of the compound, taking care to step softly and not disturb the undergrowth. The air around him was clear and dry, and he could smell loam and pine needles. Most of the trees were jack pines, and the soil was hard clay, making it easier to walk without making a sound. Overhead, bright stars twinkled and the moon was nowhere in sight. He wished it were raining, as he knew that would give him an advantage. Not many men had trained for years in the rain and snow and freezing temperatures like he had. But he couldn't choose the weather.

Before leaving the black ops building in New Jersey, he and Kate had raided the armory. He held an assault rifle with light fingers, appreciating its reassuring heft. The short-barrel FN-SCAR was the preferred rifle of the Navy SEALs. This one was configured for light duty, chambered for a 5.56x45mm cartridge, and fitted with a long suppressor. He had several spare magazines in the pockets of his flak vest, along with three flash bangs and three frag grenades. A SIG Sauer P226 was strapped to his leg within easy reach. Max also wore black tactical garb, his face was painted with black and green greasepaint, and a set of night-vision goggles were clamped securely to his head. A tiny earpiece attached to his left ear also had a tiny mic, by which he was connected to Kate through a secure channel. In his left hand, he held a small GPS receiver. The unit's screen was configured to transmit only one percent of the available light so the screen was visible through his night-vision goggles.

He knew the configuration of the motion sensors around the property, and he needed to keep to a strict path to avoid setting them off. The barn was to his left, about a half klick through the trees. It was the same barn where he'd disrupted Ed Willson's security operation only a few weeks ago. It felt much longer than that. To his right, twenty-five meters away, was a motion sensor. On the drive from Newark, Kaamil had provided the compound's security specifications and he and Kate had memorized the details. Now, Kate followed an identical path through the woods on the far side of the compound.

They had also discussed whether they should report their hunch to Kate's superiors at the CIA. In the end, they decided they had very little to go on, and that involving anyone else might put Wing's life in jeopardy. Instead, he and Kate decided on speed and stealth. Max placed another foot on the ground, tested to ensure he wasn't about to step on a twig, then put his weight down. He was moving as fast as he dared, hoping he wasn't too late. He took another step, then froze, catching a glimpse of movement near the edge of the tree line.

He moved so part of his body was hidden behind a tall birch tree, and waited. A few seconds later, the form moved again, and Max saw the distinctive shape of an arm. Another shift, and Max saw an assault rifle draped around his chest. The sentry was standing in the best position to give him a view of both the house and the barn.

Max gauged he was twenty meters from the guard's position. If Max had taken a slightly different trajectory to the edge of the woods, he might not have seen him, and been shot down as he sprinted toward the barn. He raised the FN-SCAR, sighted through the scope, and found the outline of the man's head. Max paused a beat, then pulled the trigger. The gun spit and the target crumpled to the ground.

"One man down," Max whispered into his earpiece.

"Two," Kate's voice came back. "I just took out a sentry positioned by the drive."

Max moved to the spot where the guard had stood. A quick pat down revealed nothing. Max looked out into the clearing. Through the grainy green lenses of the night-vision goggles, he saw the main house to his left, sitting silent and dark. In front of him was the paddock, where Alex would ride horses. To his right was the barn, which housed the horses and the security team's facilities. The barn was also dark and silent. He surveyed the grounds and saw nothing moving. Keeping a line of trees between him and the clearing, Max walked twenty meters in one direction, then the other, looking for more sentries. He saw none.

Returning to the location with the dead guard, he checked his watch. In two minutes, Kate would be in a similar location, at the edge of the forest on the far side of the barn. He tried to crouch on his haunches, but felt a stabbing pain in his injured thigh, and stood back up. He leaned on a tree instead. In four minutes, Max would move through the clearing toward the barn, with Kate remaining in the woods for cover fire.

While Max watched, the barn's sliding door opened and a form slipped out. The man leaned against the exterior wall of the barn and lit a cigarette. He was short in stature, and had an assault rifle hanging around his neck.

"Hold," Max whispered.

"I see him," came Kate's response.

———

Cezar gazed out into the darkness and sucked on the butt of his cigarette. His nerves were frayed. He'd been sitting in this godforsaken barn gagging on the smell of horse manure for hours, with no word from Mueller and no sign of the promised reinforcements. The operation seemed to be falling apart around him, and more than once he'd considered putting a bullet in his hostage's head and using one of his many fake identities to disappear somewhere the fucking German could never find him. Instead, he'd removed the captive's hood, forced her to drink water, applied bandages to her worst wounds, and tried to make her eat some food. She'd taken the water, but she spit the food back at him, hitting him in the face and sending him into a rage. The ungrateful bitch. That's when he'd decided he needed a cigarette.

The compound was silent around him. He knew one of his men was stationed somewhere on the periphery of the clearing, hidden in the trees. The other was hidden along the drive, watching for Mueller's men. He wished he'd saved more of his money so he had a fallback plan. As it stood now, if he ran, he'd be living like a pauper. That idea didn't sit well with him.

The phone in his pocket buzzed. He clamped the cigarette in his mouth and flipped open the phone.

"Yes," he said, trying to appear calm.

"Ten minutes out," came the haunting voice of the German.

"I was beginning to worry," Cezar said, instantly regretting his words. He didn't want to admit weakness to the German.

"They were held up," Mueller said, not elaborating. "The woman is still alive, no?"

"Of course."

"Keep it that way. You might be there a while."

"What's the plan?" Cezar asked, but the phone had already gone dead.

———

The man leaning against the barn answered his phone, spoke briefly, then returned the phone to his front pocket. A few seconds later, he stubbed out the cigarette, flicked the butt into the weeds, and disappeared into the barn.

"Go time," Max hissed into his mouthpiece.

"Roger that," Kate whispered back.

Max took a breath and slipped from cover and dashed across the open field toward the barn. He moved as fast as his injured leg would allow, leaping over furrows in the ground and trying to keep his gear from making noise. He made it to the side of the building, put his back to the wood siding, and caught his breath. There were two doors into the barn – a huge door on the front that slid on metal runners, and a second door that opened to the rear from the back of the stables. Max moved around the side of the barn and tried the handle on the rear door. It was locked.

Max had the element of speed and surprise on his side. The low number of guards had given him confidence, but he didn't know what he faced on the inside. Keeping his profile from being visible through the door's window, he removed a tiny C-4 charge from his pocket and used double-sided tape to affix it between the handle and the doorjamb. He removed a remote from his pocket and rested his thumb on the detonator.

"Ready," he whispered into his mic. On the bottom rail of Kate's FN-SCAR, she had mounted a 40mm single-shot grenade launcher. The 40mm grenades had a small blast radius, but a long range and good accuracy for someone trained in their use. Kate would be shooting decoy fire from a relatively close range of one hundred meters.

"Go," he heard Kate's voice come through his earpiece. Then he heard a grenade explode at the front of the barn. He depressed the button on the remote and heard a *bang*. The small door was flung open by the force of the blast. Max raised his rifle, crouched, and went low through the door.

He heard a second explosion, then a third as Kate shot grenade after grenade at the front of the barn. The 40mm projectiles had plenty of stopping power against humans, but he knew they'd do little damage to the front of the reinforced barn door.

Max took cover behind one of the quads used by the grounds' maintenance crew. The room was dark, and he saw no movement through his night-vision goggles. If he hadn't killed the sentry and seen the man with the cigarette, he'd think he was in the wrong place. Another explosion sounded from the front of the barn, and Max could feel the ground shake under his feet. He knew Kate would keep lobbing grenades until either she ran out or Max gave her the signal to cease.

Ahead of him was a corridor containing two rows of horse stalls. He moved forward, then paused at the entryway under partial cover from a protruding wall. He knew the stall with Alex's initials was the third one on the left. Seeing nothing and hearing nothing, he stepped forward.

The wooden walls were just as he'd seen in the dream – rough-cut and built to shoulder height. Above the walls, rows of steel bars extended to the ceiling. He crouched, keeping his head below the line of sight afforded by the bars. He paused just before the threshold to the third stall, hidden from view. He waited for a beat. When the next explosion from the front of the barn came, he stepped forward and turned into the stall, his rifle held ready.

The sight in front of him froze him in his tracks.

FIFTY-SIX

Wilmington, New York

Max instinctively took a step sideways, so he was partially covered by the wooden edge of the horse stall. The scene in front of him was just like one of his hallucinations.

Wing sat in the middle of the stall, lashed to a wooden chair. She was slumped forward, naked, and her body glistened in the sparse light from the blood and sweat that covered her skin. She was shivering uncontrollably, which Max thought was a good thing. It meant she was still alive.

What caused Max to hesitate was the lone figure standing behind Wing. The same man who had been outside smoking now stood behind her, holding a pistol to her head. His white cowboy shirt was soaked with perspiration. His hand was steady, but Max sensed desperation. Another explosion against the barn's door jolted them both, and Max saw the man's finger tense on the trigger.

"Cease," Max whispered into his mic. "We have a situation here. Hold your position."

"Roger," Kate whispered back.

In a loud voice, Max said, "Put your gun down, and I promise you won't get hurt."

As he spoke, he saw Wing raise her head slightly and stare at him through dull eyes. She looked drugged.

"One more step, and she bites it," the man growled. Max thought he detected a Bulgarian accent.

"What's your name, soldier?" Max asked, seeking to bring the tension down.

"Fuck you, man." The arm holding the pistol to Wing's head started to quiver. He shifted his weight, causing Max to put tension on his own trigger.

"That's an interesting name," Max said. "Where are you from, Fuck You?"

"Turn around and get the fuck out of here or the woman dies."

"Your accent sounds Bulgarian," Max said. "I love that part of the world."

"I'm not kidding," the man said, his voice cracking. "You better get outta here or I'm going to put a bullet in her head."

The gunman was becoming more and more agitated. Max needed to move this along. "There are two ways this ends," Max said. "Either I walk out of here with the woman and you're alive, or I walk out of here with the woman and you're dead. Either way is fine with me. It's up to you."

"Take a step back," the man said, adjusting his grip on the gun and pressing it harder into Wing's scalp. "You have until I count to three before I pull this trigger. One—"

The man's voice was desperate, panicked. "If you get to two," Max said, "I'm going to put a bullet between your eyes." He flicked a switch on the FN-SCAR and a green laser appeared on the man's forehead.

The man reacted by kneeling down, so he was hidden by Wing's body. His pistol moved from pointing at the side of her head to pointing at the back of her head. Now Max had no shot, but at least the man had stopped counting.

"Looks like we're in a standoff," Max said. "Tell me your name so we can make this civilized. I'm sure there is something you want. Every man has his price." Max wondered what the man's endgame was. If he shot Wing, Max would shoot him. Otherwise, he had no play. It was a waiting game.

"Fuck off," the man said.

"Time is not on your side, I'm afraid," Max said.

"Wrong," the man said. "I've got a team on the way."

Max considered that. It seemed unlikely, but it would explain the man's gambit.

"If that's true, I should shoot you right now," Max said.

"One move and she's dead," the man said.

"Fair enough," Max said. He would need to take at least one step to get any kind of angle on his target. That one step might mean the end of Wing's life. He tried to catch her eye. If she could make a sudden move, maybe he could get a shot. But her lifeless eyes just stared forward.

Max's earpiece crackled with Kate's voice. "I think we have company."

Fuck, Max thought. The guy had been telling the truth. Max had one more card up his sleeve. It would be risky, but if Max didn't act fast, he'd lose his advantage. Holding onto the rifle with his right hand, he used his left to ease a flash bang from his vest, hoping his movements were hidden by the man's limited view and the darkness.

"Max," Kate said into his ear. "Want me to stall them?"

"Commence," he said into his mic.

Max flicked the pin from the grenade with his thumb,

counted four beats, and tossed it into the back corner of the stall, behind the man with the pistol. At the same time, he took a step back and to his left, using the wall of the horse stall to shield himself.

The flash bang went off just as it hit the floor. Max was counting on the concussion from the grenade stunning the gunman long enough for him to get a shot off. Max had trained in the midst of detonating stun grenades, and was prepared to move despite the concussion wave. He turned and searched for the man's form in the back of the stall. An explosion sounded near the front door, then there were running footsteps on the wooden floor of the barn, then several pistol shots both close and far away.

Through his night-vision goggles, he saw a dark form move at the back of the stall. He fired. Then he fired again.

Max felt a bullet tear by his head, causing silvers of wood to fly from the wall. Another bullet embedded itself next to his head. He ducked and whirled and saw a shadow move at the end of the stables. He flicked his rifle to its three-shot setting and pulled the trigger. Bullets spit out of the FN's muzzle. Two found the floor next to the shadow, and a third found its target. The intruder went down. Max turned back to the interior of the stall. Nothing moved. Wing was slumped forward, unmoving, and the man was prone on the ground. Max spun back toward the main room of the barn.

"How many?" he whispered into his mic.

"Four," Kate said. "I got one on the way in. I'm out of grenades."

"Two left," Max whispered. He waited, peering out of the stall. Then he heard the sound of a metal canister bouncing along the stable's wooden floor, heading toward his position. He hurled himself back into the stall and braced for the explosion. The grenade went off, blowing a hole in the wood. Max felt the sting as his back was peppered with splinters. He was thankful for the protection of the flak vest.

Pulling a grenade from his vest, he popped the pin and threw the canister with a side-arm movement. He heard it bounce, then explode. Then he threw a second one. When it detonated, he tossed a third and darted out of the stall, sprinting toward the rear door.

"I'm coming in," Kate said.

"Hold outside the door," Max whispered.

"Roger. The door is destroyed, but there is a hole I can slip through."

When Max reached the end of the horse stalls, instead of heading out the back door, he turned. A wall ran along his left, forming the side of the stables. He followed the wall until it ended, then turned left again to return toward the barn's main room. He took a knee and chanced a glance around the corner.

Through his night-vision goggles, he saw two men in defensive positions, both facing the stalls, rifles out. He pulled back.

"Do you have any stun grenades left?" Max whispered.

"Yes."

"Toss one just inside the hole on the count of three."

"Roger that."

"One. Two. *Three.*"

Something metallic clanged on the wooden floor near the door. Max looked around the corner and saw the two men whirl, bringing their guns around. Max pulled back and shielded his eyes. Then he heard a loud *BANG*. He stepped into the room, found a target, aimed, and fired. One of the men staggered, then fell, his gun clattering to the wooden floor. Max shifted slightly and fired again. The second man dropped to his knees, then fell forward.

"Clear," Max said. Kate appeared through the hole in the door, rifle at the ready, and checked the pulse of the two downed attackers. Moving together from room to room, they did a sweep of the barn. Finding it empty, Max sprinted for the row of stalls, Kate hot on his heels.

He turned the corner and found Wing still slumped forward. He stepped to the back of the stall and felt for a pulse on the body lying on the floor. He found none, and his hand came away slick with blood. He moved back to Wing.

Gently, he took her small shoulders in his hands and positioned her upright. She felt like dead weight, and Max's stomach tightened with fear. He searched for a pulse in her neck, his fingers slipping on blood. He found her carotid artery, and pressed gently, then more urgently. There was no sign of life.

Kate flicked on a flashlight and illuminated Wing's body. Max pulled his night-vision goggles off and grabbed Wing's face with his hands. Her eyes looked back at him, lifeless. Kate held the light while he examined her body. When he saw the back of her head, he fell to his knees. A bullet had entered the base of her skull on what looked like an upward trajectory.

His heart in his mouth, he examined the pistol that had fallen to the ground next to the dead thug. One bullet was missing from the magazine.

Max walked out of the stall, then exited the barn, gulping in fresh air. He put his hands on his knees, and tried to steady his swimming head. Eventually, he sat down, his back against the barn wall, and stared, unseeing, at a grey, lifeless sky.

FIFTY-SEVEN

Wilmington, New York
Newark, New Jersey
White Family Ranch, Somewhere in Colorado

Max tipped his head back and let it rest against the rough wood of the barn's siding, fatigue and sadness consuming him. He reached into his pocket and withdrew his grandfather's lighter. After he'd killed Bokun, he'd found his way into the cabin to pay his respects to his grandfather. The lighter had been on the floor, and he'd stashed it in his pocket. Now, he flipped it open, then closed it, then opened it again, listening to the Zippo's distinctive *ping*. He ran his thumb over the surface of the antiqued rendering of the old Belarusian flag, his home. A place he'd probably never return to. He pulled a crumpled pack of Camels from his pocket and shook out the last cigarette.

Kate came out from the barn, leaned her rifle against the siding, and sat down next to him. He lit the end of the smoke with the Zippo and offered it to her. She took it and inhaled deeply, and handed it back.

"I couldn't find anything useful in there," she said. "One laptop. It was password protected. All their phones were likewise protected. No IDs on the bodies."

Max nodded and took a drag on the Camel. A mobile phone sounded, and Kate reached into her pocket and put her phone to her ear. After a moment of listening, she bowed her head, and finally hung up. When she turned to Max, there were tears in her eyes.

"They fired Kaamil," she said quietly. "Confiscated his credentials and walked him from the building. Said they'd mail him his stuff."

Max nodded and handed her the cigarette. "Not surprising."

"He said they're terminating me, as well. My access will be shut down within the hour."

Despite the fatigue, sadness, and drama over the past few days, Max couldn't help but laugh.

"What the fuck is so funny?" Kate demanded.

Max tried to stop, but he couldn't. All the pent-up tension and emotion from the past few weeks came over him in a wave.

"Wing's dead," he finally managed. "My family's protection is gone." He could barely get the words out through the laughter. "Goshawk is missing." He tried to stem the laughter, but he couldn't. "Lynch is still alive, and the memory card is gone."

Kate's stared at him a moment, and he saw a smile begin. "Kaamil got fired. I'm unemployed," she said.

"And so am I," Max said.

"And you knocked out the only date I've had in years." At this, Kate finally gave in. They both leaned back against

the barn, exhausted and overwrought, unable to control
their laughter.

————

"Do you think this is a wise idea? Max asked. "Isn't this
some kind of federal offense?"

"Probably," Kate said. "Stand back, and watch to make
sure no one is around." She bent down near the door and
affixed a small explosive charge to the knob.

Max took a couple of steps away and looked out over
the warehouse district. It was three a.m., and nothing
moved. He assumed they were being recorded by unseen
security cameras, but they both had taken pains to
conceal themselves. Kate had a scarf wrapped around her
face and Max was wearing a thin balaclava. She had
assured him that the black ops site was un-manned. The
security cameras would be recording, but were not being
watched.

"I could get used to this operational stuff," Kate said.
"Too much damn time in front of a desk—"

A *bang* sounded, smoke puffed out, and the warehouse
door popped open. Max followed as Kate ducked into the
building. A second later, they were set upon by a yellow
Labrador retriever, bounding and yelping in recognition.
Max knelt and petted the dog. Unsure what to do with
Charlie, they'd left him in the CIA safe house before
heading north.

"Come on, we have to move," Kate said. She opened the
roll-top door and Max backed the jeep into the warehouse.

Ten minutes later, the vehicle was filled to the gills with
clothing, food rations, weapons, ammunition, and other
gear. Max helped Charlie into the back seat, then got into

the front passenger seat. A second later, Kate tossed a black duffel bag onto his lap.

"What's this?"

"Open it," she said, walking around to the driver's side.

Max unzipped the bag, and found himself staring at a mountain of currency. He sifted through the pile, finding straps of twenty and one hundred-dollar bills.

"One of my go-bags," Kate said. "No sense leaving it here. Should be about a hundred grand." She hit the gas and the Jeep lurched out the roll-top door into the New Jersey night. A few minutes later, they were speeding west on I-78.

———

"Will the CIA come looking for you?" Max asked, forking a mound of over-cooked eggs into his mouth. They were sitting in a diner, listening to jumbo jets roar overhead on approach to Newark.

Kate was thoughtful as she sipped a mug of coffee. "They may not. I doubt they'll connect me to either the mess at the cabin or the operation at the Secret Service compound. I'll Fedex them my credentials today, and call in an anonymous tip about both sites. Knowing how they operate, I'll bet they clean up both and no one in local law enforcement will know." She took a bite of oatmeal and washed it back with a swig of orange juice.

"All those carbs are going to make you fat, you know," Max said.

She rolled her eyes at him. "Do I look like I have a weight problem?"

"Can't say I've been looking," Max said.

"Riiiight," Kate said, shooting him a glance. She took another bite of her breakfast and smiled at him.

He avoided catching her eye. Flirting with Kate came naturally to him, but the last two times he'd taken an interest in a woman, things had ended badly. He cautioned himself to keep things with Kate on a partnership level. "What about all the gear we took from the black-ops warehouse?"

"I'm sure they'll think it was me, but I'd be surprised if they waste manpower coming after me."

"Will they be looking for our car?" Max took a bite of bacon, one of his favorite things about being in the States. No one outside the US seemed to have figured out how to properly cook a decent strip of pork fat. "I assume it belonged to Yuri, which means there is a record of it in the Witness Protection database."

"I doubt it," Kate said. "But with the blown-out back window and the bullet holes in the rear door, we should probably get rid of it. We'll pick up a new one for cash from a used dealer and dump this one in the Newark airport parking lot. If the CIA does find it, they'll assume we jumped on a plane."

Max stayed quiet as a waitress in a stained jumper poured him more coffee and cleared his plate. He thanked her, and got a smile in return.

"I need to disappear for a while," Max said when the waitress had left.

Kate glanced up from her oatmeal. "Where to?"

"I have some unfinished business in Moscow."

"You think that's a wise idea?"

"I've only got one chess move left," Max said. "I have to go on the offensive." He sipped the coffee, grimacing at the weak brown liquid.

"Want my help?" Kate asked. "Not like I have anything to do right now."

"Maybe. The first part of the operation is a one-man gig. I'm not taking you to Moscow with me. Too dangerous."

"Don't you think you should rest up a bit first?" Kate asked. "That eye still looks pretty bad."

Max took another sip. "What do you have in mind?"

"Check in with Spencer. Go see Arina and Alex. Drop Charlie off. Get some sleep. Heal up."

Max looked at her sideways. "Do you know where they are? They were supposed to be completely off the grid. That includes you—" He set his fork down as it occurred to him. "You've been in touch with Spencer all this time, haven't you?"

Kate looked uncomfortable. "You didn't honestly think I'd let them just disappear and not be in contact, did you?"

"Who else knows, Kate?"

She put both palms up. "No one. I swear. Spencer sends me a secure email once every two days, just so I know they're doing ok."

Max glowered at her. The main risk to his family was the mole in the CIA that seemed to be leaking everything to Lynch's team. "So where are they?"

"Colorado."

"How far is that?" Despite his anger at Kate's betrayal, he had to remind himself that it was a minor indiscretion. He trusted her and Spencer. And the prospect of seeing his nephew brightened him up a little.

"About a day and a half of driving, if we don't stop."

Max tossed a twenty-dollar bill on the table. "What are we waiting for?"

———

Kate drove their new Jeep up to the cabin and killed the

engine. The last couple of hours of the drive had been on rough dirt switchbacks and rutted two-track forest service roads that had made for a jarring ride. Max hadn't minded it one bit, and found himself staring in awe at the beauty around him. Rugged cliffs were covered in bright green foliage, showing spots of red dirt. Rivers, still thick with snowmelt, plummeted off craggy granite rocks and wound their way through lush valleys. Overhead, a deep blue sky was marred by a single white cloud. Kate had pointed out a herd of mountain goats, balanced precariously on a rocky outcropping. They'd driven through groves of aspen trees, their green leaves fluttering in the cool breeze. Max had rolled the window down and breathed in the air, amazed that anything could smell so good.

As soon as the dust settled from their arrival, Max saw a blond boy running toward them, a medium-sized golden retriever in his wake. Max almost didn't recognize either of them; both Alex and Spike had grown since Max had last seen them.

Max got out of the Jeep, then helped Charlie down from the passenger seat. A second later, Charlie and Spike were bounding around, the younger dog nipping at the older dog's heels.

"Uncle Max!" He turned and caught Alex in a big bear hug. Then he hoisted the youngster up onto his shoulders and carried him up toward the cabin's wide front porch, where Spencer and Arina stood watching. Max noticed they both wore sidearms in quick-draw holsters. Spencer looked pleased to see them. Arina wasn't smiling.

"Uncle Max, you have to see this place. It's amazing!" Alex exclaimed as Max set him down on the ground. Max let the youngster pull on his hand, and was soon on a tour of the ranch. The home's front porch led to a wide-open great

room with cathedral ceilings and an immense stone fireplace with a hearth that reached all the way up to the thick,
wooden rafters. A rustic kitchen was set off from the main
room by a long center island covered in granite tile. Alex
showed Max his room, which had a twin bed with a doggie
bed at the foot. A fishing pole and tackle rested in the
corner next to a pair of waders. The cabin had four other
bedrooms and a lower level with pull-out couches. Max
noticed with approval that all the shades were drawn.

Then they toured the rest of the grounds, which
consisted of a large pole barn and acres of land covered by
forest, fields, and a small lake. When Max ducked his head
in the barn, he saw what looked like a makeshift shooting
range.

When they were done with the tour, he sent Alex off to
play with the dogs and joined Spencer, Kate, and Arina on
the porch. A gigantic glass of lemonade was waiting for him
next to a comfortable-looking Adirondack chair. From his
seat, he could look out over the lake. In the afternoon light,
the nearby mountains were reflected on its surface. Not for
the first time, he marveled at the beauty of the place as he
listened to Kate fill Spencer in on recent events. Finally, she
got up and started unloading the Jeep.

"We're only ten miles from Aspen, the nearest town, as
the crow flies," Spencer said to Max. "But it's at least thirty
minutes by 4x4. We have our own well water, and there is a
backup gasoline generator in the barn."

"Internet?" Max asked. He shifted in his seat, trying to
make his leg more comfortable. The knife wound was healing, but he was still in a lot of pain. He reached into his
pocket and removed a valium, popped it into his mouth, and
washed it back with a swig of lemonade.

"Satellite. It's spotty on cloudy days, which aren't

many," Spencer said, gesturing at the sky. "My parents left this place to me when they passed away. I hadn't been here in years. Alex has been a great help getting the place habitable."

Max looked at Arina. "How are you holding up? I see you're carrying."

Arina didn't answer.

"She's a natural shot," Spencer said, breaking the tension. "Got her a Glock 19, and I modified the trigger. Fits her hand well. She can shoot lights out at twenty meters."

"Chip off the old block," Max said, still looking at Arina. She hadn't said one word since they'd arrived.

"We also have motion sensors located around the perimeter, all on a closed circuit. We've installed security cameras around the buildings, most of them hidden. Monitors are set up in the living room. There isn't a ton of fire power, but I've got an H&K G36 assault rifle, two Remington shotguns, and a handful of pistols. Our best defense is our remote location."

"Living in a prison," Arina muttered.

"How long are you staying?" Spencer asked quickly.

Max glanced at Arina. "Not long."

"Of course you're not," Arina said. She got up from her chair and disappeared into the house.

"She's feeling cooped up," Spencer said. "Frustrated by being on the run. Wants her life back."

Max sighed and took another sip of lemonade. "Don't we all?" he said quietly.

FIFTY-EIGHT

Moscow, Russia

The dark form moved like a shadow over the rooftops, covering ground quickly. It vaulted over a transom and dropped several feet to the adjacent roof below, rolled, and came up sprinting. The next roof was up ten feet and across a six-foot gap. The shadow tossed a grappling hook over the roof's edge, pulled hard to test the purchase, and swung out over the chasm. He halted his swing using both feet against the wall, then scampered up the rope and disappeared over the edge. From there, his movements became more deliberate, using air conditioners and vents for cover as he moved closer to his target.

The assassin knew there were motion sensors and hidden cameras on this roof, and he was comfortable with that. He didn't know if there were sentries on the next roof. From behind a tiny shed-like structure that covered a stairwell, he peered over to the adjacent building through his night-vision goggles. He waited, patient. Then, he saw the movement he was looking for. A flame flared, and he saw the silhouette of a man sucking on a cigarette. It would be his last.

Max removed a rifle from over his shoulder and flicked down the muzzle bipod, then set the feet on the roof's grainy surface. Keeping the shed between his body and the sentry on the adjacent roof, he got down on his stomach. Max flicked up his night-vision goggles, eased his face onto the cheek rest, and put an eye to the rifle's night-vision scope. He found the target's torso in the view-frame, performed a few calculations in his head, and adjusted the scope slightly to account for a light breeze.

The rifle was a Stealth Recon Scout, or SRS, made by Desert Tech. It was a bullpup bolt-action design, with the feeder system behind the trigger, which allowed for a full-length barrel in a compact design. Weighing in at just over twelve pounds, it was one of the lightest, most accurate sniper rifles available. Max had removed the weapon's standard muzzle break and replaced it with a long, matte-black suppressor.

He eased his finger onto the trigger, applying no pressure. He'd customized the trigger for a one-pound pull. He waited an instant, and watched the target take another puff on the cigarette. When the man exhaled, Max pulled the trigger, and felt the rifle's sharp recoil against his shoulder. Half of the target's head disappeared, vaporized by the .338 Lapua Magnum projectile.

Max paused, holding his breath, waiting to see whether the kill would roust any other rooftop sentries. He half expected to start taking small-arms fire. After two minutes, Max worked the bolt and chambered a second one from the rifle's five-round box magazine. He stood, pocketed the brass from the shot, slung the rifle over his shoulder, and stepped onto the second roof.

————

Max dropped through a hole he'd cut into the grime-covered skylight and landed in a storage room. He was hit with a wave of moisture, which made his clothing cling to his skin. He pulled off a black nylon skull cap and shoved it in his pocket. He was moving fast, as he knew the motion sensors on the adjacent buildings and the alarm system on the skylight had already alerted the building's occupants to his presence.

From a holster at his lower back, he withdrew a silenced SIG Sauer P226 9mm, configured with a twenty-round magazine. He opened the store room's door and moved into the hallway, the gun pointing the way. He hastened down the hallway, the soft soles of his shoes making no sound on the linoleum floor. At the end of the corridor, he opened a door and looked into the stairwell.

Immediately, he heard footsteps coming up the stairs. He backed away and let the door close, holding it so it wouldn't bang shut. He retreated and disappeared into the storage room. He took cover behind a stack of crates and waited.

Through his night-vision goggles, he saw two men move into the room. They both wore flattops and had big stomachs, but moved like professionals who had been through the motions hundreds of times. One came into the room, pistol out; the other followed, sweeping the room with his own gun. Max fired twice, hitting the first man in the throat with two bullets. Then, he pivoted and shot the second man in the chest. Max put an insurance round in each corpse's temple as he moved past, and stole out into the hallway and back to the stairs.

He took the steps down two at a time. The facility's command and control must have sent both men up to check the skylight after failing to roust the rooftop guard on the radio. Max emerged into a hallway lit by dull yellow lights. The floor and walls were covered with green tile slick with moisture. He turned left. At the end of the hallway, he pushed the door open and moved through with his gun out.

Two men were in the room, and they both whirled toward the door as it opened. One wore a blue shirt the size of a small tent. The second man wore a tight red shirt, its buttons straining to contain his girth. Red Shirt's eyes went wide as he took in Max and the pistol pointing directly at him. A snarl appeared on his face, and he tried to bring a shotgun around. Max shot him twice in the chest, sending the man reeling. The shotgun went off, and shards of ceiling tile fell to the ground as the buckshot went wide. Max spun and shot the second man in the shoulder and the chest.

From there, Max moved back into the hallway, with the gun in front of him. A door opened at the end of the hall. Max dropped to a knee and fired. The guard reeled and fell to the ground. Max ran to the man's body, knelt, and felt for a pulse. Finding a weak heartbeat, Max rolled him onto his back.

"Where's the surveillance room?"

"Fuck – you—" the man managed.

Max put his gun to the man's temple and put pressure on the trigger. "You really want to die?"

"Through the locker room. Turn right. Door on the left."

Max slid riot cuffs on the man's wrists, then kicked the gun away as he headed toward the locker room. At the door to the security room, Max paused. Six men were down. He guessed there were two, maybe three in this room. He tried the knob, softly, and found it locked. He removed a small charge from his belt pack, peeled off the adhesive backing, and stuck it to the door. He triggered the fuse, causing a loud bang and sending a small shower of sparks onto the floor. Max kicked in the door.

The room had a row of surveillance monitors secured to the far wall. Two tables were in front of the wall of monitors, holding computers and other equipment. A thin man stood in front of the monitors, wearing a flowered shirt. He spun, grabbing at a holster secured to his hip, but froze with his pistol half drawn when he saw Max's gun. A second man, seated at a terminal, slowly raised his hands in the air.

"On the ground," Max ordered. Both men complied. Max secured their hands and legs with riot cuffs, then wrapped silver tape around their eyes, ears, and mouths. He kicked away their weapons, and left the room.

He encountered one more guard as he cleared the rest of the hallways on the main floor. The man lay down his weapon and accepted the riot cuffs and silver tape without protest.

He made one more stop in the servant's quarters, before finally pushing open a set of double doors leading into the main pool area. Gun out, he entered the massive cavern and surveyed the pool. He saw no heads bobbing in the water. There were no naked, pink-skinned men reclining on loungers on the bath's deck. The room was empty.

He stole along the walkway next to the pool and peeked into the next room. Through the swirling fog, he saw a head bobbing up and down in the water with long white hair spread out on the surface behind him.

"Hello, Dmitry," Max said, stepping into the room, gun drawn.

———

Dmitry Utkin forced his body to relax, letting his thin frame be supported by the hot water. He lacked body fat, so the water wouldn't hold him up. He used his arms to gently paddle, keeping his head above water, and forced his mind to consider the man pointing the gun at his head. Each morning when he awoke, he was surprised to find himself alive. When he was younger, he figured he'd die from a bullet. As he aged, he thought his heart would eventually give out. Now, he was staring down the barrel of a pistol, held by the son of his old friend, Andrei Asimov.

"How many of my people did you have to kill?" Dmitry said.

Max moved out of the doorway and stood with his back to the side wall. Dmitry heard him drop the magazine from the pistol and slam in a new one. He floated on his back, letting his thin legs and bony feet rise to the surface, and tried not to look at the intruder.

"Something tells me if I'd knocked on your door, I'd be dead by now," Max said.

"I figured it was you," Dmitry said finally. "It's what your father would have done. All brawn, no brains."

"Did you have to turn me over to the FSB?" Max asked.

Dmitry let his feet sink and glided over to the side of the pool where Max stood.

"I'm an old man," Dmitry said. "I don't *have* to do anything. Besides, what makes you think I turned you in?"

"I don't know what to think, but I'm done fucking around, Dmitry."

"If you're here to kill me, go ahead. Put a bullet in my head. Makes no difference to me."

"I don't care if you live or die, either," Max said.

"Then why are you here? You want to ask more questions?" His tone was mocking.

"You're going to tell me where to find Wilbur Lynch."

Dmitry laughed. It was a soft, thoughtful chuckle.

"What makes you think I even know where he is?"

"Yuri Aristov told me you did."

Dmitry turned away to hide his surprise. When he turned back, his face was blank. "You are a resourceful one, Mikhail. I'll give you that. Old Yuri Aristov, huh? I'm surprised he's still with us."

"He's not," Max said.

"You?"

"Bokun."

Dmitry sighed. "He was a traitor, he deserved what he got."

"Let's quit fucking around. Tell me where Lynch is and I'll leave you alone."

"What makes you think I'm going to tell you that? If I tell you, he'll shoot me. If I don't, you'll shoot me. Either way, I'm a dead man."

Max left the tiny pool room. A few seconds later, he returned, holding a young boy by the collar, a gun pressed firmly to his head.

"What was it you said about employing your family?" Max asked.

FIFTY-NINE

Countryside 100 kilometers outside Vienna, Austria

"I'm in position," Max said into his mic.

He sat down in the leather wing chair in the dark office and placed a pistol on his lap. He was dressed all in black, his face darkened with matte-black paint. A nylon balaclava covered the bare skin of his head, mitigating the chance that light may glint off his shaved head. The gun was a compact 9mm pistol, silenced, with a full magazine. The odor of sewer from Max's clothing mingled with the room's scents of sandalwood and leather.

Getting into the castle unnoticed had taken some work. The massive stone fortress was heavily secured with men and electronics. He elected for stealth instead of brute force, so he and Kate had sought inside help. They'd located a former caretaker of the castle, a man of indeterminate age who had been released from duty with no pension and little prospects when Wilbur Lynch had bought the place five years prior. The caretaker was still angry, and had been happy to accept a fee to provide Max with information, which had included the location of a hidden passageway through the aged sewer system. After splashing his way through garbage and excrement for thirty minutes, Max had disabled the backup generator located in the castle's former stables and gained entrance to Lynch's main living quarters.

Max checked his watch. The chair where he sat was in dark shadows. Across from him was a large, ornate desk, the top devoid of clutter and containing a row of telephones. No desk chair was evident. Several television monitors were on the wall behind the desk, each showing a variety of floating neon-colored screensavers. Underfoot were silk rugs Max assumed cost a fortune. A set of double doors stood to his left. Through the windows, he could see several spotlights illuminating portions of a courtyard.

As he re-crossed his legs, the spotlights outside blinked off. He turned and saw that the monitors had turned black.

"Juice is off," he reported into his mic.

"Roger that," Kate's voice came through his earpiece. "I'll let Dieter know." Dieter was an old colleague of Kate's, a retiree from the German Secret Service. They'd paid him to hire a couple of men to act as a construction crew and disable the power between the grid and the castle. The wily old German had foregone the crew and done the deed himself.

"Now we wait," Max said.

———

A few minutes later, the double doors burst open and Wilbur Lynch whirred in, aiming his chair toward the desk. His wispy hair stuck out in all directions, like he'd just risen from bed. Behind Lynch strode a capable-looking man wearing dark suit pants and a starched white shirt with the sleeves rolled up. A leather shoulder holster held a pistol within easy reach.

Lynch was talking as he wheeled into the room. "I don't understand how—"

Dark as night, Max stood, pistol extended. He shot the bodyguard twice in the chest. The man staggered, reaching for his own gun. Before he could draw his weapon, Max shot him twice more, hitting him in the shoulder and neck. The man staggered, tried to catch himself using the edge of the desk, then faltered and fell to the floor.

Max pivoted and pointed the pistol at Lynch. "Hands where I can see them."

The old man stared at Max with unbridled fury, his hands poised. Ready, Max assumed, to grab whatever weapon he carried on his person.

"Put your hands on your head, interlace your fingers," Max said.

Lynch hesitated, staring at Max. "This is a dangerous game you're playing, son."

Max stepped toward him, pistol extended. "I'm not your son."

He grabbed one of Lynch's wrists, sure he was going to snap the frail bones, and forced it to the old man's head. From the corner of his eye, he saw Lynch's other hand dip into his lap. Max let go of Lynch's wrist and shifted his weight. With surprising speed and dexterity, Lynch brought a gun up. Max batted his hand away just as a pop pierced the stillness of the room. The bullet passed harmlessly under Max's arm, lodging in the wall next to the double doors.

Max grabbed the gun, and simultaneously hit Lynch in the temple with the butt of his own pistol, pulling back on the force of the strike so as not to kill the old man. Lynch grunted and let go of his weapon, sagging back in his chair.

Max pocketed the pistol, then patted Lynch down, wondering how the bag of bones stayed alive. He didn't seem to have any fat anywhere on his body. Satisfied Lynch had no more weapons, Max backed away, but kept his pistol trained on Lynch's chest.

"Congratulations, Mikhail. You got me." Lynch flicked his tongue over his red lips, regarding Max with blazing black eyes. "Kill me quick, before the others arrive."

It took all of Max's willpower not to pull the trigger and put an end to the life of the man who had caused his family so much misery. The man who had tortured Wing, and been responsible for her death. But he knew the Consortium would just replace Lynch with someone else. Max needed answers first.

"Where's the memory card?"

Lynch laughed, spittle forming on his lips. "Why don't you ask Victor Dedov?"

Max furrowed his brow. "Dedov is dead. Didn't you know?"

Another laugh from Lynch. "Is that what you think? You're as dumb as your father."

Max ignored the insult, his mind running through the facts. He'd last seen Dedov in Istanbul with a gunshot wound and a bum ankle. Later, he'd seen the newspaper article in Moscow claiming the man was dead.

"You believe everything you read in the Russian papers?" Lynch asked. "When's the last time a Russian rag printed something that wasn't controlled by the government?"

"I assumed he was dead, just not by his own hand. So where is he?" Max asked.

Lynch shrugged. "Your guess is as good as mine. If I knew, he wouldn't be alive, now would he?"

"If he still has the memory card," Max said, "there isn't anything I need from you. Might as well kill you."

"Might as well," Lynch said. "Looks like my number is up."

"Before I do, anything you want to tell me about the Consortium?" Max asked.

Lynch's hand crept up to the chair's joystick, and he played with the knob with his long, bony fingers.

"As you probably know, Mikhail, information about the Consortium is hard to come by. Even your father struggled to learn anything about them before we killed him. It's an organization, a movement really, that is dedicated to secrecy. That is, until we're ready to be public. At which time, it'll be too late."

Max stayed silent, waiting to see what else Lynch would say.

"You can't threaten me, Mikhail. Let me assure you, death is a better outcome than violating the code of the Consortium. The movement is more powerful than an individual, and its force will live long beyond that of mortal man. We will stop at nothing but complete world domination. Much as capitalism beat communism, we will triumph over capitalism!" Spittle flew from the old man's lips as he blurted out the words, and Max could see him getting caught up in the passion of the doctrine he believed in.

"Are you saying that this Consortium group, or whatever they are called, has developed some new kind of economic system more powerful than capitalism?" Max's tone was mocking.

Lynch smiled, showing a set of big yellow teeth. His fingers danced over the wheelchair's control mechanism.

"We didn't develop anything. We are simply harnessing the existing power of the human mind. We are nourishing a force that has been in existence for as long as humans have been around. Since before Eve ate from the forbidden tree. It's simple human nature, a force unequaled in power. Free from the controls of values manufactured by a few in order to control the many. We believe in freeing humans from those controls."

"Sounds like hypocrisy to me," Max said. "Or anarchy."

"Only if permitted to grow unchecked," Lynch said, obviously enjoying the sermon. "That's where the Consortium comes in. We provide the checks and balances."

"You say *we* like you are part of the Consortium," Max said. "But you aren't, are you?"

Lynch's smile vanished, replaced with a scowl.

"I was your ticket into that club," Max said. "Except my guess is, they were never going to let you in. It's too exclusive. Simply killing a few people doesn't admit you into a club like that. Isn't that true?"

Lynch's finger's stopped toying with the chair's joystick and hovered over the plastic knob. Then Max saw something he hadn't noticed before. There was a tiny black button on top of the joystick that blended in with the rest of the knob's surface. Max looked into Lynch's eyes and saw him smile a hideous grin. He pulled the trigger, his gun spitting twice just as the old man's fingers plunged down on the button.

———

The bullets tore into Wilbur Lynch's chest, causing his body to spasm and forcing him back in the chair. Lynch's hand flew up, away from the wheelchair's joystick, then fell to his side. Two red dots appeared on the old German's white shirt, then a dull red blossomed over his chest. His black eyes found Max's and stayed there, fixing him with a stare of utter concentration.

With forced deliberation, Lynch started to move his arm again. His hand rose up, as if under a spell, and moved toward the joystick. Max watched, willing the man to die, but the arm didn't stop. Blood appeared in the corner of Lynch's mouth and dribbled down his chin.

"The. Code. Of. The. Consortium," Lynch uttered, his words coming out as individual puffs of air.

With a sudden movement, Lynch's hand shot for the joystick. Max pulled the trigger and shot Lynch dead center in the forehead. The old man's eyes rolled back in his head and his arm fell back to his lap. He didn't move again.

————

Max pulled Lynch's body from the chair and laid it on the ground. It took him several minutes to examine the conveyance. Underneath the seat, hidden in the motor compartment, Max found a large block of plastic explosive. It was enough to practically decimate the entire room, taking Lynch and Max along with it.

Lacking the proper tools, Max left the explosive alone. With the utmost care, he examined the chair's undercarriage, the motor, the joystick, and the other controls. He found a second pistol in a back pocket on the chair.

Max didn't want to stay in the room any longer than necessary. The gunshots would attract attention. But something gnawed at him. Why would Lynch want to blow himself up? Was it because he would take Max along with him? Maybe, but why rig the explosive on the chair in the first place? The only thing Max could think of was that Lynch wanted to destroy something. Something he didn't want to get into the wrong hands. Something important enough to destroy himself also.

Max was about to give up when his fingers found a small compartment hidden close to where the block of C-4 had been secured. Max worked at the tiny cubby hole with the blade of his knife and finally pried it open. He felt something small and lightweight fall into his hand.

When he withdrew his hand from the cavity, he saw a familiar-looking memory card. This one had a gold label.

SIXTY

White Family Ranch, Somewhere in Colorado

The quad bounced over a rock and Max fought the controls, trying to keep up with his nephew. The youngster had his own quad on a beeline for the summit of a ridge, navigating the narrow two-track like a seasoned rider. To Max's left, a sheer cliff plummeted to a rushing river hundreds of feet below. The road, a former 4x4 Jeep trail, had become unnavigable by passenger car, and was now only accessible by quad, horse, or mountain bike. Spencer had assured Max the views at the top were well worth the trip. After another thirty minutes, they passed the tree line and the track widened and moved away from the cliff. Alex turned on the speed, and Max twisted the throttle to keep up.

He finally caught Alex at the summit, pulling his quad even with his nephew's. They hiked to the edge of a cliff, where they both sat, dangling their legs into the abyss.

"Isn't it amazing, Uncle Max? I never want to leave this place."

The view was stunning, and Max didn't immediately answer. As far as his eye could see were the jagged peaks of the Rocky Mountains. With their white caps on top of grey silt and scree, the ranges seemed to go on forever. A clear blue sky framed the mountaintops, and a patchwork of different shades of green covered many of the lower reaches. At that moment, he had to agree with his nephew. He didn't want to leave, either.

"It sure is, Alex," he said. "I'm glad you like it here."

They were both silent for a while as they took in the view.

"You getting along with Spencer ok?" Max asked. Alex's face had weathered since they'd come to Colorado. His skin was tan and his hair was a lighter shade of blond. Max was happy that Alex was settling in, but wished he was able to spend the same quality time with the boy that Spencer was.

"He's great. Teaching me a lot. Showing me how to track animals and use a fly fishing rod. I'm target shooting with a bow, and he said he'd take me hunting this fall, as long as you say it's alright."

"Of course it is," Max said. "How's your mom doing?"

Alex hesitated. "She's ok. Doesn't say much these days. Spends a lot of time on her laptop."

That piqued Max's interest. "What's she doing on her laptop?"

"Dunno. She won't say."

Max considered that. "How are the school lessons with Spencer?" Max didn't want Alex to get behind, and had been happy to hear Spencer had been home schooling the boy.

"Kinda boring."

"Understandable. Your English sounds really good. Almost no trace of an accent."

"Spencer and I spend at least an hour a day on English. He said it's very important to lose the accent."

"He's right." Max was quiet for a while. Then he removed his pistol from his side holster. He wore the gun during every waking moment while on the ranch. Max removed the magazine and racked the slide to eject the chambered bullet. Then he handed the gun to Alex, butt first.

"Mom said I should never touch a gun."

"Take it. The Asimov family was destined, or maybe cursed, to carry firearms. It's in your blood. And given the situation we're in, you need to learn how to use it."

Alex hesitated, then took the pistol. Max showed him how it worked. "This is a Glock. Made in Austria. This one is kitted out in .45 caliber. The caliber refers to the size of the bullet." He handed Alex the magazine he'd been holding. "Slam the mag into the handle – now watch where you're pointing it." Max gently guided the muzzle of the gun away from them. "Slam it in hard, otherwise the bullets may jam."

Alex shoved the magazine into the gun's handle using the palm of his hand.

"Now rack the slide. Do it like you mean it."

Alex pulled back on the slide and let it go.

"You're a natural," Max said, beaming. "That put a bullet in the chamber. The gun is live, so be careful. Only point the gun at something you're willing to destroy."

Alex held the gun with both hands and moved his finger to the trigger.

"Never put your finger on the trigger until you're ready to shoot."

Alex dutifully moved his finger so it was alongside the barrel. He looked at Max expectantly.

"Want to shoot it?" Max asked.

"You bet!" Alex said.

"Promise not to tell your mother?"

"Promise!"

"Come on. Let's go find a target you can shoot at."

———

"Any word from Goshawk?" Kate asked. Outside, it was pitch dark, save for a million tiny lights sprinkled though the sky. She, Max, and Spencer were sitting around the kitchen table. Arina was on the living room couch nursing a white wine, buried in a small laptop. Alex was asleep in his room, along with Spike and Charlie.

"None," Max said, absently checking his Blackphone. His service at the ranch was spotty, but so far, there'd been no word. He didn't like to admit it, but he was really worried about the lounge singer. If he had any leads as to her whereabouts, he'd consider attempting a search. As it was, he had zero information, so he waited, hoping for the best.

In front of him was a laptop and a glass of American bourbon. Resting on the table next to the laptop were two memory cards; one with a red label and one gold. Spencer nursed his own whiskey while Kate held a glass of chilled vodka. This was the moment they'd all been waiting for.

Max checked the laptop to ensure it was not connected to the internet – a safety precaution Goshawk had drilled into his head years ago. Then he inserted the red memory card into a slot in the side of the laptop and accessed a script that copied the encryption keys from the chip to the computer's hard drive. On his way back from Europe, Max had made backup copies of both memory cards, but lacked the technology during his travels to decrypt the information.

Involuntarily holding his breath, Max inserted the gold memory card into the laptop, copied the contents to the hard drive, and clicked on the decryption app.

Forcing himself to take a sip of bourbon, he watched as the laptop's screen clouded over and a countdown bar appeared. Max spun the laptop around so they could all watch. No one spoke as the blue progress bar slowly made its way from left to right. Halfway through, Max rose and poured them all fresh drinks.

He'd finished his third bourbon by the time the blue bar reached the end and the screen unclouded. They all leaned forward, their drinks forgotten. With a hand made steady by the bourbon, Max reached over and double clicked on the new file folder that had appeared on the desktop. The folder opened, revealing two documents. Each of the documents were labeled in Cyrillic letters.

Max knew both Spencer and Kate were fluent in Russian, but he translated the labels anyway. "Officer's Roster and Financials." He stared at the files, his heart pounding.

Arina looked up from her computer, then rose and walked over to stand behind Max's chair.

"What are you waiting for?" Kate asked.

Max looked back at the screen and double clicked on the file named *Officer's Roster*. A text document opened, this one also in Cyrillic. All four of them crowded around the monitor. Listed were twelve names, followed by titles, phone numbers, and email addresses. The titles were in order of seniority. *President, Vice President, Secretary*, etc. Some of the phone numbers started with +7, the long distance code for Russia, but Max also saw others, including +375 for Belarus, +371 for Latvia, and +49 for Germany.

He recognized a few of the names, including a Russian billionaire, a couple of high-ranking Russian military officers, and a ranking member of the Russian President's cabinet. But many of the names he didn't know.

He left that window open and double clicked on the file marked *Financials*. A spreadsheet opened up, also containing Cyrillic text. He sucked in his breath when he realized what he was looking at. The document contained a set of financial statements – a profit and loss statement, a balance sheet, a cash flow statement, and others. The size of the numbers was staggering; some of them went into the billions. He could only assume the document showed the financial status of the Consortium itself.

They all sat back. Kate broke the silence first. "Keys to the kingdom," she said.

Spencer leaned forward, tapped the track pad, and brought the list of twelve names forward. He sat back and looked at Max. "Looks like you've got your kill list."

EPILOGUE

Somewhere in Malaysia

"Last time we did this, we were walking into a trap," Kate whispered. She was crouched next to a broken-down concrete wall, holding an assault rifle. Her hair was tucked under a ball cap and her grey T-shirt was soaked through from perspiration. A full moon illuminated a crumbling but vast compound in front of them.

"I said a hundred times you didn't need to come," Max said. "This is my deal, not yours." His T-shirt clung to his body in the humid air. An assault rifle was held ready. He had a pistol in a side holster and a tactical knife strapped to his leg. The compound sprawling in front of them contained mostly burnt-out and falling down buildings. It looked like a war zone.

"I still don't get why you're doing this," she said.

"Your father is still alive, no?"

"Yes."

"See him often?"

"Every few months. He and my mother have a little beach house on the outer banks of North Carolina."

"Then you wouldn't understand," Max said. "Be thankful you don't." He checked his watch. "You ready?" He drew the tactical knife from its sheath.

"Affirmative," she said.

They heard footsteps crunching toward their position, and the smell of a cigarette wafted at them. A few seconds later, a dark skinned man in a black uniform strolled by, a rifle slung across his back. Silently, Max stood and put his arm across the man's throat to choke off a cry. He held tight until the man stopped struggling, drew the knife across his throat, and lowered him to the ground.

They both moved forward. At another wall, Kate kneeled at the transom, rifle held steady, while Max entered the compound. A guard appeared and Max's silenced rifle spit twice. The man went down. A second guard appeared and Kate fired three times, hitting the guard in the chest and neck.

Their objective was a small outbuilding in the south-eastern corner of the walled yard. The compound only existed to house one prisoner, and their mission was to free that prisoner. Anyone who got in their way would die. As Max moved, he felled two more guards. Each man seemed poorly trained, as if Lynch never expected them to have to actually defend the compound.

Max paused at a doorway to a low-slung building. Even at this early hour, he could hear the sounds of dice clicking and men laughing. Kate slid up and put a small explosive device next to the door's handle, then backed away. Max withdrew two flash bangs, pulled the pins with his teeth, then nodded at Kate. She fired the explosive and the door burst open. Max tossed the grenades through the plume of smoke. Right after the two bangs from the grenades, he stepped through the door, gun held ready.

The room was small and served as a cramped barracks for the guards. Max saw six human forms through the smoke. Two men had scrambled for weapons. Max fired four times and both men went down. The other four looked at him with wide eyes and put their hands in the air. Max covered them while Kate secured each man's hands with plastic cuffs. The duo left as quickly as they'd entered. It took them another ten minutes to clear the compound, killing two more guards and capturing another six.

A hundred meters from the barracks, Max found the building they were looking for. They repeated the entry drill, and found two guards in the tiny room with their hands in the air and scared looks on their faces. Max marveled at how young they were. They'd been playing cards, leaving their rifles leaning against the dirty wall. Kate secured them and left them face down on the dirty floor.

In the center of the room, Max found a large, square, metal trapdoor. He grasped the handle and pulled. He and Kate shone their lights into the hole. Looking up at them, blinking against the sudden light, was a white-haired old man. His emaciated body was curled up in a fetal position on a dirty mattress. There was deep fear in his eyes.

Kate held a flashlight, and Max lowered himself into the hole and squatted in front of the man. If the captive had enough energy to move, Max believed he would have tried to crawl away. Max reached into a pocket of his flak vest and withdrew the locket he'd found among Wing's possessions in the barn in New York. He snapped it open, then handed it to the old man.

It took a moment, but recognition appeared in his eyes. He held the locket to his breast, and started to cry.

"Come on," Max said. "We're going to get you out of here."

THE END

IF YOU LIKED THIS BOOK ...

... I would appreciate it if you would leave a review. An honest review means a lot. The constructive reviews help me write better stories, and the positive reviews help others find the books, which ultimately means I can write more stories.

It only takes a few minutes, but it means everything. Thank you in advance.

-Jack

This is a work of fiction. Any resemblance to persons living or dead, or actual events, is either coincidental or is being used for fictive and storytelling purposes. No elements of this story are inspired by true events; all aspects of the story are imaginative events inspired by conjecture.

The Pursuit continues the story of Max Austin as he fights to save his family from unknown forces. This is book two in what will be a five-book series. The story of Max's family will culminate with three more novels, after which Max Austin's future is uncertain.

I hope you enjoy the story. Drop me a line if you have feedback or just want to say hi.

Jack Arbor
November, 2016
Aspen, Colorado

ACKNOWLEDGMENTS

Leonardo da Vinci once said there are no finished art projects, only abandoned ones. As I abandon this one, I have a whole host of people to thank for their help and encouragement along the way.

First and foremost, I'd like to thank my lovely wife, Jill Canning. She brings the fun to our relationship and keeps me from losing my mind to toil and industry. She's also my number-one reader and suffers through early drafts, offering wisdom and perspective along the way.

I also want to thank my cunning editor, Jen Blood. Her ability to use up an entire pen full of red ink is exceeded only by her skill at smoothing the rough edges of a story.

Since writing my first book, I've formed what I call my Advanced Reader Team, or ART. Very clever, I know. There are almost fifty of them now, so too many to name, but I'd like to thank a few who have been with me since the beginning and provided valuable input to this draft: Eric Rutz, Kristen Werner, my mother Gay Birchard, Angie George, Jen Close, and Connie Cronenwett. Also, several advance readers provided quite a bit of input to the final draft, including Wahak Kontian, Kathryn Pynch, JoAnn Howard, Lynnea Linquist, Murielle Arn, and James Farmer. Their help is hugely appreciated.

No section of acknowledgements would be complete without thanking my father, John Lilley. From day one, he suggested I follow my heart. Forty-some years later, I finally did.

Lastly, I'd like to once again thank Joanna Penn, whose spectacular weekly podcast continues to inform and motivate me and legions of other writers.

Before I sign off, I'd like to thank the wonderful and patient staff of the public library in Basalt, Colorado. If I could only talk them into increasing their hours, maybe I could get more writing done.

JOIN MY MAILING LIST

If you'd like to get updates on new releases as well as notifications of deals and discounts, please join my email list.

I only email when I have something meaningful to say and I never send spam. You can unsubscribe at any time.

Subscribe at www.jackarbor.com

ABOUT THE AUTHOR

Jack Arbor is the author of two novels – *The Russian Assassin, Max Austin Book One* and *The Pursuit, Max Austin Book Two* – and a novella titled *Cat & Mouse*, a prequel to the series. All three feature the wayward KGB assassin Max Austin as he comes to terms with his past and tries to extricate himself from a destiny he can't avoid.

Jack works as a digital technology executive during the day and writes at night and on weekends, with much love and support from his amazing wife Jill.

Jill and Jack live outside Aspen, Colorado, where they enjoy trail running and hiking through the natural beauty of the Rocky Mountains. Jack also likes to drink old bourbon and listen to jazz, usually at the same time. They both miss the pizza on the East Coast.

You can get free books as well as pre-release specials and sign up for Jack's mailing list at www.jackarbor.com.

Connect with Jack online:
(e) jack@jackarbor.com
(t) twitter.com/jackarbor
(i) instagram.com/jackarbor/
(f) facebook.com/jackarborauthor
(w) www.jackarbor.com
(m) Mailing List Signup

The Russian Assassin, Book One

What if your father wasn't the man you thought he was?

Max, a former KGB assassin, is content with the life he's created for himself in Paris. When he's called home to Minsk for a family emergency, Max finds himself suddenly running for his life, desperate to uncover secrets about his father's past to save his family.

Max's sister Arina and nephew Alex become pawns in a game that started a generation ago. As Max races from the alleyways of Minsk to the posh neighborhoods of Zurich, and ultimately to the gritty streets of Prague, he must confront his past and come to terms with his future to preserve his family name.

The Russian Assassin is a tight, fast-paced adventure, staring Jack Arbor's stoic hero, the ex-KGB assassin-for-hire, Max Austin. Book one of the series forces Max to choose between himself and his family, a choice that will have consequences for generations to come.

Cat & Mouse, A Max Austin Novella

Max, a former KGB assassin, is living a comfortable life in Paris. When not plying his trade, he passes his time managing a jazz club in the City of Light. To make ends meet, he freelances by offering his services to help rid the earth of the world's worst criminals.

Max is enjoying his ritual post-job vodka when he meets a stunning woman; a haunting visage of his former fiancé. Suddenly, he finds himself the target of an assassination plot in his beloved city of Paris. Fighting for his life, Max must overcome his own demons to stay alive.

CHAPTER ONE FROM CAT & MOUSE

Rome, Italy

Max checked his weapon. The .22 caliber Walther P22 subcompact pistol was right where it was supposed to be, in a custom holster inside the waistband of his jeans. The pistol's suppressor made it impossible for him to sit; a small price to pay since the summer heat prevented him from wearing a jacket.

Even at midnight, July in Rome made for a gritty, humid time for the throngs of tourists packed into the city like sardines. Max stood at an outside bar nursing a beer, watching the melting pot of tourists laugh, smoke, and drink their way through the night. A smattering of European dialects reached his ear. Max was fluent in each. Most of the revelers were watching the World Cup finals match between Spain and Netherlands that played on televisions in the various cafes. From his vantage point, he could see across the cobblestone street to a bar filled with a younger set of partygoers.

Max's attention was focused on one corner of the outdoor bar, where a tall, lanky man with a salt-and-pepper goatee and long wavy hair sat hunched close to a young woman. The man wore round spectacles, sandals, and linen pants. The woman had on a tight-fitting T-shirt and rested her hand on the man's knee. Max checked his watch. Three minutes.

At the appointed time, the woman rose and tugged on the man's hand. He resisted, leaning back in his chair.

Go on, Max muttered under his breath.

The woman smiled, biting her lip. Finally, the man with the goatee rose and followed her out of the cafe and into the street. The girl clung to her companion as they strolled away from the bar. Max gave them a minute, then drained his beer, and left the cafe, following at a safe distance. The pair rounded a corner and disappeared down a side street. Max kept his pace slow. He knew their destination.

At the entry to the side street, Max stopped and lit a cigarette. Here, several blocks away from the string of outdoor cafes, the street was quiet. He knew that if he continued down the main street, he'd eventually reach the Pantheon, the hulking ancient Roman building historically used as a church dedicated to St. Mary and the Martyrs. He hoped what he was about to do wouldn't create a new martyr for ISIS. The mark was a prolific recruiter of Western teenagers for the cause of the Islamic State and was also responsible for directing several terrorist bombings around Western Europe that had killed scores. Known only as the Chameleon, the target was on the kill list of several Western nations. The Chameleon had remained anonymous, hiding in plain sight, until Max's client had identified him. Max sucked in one last drag, then stubbed the cigarette out on the side of the building and pocketed the butt. He saw no one.

Max walked down the alleyway until he reached the door he'd been looking for. He tried the handle and found it unlocked, just as planned. He entered, pulling the door shut behind him. A small entryway opened in front of him with a narrow flight of steps going up. Max removed a thin balaclava from his pocket and pulled it over his head, slid on a pair of black latex gloves, then removed the .22 from its holster. He stole up the stairs, holding the gun in front of him. As he neared the top, he could hear the sounds of frantic lovemaking coming from the room to his right.

Max preferred to work alone. This partnership had been mandated by his client, and Max had reluctantly agreed on the condition that the woman not know his identity or physical description. The fact that she'd spent the last six months undercover as a student in the professor's class and had successfully seduced him into an affair had impressed Max, and he'd agreed to work with her. Max didn't know what hatred motivated the woman to sacrifice her body in this way. Whatever it was, she had executed her part of the job perfectly.

He entered the room with his pistol at the ready. The scene had been orchestrated just as planned. The woman was on the bed naked, kneeling face down. The professor was behind her with his back to the door, also naked, sweating and straining with exertion. His long hair was plastered to his head with sweat. Max could smell a strong scent of bleach. He took two quiet strides into the room, aimed the muzzle at the man's head, and pulled the trigger.

The small .22 caliber bullet caused the gun almost no recoil. Max chose the .22 because he wanted a compact, reliable, and accurate pistol for the job. He also wanted minimal mess. The bullet entered the rear of the man's skull and tore through his brain before it came to a rest lodged in the interior of his front skull. The professor went silent and pitched forward over the woman's back. The young woman let out a yelp and tried to roll away. Max pulled the man's body off her and rolled it onto the floor, then put another bullet into the base of his skull. Insurance.

Holstering the gun, Max walked into the tiny bathroom and pulled a gallon-sized jug of bleach from beneath the sink. When he returned, the woman was pulling on her clothing. Shock registered on her face. Her hands were shaking but she was moving, and that's what mattered. Max rolled the body onto its back and dumped half the contents of the jug onto the man's front, paying particular attention to his genitals, hands, and mouth. Then he rolled the body over and dumped the remainder of the bleach on the man's back, buttocks, and legs. Bleach, Max knew, was effective at covering up DNA. From the smell of it, Max could tell the woman had sanitized the room earlier that night. She wouldn't be coming back to this place.

The woman began shoving a few belongings into a duffel. Max looked around the bare room for any remaining items. Finding none, he grabbed her arm and led her down the stairs. In the tiny entryway, Max moved to open the door, but she grabbed his arm. Turning back, Max felt her bury her face in his chest. She was sobbing. He hesitated, then put his arm around her.

After a moment, he said, "We have to go."

She nodded, face still pressed into him.

"What you did was a brave thing," Max said.

For a moment, she didn't speak. Then finally she pulled away, stifled the sobs, and said, "Revenge is a powerful motivator."

"You ready?"

She wiped her eyes and nodded. "Yes."

"You remember the details of your exfiltration?"

She nodded. "Thank you."

"Don't thank me. You did the hard work."

"My name is Naomi," she said, looking at him with big, brown eyes.

Max shook his head, put his finger to his lips, then ducked out the door. When he looked back, he saw her walking in the opposite direction, head bent, eyes on the ground.

———

Max lit a cigarette as he walked south. He kept a steady pace and walked past the Parthenon, then stayed to the west of the Colosseum. He threw the balaclava in a dumpster, then tossed the gun into a public trash can. Holding his hand in front of his face, he noticed it held steady. *Your hand is your retirement indicator*, his father would often say. For now, Max was still in the game. No easy feat in this profession, especially at age forty.

He walked up the incline away from the Colosseum and entered the neighborhood of Monti. Historically the home of beggars and prostitutes, Monti was now full of trendy bars, fashion boutiques, and hip restaurants. Max found the doorway he was looking for and pushed into a bar. The low-ceilinged room was illuminated by red-tinged light, and soft Russian music came from hidden speakers. The u-shaped bar was nearly empty, and Max found a stool at one end. When the bald, barrel-chested bartender appeared, Max spoke in Russian and ordered a tumbler of vodka, chilled. This place had been Russian-owned since long before the neighborhood had gentrified, and was one of the few places in Rome where Max could get a proper drink. An annoying buzzing sound came from a small TV that showed Spain playing the Netherlands in the World Cup. As Max sat down, the bartender thumbed the mute button and grumbled, "I hate those fucking vuvuzelas. Leave it to the South Africans to ruin a good football match."

It wasn't until Max was well into his fourth chilled vodka that she walked into the bar. Tall and balancing on heels, wearing a form-fitting black dress, the woman came in alone and perched herself on a barstool directly across from Max. She pushed her hair behind one ear and smiled at the bartender, ordering something Max didn't hear. He watched as she scanned the room, her gaze lingering on Max before looking away. The bartender put a martini glass in front of her containing a clear liquid and a skewer of olives.

When she'd walked in, Max's heart had dropped into his stomach. If he didn't know better, he'd swear he was looking at Maren, the woman he'd fallen in love with a year ago. He still had the ring; it was too painful to part with. His mind reeled. This couldn't be his ex girlfriend – she was dead. He was looking at the haunting image of her double.

He downed his vodka and signaled for another.